2008

Books by Susan McCarty

Anatomies
2008

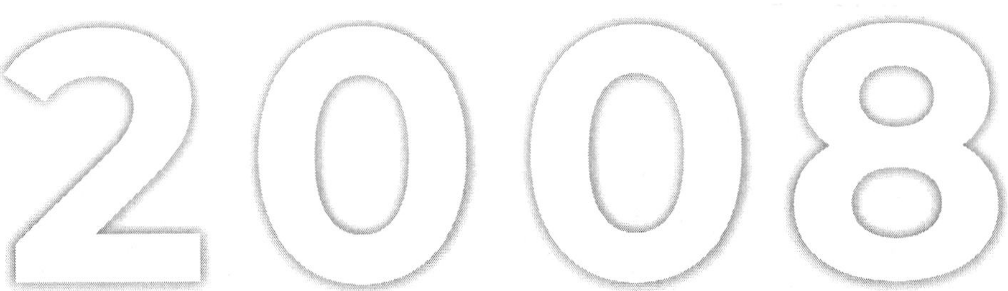

2008

Susan McCarty

Carnegie Mellon University Press
Pittsburgh 2026

Book design by Connie Amoroso

Library of Congress Control Number 2025939029
ISBN 978-0-88748-728-6

Printed and bound in the United States of America

10 9 8 7 6 5 4 3 2 1

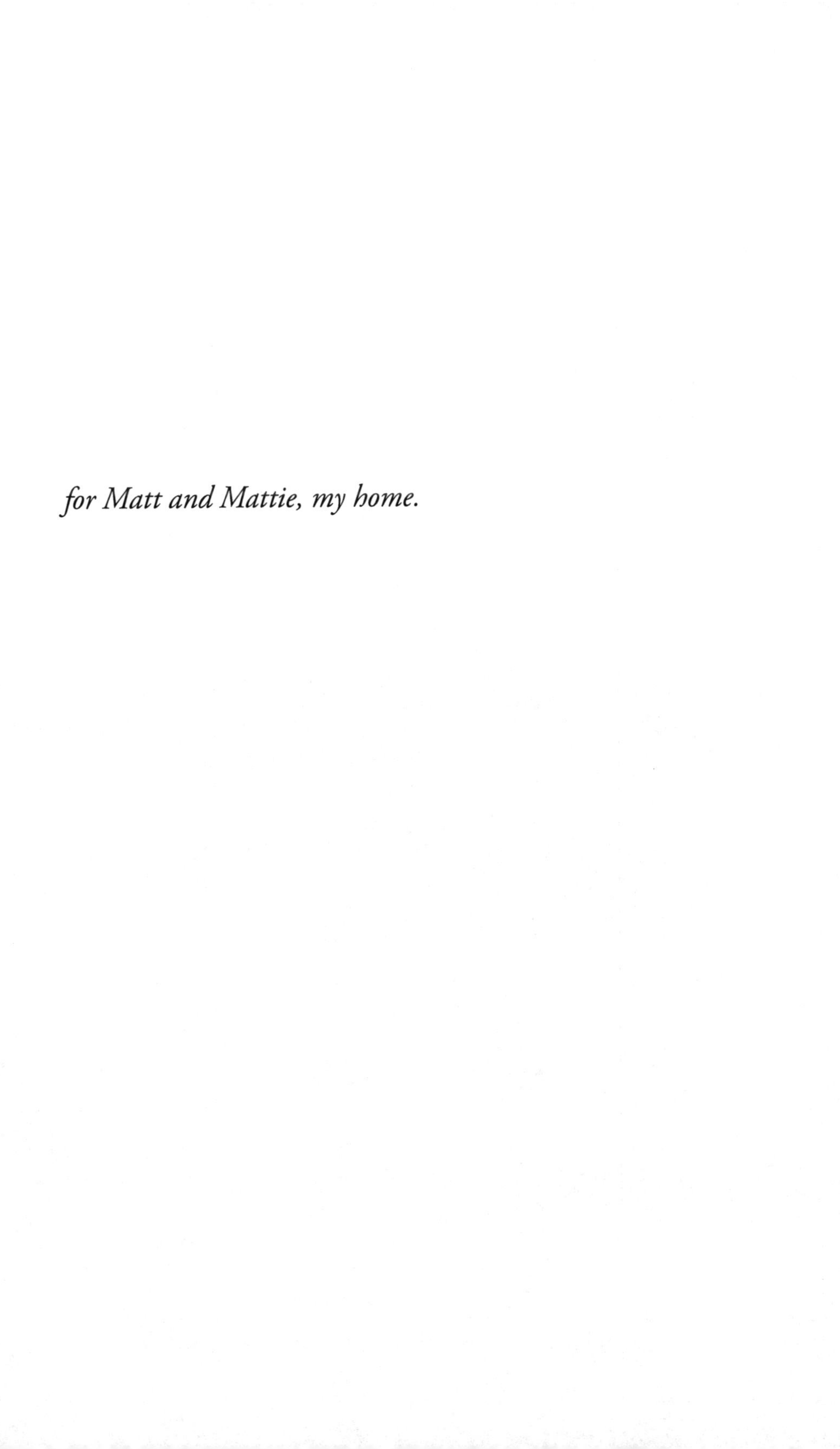

for Matt and Mattie, my home.

PROLOGUE

Summer, 1993

In the humid basement of a split-level ranch near the banks of the Wapsipinicon River, three friends sat, mostly naked, on a faded Rainbow Brite sheet on the floor, the knots of the practical Berber itching up at them through the thin cloth. This was Stevie's house and thus, Stevie's sheet, and in deference to an innocence that, though not long-departed, already seemed never to have belonged to her at all, she had turned the sheet upside down, so that the Rainbow Brite faces were kissing the carpet and would not be witness to what they were about to do.

If Stevie were being honest with herself, with her flipping, wag-dog stomach, she would admit a certain terror at what they were all on the cusp of here, in her parents' mildewed basement (in short: a threesome), but Stevie was a seventeen-year-old girl and if she had let one terror slip by, a multitude might come pouring in to cripple her. The idea was to float on top of the terror, to run headfirst at whatever it was that intimidated or scared you. To "just do it" as the sneaker slogan went. Equal parts *get it over with* and *see what it's like* and very little earnest desire governed how one lived as a teenager in those days. And since she lived in the small college town of Taylor, Iowa, and since this was before methamphetamine had dug its claws into the rural quilt patches of that state, this approach to life had mostly, harmlessly worked out and given her quite a few interesting experiences, including a handful of breathless, joyful acid trips and a boyfriend, Sam, with whom she had tried almost every sexual position in the literal book of sexual positions which Sam had found in his parents' bedroom as a child and now and then brought with him on their dates for consultation.

It was in this spirit of not-quite-reckless abandon that Sam and Stevie found themselves sitting casually in their underwear across from their good and beautiful friend Jen, who, Sam noted, was wearing a matching turquoise bra and panties cut, he'd realize a few years later, in the G-string style that would come to be popularized as the "thong," and immortalized in the Sisqo dance hit of 2000, "Thong Song," which would always confuse Sam, who had grown up using the word to describe his summer sandals, which had, in turn, by then, become more widely known as "flip-flops" in order (he assumed) to avoid embarrassment and miscommunications, while the word "smoothie" would, in the broader culture, go through an analogous but opposite transformation. In the early aughts, the country came to embrace the historically Californian practice of juicing, but for Sam, the word would always and forever be a synonym for blowjob and he was never able to walk into a Jamba Juice as an adult without snickering.

Sam was really trying not to make comparisons, but he couldn't help wincing, just a little, at Stevie's big white diapery underwear, her mismatched beige bra, the one that flummoxed him because why would you want your bra to be skin-colored anyway? Let's say you managed to fool someone with very bad eyesight into thinking that you weren't actually wearing a bra, which was the only reason he could see for making them that color. Wouldn't the resulting effect be nipple-less and frightening rather than sexy? Sam would never *say* this aloud to Stevie, of course. In fact, under normal circumstances he never even noticed what underwear Stevie wore because they were usually both in such a hurry to take it off. But here on the rug, the more he looked at the two girls in front of him, the more he found himself thinking random, stupid thoughts, focused on anything but the task at hand, which was to have a threesome, right here, right now. In his imagination, it had all been very sexy. He'd assumed being with two girls at once would make him feel extremely manly or, at least, that some sort of man-instinct would just take over and he would know, automatically, what to do. But that wasn't happening. Instead, here they were on this ugly, creepy sheet, sipping off of their Snapple bottles in order to make enough room for a healthy quantity of Hawkeye grain vodka, like some sort of pornographic tea party. It was giving him the opposite of a boner, whatever that was.

Jen put her Snapple down first and leaned across the sheet to grasp the bottle of vodka Stevie held snuggled between her soft thighs. Was Jen's hand brushing her leg accidentally or seductively? Stevie tried to make eye contact with her, but Jen was looking at Sam.

"I can't believe we're doing this," Jen whispered. "You guys. I can't believe it." Jen had a weird half-smile on her face that made Stevie's stomach shimmy again. When Jen did finally meet her gaze, the two girls began to giggle, and this quickly escalated into uncontrollable, snorting laughter.

Sam looked panicked. He held up his Snapple bottle, which glinted in the light of the two fat cinnamon Yankee jar-candles they'd lit earlier. "Uh. I heard the 'K' on the label stands for the Ku Klux Klan." He was red-faced and bewildered, as if some stranger had just spoken with his mouth.

"Where'd you hear that?" Jen asked, as if she too was trying to prolong their inevitable plunge.

"Aaron Yoder. He showed me that pissing man on the front of the Camel pack too."

Stevie rolled her eyes. "Not this again."

"It's there! I'm not making this up. Do you have a pack on you?"

"It's K for Kosher," said Jen. "It tells Jews who keep Kosher that they can drink Snapple."

Jen's family was Jewish and originally from New York, which was why Stevie had struck up a conversation with her on their first day of ninth grade, nearly three years ago. For as long as she could remember, Stevie had known she was going to move to New York City and become a famous novelist or possibly advertising executive and/or off-Broadway actor. (She wasn't sure what it meant, exactly, this "off-Broadway" business, but in movies and TV when someone said they were "off-Broadway," they were also usually sleek and devastatingly apathetic and smoked cloves.) Stevie even loved the word, *Manhattan*, which seemed to be architecturally mimetic of the place itself—the "h" slendering to its tip like a lopsided

Empire State Building, holding down the middle of the island; the two "t's" of the World Trade Center slightly south. She wrote Manhattan in her school notebooks the way some girls wrote the last names of the boys they secretly loved, behind their own first names, like making a wish. If this new Jen girl was from New York, surely she could let Stevie in on the mysteries of the place. As it turned out, Jen was from Albany, which was far different from Manhattan in almost every respect ("I'm what they call 'upstate,'" Jen had told her ruefully, and Stevie had nodded like she totally knew what this meant), and though Stevie found this out not long after befriending Jen, even then the two girls had already fallen in love with each other, the way girls do when they are young and boys are still weak, mean little things, hooting and batting at them in the hallways like wild animals. And, as it turned out, even if she was only from Albany, Jen really was more sophisticated and cultured than every other kid and probably many adults in Taylor. Jen, for instance, lost her virginity that first year, to a neutral party at another school named Malcolm Baker. She had, in fact, coached Stevie through the process of unbecoming a virgin herself, just four months ago.

Sex, as it turned out, was extremely interesting. It seemed to have much more to do with Manhattan and much less to do with her family's run-down shag-carpeted ranch on the river. It seemed infinitely mysterious and powerful and somehow very true. Almost immediately, Stevie had recognized that sex with Sam, though somewhat mechanical and with admittedly low returns, had great potential. She saw it would be a good investment and she had been, really still was, eager to plow through the rough patch of the beginning—which she and Sam were both well-read enough to have expected—and get to the multiple and simultaneous orgasms promised to them in the romance novels she openly criticized her mother for reading, but occasionally perused with one hand on her crotch under her tented covers at night, flashlight propped and lit, usually after smoking a good quantity of cheap weed through a blowtube out the window of her bedroom, where she liked to watch the cloud of her delinquency drift out over the night like some kind of dreamy, Gothic fog.

The first sex time had been on Sam's crumby chenille couch in March when his parents were away at some kind of fundraiser. Sam had lit candles and put on an Edith Piaf CD—the most romantic singer in the world, according to his mom. For her part, Stevie had snagged some of *her* mother's lingerie—a black lace teddy, too large in the bust—and they'd made unsurprisingly painful (for Stevie) and surprisingly warm (for Sam) love, neither one aware (blessedly) of the Freudian implications of the maternal bent of their mutual seduction.

In the following months, during their dates, which formerly consisted of movies and dinner followed by some sort of oral or digital co-pleasuring, they'd begun skipping the other stuff and jumping right into the sex. They had, in a shockingly short amount of time, become freaks. From the tiny adult bookstore across the railroad tracks on the south side of town, they'd purchased handcuffs and butt beads, lactation pornography and slim, bullet-sleek dildos. They had spent what seemed like weeks, possibly a month, on anal alone. They felt as though they were disappearing into something much larger and more important than the both of them, than school or their families, or even most of their other friends. But while Sam fell head-on into this abyss without much thought except for an occasional gratitude toward Stevie so strong it nearly brought him to tears, Stevie's insatiability was actually fed by a growing fear that what she was feeling through all these contortions was not actually pleasure but some sort of false epiphany constructed of desperate hope and rhythmic breathing in place of actual orgasm.

So, when Sam cleared his throat one night after they'd finished their contortions in the back of his Corolla and asked if she'd ever thought of a threesome, Stevie, feeling the weight of a thousand unfinished humps, sensing, though unable to say exactly what it was that was missing, did not immediately say no. And when Sam brought up Jen's name as the probable candidate, Stevie felt a promising jump in her groin.

It didn't even occur to her to be jealous of Jen. If anything, Stevie felt a little protective of Jen, who Sam now wanted to share her with. Jen who had taught her how to give a blowjob by practicing on bananas. Jen who had coached her through that first anxious time, who had recommended the lingerie. Jen who had listened to every detail of Stevie's personal life with approbation and congratulations, instead of the dour disapproval broadcast by the other girls in their school, girls who coyly wound around their fingers the silver cross necklaces they wore. They were girls who labeled other girls sluts, and then, protected by their accusations, went out and did the very same things themselves. Jen was different and special and so was their friendship. Plus, threesomes were exotic, and very New York. Might this not be the key to multiplicity and simultanaeity? A veritable orgasm smorgasbord? Stevie had taken a few days to think about it and when she showed up for her lifeguarding job at The Willows country club on Wednesday afternoon, Jen was there lying poolside on a lounger as if summoned, white skin flashing in such contrast against her black deep-V one piece (the other girls in purples and aqua metallics, looking so young and Midwestern), it hurt to look directly at her. She waved at Stevie, who had just climbed up on the stand and Stevie waved back, heart already clapping hard inside her. Jen sauntered over and stood beside the platform on which the first-station lifeguards swiveled, whistled, and yelled.

"'Sup, Buttercup?" said Jen, looking small and vulnerable there on the pool deck. Stevie thought she might throw up.

"Um. Chicken butt."

"Butt why?"

"Chicken thigh." Stevie felt some relief in this greeting. Things were still normal between them. It wasn't too late not to ask, for things to stay the way they'd been for years now. But no, another part of her contradicted, *it* is *too late. The idea is already in you. Things are already different, Jen just doesn't know it yet.*

"What's wrong, Steve?"

See? "What do you mean?"

"Uh, like, you working on your tan line or your frown line?"

Stevie unfurrowed her brow.

"Better."

"Sorry, I was just thinking. I have something I want to talk to you about."

Though Stevie couldn't see Jen's eyes behind her sunglasses, something about her face seemed to change slightly, to turn down.

"Am I in trouble?" she tried to joke, but it fell flat on the pavement between them like a slipped toddler. Then, quieter: "Are you mad or something?"

Stevie was so surprised by the fear and vulnerability in Jen's voice she actually had to think for a moment. Was she mad?

"No, I'm not mad. Nothing like that. I'll come and sit with you on break."

"Okay then, Miss Mystery," said Jen blew a kiss at her from over the top of her middle finger and went back to her lounger to wait.

But there was a problem with the baby pool chlorination and then the manager noticed that a couple of the trash cans were nearly overflowing and it wasn't until her third break that Stevie actually got to sit down on the plastic-strap chaise next to Jen's. And since she hadn't, in all that time of sitting and thinking, hit upon a better way to ask, she came right out with it.

"Will you have a threesome with us? Me and Sam?"

Jen laughed and Stevie's hands stopped shaking.

"Oh my god. Is that what you were all upset about before? I thought something was going on."

"What do you mean?"

Jen's face went blank and she blinked, and for just a moment, for less than a second, Stevie thought she looked . . . it was hard to say, but maybe embarrassed? Guilty? The look passed over her and was gone, like a pasture on a clear day when a small cloud passes right in front of the sun. "Didn't you say something the other day when we were out at Mars about your parents? I wondered about that. Like, maybe they'd been fighting a lot or something?"

Now it was Stevie's mood that darkened and she felt a little embarrassed. She had been so high that night, she'd had to lay down in the backseat of Sam's car. Had she said something to Jen, who'd walked her there so she wouldn't trip in the dark? Had she really talked about her parents? Like the rest of her friends, she preferred to pretend they didn't exist when she was anywhere but home.

"They're always at each other but, yeah, it's been worse since Christmas." Stevie's household had never been calm, exactly. Her dad was a yeller, and seemed perpetually impatient with his children and wife; her mom, the quick victim. Neither seemed capable of de-escalating and Stevie had inherited their temper. In recent weeks, it was hard to remember a night that hadn't ended in a slammed door. James alone was the peacekeeper. The few nights they bothered sitting down for dinner together anymore were usually silent affairs, punctuated only by his seemingly endless supply of animal facts.

The average giraffe is fourteen to eighteen feet tall, with males being taller than females, but the tallest on record was nineteen feet—a Masai bull named George. There are over three million species in the Amazon rainforest, but almost a million are currently facing extinction, largely due to human encroachment for industrial agricultural purposes, mainly cows and soy. Just like Iowa. The cows and soy, not the three million species. Here it's more like 1,100 species including lots of birds and many small mammals.

Etcetera. She knew if something happened to her parents, like if they did finally quit each other, that she would be okay, but she worried endlessly about James, who seemed to come from a different, kinder planet than the rest of them.

"My mom told me once they wouldn't get divorced but I don't know. I don't want to think about it right now. I just want to know if you're down with OPP." Maybe it was just that sex distracted her from the other stuff. In which case, she thought, bring it on.

Jen smiled her huge smile again. "Yeah, you know me, Miller. You crazy kids. Did you talk this over with Sam?"

"It was his idea actually,"

Another cloud.

"Oh . . . kay. Wow. But, you're like, into this too, right? You don't think it would be weird?"

Stevie looked out toward the tennis courts where the handsome college "pro" batted balls at an overweight middle-schooler who flinched when he served toward her and looked, in general, like she wanted to die. That, thought Stevie, is what sex was here to save us from. She looked at her own reflection in Jen's sunglasses. "I've thought it over and yes, it might be weird. But I totally trust you and it sounds really—"

"Hot."

"Yeah, totally hot! Plus you're, you know . . . experienced." Oh god, did Stevie sound like those cross-necklace biotches at school?

Jen laughed, "Practically a grown-ass lady."

"Well. Fine then." There was a long silence between them that neither girl knew how to fill. "So. . . ."

"So . . . I would love to have a threesome with you. So there." Jen nodded her head once, as if the deal were done or the spell cast and Stevie forgot all about the clouds, until many years later, after Jen's funeral, at which point it was far too late to ask her about them anyway.

And now all the Snapple bottles were full again, and now they were well shaken, and now sucked at greedily, and now something, at last, was happening to Sam's penis. Someone made a joke about cruise missiles. Someone else make a joke about plotting to assassinate Bush. There was nervous giggling and Sam moved closer on the sheet to the girls so that his feet were resting against Stevie's feet and Jen scooched closer too until their feet were all overlapped in a way that looked casual and accidental but each foot felt the soft curve of another's instep or rough of ankle hair or scrape of toenail so exquisitely that the sensation these feelings most closely resembled was a warm, shooting pain that ran from feet to crotches, connecting them to each other through a web of sensation. Something would have to be done about Sam's boner, and soon, but just as they were all connected they also all seemed to be suspended above a very steep drop and to move even an inch would be to risk tumbling in. The only sound was the clicking of throats as the booze moved through them. But finally, finally, when they had almost stopped breathing for the tension, Sam surprised himself and leaned forward and kissed Stevie, which was the easiest thing, the most comfortable place to start, and Jen scooted forward and sideways until she was right up against Stevie, and then was somehow kissing her too, kissing them, like they were some kind of sexy Siamese twin, Jen's head perched atop Stevie's strong bare shoulder. And no one could say, later, exactly how it all happened after that because they moved against and around each other with something like pure instinct, as if the very human thing that was happening was not human at all, but something primordial which needed only the small hop of that first thought of Sam's—*kiss Stevie*— to turn them into a perpetual motion machine. There wasn't a thought in Stevie's head as she licked at the parts of Jen that rolled closest to her and got her hand around Sam and felt someone's tongue at her thigh. She opened her eyes and Jen's white-star face was shining up from Stevie's navel, her mouth fishing open on Stevie's goose-bumped skin. Though her mouth was obscured here by Stevie's breast, there by the soft rise of her ribcage, Stevie could tell by her eyes that Jen was smiling and when their eyes did meet, Jen seemed to dissolve into Stevie's flesh, like all that had ever existed of them was some kind of fleshly Venn diagram, the overlap between two parts, and when Jen delivered her sour, sweet mouth back to Stevie's, there beat her heart, a fist against the empty side of Stevie's chest, the side with no heart, that anomalous asymmetry banished, fixed, solved.

Stevie slid her hand lazily through Jen's red hair, almost overwhelmed by her beauty. So she closed her eyes and nuzzled whatever flesh was nearest, accepted whatever was placed softly inside her and sighed and sighed until, at some point, the perpetual motion machine seemed to stop, and her body grew cold and when she opened her eyes, she saw Sam fucking Jen beside her.

Before Stevie felt the cold vine of jealousy begin to wind its way through her intestines, she thought how beautiful they were, how they looked into each other's eyes in a way she could not yet bring herself to look at Sam, but maybe something like how she'd just looked at Jen, how they moved like one joined thing, together, like they had known each other's bodies forever. Like they were in love, Stevie realized and then turned over and threw up pink Snapple-lemonade bile onto the Berber.

Though she tried not to dwell on it later, it seemed like a not-insignificant amount of time passed between the moment when Stevie began to puke and when Sam and Jen stopped fucking to help her. Stevie could never in a million years bring herself to ask either of them whether they'd "finished" as it went, or whether the fact of her retching had simply taken a moment to waft up to their cloud; whether Sam's ruined erection was post or interruptus, coitally speaking. It's not that she didn't want to know—she both did and didn't—or that she was afraid of the answer (again, as a seventeen-year-old girl, she was not, technically, afraid of anything): these things barely even registered as reasons to ask or not ask compared to the simple shame of having single-handedly brought to an end the most erotic thing that would probably ever happen to any of them, especially in the face of the tenderness they showed her as they crouched around her heaving body. But, though she tried not to dwell, she would. She would also find that instead of bringing them all closer together, the threesome had just shuffled them instead, redistributed the space between them so that instead of surrounded by her two best friends and their care and warmth and static, Stevie eventually found herself alone.

That was to come. Back in the basement, before it all fell apart, Jen came to her first, gathering up Stevie's fine brown hair in one hand, brushing back her bangs with the other. Then two more hands: one rubbing her back and the other, the only one Stevie could see, blotting at the puke on the carpet with the corner of the bedsheet.

"Babe," said Sam through a thick throat and Stevie hiccupped and laid the crown of her head on the floor to that her forehead grazed her thighs. In her first Bikram yoga class a decade later, she would tuck into rabbit pose and remember, with her whole body, this moment, and feel so nauseated she would have to leave the dripping, sweat-stinking room.

She turned her head and watched Sam's hand press at the carpet and imagined, without meaning to, the looks he and Jen were exchanging over her head, then squinted as she noticed that the carpet a couple of feet away seemed strangely stained. She sat up and crawled closer to the edge of their circle, feeling her stomach lurch again at the plasticky potpourri smell of the melting wax. She swallowed and put a hand out toward the stain. Wet. She smelled her hand and got a faint, fishy tang and stood up to turn on the bright overhead track lights. Jen yelped her surprise and both she and Sam automatically grabbed at the sheet to cover themselves, lightly spattering parts of themselves with Stevie's vomit.

"Jesus, Stevie! What the fuck?" Sam snipped and made a little gagging movement with his jaw.

Stevie pointed to the dark corners of the room where tiny bubbles were now bursting at the place where the baseboard met the carpet. She pulled on her shorts and tank top and walked to the basement door, which led out to the backyard, and she could actually see water worming its way in past the door frame to be soaked up, immediately, by the carpet. In fact, when she stepped back for the bigger picture, she saw that the walls were bordered by the spreading stain, that the dry-carpet island in the middle of the room covered by the sheet was rapidly shrinking, Sam and Jen shipwrecked there in the middle of it, wrestling themselves out of the sheet and into their clothes, trying not to look at each other but wanting, very badly and obviously, to do so anyway. Stevie threw the deadbolt and opened the basement door. She could see very little of the back yard but the small concrete patio was dark with water and the lawn, when she stepped onto it, sucked at her feet. Ahead of her in the dark, across the wet expanse of what had previously been her backyard, the black river sounded and moved like a train, so high and fast that it seemed to be floating above its own bed, like in a child's drawing of a river. Below an enormous moon, the gnarled and stubborn oak that clung to the riverbank and had grown out parallel to the water was now partially underwater. River waves crashed sullenly against the huge bulb of its exposed root system, parted, then met on the other side of the trunk in a fat burble, and disappeared into the manicured expanse of the neighbor's yard. As Stevie waded out into her yard, the water came up past her ankle bones. It was extremely cold. She heard Sam and Jen splash up behind her. Stevie imagined them holding hands but she didn't turn toward them to verify this. If she took her eyes off the river right now it would surely swallow them all.

"Oh," said Sam with a soft little gasp as if they were all still naked and nested like dolls in the salty warmth of one another instead of out here in the dark, wet and shivering, "it's flooding."

Late June in Taylor, Iowa: Fathers awoke on Sundays, took in coffee and the sports section while they waited for their dewy lawns to dry, then set out to tame them, their mowers farting a symphony up to the wide blue Iowa skies. But this year, rains had beat back these domesticities. On other, larger plots, the corn had been planted, and the people of Taylor drove by it in their minivans and sing-songed to themselves, "Knee-high by the fourth of July." The younger farmers, the ones who kept their noses in the papers, knew this would soon be a thing of the past. That once the insect-resistant GMs had been perfected, the growing season would be faster, shorter.

The older farmers could not be so optimistic. They'd worked too long and seen too much. Also, they were Hawkeye fans, which meant more or less the same thing. You weren't an Iowan farmer until you'd lost a crop to drought after a rainy spring, and watched the Hawks lose a playoff game they were favored to win by a mile. It was difficult to know whether this pessimism was reactive or protective: the farmer's soft heart inside a hard, all-weather case. But whatever its origins, their stoicism had trickled down to their sons and daughters and the children of their children. So when the Wapsi River leaped its bed and went careening through the livelihoods and domiciles of a good portion of the low-lying county—urged on, in part, by an Army Corps of Engineers who were not prepared for the fury with which the late spring melt waters from Canada and Minnesota had arrived, stinking and cold, at their banks—there was little outcry and no panic whatsoever. For the most part, the people of Taylor simply moved out of their sodden homes and farmers filed insurance claims for their ruined crops and life went on. For Stevie's parents, however, it signaled the beginning of the end.

There were four-and-a-half feet of water in the Miller's basement before the river crested and began what seemed to the family like a glacially slow recession. Though the thought was slightly babyish, for Stevie and James it felt, at first, like a vacation—like when they'd been to South Dakota to visit their grandparents last summer. The browns and whites of the national parks signs at Rushmore and the Black Hills and of the Badlands themselves. But Stevie could hear, from their adjoining rooms at the Super 8, a sharp furious buzz through the paper walls from their parents' room, almost always late, after James had fallen into his nightly boy coma.

What had felt like rising waters since Christmas had finally split the dam. Stevie spent most of every day at her lifeguarding job while James spent his summer days at friends' houses and the local rec center day camps. Stevie would pick him up after her shift on her way home and they drove back to the Super Hate, which is what they called it now, James dirt-smudged and damp, instructing Stevie on the lifespan of a mayfly and the names of rock types (*metamorphic, sedimentary, and ignorance*). When she was older, and James had disappeared into the wider world far from Iowa (her mom would never call him a runaway, preferring to think of him, instead, as a backpacker, an explorer. Not a child driven away by angry parents and some risings inside of himself he didn't understand, but as a whole and capable human who needed to wander to find himself. Her mother, the romantic, erstwhile hippie, had never admitted to herself or anyone else in the family that James was, in fact, by all appearances, itinerant and largely estranged) and she didn't hear from him, sometimes for years, she always thought of him in the passenger seat of her fifteen-year-old Dodge Charger, sunk deep into the maroon interior, looking like a wise old elf. "What do you think of owls, Stevie?"

"I think owls are a hoot, Jay."

In answer: a quick squint and his charming refusal to be bought with a pun. "Some people say they are bad luck, but I think they are beautiful. There's one at the house. When we get back there, I'll show you. When I was little, I always thought it was a ghost, but actually now I think it's an owl."

"Good detective work," she said as her heart broke for him and his littleness.

"Yeah, and if the owl is there, and I know it's not a ghost, then maybe I can talk to it. Maybe it won't scare me anymore."

She reached over to squeeze his hand, but he drew it away silently and looked out the window at the pulse of the setting sun. He was always already leaving but Stevie could never blame him because so was she.

Back at the motel, a pattern emerged: they'd eat dinner with their mom—who got home first from work in her clogs and scrubs, a bag of Kentucky Fried Chicken or Taco Bell in her fist—on one of the two beds in her parents' room, television on. When their dad got home, they'd move over to the kids' room and watch sitcoms with him so their mother could have "alone time," which, from the glimpses Stevie had caught through her parents' open motel-room door, consisted mostly of her mother laying on her side on the queen they didn't eat on, fully dressed, pointed away from them and hunched like something dead on the side of the road. Sometimes there was an ice cream run or a movie, but mostly they watched TV in their motel room until their dad fell asleep and had to be jostled awake to move back to his own room. The insurance company had told them three weeks, but three weeks turned into five. For a few nights near the end of their flooded-out motel stay, their dad never came home at all. "At a friend's," their mother told them, and it was strange to think of their father as having friends, much less a friend he would have a slumber party with. Stevie thought of Don Miller in pajamas, eating popcorn and making prank phone calls with his friend, Frank-Rizzo-Jerky-Boys style ("Hey there, Sizzlechest.")

In the over-airconditioned motel rooms, between greasy sacks of dinner and endless HBO movie reruns (when their parents were around: *Rudy* and *Free Willy*. When they weren't: *Menace II Society*, *Jason Goes to Hell*) this thing that was happening to her family seemed to be happening in slow motion. She often thought of the time last year when Stevie had asked her mom if they were going to get divorced and her mother had laughed a sharp bark and said no, of course not, but her eyes had been far away and thoughtful. She wouldn't dare to ask her now, afraid of what the answer would be, even while the concept remained abstract, too big. Something out of an episode of *Degrassi Junior High* or an after-school special.

On nights he didn't fall asleep on the burgundy and forest green geometric pile of their carpet, on nights her dad worked late or ran out for beer, or attempted another form of escape, those Dan Miller nights, Stevie and James learned to brace. How interesting or useful is it to recount these fights? Someone felt resentment and expressed that resentment in a passive aggressive or overtly aggressive or reasonable way and the accused reacted not as though this was valid or important or worthy of consideration, but as if s/he her/himself were being unfairly railroaded by the complainant—a known take-it-to-hearter, a borderline martyr, the accused would accuse and thus the escalation would occur until every slight and miscommunication, irritation and shit-sling from the last six weeks had been aired and accounted for. And the two-tone pitch of their voices, semi-muffled by the sincere, heart-eating dialogue of, say, *The Breakfast Club*—the sharp rises and sudden low moanings—would come to be something like the soundtrack of their summer. And so, knowing her parents' shame and anger would keep them on their side of the door, Stevie left her motel room every chance she got.

She snuck out often, sometimes going to Sam's to hang out, sometimes just driving around the gravel roads, listening to P.J Harvey, Wu-Tang Clan, and Pavement, until the college radio station turned to static and all that was left was the semaphore of the fireflies over acres and acres of fallow fields.

And on nights she didn't sneak out (was it sneaking really if she had never asked permission and so never been told no? Another question she kept to herself) Stevie snuck Sam in. Things had been different since that night between them, the night of the flood. For one, Jen had left on vacation a week after that night and hadn't yet returned. She'd sent one postcard: an old black-and-white photograph of two men in flannels sitting on a pickup bench with their dogs between them and the caption "Montana Double Date." Was this a sort of reference to their threesome? Jen's own message was short and neither Stevie nor Sam could read anything into it, though they tried. "Dear S&S, Yellowstone is nothing to write home about. But here I am. Saw two buffalo today. Smelled some sulfur springs (farts, Sam, farts). Parental units are doing their best to keep us in a cloud of Deep Woods Off 100% of the time. Expecting death by asphyxiation/bear at any moment. (Hammond, after some consideration, I've decided not to endorse your park.) XO, The Fiend Formerly Known As Jen."

Inscrutable, generic.

They played cards and watched so many movies and sometimes just hung out on the picnic bench behind the motel near the smokers and insomniacs that passed through every night. Sometimes Stevie would show her bravery by bumming a cigarette and then they'd hear stories: bikers in full leathers even in this humidity on their way to their own oily meccas—Wetzelland, Sturgis, Algona. But with Jen gone there was always something missing now, when it was just her and Sam, even with the bikers. Even in the damp depths of the Hate and the big bed that made them feel like parents. James still sometimes wet his bed or cried in his sleep and Stevie would shush him and pat his brow with the cool bleachy bedsheet, or run a bath for him, find new pajama pants. She could never make him put on the pull-ups that so deeply humiliated him. And, afterwards, tucking him back into bed, set of spare sheets folded over his flat boyish chest, she felt like a mom, a wife. Next to Sam when they slept, she felt sure of their world and their place in it together, in control of something beyond themselves. But when they were awake, Sam's face told the story of the missing thing. When Stevie said, "I love you," he could not, no matter how hard he tried, keep the tiny edge of discontent out of his voice when he answered back "I love you, too," though they both pretended it wasn't there. So when Sam half-jokingly suggested they break into Jen's house one night (has anyone ever been so full of suggestions?), Stevie told him she knew where Jen hid the spare key. The incursion felt right to both of them, though for different reasons.

Before they were taken away by cop car, before both sets of parents appeared weasel-eyed, angry, blinking in the dazing fluorescence of the county jail, something did feel right. An empty house at night always feels holy. Though the Siegel's kitchen was a little rank—something left behind in the trash or the fridge, the windows closed now for weeks—Sam felt the presence of something large and wise looking down on him. He had the ridiculous notion to sink to a knee and pray, actually. Ridiculous, maybe, but he still felt intensely irritated when Stevie opened a cabinet and pulled out a bottle of Hendrick's gin and began to giggle. "Open, sesame. Glug glug." She put the closed bottle to his head and tilted it; he pushed the bottle away. "Knock it off."

"Don't hiss. Let's have some fun. Isn't that why we're here? To do something fucking fun for once?"

"We're here. . . ." Sam trailed off. *We're here because I'm in love with Jen and when she's not around I feel like I can't breathe.* It wasn't something he could say to his girlfriend. *We're here because I am a weak person who is not worthy of either of you. We're here because I can't leave you when you're homeless and your family's falling apart and Jen's not even in the state of Iowa.*

"Communion," said Stevie and opened the bottle and drank, passed it to Sam.

"Okay," Sam said, because he couldn't say any of the rest of it, and drank.

Jen's room, dark and the nibblable sweetness of the space (the orange egg of Obsession and a half-empty bottle of Warm Vanilla Sugar body lotion), playbill posters from shows her cool aunt had taken her to see before she'd moved to Taylor: The Flaming Lips, Mudhoney, Ween. Sam and Stevie lay on top of the serape that covered her bed, drunk and pawing at each other and wishing she were there between them. It was where the young cop found them, gun out, as scared as they were.

No charges pressed but Jen didn't call when she got back into town. Sam knew the exact day—of course he did. From the prison of the eastern dormer in his family's beige and oversized cape cod, Sam could only make phone calls. No car for the rest of the summer meant he was marooned in his suburb, way out of town. He only got to keep the phone line on account of Stevie, who, he made the case, was going through some very heavy family stuff and currently living in a motel. His parents—his dad a successful realtor and his mother a busy Taylor socialite—were uncuriously horrified to the extent that the question of whether or not to phone-ground Sam was dropped immediately and never brought up again. In the same way that they never pressed Sam to get a job, his parents seemed content to let him live his life apart from them, caught up as they were in their own social lives.

Stevie, though, had work and James to take care of and most of what she owned was still in her bedroom on the second floor of their flooded house, collecting drywall dust and mold as contractors gutted their basement and first floor. So there was little to punish her with but the bite of their own disappointment and fear. She was forbidden from seeing Sam for at least two weeks (light, maybe, but her parents, on the verge of unraveling themselves, seemed to intuit that she would need someone to lean on, even if that someone had just aided and abetted a B&E), but in truth this was a kind of relief—the sense of something being wrong between them was distinct now. In a sense, the whole affair brought them together a bit, and Stevie found a strange solace in her parents' fury. That they were directing it at her and not each other, for once. Late at night, the dingy motel room filled with their concern, Stevie cried and cried, her anger and shame hidden in her tears, her fear at the arrival of some unspoken familial emergency, another seemingly equal fear that she was alone, that the two people closest to her were beginning to distance themselves from her, it all sobbed wide out of her and her parents fell quiet and eventually left her alone in their room to cry herself to sleep toward whatever the future would hold for her.

The moment one becomes a lifeguard, time begins to tick differently. Every day there were the opening tasks: kicking the garbage cans for raccoons, skimming the pool of leaves and frogs, screeching the heavy beach chaises across the concrete, already heating up at eight a.m., wiping down locker room surfaces, the smell of bleach and chlorine and sun-baked skin fogging the brain. Stevie sat on a white plastic deck chair at the shallow end of the pool and twirled her whistle around her finger. It was a game to see how loosely she could hold it so that the whistle came to rest softly at her wrist. Sometimes, the whistle flew off into the bushes, the metal ball that gave it its trill rattling like a dog tag and she'd have to wait for break to go hunt for it beyond the concrete block of the deck. The kids in the shallow end shivered and leapt at each other like puppies. They showed off and fell in and scraped their knees and walked as quickly as they could get away with—a quick stiff heel-to-toe stride that fulfilled the letter of the lifeguard's law: "Walk!"

In the heavy July heat, behind the mask of her sunglasses, it was easy not to think much at all. She ate grilled cheese sandwiches and cooled off in the pool on her breaks. There were just the minimum number of guards on duty to cover each station (front desk, tower, shallow end, baby pool) and they rotated every forty minutes. She liked her coworkers—two potheads from the swim team at the rival high school, an acne-studded kid from her own school (a boy she had once kissed in a closet in fifth grade and so now was almost legally obligated to ignore), and one nursing student from the university—but she couldn't spend much time with them on duty. Instead, she sat and looked at the water and allowed it to dazzle her and examined the many different facets of her anger as if she were hypnotized, or sitting on the bottom of the pool, being pressed by all those tons of water, soft on her like an animal skin.

Her parents were a wreck. Shortly after Stevie was caught at Jen's house, any semblance of parental unity left had dissolved and they spun out icy silences in their motel suite, a place Stevie had come to hate and fear. She had never before thought of her parents as owing her anything, but when she tried to think of the last time they'd all been happy together, she couldn't. Maybe the state fair, seven years ago, when she'd helped her cousin show his prize Boer goat, and she and her brother and parents had all gotten chocolate-covered bacon and lamb burgers from the food trucks. But even that memory was tainted by other parts of the day. The horror of the hog pens; the dead-baby-chicken look of her cousin's penis, which he showed her behind a Port O John. From then until now, what family was there? Just a father who always said "no" and never said "yes." How his hand had smelled like motor oil when he'd slapped her the night of her arrest. A mother who seemed powerless to change anything about the way they were living. And she'd look at the U.S. road map she'd put up on a wall in her bedroom at home as she began to plan her route of escape. When the rage in her felt too heavy, like it would drown her, she thought of the night she and Jen and Sam had spent together. How beautiful it had been before it wasn't. How the three of them had felt so perfect together. Like Voltron? It seemed they had found some pinnacle of togetherness there.

Her days were on repeat and time did not pass until, of course it did. One day Jen—had it been a month since she'd seen her?—sauntered up to the gazebo at the Willows, where Stevie was counting the cash in the lockbox. Jen peeled off a Twizzler and handed it to Stevie through the gazebo window. Stevie's hand trembled as she took it.

"So, what was that about? Breaking into my house?"

"I know, it was so stupid. I'm so, so sorry."

"It's a little weird, Miller. You know that, right? The cop said he found you on my bed?"

Stevie blushed and thanked god for the oversized sunglasses that covered half her face. "I'm really sorry." She didn't want to mumble. She didn't want to fall into the dark hole in the center of herself. Jen fiddled with the Twizzlers then bent down and reached into the gazebo. "Come here." Stevie leaned forward and Jen put her face close, then looked down and tied a Twizzler around Stevie's wrist. "The last time I saw you, I was biting your nipple."

A hard laugh leapt out of Stevie.

"I hope you have fully recovered. Your nipples I mean."

"I have. They have. Thanks for asking."

"Well then, that's the good news. The bad news is I'm not allowed to see you for the rest of the summer. My parents are super mad. They think you're a bad influence and they know you work here so I can't come to the pool for a while." Jen was backing away and Stevie wanted to reach out and grab her. Not yet. Don't go. The Twizzler unwound itself and fell to the ground.

"But you're here now."

"Shh. It's a secret. Now we have two. I'll try to come see you soon." Jen waved, half-looking back, and then tripped across the mushy blacktop parking lot toward a waiting car—a kid's car from the looks of it—an ancient beat-up Nissan Stanza with tinted windows. Stevie didn't recognize it. The car began its peel out before Jen had even got the door shut and Stevie didn't see her again until school started in the fall.

By August, Sam's parents, sick of having him around maybe, had relented and given him back his car and he used it to spy on Jen. Since his "arrest" and subsequent grounding, he'd been absolutely distracted by thoughts of her. Even on the phone with Stevie at night, who he was still not allowed to see, he could barely focus on her voice. "Fluids derangement," his neighbor

Andy called it. Andy who had, over the course of another wet summer several years ago, introduced Sam not only to porn, but also to masturbation and then, eventually, to the sock method. Fluids derangement was what happened when the jizz built up in your brain, when you got backed up. Sam knew Andy was a lunatic, but wasn't there something true about this too? Although, at the rate Sam was masturbating, literal backup was absolutely out of the question.

With his driving privileges restored, he'd been driving around town at night just to have something to do when he'd found himself a few blocks from Jen's house. Heart pounding, he'd turned onto her street and saw, as his blood-pressure spiked, that she was on her front porch. He pulled behind one of the parked cars that lined the street and turned off his lights. Her family's big Craftsman was set far enough back on its lot that she wouldn't necessarily notice the action on the street, he hoped. She sat on a porch swing, reading a book—from here he couldn't tell which—under a mothy porch light. She rocked gently, the toe of one foot anchoring her to the porch, acting as a fulcrum, the other foot tucked up under her in a gamine style so fetching that Sam wept frustrated, horny tears from the beige seat of his Corolla to see it. He came back the next morning and the next night and kept returning until he saw her again. One night, he'd walked back and forth on the sidewalk that faced her bedroom, seeing nothing but the top of Lou Reed's shiny black and white head and some vague shadows until her light had gone out. Another day, he caught her backing out of the drive in her parents' old Volvo and followed her to Hy-Vee, tailing her car by several lengths, the way he'd learned from shows like "Law & Order" and "The Commish." He'd meant to follow her into the store—a chance run-in—but some guy he'd never seen before got out of her car: long, loose brown hair, buttoned-up short sleeve plaid shirt, board shorts, sunglasses, Vans. He flicked his lit cigarette and it arced across the blazing sky and Sam chickened out. Instead watched her trail the guy into the store in her Daisy Dukes and flip-flops, ankle bracelet glinting in the sun. The whole scene hurt him in some deep space inside that felt hollowed out by pain, some white-hot infected spot that glowed in the center of him. He needed relief but couldn't find it with Stevie, even after her penance was done and they could take up where they'd left off. Where had they left off? With Sam and Stevie playing husband and wife in a motel room. Something about that seemed strange now. Too intimate and in the wrong ways.

The Millers had been lucky—the water hadn't damaged their foundation, and after their basement had been stripped to the studs and power washed, new drywall put up, the floor recarpeted, they'd moved back home. But after everything that had happened, how to get back to usual? Everything was different. Sam felt like a bad dog—hanging out with Stevie and creeping around Jen's, hoping to get a whiff. It was sick, he knew, but he didn't know how to stop it. How to end it with Stevie, or even if he should. Maybe what he wanted was something perverse that didn't exist, as far as he knew, in the real world at all. Maybe he was just an asshole. This seemed the most likely of answers.

To Stevie it felt as if everyone in her family ran to different corners the second they moved back into the house, which still smelled faintly of mildew and felt swampy, as if the river was still in it, haunting them. Coming home from a night out with Sam, she usually found James in front of the living room TV, her mother cloistered in her bedroom, her dad absent. These were new silences: dry and brittle. They seemed to expand to fill the space around them. Sam, too, was quiet and distant, the thing she'd sensed in the hotel room starting to take shape. Their usual movie/dinner/car-fucking routine felt stale to them both. They'd finished the book of sex positions. There was little between them left undone but much unsaid. She called Jen but couldn't bear to leave a message with her parents. Jen never called. Stevie wondered if it had more to do with the threesome, the break-in, or the Nissan Stanza guy.

The fluorescent and gossipy halls of Taylor High woke Stevie up from the dream of summer. At school, she and Sam were simply boyfriend and girlfriend and Jen not part of the equation at all, though she would miss Jen more than Sam and think often about their summer night together during the ensuing school year. She and Jen would spend time together at school, but it would never again be like it was—sleepovers and secrets. Jen had a new boyfriend, after all. It was the nature of things. Her parents finally seemed to make a decision and announced their divorce in a teary family meeting after breakfast one Sunday in October. Her father would move out by the end of the month. Stunning how someone could just make a decision like that about your own life.

Though Sam would, redundantly and officially, break up with Stevie in his car one chilly night, when they were parked in front of a giant mound of dug-out red clay at the edge of a new development behind their high school, a place the kids called Mars, things had already been over for a while. Still, she made him answer for it.

"Why," she said. It was not even properly a question.

"Because," he said. "You know why."

"No." Through the windshield, beyond the dirt pile, stars sparkled cold and hard from an infinity away.

"Because," he said. "Things just aren't the same."

"The same as what?" The stars swam into her eyes and she cursed her own tears.

"Stevie."

"My parents are getting a divorce."

Nothing. Silence. But a kind of heavy, angry silence. As if he was willing himself not to take her bait. Did he think she was making it up to get him to stay?

"Anyway," she said. "It doesn't matter. Because things aren't the same."

"Right," he sighed and turned to embrace her.

"No!" she yelled like a tantruming child and brought her knee up, not to hurt him, she would tell herself later, but because she couldn't bear his nearness. Because she felt if he touched her she might die. But the knee caught him hard as he moved toward it and he coughed and sunk forward, holding his chest. "Fuck," he whispered. "You bitch."

And then she was out of the car and sprinting back out the way they'd come in and turning the corner up a street that hadn't existed four months ago, and then making a quick right onto another, and she both wanted him to come find her and not, and when he didn't, it became a reason to let go and she sank onto the new road, so freshly paved and hardly used that it felt soft on her cheek. And she must have fallen asleep there, for a little bit, because when she woke her whole body was wet, not just her face, and she was violently cold. It took two hours to walk back to her house, where her parents' ugly, nightly aria had already wound down. Why they even bothered anymore was a mystery. Though exhausted, she laid awake until dawn, emptied of grief, defiant and plotting escape. Early graduation. A couple of part-time jobs, the money straight into savings until she had enough for a one-way ticket. Bonus: the jobs would keep her out of a house that echoed perpetually with the death rattle of her parents' marriage, though as it would turn out, the silence after her father left was worse. Her thought was this: Fuck them. Fuck them all.

Fourteen months later, on the way home from a night class, a young red-haired girl would sit down on the 2 train across from her and Stevie's breath would catch. Stevie saw right away it wasn't Jen, but the diffuse and foggy ache stayed with her a beat and instead of running from it, she tried to hold onto it, like a dream right after waking, that sweet wave of nostalgia. But on the other end of the train, two men began to yell at each other, and the feeling was gone, punctured by the sharp edge of the city, the train a dark knife tearing through its belly.

PART I

2008

Chapter 1

Dr. K stopped rummaging and held the Q-tip aloft in the air. "Chlamydia!" he yelled, triumphant, a vaginal eureka.

"Ha ha, April Fool's," said Stevie, for whom the exam was an eye-rolling complication. She'd come for a single dose of flucanazole but after describing her symptoms, Dr. K had insisted on an exam. After he said nothing else, though—no outburst of his usual cackling Russian laughter—she looked up at him, heart pounding. "That's a joke, right?"

"No April Fooling Day. Sexual disease is no joke, my dear! We won't know for sure until the labs come back but is discharge, is inflammation, and the little c going around . . . is probably chlamydia. Everybody get something. But is okay, just a quick Z-pack and good as new. Here." He handed her a lollipop, this man who had just been cervical-deep inside of her. She shuddered and took the pop and was relieved but also kind of disappointed to see it was actually a wrapped condom glued to a stick. Stevie did not share in his self-satisfaction. She turned her face to the framed "White and Blue Flower Shapes" print and shut her eyes for a moment before sitting up on the table. Anderson Anderson. It had to be him.

"I wish it was an actual sucker," Stevie sulked, feeling like one.

"How many licks does it take to get to middle? That was first English I knew here. First thing I see on TV." Dr. K laughed. "I knew then: Dmitri, you will give condom like candy in this free land."

"You had a dream, Dr. K."

"Yes, like your great M.L.K.! Also a doctor. Different kind." He clapped his hands. "Okay, no sex for two week though, Steve."

She had first seen Dr. K for her HPV eight years ago, and though his office was small and dingy, the fishtank he kept in it was clean and the pink light it gave off cheered her, as did the O'Keeffe poster, and Dr. K's general manner. He was her neighborhood mechanic, of a kind.

"Two weeks! But Dr. K, I have that gangbang this weekend."

"Then you will make everyone sick. Steve, I command you. No gangbang."

Stevie put the condom sucker in the pocket of her H&M blazer and tore off a string that had been flapping from a seam for weeks. "Just kidding, Doc. No gangbang for me."

"You know who give it you?"

Stevie's heel caught on the bed of her shoe. Manmade uppers. How surely the paradigm had shifted—you had to be aristocracy to get genuine leather and 100% wool these days. Whoever invented the phrase "better living through chemistry" didn't have to stand around smelling all the office workers he'd kitted up in polys and plastics. That white-collar struggle-funk, purchased on credit and paid for five times over. A layer of skin rubbed off as her foot found its home. "My boss. My boss gave me chlamydia." *Happy lunch hour to me.*

What is the protocol? Consider extenuating circumstance a): not only was Anderson Anderson (oh his parents, those sodden, clench-jawed Southamptonites) Stevie's boss, he was also b): no longer fucking Stevie, but c): fucking a fawn of an intern named Eugenia, instead. A turn of events that did not upset Stevie so much as surprise and humiliate her. A turn of events which was not announced per se, but rather observed at after-work drinks one night.

When they'd first gotten together, Stevie had been flattered, hungry. Here was someone who could put an end to her expensive, tiny closet on the Upper West Side. When she looked out onto the street through the warped window from her rented studio, she felt as though she were living inside a bubble, a toy action hero paralyzed in its molded plastic shell. Sometimes it felt like all of New York was clawing to get in and she was a mouse in a hole too small for the paws and snout of the city. Instead of at home in New York, Stevie had always felt as though she was ducking for cover, hiding from something, waiting for the storm to blow over. In the thin, clean, blond angles of Anderson Anderson, might she not find a partner ready to invest in her and, at last, find safety?

No, she might not.

She should have known. She wasn't the trophy-wife type. She was a scrappy Midwesterner, nearly unconventional in this unconventional city, but not the sort you took to meet your parents for greyhounds at the Bathing Corporation. Those who scrap do not get to marry Andersons. Something about the openness of her face, the natural heaviness of her bottom that she could not, finally, spin or Bikram off. She was like the prairie—all wide and rolling hills. Eugenia, though, was angles and secrets, bangs over French-girl long hair and a silk dress that smelled like cigarettes and jasmine.

She had blogged about it of course, and had received a lot of support from her blogroll compatriots. Not the big ones, whose blogs she linked but who would never, ever link back—who was she to Jason Kottke (fleeting Iowan himself) or everyone's favorite bookslut, Jessa Crispin?—but the friendly few who, like her, played in the low-hundreds-hits-a-week range, left their supportive vitriol in the comments below her post, "Cad's Bad Brad Act."

In a development that will surprise neither of the readers of this blog, East End was last seen sucking face with a work bitch so rich she can afford to be an intern. Starter wife age. Legs for miles. Kill me now.

Yes, of course, I stalked her on New York Social Diary. It seems East End has made a match for himself with Miss Westhampton and yours truly will have to find something else to do on the weekends for a while.

Seriously though, why did he bother? This is a rhetorical question. I have a theory that dating a Midwesterner of unknown origins is the closest thing some of the sophisticates out here can get to the exotic. They think it's fascinating? Sexy? Deliciously plebian? that we don't know a single pew at

St. Patrick's or Spence alum and they are drawn into our plain, wide orbits, the same way there is always ALWAYS a line to get into Times Square Red Lobster on the weekends. (I know we are the generation of irony, but we are also the generation of really fucking good food and I just Do Not Get It. That's cool, though. More smoked-fish platters for me at Prune.) It's part of what makes New York so exciting. Those of us who regularly rely on bar snacks for dinner might, on some random Alphabet City night, stumble into and accidentally make out with any number of minor or major city celebrities or NOCDs and what makes this hilarious is that it is seemingly also exciting to them to accidentally stumble into and make out with us: people of no social standing whatsoever whose existence on earth can neither harm nor help them and for whom they (I guess) mistake the low tug of pity for something genital. They are shame-kinks, peasant-fuckers. And what is there left to do at the end of such a fucking, except to exeunt, stage left, as quickly as possible with my head down and breathe a small sigh of relief that I can once again wear my normal, slutty bathing suits to the ignoble public beaches (colloquially known to East End and his friends as "The Bay of Pigs") of this fragrant and disorienting archipelago.

So the question remained: should she tell her boss about the chlamydia or no?

She got her answer twenty minutes later, back at Britely, vagina en fuego and her own sense of her role as wronged woman growing stronger with every twitch of her crotch. As if summoned, Anderson Anderson was suddenly at her desk in his popped pink polo collar and sockless Converse. He was a man who could pull off the women's perfume he wore. Something that smelled like cinnamon and Earl Gray tea. "Stevie," he said.

That nose. She had touched it, which was how the whole thing had started. The nose and the perfect dirty-gold ringlets, the poreless forehead. A former finance recruiter who'd climbed the ranks. She'd been smitten at first, then disappointingly bored. He was disinterested in anything but preppy talk—finding a summer house in the Hamptons even though his parents already lived there year-round, the Jitney. *Do you think our waiter is jealous of people who can afford to eat in this restaurant? The other day at Brooks Brothers I tried on the most interesting shirt.* Doomed from the start.

But when he stumbled into their afterwork bar one evening, clearly already drunk, with his arm around the chilly intern Eugenia—impossibly thin and young and wreathed in smoke like some Puckish dream—something in Stevie flailed anyway. She in a pussy-bow collar, long-sleeve sack dress, Miu Miu Mary Janes, bangs in her eyes, he in a rumpled button-down and broken-in Levis. How very Gainsbourg the two of them had looked together in that tony Manhattan way.

Her old lover, her current boss, did that annoying, proprietary thing where he leaned around the corner of her office doorway and beckoned her with a half-raised finger. As if he didn't have enough bones to walk all the way up to her desk, homo erectus-style, and ask her with his words.

Stevie grimaced but followed his heroically broad shoulders down the hall to his office. Did he already know? Was it possible she had this wrong? Was chlamydia like HIV? Could it show up years after exposure? Had *she* given it to *him*?

Eugenia looked up at Anderson but did not make eye contact with Stevie as she passed her desk. Out of habit, Stevie counted the Kidrobot Dunnies and Labbits and the growing army of art-infant gifts Anderson brought in for Eugenia. Eugenia frowned at her screen and fiddled with one side of her headphones and averted her eyes.

Anderson Anderson's office was pale and empty, no file folders, barely even a desk—just a narrow Lucite platform upon which floated a single sheet of paper. The wall was dominated by an Agnes Martin grid of whispered graphite lines on canvas. Order and the borders of fascism. Anderson gave her a grim look she couldn't read and she perched atop the Louis Ghost Chair opposite his. Like she did every time she was in here, sitting in this chair, she gazed for a moment out the windows at his Manhattan, which was scattered in front of them like the blocks on a child's playroom floor and wondered what it would feel like to recognize the toys as her own.

He looked down at his knitted fingers and took a breath. "It's come to my attention that you write a blog." There was a pause as if he was giving her time to process new information. There was something disapproving in his voice, though his face was as affectless as the Martin grid.

And you fuck teenagers, Stevie burned to respond.

"At work." The words stuck between them like thrown knives. "According to the time stamps."

Ah. Stevie felt herself blush, which made her blush more. Goddamnit. "I—" she took a breath. Do not stutter. "Maybe once or twice. Mostly though, no. I write it at home. After work."

Anderson Anderson looked at the single sheet of paper on his desk. "This report says twelve blog posts at work just this month."

Stevie craned her neck to look at the paper but he flipped it over.

"I post them at work, sure, but I don't *write* them at work."

Anderson's canvas was blank. And why, why did she rush to splatter it? But splatter, she did.

"My internet at home is crappy. I write them, then wait until I get to work to post them."

"I don't really see the difference. You're using work time whether it's to write or post. And you write them *about* work."

And here Stevie did not have a comeback. Because, yes, of course she did.

"You write them about *me*."

"It's a blog about dating and life in New York. I write posts about people I date. It's a thing."

"It's a *thing*?" The way he said this was so venomous and dismissive that Stevie thought for a moment that he was actually much smarter and meaner than she'd previously understood. She saw, now, that he was furious with her, was attempting to keep his face impartial in order not to lose his temper completely.

"This is a lawsuit waiting to happen. One of our employees has already threatened to sue—"

"Who, Eugenia?" Now Stevie was angry. She could see Eugenia's paw prints all over this. Of course Eugenia would go to Anderson. Of course she'd be trying to get Stevie in trouble. It wasn't enough that she'd won, she had to ruin the rest of Stevie's life too.

"That's confidential."

"She blew my whistle, right, Anderson? I mean, after she blew yours."

"Okay. You're fired. You can clear your things out today. I'll give you two month's severance."

Vertigo. The strong sense that Stevie was sitting in a box inside the Martin grid and that in each box in the grid, there was another manager firing another closet-blogger, repeated, a thousand times. The grid was about to be picked up and shaken, and she and all the others would fall out onto the floor and be swept away in the reeking mop of a giant. Though this was indeed April Fool's Day and here she was the fool for the second time that day, she knew this time that none of this was a joke.

"Anderson? Are you kidding me? For writing blog posts?" Getting fired was the thing that had made Dooce famous but, of course, it made her famous because she was the first. Stevie wondered what number of fired blogger she was. A hundred? A thousand?

Stevie often found her job depressing. If she'd finished college, gone to a better college, come from money, she might actually have a job in magazines or documentary film, like she'd used to dream about. Instead, she was a recruiter. She got creative jobs for other people. Often for people younger than she was. All of them smarter, richer, better dressed. The Random House VP last year, and the editor at Esquire, the assistant to a powerful agent at UTA who'd landed his first producing credit within a year.

But it was a job and it paid okay and while she was not a Mamet-esque Always-Be-Closing type, she did just fine for herself. Maybe not genuine-leather fine, but that was coming. Or, actually, that's what she'd always patiently, stupidly assumed like the trusting Midwesterner she was. Now it seemed she had been wrong.

Anderson Anderson seemed drained of his anger, and instead of blank, he just looked tired. "I'm not kidding. Eugenia will take over your accounts."

Stevie imagined getting close enough to him to bite the perfect aquiline nose off his face. To roll a ringlet up on her finger and rip it off his scalp. To tip him from his Philipe Starck out the window and watch his soundless flight. "You can't do that," she choked. Her throat started to close and rasp. Oh god, no crying. Anderson looked out the window in his office, raised an eyebrow and sighed. She remembered the first time she saw him do that. It had been sexy. They'd been on a twilight cruise down near Battery Park City and a pretty girl had asked him for a light. Though at the time she'd thought it meant he only had eyes for her, now she realized it was maybe because he didn't actually like women very much. No time for their shitty emotions. It had hurt to see him like that with Eugenia, but she'd understood it. This, though. This felt like a whole other level of betrayal. Below, the afternoon glittered with wealthy malevolence—women in flowing white gowns—tony seagulls— moved among the shaped topiaries on a rooftop below them.

"Well, FYI, you gave me chlamydia, you dick."

She stumbled out of his office, reached into her blazer pocket and dropped the condom lolly square on Eugenia's desk. She didn't look back but heard a rodentian squeak behind her.

In her mind, Stevie smashed the Agnes Martin over both of their heads, imprisoning them in the frame before she set it on fire.

When her mother called, she was on her third martini, shifting on her bar stool, trying to get comfortable as the stink of the underground bar rose around her. It was a terrible and unforeseen side effect of the smoking ban—everyone was so gung-ho to get rid of the smoke that no one realized how much worse these spaces would smell once the smoke was gone. Or that the smoke would never truly go—not at the neighborhood places. The investor-backed restaurants could afford the industrial steam clean, the new woodwork, but the pubs and the holes—the places where everyone else drank, especially at two p.m. on a Tuesday—those would smell like vomited-in gym socks until the old tenements that housed them someday burned to the ground or were bought by those same investors and paved into Whole Foods or pieds-a-terre for foreign businessmen.

The itch was bad, but the burning sensation the friction produced was really something new. Walking was excruciating. The only thing comparable were the wicked foot blisters she'd had after 9/11, when she'd walked eighty blocks home in kitten heels, away from the stink and the smoke roiling up from the new hellish aperture that had opened in lower Manhattan.

They'd all walked like the undead—silent and shuffling except for the screams and sobs when people stopped to look back. She had walked home with her boss, Wes—this, years before Anderson Anderson had arrived, protégé on fire, from the midtown office, where he had grown bored with finance and set his sights on the sexier downtown scene—the so-called "creatives." Wes and his wife had a place on Central Park West and two kids who were younger than they would have been if Wes and his wife had lived in Iowa. Wes had looked old and gray on that walk and they'd said little but she had felt comforted by his paternal presence—the kind of presence that had been so often lacking in her own life. She remembered he had been near frantic, unable to get through to his wife at her law firm uptown or his kids' school. He had done little else but dial and redial. When Stevie's phone rang once—her mother, begging her to leave the city, to come home right now—before the signal was lost, Wes had looked at her with desperate envy and it had occurred to her that this event, whatever the fuck was happening right now, meant very different things to each of them and she felt a pang for the cozy worry that would fill Wes's Classic Six tonight.

All that and *this* is how it ended. Fired by her boss. Fucked then fucked over. She'd been nervous about being blown up on the subway during her commute every day for the last seven years and some asshole with a popped collar could just kick her out of her life. It felt like being shit out by history. That was a good line. She said it aloud to herself so that she'd remember it for the blog and a piece of chewed olive flew out of her mouth and stuck to the bar.

Her phone rang. Stevie flipped it open and smooshed the olive desultorily with her thumb. "Mom, I've been shit out by history."

"Honey? Stevie? Can you hear me?" Every conversation with her mother began this way, vaguely emergent. The cell service at her house was spotty and her mother had never truly acclimated to the cell phone, but she insisted on using it over the landline, in thrall to the technology and eager to get her month's worth out of it.

"I can hear you."

"I'm sorry to call you at work, babe. I didn't think you'd pick up."

Stevie chewed another olive off its toothpick, "It's okay, Mom."

The double beep of her call waiting blotted out whatever else her mother was saying to her now and she pulled the phone away from her ear. A 212 number she didn't recognize. Probably a misdial, but could be something work related. A client. Eugenia on her hands and knees, repentant. A loser could wish. "Mom, hold on a sec. I have to get this."

It was Amanda Collins. The voice on the other line announced this as if it explained everything, though Stevie did not and had never known an Amanda Collins. Stevie chewed quietly, puzzling. Amanda Collins barged on, impatient. Is this *Hex and the City*, she wanted to know. Because Amanda Collins was an agent. A *literary* agent. She inflected this as if she were asking a question: Am I, Amanda Collins, a literary agent?

"You *are* a literary agent!" Stevie answered, fairly certain this was correct.

"Yes I am, and I fucking *love* your blog."

Stevie choked, then coughed.

"Oh my god, are you okay?" Amanda Collins sounded extremely alarmed.

Stevie croaked that she was and Amanda Collins pushed on. "I'm assuming that means you don't have an agent yet and that you want one. Right answer. Okay. I'm also assuming that you don't know jack-dick about the lit world because if you did, you'd know I just signed book deals for *I Keep a Diary* Brian and Nathalie from *Cup of Chica* last month alone. I'm on a roll and I'm taking you with me. You in?"

Stevie swallowed. "Um, oh my gosh. Well."

Amanda Collins seemed to vibrate with excitement and irritation. "I think you have a fresh young voice. Voice of a generation. Yadda, yadda, yadda. You're better than some of the bloggers I've signed lately, you just need a hook."

Stevie found her voice. "I have a hook. Dating in New York."

"Oh no, honey, that's everyone's fucking hook. Amy Sohn already did anal and unless you look like Julia Allison, you can't do it. It's dead. Do you look like Julia Allison?"

"Definitely not."

"It's okay, no one does. Not even Julia Allison. Okay, so a hook—you have anything?"

Unless someone wanted to read a blog about scouring Monster daily and eating a single bunless Boca Burger with an egg on top for dinner every night, until she found another job, no. "Can I think about it?"

Amanda Collins made kissing noises from inside Stevie's phone, "Of course. My assistant's going to call you to set up a lunch date with me and then she'll mail out a contract. There's a project description section. You call me when you get it and we'll fill in that part together."

"Wow. I mean, thank you. I don't know what to say."

"Listen, bitch, you don't have to say anything. We're going to make each other some Benjamins, right?" Amanda Collins cackled across the wireless networks of Manhattan, through the man-made caverns where white collars were right then staining yellow with fear and despair, up the rebar in the GM building, formerly owned by squinty tycoon Donald Trump and financed by a Hungarian named Soros, currently home to Apple Fifth Avenue, a clear box of a retail environment that appeared to sell nothing so pedestrian as actual objects where Anderson Anderson, about to lick the vagina of the rich, young intern on his Lucite desk, paused and squinted—was that a blister?

"Right!" yelled Stevie. The bartender, an ancient rheumy alcoholic, jerked mid-pour and shot Coke across the sticky bar. "Yes," she whispered into the phone. "Thank you, Amanda Collins."

But Amanda Collins had already hung up. The soft voice on the other end was her mother. Her mother! She'd completely forgotten. How like her mother not to hang up.

"Oh my god, mom, are you still there? You're not going to believe this."

"Can you hear me now?" They had to go through the whole confusing conversation opener again, of course. "Stevie? Are you there? I don't want to bother you at work, sweetie, I'm sure you're very busy but I have some news."

Stevie thought of James first and her heart fell out. She slipped off her bar stool and out the door, where the smokers exhaled into the wet spring chill. Fucking James. She'd always known this moment would come. The something's-happened-to-James moment and she had maybe prematurely hated him for it. For the destruction he would inevitably wreak. And now. . . .

Stevie was suddenly sober, the soft drunk a blanket fallen off her shoulders. "What happened to James?"

"James is fine. Sweetie, it's Jen. Your old friend Jen Siegel." A pause, a figuring. "She's . . . she passed."

Stevie felt momentarily hearted again—not James—then realized the wound had been struck anyway. And like any fresh wound, it took a little while for the blood to begin to flow.

"'Passed'?"

"She died, honey. I think you better come home."

Empty houses all smelled the same. It was a peculiarity he always remembered when he opened a home for the first time. Emptied of all its stuff and closed for just a day, a home began to smell like exactly what it was: an empty building. Wood, paint, mildew and the unmistakable blood tang of the metal bits that held it all together. Each house, occupied, accumulated its own fragrance over the years— cooking habits, pets. Homes with babies tended toward the milky, toward shit, while children smelled like sugared sweat and teenagers, drugstore perfume, pot. Men brought in the smells of the garage—motor oil, gasoline, paint thinner. Mothers had a bready, yeasty smell while the houses of single women tended to smell more strongly of half-eaten dinners and the urine of cats and small dogs. He could smell a ferret from a mile away (and, more importantly, the kind of family who would have a ferret—divorced mom, tween boy, working class). The carpeted basements of larger families with kids of various ages always housed some form of rodent: guinea pig, hamster, rat, rabbit. Though a rabbit was not technically a rodent. (This he'd just learned from the daughter of the homeowners as he bent over a startlingly large cage containing a black and white Dutch named, of course, Oreo. For some unspoken reason, thought the house was otherwise empty, Oreo was still occupying the front room and he'd had to call the family to come pick it up before the open house began. While he waited, he'd eventually wandered into its space, noting with a frown the crunchy brown halo on the carpet around the cage. He'd stuck a finger into the cage and the rabbit had sniffed his hand amiably before biting the tip of one finger hard enough to draw blood. "Rodent!" he'd yelled, unable to recover his finger for a frighteningly long moment, then nearly screamed again as its girl, who had somehow entered the house and snuck up behind him in cat-burglar silence, swooped over to the cage. Seeing her, the rabbit took its teeth out of his flesh and began to groom itself.

"Oreo!" she squealed, scooped the rabbit out of its cage, and slung him over her shoulder. "It's a lagomorph, *not* a rodent. Rabbits have more in common with deer than rats." She'd frowned at him and he'd experienced a small vindicating gladness that he had no kids.

He'd bent close to her, scowled Grinchily, said, "Well, they both make a good stew," to which she'd had no answer but showed him a crinkled, befuddled chin. Wood shavings fell from the rabbit's squirming legs, the terror clear in its wild, liquid eyes. It was the look of an animal that suspects it is about to be eaten. It might have been a stupid rodent, but Sam felt a pang of solidarity. He knew how it felt. This was the first home (he'd been coached by his dad to say the word, which was friendlier, cozier, more personal than "house") he'd listed in ages. He wasn't totally sure when the listings had stopped rolling in for him. A month ago now? Maybe two? One day he'd sat down at his desk and realized he had nothing to sell. A week later, his last buyers had closed and that was it for clients. There had been talk that he'd mostly ignored—corporate managers from Tampa and Vegas offices talked of a bursting bubble. Prices in Taylor were pretty stable—a little flat maybe, but not headed down, not yet—but the managers from the far-flung urban offices had begun to sound a little doomy. How had the one guy from Clearlake put it? "The Fed's up Freddie's Fannie. That Bernanke's a real killjoy."

Tsunami's coming, said the guys in Florida, sounding the alarm. And the rest of the country out there in a canoe. Sam had not panicked then, had not even panicked when Pam had left an article about the collapse of Countrywide Financial on his seat, an article which he'd first sat on, then used to soak up a coffee spill on his desk.

He had not panicked but he had made some calls. The clients who'd returned weren't interested in selling their homes—at least that's what they told him—and though they all politely promised to pass his name along to colleagues and friends, not a single referral came of it. And that had been it.

For a while, he'd spent mornings doing nothing. He'd puttered around his office, which was bare but for a ceiling-high, mostly empty oak bookcase with a row shelf of pulp mystery novels he kept at work because Bonnie thought they looked too cheap for the built-ins at home. There was also a tall, waxy plant in a black plastic container, that had appeared inexplicably one day last year. There was something about it he didn't like—it seemed both real and not real at the same time. He had never watered it, and yet he'd scraped matter off a leaf and sniffed it one day and smelled the fecund, clotted smell of a living thing. Their evening janitor, a teenage boy who was silent to the point of sullenness, did not seem like the secret-watering type. And so, in these tiny, pitiful ways, his was an office full of mystery, if not wonder.

There had been endless games of Civilization and endless obituaries in the *Taylor Flyer* (long illness and short illness, beloved now singing in Heaven's golden choir). He regularly sauntered out onto Main Street for a late lunch at one of the nearby farmer's cafés, which he preferred to the co-ed pizza shops and yuppie fusion bars his colleagues loved. The old men—and a few women too: the neighboring county lesbians with the alpacas, and a couple of weathered widows in Carharts—sat like dissatisfied lumps at the counter, gazing into their coffees (never hot enough for their leathered mouths) like the weather had already defeated them, like the government had already cancelled their subsidies, the disappointment permanently ground into their roots, their very genes. There was something in the atmosphere of the place that Sam felt in tune with. This was it, he thought when he walked in. This was life. Only the alpaca gals were what might pass for friendly in farm country and he'd shared a lunch-time beer with them now and again. Stacy and Rose. Rose was a tough old thing who never smiled, stiff and straight, an old nail the soil had coughed up. Stacy, the younger, was plump, and owned an endless supply of long brown skirts which she wore everyday, even through the arctic winters, with her silks underneath. The alpacas were their children and main topic of conversation. "Amelia had a bath today. She's not mothering well to little Joan." This was how a dialogue began, in place of greeting. Little was required of the listener but polite interest whether feigned or sincere.

"What about Virginia?" he'd ask. "Did her hoof heal yet?" Regardless of sex, all the animals were named after history's great women and referred to as "she" (a fact he'd been apprised of one day after correcting Rose for claiming she'd recently neutered Frida. "You mean spayed? " he'd said, surprised at the error. "I mean I cut off her testicles." Rose had seemed more affronted than usual.).

After a coffee, or (more often than he'd like to admit) beer with the ladies, he'd check in with the office manager, Pam (and what great mirth was had in the office over the completely unremarkable coincidence that their names rhymed. Pam blushed every time the joke was made.) and tell her he was off to meet clients.

Then he drove.

Those first couple of listless, listingless weeks, he took short jaunts to neighboring towns. Tiny places more outpost than anything—a four-way stop at an intersection and a post-office, islands of basic commerce in an ocean of corn and soybeans, dirty snow heaped in piles in the colorless fields. He'd found an Amish grocery that sold about every type of kolache in existence; a fancy French restaurant run out of the first floor of a farmhouse on a hill in the middle of the county; huge auction houses that sold antique John Deere tractors, perfectly restored, and pristine mid-century furniture for next to nothing. He ventured further out to Indian burial mounds, an early Mormon settlement and a living-history farm, with period actors who spoke in overloud voices about the horrors of dentistry in the nineteenth century. Everywhere he went was nowhere, and yet all these places felt more like home to him than Taylor. Each hill held a secret and he wanted to know them all. Sometimes he headed west, toward the capitol, through What Cheer and the flatlands where the wild hitching breath of the prairie had been suffocated by farm settlements and the old promise of plenty, now faded into feed lots and factory farms that stank of fear and death ("The smell of money," the ranchers liked to say). This week though, he'd driven east—over the mythic Mississippi and past the concrete industriousness of the Quad Cities, snout pointed at Chicago. He'd sailed as far as DeKalb and realized, with a start, that he'd been hotfooting it for three hours.

So, no, faced with the end of his business prospects, he hadn't panicked—proud of that—but then what was this new habit of wandering about? Panic was a strong word, and he probably didn't have such a thing in him. He was a Midwestern man at the turn of the century—bred, like livestock, to be even-tempered and suspicious of any idea with even a whiff of the hysterical about it. To mildly and automatically defend the grandfatherly authorities and lawmakers that made bovine wives out of all Iowans. But perhaps he did feel a lick of urgency deep down. Some unease nipping up at him. Maybe it was the recent phone call from Jen last week. He'd been on one of those work-time day trips when she'd called. He hadn't even been surprised—hadn't he just, an hour ago, mindlessly driven by her parents' house on the way out of town and thought of her, a block after he'd realized what he'd just done? Hadn't he called to her in this way? Summoned her? It had been a year since they'd talked, two since she'd come home for the annual Christmas night drinks at Doc's for the townies and the returnies, the ones who'd escaped, coming out of their overheated parents' houses to mix with those who had stayed, their cultural divides put aside for an evening of getting absolutely shitfaced and raising from the dead their libidinal and gossipy eighteen-year-old selves.

"Samalama ding dong," her greeting had gone. That husky touch of vocal fry that always made his balls shiver gently. "I need . . . hold on for a sec," and the line had gone silent before he'd even managed to say hello. Almost as quickly she clicked back onto the call.

"Okay, so I'm going to be in Des Moines next week—"

He cut her off. "Hello? Who is this?" he pretended but couldn't keep the smile from his voice. "You've reached the Donner Kebab House."

"You kill 'em, we grill 'em." A beat of happy silence between them. "That a was a good one, buddy. But, hey, Sammy. I'm coming into town next week and I need a favor. I can't tell you why, not over the phone, but can you meet me for dinner at Kristo's next Friday night? It's important."

"Hmm . . . let me check with my assistan—"

"Perfect. 6:30. See you then." And she'd clicked off. He'd taken the whole thing as a kind of flirtation because that's what he'd wanted it to be, but was it? They'd made plans to meet for dinner, which excited him tremendously, but wasn't there something else in her voice when she'd said she needed to talk to him about something? Need. To be needed. It felt like a tethering and he clung to it gratefully. But what had she meant by it?

Now, Sam followed Becky and Oreo out the front door of their house, carrying the enormous stinking cage, which he slid into the trunk of the family's SUV. The showing could officially begin. In the kitchen, he ran a hand over the black granite-look countertops. He flicked the overhead light and saw a flaw in the countertop, almost invisible, where the thing had snapped on installation and the builders had glued it back together. He slid the deli sampler he'd brought with him across the counter so that it covered the crack. Cherry cabinets. Stainless steel appliances. Everything was builder grade, a homogenous imitation of a nice house. Sam tried a drawer. False front. He hated these lipstick-on-a-pig flips, which they all were lately. He hated his own rhetoric. Pride of ownership. Fabulous finishes. Move-in ready. Like the house itself, his realtor voice was just a cheap imitation of a human being's. A feign toward sincerity, which was worse than an outright lie.

The house wasn't his listing—it had been a pity gift from a colleague whose stock was also low, but not nonexistent, like Sam's—but there was a chance he'd hook a buyer today and earn a commission split. At the very least, he was hoping to find new clients among the lookie-loo neighbors and bored retirees. He straightened his stack of business cards and the folder of MLS print outs.

Sam took a lap to look for any potential issues, anything he might steer folks away from. The kitchen and living room were renos but the bedroom had been left untouched. The master was cramped and dark. He drew the blinds and slid open the mirrored doors of the reach-in closet, stepped out, stepped back in and closed them again.

The basement was unfinished, the well-windows were translucent, covered in some sort of yellow grime, whether intentional or not, he couldn't tell. A toilet stood prominently in the middle of the room (the dad: "Could we call it a quarter-bath?"). He opened its lid, grimaced, and ran the scrub brush around its dingy bowl. Someone had painted the concrete floor a soft mint green. It was the kind of color that made one think of institutional rest. A tuberculosis sanitorium. Sam got to his knees and from there came to rest on the floor in a crisscross applesauce position which he could never not think of as "Indian style." He had always played Indian, never cowboy, in the neighborhood because of the Blackfoot on his father's side. Some pre-industrial rape, words adorning his father's white skin like a veil of authenticity. A mask. An excuse to drink. "Half Irish, quarter Injun," his father would say in a tone that was meant to be witty, from his brocade Broyhill captain's chair, a hefty glass of pinot noir at his lips, clearly considering himself a brother of neither, the print of Regnault's Salome (the one Jen had once said looked like Stevie) glowing a piss yellow from the wall behind him. His father was retired now, in Florida—like Stevie's dad—and still worked a property on occasion. He trusted Sam to run the branch at home, though Sam had never been as good at the business part as his dad.

The concrete was cool, and the paint gave a little, as if someone hadn't waited for the first coat to dry before they'd put on the sealant. He scratched at it, made a fingernail dent in the finish. No, houses weren't *that* difficult to sell these days; tsunami or no, even an idiot could sell a house. And Sam *was* an idiot. Idiot's market or not, Sam hadn't made a sale in months. He would sell this house though. He would sell this goddamned fucking house.

He slipped an airplane vodka from an inside pocket of his jacket, tipped it back and felt like a baby sucking a tit. He was warm, the receiver of life. He wandered over to the neat laundry station. Clean white laminate countertops, a drying line that stretched diagonally across the room, wooden clips lined up like soldiers. They would want to see the washer and dryer, they always did. He threw the tiny bottle against the wall behind the dryer with a bit of force, and was rewarded with the polite cough of a smash. He shimmied the dryer out a foot or two, picked up a sliver of glass and ran it an inch across his left palm. A little line of blood welled and he flexed his hand, tilted it. A drop fell like a promise on the linty floor and he pushed the dryer back into place, wiped its side clean of his blood with the cuff of his sports jacket. The doorbell rang. The open house was starting. He practiced twinkling his eyes on the way up the stairs.

The customary droning. How are you-and-Bill-and-Bill-Junior?-Has-Sarah-heard-from-Dartmouth-yet?-Of-course-she-will. The residents of Taylor, Iowa, hid their true feelings for one another behind a drapey curtain of small talk they spun out like so much rayon. They were, after all, Midwesterners, and practical. No velvet here. No silk. The older women, the gossips, all asked him when he was planning to pollute the earth with offspring. "Oh, I don't know, maybe next year," he lied jovially, as if, like lambs or calves, there was a singular season for such things. If Bonnie had been interested, if she'd started the conversation tentatively, searchingly, they may have groped their way to some agreement. He'd been prepared, after all, to be the dissenter. He'd been ready to have to be talked into it. But, as it happened, one night, as Bonnie stood in front of the mirror, grasping at the flesh around her middle, willing it into two previously non-existent love handles as was her nightly routine, she sighed and let go of herself and said, "Children ruin your body. Did you know they call the moment of the baby's crowning The Ring of Fire?"

"They who?"

"Wanda told me. The Ring of Fire! She said she felt like all of her organs had been dipped in acid and were falling out of her vagina. She said she's all stretched out now. Everywhere."

Sam had tried, at first, to make reassuring sounds, but Bonnie was in that mood she sometimes got in, the one where everything was a tragedy. He privately thought of it as Code Red, without understanding the menstrual implications until he'd admitted this to a male co-worker who was almost a friend. "Dude," said Ken over half-priced margaritas at Applebee's one Tuesday night, "my wife would kick me in the balls for even thinking that." And Sam had colored and stammered something stupid about not meaning it that way but that made him sound worse somehow, and he and Ken had never, truly become friends after that. It was a small thing, but there was a crucial juncture in any non-intimate relationship between two independent parties where each was deciding whether the other was worth the time or not, was more or less "normal" according to the standards of each, if these two norms were close enough to each other, if they would mesh, and here Sam's clumsy admission had shown Ken something that made him back away. It made Sam feel surprisingly embarrassed and tongue-tied around the tall, handsome Ken, as if he were a teenager and Ken his crush. Now, when Bonnie went Code Red, Sam felt both anger and shame and something like satisfaction that perhaps if Bonnie knew what he was thinking she would want to kick him in the balls, which made him feel like his own person—an entity asserting its individuality—and not a man married for five years to someone he found increasingly off-putting.

When Bonnie declared she would never, ever carry a fetus like some dumb animal host to the world's most successful parasite, Sam, though not especially excited about fatherhood himself, argued with her, which, of course, only caused her to become entrenched in her position. Now, she reported back to him regularly about the difficult pregnancies of friends, forwarded him articles in progressive national magazines about the drawbacks of modern parenthood, had even opened an extra savings account which would either go toward a kitchen reno or one of those new electric cars ("Hybrid," he heard her correcting him, a nagging disembodied voice, "They use gas *and* battery electricity.") when she had enough for a downpayment.

And this, then, was why he needed the vodka: to face these people—his people—and to be able to lie to them, to reassure them of their own normalcy, of his normalcy, of their collective harmlessness on earth, to sell them houses that were too expensive in a world where the only thing keeping them from a headlong slide into the abyss behind the refrigerator was the magnet of every-day mundanities. Of course Sarah will go to Dartmouth. Of course.

Sam retreated from his post at the front door near the basket of disposable shoe covers to the kitchen, pleased with how many people were actively circulating in the house already. He popped the big plastic lid off the deli platter. The smell of processed meat and white bread; the ghastly silence of the American cheese, soaked, lathed, processed and cut, like plywood, without passing through human hands. A fly spun lazily downward and wet its legs on a cliff of crust. Sam let it be. If he didn't have this showing today, he'd be lunching in downtown West Liberty—a tiny farm town whose Main Street had turned into a Little Mexico after the turkey processing plant began to hire the immigrant laborers who used to be farm hands, before the farms sold out to large corporations, who brought in their own to dig the manure pits and denude the pastures. There were two signs on almost every storefront on Main, one in English and one in Spanish. Downtown, the smoke-and-asbestos-filled Maxie's and a long-dead Woolworth's had been replaced by the delicious El Patio and the even better Tienda La Luna. The laborers had saved the town while it was in its death rattle and what was left of the surrounding community repaid them with racist shunning and increased police presence, though you'd have been more likely to be stabbed or shot at the old white Maxie's on a Tuesday night than any of the little bars or cantinas that cropped up along the streets of West Liberty—in the backs of grocery stores and gas stations. So went rural America these days. The way it clung to and defended its whiteness as though that whiteness symbolized something. Or maybe it wasn't whiteness at all, but money. The white Lutherans of Postville had turned their plump bougie cheeks away from the human abuses heaped on the undocumented immigrants in their midst by the local kosher meat processing plant, Agriprocessor, itself run by outsiders—a group of Orthodox Jews from Brooklyn. Everyone knew what was happening in Postville—the human rights abuses, the dangerous "company" apartments with exorbitant rents taken directly from meager paychecks. Everything so Dickensian, such a perversion of that perpetual heartland motion machine, the Protestant work ethic. Sholom Rubashkin could only be getting away with his monstrosity among them, and the whites of Postville seemed to be choosing, daily, to conspire with the slightly more palatable wealthy Jewish menace against the poorer brown one in their midst. Though the way those white kids jokingly Heiled at the windows of the Orthodox shul, one would never suspect collaboration. By May, Sam would have other things on his mind and would not hear, until weeks later, about the Postville ICE raid, the 400 undocumented workers arrested, nearly all of them deported. Would not see the town begin to fill again, this time with Somali families, whose children were called illegals and terrorists (and worse) at recess. Every international drama of the twentieth and early twenty-first century writ small, tumbling from the mouths of the quarterbacks and cheerleaders who were raised on the racial resentment of their parents and grandparents, as much as they were raised on the Quaker Oats produced in an odiferous factory in Cedar Rapids, whose white inheritance of the furred green fields and limestone cave systems of northeast Iowa was, finally, at an end, but not because of refugees. The century farmers of rural Iowa could not fight or flee the awesome capitalist wheel that drove them, after a life of stress and struggle, to sell out and retire to Arizona. They had seen neighbors lose everything—their buildings and equipment sold off piece by piece. The suicides. The murders. They had paid their dues, had survived all that and when their ships had come into this landlocked port—a good-enough price from Agrifund or Commodity Credit—they gladly disembarked, traded, not the ocean, but a monocultured desert for the real thing in the Southwest. Or to Florida, a monocultural desert in a sense more political than agricultural. Goodbye to the stench of the factory farm, the processor, the sound of a billion ears of corn being fed to twenty million bristly snouts. Seed and stock were better than cash in these parts and the nice Iowa the country had come to trust as a political bellwether, as the rational moral center, had, finally, begun to rot.

Was Sam thinking about any of this as he bit into a slice of fat-flecked deli ham from his Hy-Vee platter? He only tasted the plasticky schmear of preservatives and ached for the al pastor he wouldn't get for lunch today.

Upon reflection later, however, he was, if not glad, then grateful for the open house, because as disengaged from the rest of his life as he'd felt lately, he might never have heard the news otherwise. He'd walked a few young couples through the house, careful to show them the kitchen and fenced-in backyard (with Jacuzzi!) first before allowing them to drift innocently into the underwhelming master by themselves. He'd just set free the last of these, and was slowly closing the sliding-glass doors onto the porch and eavesdropping without appearing to when he saw Laura neé Winklehaus—and . . . here he drew a blank, though he knew the guy's face, knew these two had been a couple now longer than they'd not been one. High school sweethearts, so common in Taylor as to be unremarkable—near the deli tray and approached them. Personally, lately, inwardly, he always shrank from these people, his people. People who had known him in the awkward intimacy of his teenagerhood—these people always had something on you. That was the problem. His impulse was to run the other way, avert his eyes and turn before they recognized him, but he'd learned, as a small-town man of business, to bury these impulses deep inside so that his fellow Taylorites had been known to comment how boisterous and friendly he was, and a couple of them to snidely remark amongst themselves that they'd like the number of his dealer as long as that dealer wasn't God, like the rest of his office.

He approached his old classmates with the enthusiasm of a long-lost brother. But when he got to them, they seemed somber, and he dialed it back a little. Drew his face forward to look thoughtful instead of ecstatic.

"Nice to see you two again. It's been a while." What *was* his name? There'd been something about him, some rumor. . . .

"Sam, oh." Laura drew him into a hug. "We just heard the news about Jen Siegel. How awful."

For a moment, the sound of her name blocked out all logic and sensation. He fought a strange urge to say, "Who?" as if to prolong whatever thing he was about to hear that he didn't want to hear. Though of course he'd spoken to her just last week. He began to sweat. Jen Jen Jen Jen. Once, he had stayed up nights whispering her name into the humid dark. Now the word tumbled out of his mouth like something lost. "Jen. Yes?"

Laura looked at her husband and they did that thing that some husbands and wives can do: in a split second they had made a decision. The man took a step toward Sam, held a hand out. Sam shook his head and realized that somehow he'd gotten mixed up in their married assholes ESP, that somehow he knew that something terrible had happened to Jen and furthermore he did not want to hear about it.

"You were pretty good friends with her, right? I mean back then—"

Laura cut him off and put a hand on Sam's shoulder. They were flanking him now, as if he were slightly dangerous animal, or a teetering invalid.

"Something happened. I don't really know what." Laura, bewildered. The husband—Jason! His name was Jason—and here the rumor took shape: Jason One Ball they had called him. There had been an accident in shop class, maybe. Or a bloody incident at the gym rope? It came back to him in spurts as his mangled old classmate tried again. "Ryan called Laur last night. You remember Ryan Elcott? Well, he's in Chicago now, and I guess he heard from a mutual friend that she had—that she . . . died. Yesterday. He didn't know details but. Maybe suicide?"

A question. As if Sam had an answer.

Why were so many Midwestern men of his age saddled with those names, those –en names. Ryan, Jason, Kevin, Brandon. Names that insisted on their own full stoppage. RyN. JasN. Nothing is getting past us, the names seemed to assert. This name is over. Jen, on the other hand, was a perfect distillation. One syllable that needed nothing more than itself. That did not need to assert. That just was. He had taken French in high school and he had once, in the middle of class while they were conjugating verbs, thought something so stupid, that to remember it now still made him blush. He had once thought to himself: if you squished their names together, the beginning of Jen—je—plus the end of Sam—am—you get a Frenglish phrase that means "I am." He'd scrawled it—"je am"—in ballpoint on the bottom of his Adidas Gazelle where he could find it but where no one else was likely to notice. That's how much we need each other, he'd thought. What the fuck had been wrong with him? Had he just said, "What the fuck?" out loud? He looked up and Laura and One Ball wore masks of concern. Yes, he thought so. The heat spread from his face down his neck and into the hollows of his shirt, where his breath mysteriously caught and would not come to him, would not move from shirt area to head/mouth area. He coughed and gasped and took a step back from his flankers, and yanked hard from side-to-side on his tie.

"I don't think so," he said.

Laura put a hand out toward him as if inviting him back into the safety of their fold. "I know, it's such . . . horrible news. I couldn't believe it either. She always seemed so. . . ." The worst thing was not the attempt at calming him, but the attempt to speak the things they were saying at all.

"Just," he gasped and the tie flew free of his collar and whipped at Laura's face, a giant pale pink tongue. She made a sound and brought a hand to her eye.

"Maybe you should sit," One Ball motioned to Sam, but there were no chairs or barstools, just a cracked granite counter and a half-eaten deli platter and rooms and rooms of nothing.

Laura took her hand off of her eye and blinked rapidly, "I'm okay. It's just—" she winced and turned her face away, "I think it might be scratched? The cornea?"

One Ball attended to his wife, bending over her and peering into her fluttering face to see what there was to see in her eye, which was nothing, and Sam wandered away from them, into the miserable master. There was a man across the room, tie in his hand like a garrot, shirt stained with something at the heart. Sam's new, untrimmed mustache made him a stranger for a moment and he thought, *who let that guy in here?* And even after he realized he was looking into the mirrored closet doors, he still did not recognize himself, the person he'd become, which was somehow at this moment both the closest to and farthest away from the person he had been. And when had the two begun to diverge so radically? And why had he never seen it before?

Chapter 2

A house after a flood smells different than a house up for sale; it is a house that has gained material. It is a house plus and it's almost inconceivable how bad it smells. It smells so bad and yet must, at some point, become your house again. A house after a flood smells like death's toilet. It is not so much the water, but what the water leaves behind. All that silt and sand and fertilizer and the toxic sludge of a thousand half-open cans in a hundred garages. The sewage of a generation. A house after a flood is Dorothy's house, picked up in Kansas and put down on Oz, on the Wicked Witch of the East, her body turned to carrion, left to rot. Does it ever feel the same again, even after you've stripped out the sodden drywall and insulation? Can you ever really come home? Yet, here she was. 215 North Prairie. The old split level. Dingy white—siding shattered in some spots. Her mother had never been handy, had not yet remarried someone who was. Stevie tried the front door. Open. In the middle of the day. She waved the polite Iowan cabbie away and let herself inside.

Their smell had returned, eventually, after the family had been around to stink it up awhile, like it had never washed away. Walking into her mother's house always made Stevie feel firmly rooted, as if she'd finally arrived somewhere after years and years of travel. Something like laundry detergent and beef broth—clean and hearty. The smell after the flood had been, at first, rotten, fishy, slightly genital; then, mildewed and, when the work had been finished, the basement remodeled finally, and freshly painted, the sharp sterile smell of plastic drop cloths and new drywall. But, eventually, the house had reverted. Was it in the walls? Or in the people between them? Did they all smell the same? Was it genetics? Her father's home in Florida smelled different. Had his smell changed long ago when he'd moved out? Shouldn't the smell of the house have changed when he'd left, its delicate chemistry changed by the loss of one of them? Perhaps it had, but it was still close enough to the old smell to send Stevie reeling when she walked up the carpeted stairs and into the split-level living room ("sitting room" her mother insisted, ever the farm daughter). Even under the jolting sense of relief: a familiar swell of anxiety and sadness. Stevie stood at the top of the stairs until it all slid back down into some deep, still pool at the very root of her.

Jen's house had smelled different. Like a library or a clean gymnasium, all that wood. In the fall of their junior year, they had huddled under scratchy wool blankets in her back yard around the brick firepit, the flames low and yellow, just sticks and pinecones the squirrels had broken off the trees. When they had grown too cold, the fire and stick-pile too low, they hunched into the living room with their blankets, and lay hip to haunch on the pebbled leather couch and watched the old movies on public access. *From Here to Eternity*, *The Birds*. Always, Stevie fell asleep and woke to Jen's mom patting her blanketed shoulder. "Time to go home, hon." Those nights she dragged the scent to bed with her: damp wool and cinders, leather and the Pantene hair of the girl she loved best, and she felt cocooned. In the morning, it was gone.

When had they last spoken? There had been awkward moments through the years: a run-in at a store in the mall with her mom. Both of them quiet and uncomfortable, her mother cluelessly chatty. She'd still been angry with Jen for whatever it was that had split them up. Had it been Sam? Maybe, but that wasn't it exactly. Ever since that last summer, the summer of the flood, there had been a strangeness between them and Stevie hadn't thought it was entirely the threesome. It was something else, some measured distance. The way girls could fall so completely in love with each other, they might just as suddenly find themselves estranged. One girl pulling back and the other, dazed and hurt, teetering like she'd lost a limb. Like everything from back then, the motives were difficult to tease away from the actions, the actions from the outcomes. They had done certain things, and then they had not been friends. It was not necessarily cause and effect, not something you could figure out.

But then there had been a reconciliation, or the start of one. At Doc's at Christmas a couple of years ago. It had been a loud, smokey, happy night, and she had piled into a booth with Jen and four other high school friends, and they'd gone hoarse from the talking, the bullshitting. The other friends had left and she and Jen had talked right up to closing time: the gossip about their old hook-ups and where the mean girls were now, and with it the irresistible and smug assessments about who had failed and who had succeeded; the glow of "succeeding" in Jen's eyes just because she lived in New York; the shame of knowing she had succeeded at exactly nothing and not disabusing Jen of the notion. The lopsided admission, from Jen, that she *was* failing, too, that her job had taken her soul and she wasn't sure she could ever get it back. Stevie had been so close to confessing the same thing to her when the bar lights flicked on and everyone blinked nakedly under the fluorescents. Jen had kissed the side of her head as they stumbled out of their booth and, outside the bar, made an I'll-call-you sign with her pinkie and thumb as she drove away, the wrong way down a one-way street downtown, beautiful and drunk and stinking of cigarettes and looking to Stevie like a thing dreamed. Yes, that was the last time she'd seen Jen. She'd thought it had been some sort of reconciliation—the beginning of something new between them. But she hadn't heard from Jen, and she'd been shy about calling in the sober daylight. Of the two of them, Jen had always been the outgoing one, the firecracker. Stevie assumed it was understood between them that Jen would call first.

And then her vacation days were up and she was back in New York (she never thought of it as *home*), once again wholly absorbed in its distractions and discomforts. And now it was now and Jen was gone.

Stevie's bedroom (now she banged the door open with her carryon in hand, struggled slightly through the doorframe) looked the same, of course, that hallowed shrine to her indolent adolescence. She kept insisting her mother should convert it into a useful room, but her mother refused, like some movie parent whose child has died. Which was maybe not totally ridiculous because Stevie always half-expected to see a ghost of her former self smoking a joint on her bed or cross-legged in front of her modular dual cassette stereo, making a mix and pasting scraps of newsprint into a collage for the front of the tape case. The old silver beast sat in the corner, below the wall-sized black and white poster of a shirtless Jim Morrison that always made Stevie smile. She turned on the stereo, rewound the first tape deck for a second, then pressed play. Sophie B. Hawkins, "Damn, I Wish I was Your Lover" oozed out through the ancient, crummy speakers. Stevie felt something in her rising up and out. The tape had been a gift from Jen, a joke, after their interrupted night together but Stevie had found the song beautiful and moving and she had listened and listened and later cried to it until she'd wrung it dry. But, in the intervening years, it had filled up again. When the song ended, she rewound the tape and pressed play and once again cried quietly on her old, sagging bed, like the world's oldest seventeen-year-old, beneath the shadow of Jim Morrison, who was vast and stoned and unbelievably young and still in denial about his own death.

Stevie woke to her mother dangling two steaming Hy-Vee bags full of grocery store Chinese takeout over her feet. "Heya, toots," she said. Her mom looked older, smaller somehow. She'd let her hair go gray, finally, after years of dyeing it herself, and she was small, elvin. Stevie had been taller than her since she was twelve but she seemed to have lost half an inch since Christmas.

"How'd you know I was here?"

Hugging her mother was always like losing herself a little. Her mom's smell was somehow distinct from the whole of the house, and yet it undeniably contributed to it. She smelled like tuberose, from the tuberose perfume she wore lightly, even though it was against code, and the Lubriderm she used to keep her hands from cracking from all the washing.

"It's a mom thing." Her mother kissed her cheek and pulled back. "You look wrecked. Long flight?"

"Not really. I think I'm just tired."

"It's that city. It's wearing you out."

In her mother's mind, she and Manhattan were locked in an epic battle for Stevie's love and attention, especially since 9/11. (The memory was always right there, so close. Her mother's shaking, teary voice once she could finally get a line out of the city. "You get out of that city this instant, young lady. You leave right now!") She got in a dig whenever she could. This was the thing about being home, of course: every sentence, every word was overripe with accumulated meaning. Stevie took a quiet yogic breath and touched her mother's hair. "I like that you let the gray grow out. It's so pretty like that."

Her mother beamed and then seemed to remember why Stevie was there. "I'm so sorry about your friend. If you want me to go with you, I can probably get a half a day. I'd just have to call—"

"It's okay. I just want to get in and out. Not make a big thing, you know?"

"Oh honey. How are you feeling?"

It came in pulses, fading from awareness, for minutes at a time, then the impossible thought surfaced again—Jen's dead—and she felt a fresh shock, a ripple of pain. Melissa had emailed her with the awful details—suicide, jumped from a parking structure. Though this did not sound like her old friend, not at all, and she had no idea (and hadn't asked) how Melissa had come across the information, Stevie knew it was the truth. Death made you believe it, no matter how unlikely. Stevie found it impossible not to picture the mise en scene. Sometimes Jen was face up, sometimes face down, arms and legs bent and broken, halo of blood against the concrete creeping ever outward. She was drawn to the dark abyss of the moment of Jen's death. Her mind darted at it, a tongue at the raw, bloody hole where a tooth had been. But even as these visions filled her head, made it impossible to think about anything else, to have a conversation, to blog, there was something underneath them that was even worse: the monstrous shadow of longing and regret that would stay with her much longer, perhaps forever. The friend she'd always meant to patch things up with, the person with whom she shared the story of her youth. . . . Stevie hadn't realized it until it was too late but apparently she'd always assumed there would be a homecoming.

"I'm okay," she said and dipped a crusty cabbage roll into a gilded porcelain finger-bowl of pink sauce—her mother refused to eat on Styrofoam.

"How's work?"

And here Stevie shrugged. Made the hand motion for so-so and hoped her mom would drop it.

Luckily her mother was happy to move on. "I got a call from James recently. 312 area code, so: Chicago."

Stevie saw that she was trying to downplay how excited she was about this news. "Do you think he'll visit?"

"Oh, it's James. Who knows," her mom fidgeted her fork through her lo mein in a hair combing motion. "I don't know where you learned those things," she pointed her fork at Stevie's chopsticks. "My city girl." This was both a compliment and an insult.

"What did he say?"

"The usual: he's fine, not to worry. He has a job and a place to stay."

"And?"

"And he's clean."

"He fucking better be." It would be just like her brother to eclipse the death of her friend by OD'ing himself into a neighboring coffin. "Well, I'm just glad for you that he's okay."

"Be glad for him too. And for yourself. Maybe he'll come see us—me—soon." Stevie didn't think James would until he needed something and when he needed something it was almost always money, which he used to buy drugs and then the next time he came around he'd be obviously strung out. Too friendly, too excited, too bubbling over with gratitude for his family that it must be a show. He'd been out on his own for years and years now, moving from town to town, working seasonal hospitality jobs then going no contact for months at a time. Every time she talked to him, it was from a different number. She didn't know how her mom did it, kept the hope alive. Stevie found it easier to disconnect. But her mom, well, she was always a mom. She'd always want her kids nearby, even if they were druggie fuckups. It was why Stevie didn't want to tell her about getting fired. She didn't know what to say, how to spin it. "Don't ever tell them you're leaving until you know exactly what your next move will be and how well it will pay," she used to coach her clients, the ones who hadn't already been turned into moray eels by the media industry. If she told her mother, she might start the hard press. And Stevie was weak—sad, hungry, and staring at the best worst take out in the world. Her mother had a sense for these things and she didn't know if she could bear another please-move-home talk right now. Didn't know if she could say no. Amanda Collins, though—that was something she could share.

"I have some potentially good news. I have an agent! For my blog."

"A blog agent? What's that for?"

"She's a literary agent but she represents bloggers. She wants me to write a book."

"A book about a blog?"

"No, well, a book based on something I might blog about. I guess. I don't actually know because I haven't figured it out yet."

Her mother looked puzzled, then smiled. "Congratulations, honey. I'm so proud of you," sheer mom pride, then: "What *could* the book be about?" and Stevie felt a flutter of anxiety. "Maybe this?" She meant Jen's funeral, and Stevie grimaced. She had been tucking away notes for a blog post, but it felt so—off-genre. And truthfully, she wasn't sure she really understood how she felt about Jen's death, or at least, she didn't feel able to articulate those feelings yet. Obviously, it was terrible. But there had been something creeping in since she'd booked her flight. A sense of something left unfinished. And she'd been surprised to realize, as she sat at her gate at LaGuardia earlier that day, that she was angry, like really angry, at Jen. "Maybe. I don't know."

"Whatever it is, it will be great."

"I don't know. I'm just signing a contract. I still have to write a book—a good book—then sell it. I think that basically describes 30% of the people in New York right now."

"You're so smart, and you're such a good writer. I have no doubt you'll figure it out."

Why are we so loathe to believe our mothers? The more praise her mother gave her, the more Stevie felt doomed to failure, as if her mother was cursing her instead. "We'll see."

Why was Stevie so annoyed? She'd brought it up, hoping to add a little light to their dinner. There was something about being home. That old rebellious posture. She pushed it down. Treat your parents well. That old song her mom loved so much.

"Dancing with the Stars will be on in a minute," said her mother, and of course she acquiesced—she had to, now. And afterwards, after she thought she might die a thousand deaths of embarrassment and boredom as the naked girl from American Pie stomped around the screen to "Goody Two Shoes," she took her laptop to her room and lit a stick of Nag Champa to appease the spirit of Jim Morrison and started to write.

Back to My Home on Whore Island

When last we left it, dear reader, your aging narrator was alone in the city once more—her pluck, her determination temporarily askew, her chin, bruised but not split. It was that age-old story: Girl meets Boy; Boy makes out with intern he supervises; Boy gives Girl STD; Girl finds out they are now calling them STIs probably in order to reduce stigma and therefore encourage treatment; Girl knows "everybody gets something" as they say in this city, but still feels pretty terrible about the whole thing, not to mention gross and contaminated; Boy fires Girl from her job for "blogging at work;" Girl hopes that this might lead to Dooce-level blog fame but understands that hope and likelihood are very separate things. . . .

Are you still there?

(Girl gets a reality check in the form of very bad news, worse, by far than the STD.)

What I mean to say is: I lost her.

My first love. Before Boy or his predecessors, all the way back to the OG Boy, the First Boy, Sam. Before Boy came along to muck things up like he does, there was a girl named Jen. She was my best friend. The kind of friend you only get one or two of in your whole life and only in the first couple of decades or so of it. Before all the splitting off and procreating and whatever.

Hoes before heteros and embryos.

Something Jen used to say.

I'm at my mom's house in Iowa because Jen died and tomorrow is the funeral. And instead of telling her to her face that I'm sorry and I miss her and I don't really know why or how we drifted so far apart it's like we were in totally different atmospheres but let's stop being that far apart, it's a waste of time. Let's share air (she would have liked the rhyme), tell me about your life and what you love about it and what's hard and shitty and who's your favorite band right now (have you heard that Vampire Weekend album and is it super cool or really uncool I can't tell?) and the last interesting book you read. Instead of having this awkward and maybe uncomfortable and possibly even banal conversation that might possibly, if it went okay, lead to more less-bad conversations, there's just whatever: her dead body in a coffin, I guess. And a bunch of people from my high school with whom I can and will have the bad conversation. I don't want it. I don't want them. Not one.

What are you afraid of? What's your favorite spot for takeout? Why Chicago? Have you been to New York? Does your parents' house still smell like that, you know, like old books and cooking rice? Is your cat alive, the one who used to bite your feet under the covers while you slept? I still can't really believe you went into finance—I thought only assholes did that—are you an asshole now? Remember "Zip it up!" Remember freshman skip day. Remember my Charger, so old it didn't have a/c, the way the night fields beyond the road smelled through the open windows at 60 miles per hour, your bare foot out the window, CDs scattered in your lap, Discman jacked into the tape player, cigarette in hand as you picked up The Jesus & Mary Chain between your pinkie and thumb and pressed it into place, the spinning sound before "Head On" began to pound around us more atmospheric disturbance than song? Do you remember that?

Stevie wept herself into a sleep that may have featured Jen in its dashed-out narratives, but which had disappeared from memory within moments of waking, pushed out by the awful understanding that came pouring in with consciousness. The rain tapped politely at her window. Jim Morrison loomed like a sexy monster. Today she would attend the funeral of someone whose importance to her seemed to be unfurling voluptuously—rose-petal-like and too late for her to do anything about it, death now standing in for pride or fear or whatever it was that had blocked her way before. Death and with it, anger that, once it had announced itself, would not just shut the fuck up and go away.

She'd been hurt so badly by Jen's withdrawal and slippage into silence all those years ago, by her parents' own unfathomable dissolution, that Stevie had put that part of life away from herself. But now, here it was, crushing in its present absence. Here was the home that no longer housed a family, here was the day she would see her old friend buried. The thought of home, the brief panicked disorientation that always followed a night in a place she was not habituated to, brought her to thoughts of her place in New York and she wondered if she'd be able to keep the apartment. Unlike many young professionals in New York, she had no trust fund to fall back on, no rent halved by parents. What had begun as a little credit debt from an emergency dental visit swelled monstrously each month, accruing interest and late charges she couldn't pay or at least found it difficult to prioritize. She'd moved to the city so young, taken night classes at Marymount Manhattan so she could take out student loans, waited tables, lived in hovels with strangers. She'd struggled because struggle was the way to succeed. Everyone knew that. It hardly even needed to be said. Except, of course, that it was turning out to be a total lie.

She put the thought aside. One disaster at a time. Now she was here, in her mother's house. Safe. And that was something. More than many had. The bed sighed as she dragged herself from it and began to dress.

Early on, she had shared a tiny studio with an Irish girl named Siobhán, a bartender at an Irish pub in the twenties, whose sleep schedule was exactly opposite of her own. Their apartment, deep in the East Village, just beyond the reaches of gentrification. Garden-level, that pretty way of saying "illegal basement space." Converted nursing home crouched around a city-sized island park—a square of grass, a maple tree—this tiny oasis not at all accessible or even visible from Stevie's studio, not worth a special trip through the main lobby. Even when there were not visible turds littering the garden, which was rare, the sharp smell of dog piss kept away everyone but the building's dog owners, the dogs themselves, and all but the most waist-bent of junkies.

The girls had decorated their apartment like the poor and transient strangers they were. Siobhán had found a Weezer poster in the trash behind the building and stuck it onto the wall with a bit of chewed gum. In her corner, Stevie hung two strings of fairy lights she'd bought for a dollar at Key Foods on New Year's Day. Beneath the cheery glow of the lights, above her mattress, she'd Scotch-taped photos of her parents she'd taken from the house before she'd left. They were old photos, taken long before they'd all crashed into the brick wall of the divorce. In one, her mother wore a short blue jumper and a big-collared white shirt. Her long black hair was parted in the middle and she wore gray brogues. Her father wore a pink shirt, a wide white tie and striped pants. In another photo, they wore different dapper outfits, but their heads were out of frame. Instead, there were hands. Her father held her mother's wrist with one hand and his other was below hers, displaying her engagement ring. It looked like an ad for either diamonds or polyester. Were they happy? The people in the photos, the people who would become her parents, seemed alternately stiff and excited and this seemed to change depending on Stevie's mood and angle. Who had taken the photos? Certainly not her mom's dad, who'd disavowed the whole thing because her father had not been a farmer or a farmer's son, or even a Lutheran. His mother maybe? A little bit drunk but optimistic to a fault? Was the end already there between them, a foregone conclusion and could she see it on their dewy, unlined faces, or in the way her hand seemed to float above his instead of touch it?

One time, Siobhán had come home early from work, loaded with coke and, clearly, already incredibly high. She'd convinced Stevie to come out with her to a party a regular had given her tickets to. It was bondage night at a club nearby. A woman with a laser-forked tongue, in a corset and glasses, had handed them each a cheap plastic riding crop as they entered the place. Lights strobed off the thick machine fog, and in cages hung from the ceiling and on velveteen benches seating that lined the walls, men and women stood and swayed and sagged and smoked in bondage wear, sipping well drinks in plastic cups through the mouth holes of their pleather balaclavas. Sometimes someone would do something to someone else—pinch a nip or take a swipe with a crop—but every move seemed a little lazy and lacking in conviction. A short man with hairy shoulders and a strange, blockish belly asked if he could be her slave for the evening. "At your service, my queen," he'd said, and bowed, and Stevie had gone to the bathroom and done the rest of the coke Siobhán had given her to hold onto for some reason, at some point, before she'd wandered off and could be seen across the room some time later, awkwardly hoisting herself onto a grid iron suspended four feet off the ground, like a bed. Stevie had sat on the toilet in the glow of the single red light of the bathroom and listened to two people whispering in sexy anguish at each other in the stall next to hers ("Cut it, cut it off. Yes please?" followed by a soft cat-like mewling) and looked up to see a close-circuit camera peering at her from a corner of the ceiling—the faint red glare in its lens, the hellish giveaway—and felt more alone than she'd ever remembered feeling in her life. She'd left the club alone that night at four a.m., having lost sight of her roommate, and they'd never discussed it again, as if the night had never happened, not even the bogarted coke. Really, they'd almost never had another conversation again, so rarely did their presence in the apartment overlap.

It was mostly like that, in New York. Hopping from one thing to another with a person or people she kind of knew—birthdays and book parties and free shows at the downtown spots—Tonic, Lit, Arlene Grocery. All the best friends she could make in four drinks while noise-deafened.

After Jen, there had never been anyone else like her and as she put on her black dress (did people still wear black to funerals? It seemed like something that happened in movies) the thought struck Stevie in a nearly physical way, as if someone had hit her, that now there was also no Jen. Jen and Stevie sitting in folded-over boys' boxer shorts on the felled tree over the river behind Stevie's house, faces green in Queen Helene Mint Julep face masks, figuring out how to blow smoke rings. "It's all in the tongue." Jaws cocked and pulsing, skin tight in its frosting, smiles cracking all the way up to their eyes.

Stevie ate a poached egg, vomited, and called a cab.

She kept her eyes low as she entered the synagogue—no energy to play catch up just yet—but as she entered the room, her attention was immediately drawn to Sam, who perched nervously by himself near the back, his coat off and laying across his lap, yarmulke askew. She couldn't not notice him, as if she were keeping a date they'd arranged. There was sweat shadowing his dress shirt when he moved his arm to fiddle with the yarmulke. How is it that some people turn us into quivering teenagers upon sight, no matter how worldly, confident, or grown up we feel ourselves to be? Except for an inexplicable mustache, Sam looked the same: dimple-chinned, shaggy-haired, and so wide in the eye, he was sometimes mistaken for a stupid man. She'd heard years ago that he'd become a realtor like his dad, which had always struck her as somewhat pedestrian for a boy who'd been a champion debater in high school. But now she understood: sitting there he looked like a single gal's small-town American dream. Handsome, boyish, broad, like something straight out of a romance novel. He looked up as she approached and she saw he was exhausted. His pupils were dilated and the lines around his mouth were pronounced. His bottom lip quivered slightly, as if he'd developed a tic. She probably looked old, too. Though she didn't feel it: her stupid stammering heart, her uncertain tongue. She notched herself into his row, the back row, and was wondering what totally embarrassing thing she would stammer at him when he said, "Steves," but the music swelled and she didn't need to say anything, just sink into his outstretched arms and be held, too long, as her heart struggled toward him every second, the pounding almost too much to bear.

*

Sam's fist curled and uncurled, a sweaty slug against the greasy skin of his flask. Though already drunk, he was itching for another swig, but the service was about to start and there was not a way to take a drink gracefully and without making a silent sight of himself. He felt the eyes of strange mourners on him. Who were these older men in suits scowling from the back wall of the sanctuary, behind him, not sitting? They seemed to be watching him, waiting for him to do something . . . bad.

There were a few old classmates scattered around, their faces recognizable even through the bloat but their names known only to the stack of yearbooks in his parents' attic, and a few more blew in on the froggy sob of the pre-recorded organ music. It was said that killers often returned to the scene of their crimes and what was Jen's body now besides a crime scene, a location where someone else had exercised his will, where something bad had happened. The silk-lined pinewood box up there. He couldn't look at it.

Every medical examiner in the state could cry suicide until the cows came home, but Sam knew, *knew* in a way that surpassed knowing—he *understood* that Jen had not killed herself. She was simply not capable of such a thing, and goddamn the tendril of doubt that was sometimes able to sprout its way through the liquor haze he'd been in the last few days. Goddamn the thing inside himself that whispered, in sharp and horrific moments of clarity, that he was only convinced of her murder because if she'd killed herself that meant that she hadn't really wanted to see him after all. That even, maybe, the promise of his sudden presence in her life had irrevocably tipped some fatal scale inside her. That maybe their meeting—which was supposed to happen today, actually, tonight, at a Greek restaurant in Des Moines where they knew no one, or next to no one, and would be able to order flaming cheese again, together, like they were eighteen and fuck hungry, raw and ravenous—maybe this had been the thing, somehow, that had made her—No. He might have been a stupid worthless drunk of a realtor who couldn't, these days, sell a piece of shit to a fly, but he knew somewhere deep inside, somewhere that was deeper than the already-deep place that suspected she'd killed herself because of him, that Jen had been murdered and that it was his duty, as the person who had undoubtedly loved her the most, if not the best, to find her killer.

The surprise of Stevie suddenly at his side—her knobby knees and elbows looking like weapons sticking out of her black wrap dress—made him feel a little faint. She looked slimmer and angrier than he remembered her. Life in New York. And how long had it been since he'd seen her? Five years, maybe? It surprised him that she wore glasses as black as her dress. They made her look smart, which she was, but also vulnerable. It was like every part of her was in conflict between these two poles of tractability and edge. As she uncoiled herself from his flail and settled beside him, he watched her roll through the entire *ouevre* of ex-girlfriend emotions—puzzlement, anger, sadness, embarrassment, relief— then she patted his knee and turned back to the service. The mourners shuffled in. He surprised himself by recognizing Jen's parents immediately.

No one from the family eulogized. Was it shame that silenced the funeral? Or simply the shock of the loss?

Sam felt the sag, the slowdown, the slight drag on his brain that told him it was time for a drink. Stevie shifted beside him and it took all his willpower not to lean over and put his head in her lap. A date. He was supposed to be on a date with Jen tonight and instead she was dead in a box in front of him. Something in him tipped and spilled and a sound came from his throat, some cow-like low. She had sounded happy over the phone. *She* had called *him*, after all. She had an appointment in Des Moines—something business-related, a banking connection, and she wanted some company, didn't feel like bothering her parents for such a short trip, was being put up at the Hilton downtown—they could order champagne and jump on the beds. He couldn't believe she'd said the word "bed" to him. He'd been on one of his regular aimless workday trips out to nowhere when she'd called and he was so surprised he pulled over. His dick had jumped lightly in his pants. How long had it been since he'd heard from her? A year?

But no, she wasn't completely happy. There'd been a tension in her voice. Some new taut key turned to breaking. She'd been trying to sound happy but even the bed and champagne bit had sounded a little forced. Like she knew she was playing him and felt bad about it. But he'd agreed—of course he had, of course she knew he would—and put the weird vibes out of his mind until the open house. Until the bad news from Laura and One Ball.

It was the only reasonable explanation—not suicide, that was preposterous—but foul play. An ex-boyfriend, maybe? A Nerve.com date? A neighborhood stalker? Or maybe it was job-related. Money. The oldest motive in the book, after jealousy. True, she worked as a mortgage consultant. It wasn't a sexy title but she was a player at Satchel Ferry. "We're basically printing money," she'd told him once, disgusted.

"What laws are you breaking?" he'd asked, flirty over the phone and celebratory after closing on a fat listing a couple of years ago. Two glasses into the middling bottle of Prosecco he'd intended for the clients but kept for himself.

"Like, all of them," she'd said and laughed and he could hear that she was smoking again—a habit he'd nagged her out of in high school, but that she'd quickly picked up again in college and couldn't rid herself of now. "It goes so well with the job. You wouldn't believe the stink off the assholes I deal with."

"Maybe I would. I'm a realtor, remember?"

She'd laughed. "This whole industry is an asshole pageant, isn't it? From tip to tail. That's why I like talking to you, old friend. You get it."

He did. He really did. Or, well, he did because he listened to her. Because every once in a while they would talk like this late into the night and feel, he liked to believe it was—how had Prufrock put it?—each to each. They were getting older but what they didn't say because they didn't have to was that they still remembered the peaches. They floated there, just under the surface of everything. She was his mermaid. She did sing for him. Didn't she?

And that night, that last night, the last time he'd ever speak to her: she had been worried. She'd been worried about whatever was bringing her to Des Moines and—

Sam followed this worn groove to its end—and she had invited him to keep an eye on her or to help her keep an eye on whomever—someone who was onto whatever shady thing was going on in her office. No one local—they were meeting incognito. Maybe her meet-up was from Chicago, too. Sam there as decoy? Protection? Simple distraction?

Or had the worried note only ever been his invention?

Stevie was crying lightly now and he took her hand, crushed the wet Kleenex in her palm, which revolted him only slightly, and put his lips to the back her hand for a long while, until the rabbi began to sing. *El malei rachamim shochein baromim, hamtzei m'nuchah n'chonah tachat kanfei hash'chinah.* Jen had taught him the words of the prayer, many years ago, after a funeral for a frat brother, freshman year of college, when they were still talking on the phone every couple of months or so. In these tiny ways, for the last fifteen years of his life, by degrees of association, Jen had infiltrated almost every aspect of Sam's experience. In this way, she had haunted him long before she'd become a ghost.

He lifted his lips and said the words silently and promised her that he would get to the bottom of all this.

"What do you mean 'murdered'?" Stevie was trying not to be alarmed but between Sam's raggy look, the stink of him—half-digested alcohol and the groinal tang of smoker's sweat—and the whisper of a tic in his squinted eye meant she was losing that fight. She sat a foot away from him in the passenger's side of his Outback and saw, smelled, how frayed he was at the edges. But she hadn't realized how drunk he actually was until she'd ridden with him to Jen's house, where they now sat parallel parked up the street to wait for the other mourners to arrive.

Once, she'd driven Jen and Sam home after a party—some cornfield kegger that summer, the summer of the flood. She'd been the designated driver but Jen had other ideas.

"Give me the keys Stevie—I want to drive fast. Please, please, please." Jen was practically slobbering with drunken sibilance. Sam had laughed and sung "Do not . . . go-oh" in a pretty good Gordon Gano voice. And he and Jen had collapsed into each other in the back seat, nearly peeing with laughter. A moment later, Jen had crawled into the empty front passenger seat, Simples beaning Stevie in the head as she crabbed over the center console. She crossed her arms and nodded at Stevie—her KidNPlay move, like "let's do this"—then mimed a steering wheel, elbows cocked at exaggerated angles, and started to sing along with the song that had come on the radio.

"Everybody was drunken driving! Na na na na na na na na na. That bitch was down for fighting." She punched and kicked the air, rolled down the window and stuck her feet out. The memory jolted Stevie now. Those two dove-gray sneakers tapping time against each other over the passenger side-mirror. The orange strobe of the streetlights as they made their way through their immortal teenage night. A fist clenched inside her.

Sam had run up on the curb a couple of times during the two-mile trip between the synagogue and the Siegel house. Everybody was drunken driving, all right. Stevie's heart stuttered as she caught sight of the place. There it was, set back, the big old craftsman, familiar porch swing painted a new green to match the door. There were lights on in the house—clearly some cousin was holding down the fort, sitting shiva or setting out food as the Siegels poured little shovelsful of dirt onto the fresh grave, their request for a private burial kaddish a result of their shock and horror.

So they'd parked and without speaking of it, and neither of them had moved to get out of the car, not yet brave enough to join. How tacky to be waiting like some surprise party gone wrong. But when Sam had fished a flask from his pocket, she wondered if he'd even be able to walk into the house on his own without being carried. Then, pointing the flask at her, he'd made his maddening declaration: Jen had been murdered.

She took the flask and pulled from it, already moving to obliterate whatever he was about to say.

He nodded. "The good stuff. I need all the help I can get, you know? I mean, maybe I'm crazy, Stevie. It's possible, yes it is. But I just have this feeling. This *sense*. Like . . . remember that time you and I were sitting at that intersection at Keokuk and Highway 4? And the light turned green but I didn't go, I just sat there, looking at the light. And when you turned to me, just when you were about to say, 'Hey, idiot, green means go,' a huge sixteen-wheeler blasted through the intersection going sixty, at least. Just powered through the red. Do you remember that?"

She did. It had shaken her for days. She still thought about it sometimes. They had been out early, a study date at Donutland maybe. It had been a sunny winter day—she remembered the snow and the alien-hands of oak trees in the park just beyond her window. The semi had been going so fast, his car, that little Corolla, had rocked when it passed. They would have been toast, shrapnel. They would have been James Freyed—a million little pieces. A Jen joke for sure.

"I remember."

"I didn't go. You know? Like something held me back. I was sitting there, looking at the green light, thinking oh, I should drive now, but my foot just wouldn't give it gas. It's the same thing. Something very deep inside is telling me something I shouldn't know yet, but I do. It's telling me someone murdered her."

"I wish you would stop saying that word." Stevie took another draw from the flask. She still couldn't—just like *could not*—process the fact of it. Had Jen been secretive and moody and had there been something behind her eyes, *always*, that hadn't ever opened up all the way? Yes. Yes, of course. But wasn't there something like that in all of us? Most of us managed to submerge it completely. Jen had never cared enough what other people thought. Her strange had always bobbed near the surface. Fine. Honest. Did that mean she'd killed herself? Did it mean someone had killed *her*?

The look on Sam's face—the way it was starting, just now, to fold in on itself—told her that this was something he believed with all his heart. That he had to, for some reason, and Stevie felt how easy it would be for her to believe with him and for him. There was something about his paranoia that called her to join in.

Danger said the more rational, intervening voice. It was clear he was at the end, or possibly even in the middle of, a bender. If she believed him now, it was all over for the both of them. She didn't know what to say.

"Sam. I don't know what to say."

He told her about the phone call. The meet-up they had planned. Stevie shook her head. "Do you have any proof? I mean . . . that's a—" *don't say crazy* "that's quite an accusation."

All around them, people were arriving, silently stepping out of their cars then: the sucking thud of door after door being shut. They were walking up the sidewalk with their heads down under the weight of the clouds whose rain was reaching down for them now, their hands clasped in each other's hands. Stevie gave him back the flask.

"You're not going to say something in there, are you?" Stevie motioned toward the house. "You can't just say that after a person's funeral."

"Do you believe me, though? You knew her too. It just feels wrong."

"I don't know, Sam. But it doesn't matter right now. This is about her parents, her family. We need to pay our respects. No murder stuff."

Sam looked out into the soggy gray blanket of the day. Muddy lawns, the earthworms eating their way up into the air and across the gritty expanses of sidewalk.

"Okay, Steve. No murder stuff." That was the same voice with which he'd once told her he loved her, then that he didn't love her anymore. She'd been thinking that Sam barely had a grip, but she suddenly found that she, too, seemed to be perched, toes clenched, on the edge of . . . something. She put her hand on his knee and looked at him. His forehead was longer, the straight and sandy hair receding in a pleasant way. The mustache was thick, without nuance or finesse. It might have been edgy and ironic in New York but was still two decades out of date here in Iowa. She reached out to touch it. "Your mustache," she said.

He brought up the back of his other hand, the hand holding the flask, as if to wipe it clean. "We should go inside."

Was she imagining it or had the tips of his fingers bitten into her arm before he'd slipped away from her to toss the flask onto the floor of the back passenger's seat. Then he popped the glove and took out a wadded-up tissue, blotted the shine off his forehead and did something to his face she'd never seen before—instead of sleep-deprived, puffy and drunk, his face became a mask of helpfulness. Salesman face. He looked concerned and glad to see her. She wondered if he even knew he was doing it.

As they crossed the Siegels' lawn, she wrestled her heels from their divots in the grass and he put out a hand to steady her, getting close to her as he did. For moment, he was still there, the essential Sam. Beyond the booze: the particulated cedar smell of something organic and masculine beneath.

The Siegels were vacant-eyed in the living room. Both in glasses, she with long, curly hair shot with white and he mostly gray, but with a hint of Jen's red in his beard. Sam and Stevie whispered their own names as if bearing some fragile gift.

"Stevie. Oh Stevie, there you are. It's been so long," and Jen's mother grasped her shoulders and drew her into a loose, fragile hug. She repeated the act with Sam and pointed the two old friends toward the buffet in the living room before she was whisked away by an officious aunt-like woman who carried a bowl of red Jello that waggled with each heel strike of her sensible pump.

The house was just as Stevie remembered it—the red accent wall in the kitchen with the framed Toulouse-Latrec posters visible through to the living room, scattered with faded oriental rugs, angular mid-century lounge chairs and the long oak slat bench they used as a coffee table. Everywhere there were bookcases filled with books so tattered and haphazardly placed that it was clear they'd all been read at one point or another. The television was still an old TV/VCR combo box set, ashamed and unwatched in its dark corner. This was the first home for which she'd ever longed, the hardwood floors so different from the '70s shag of her own childhood home, which had never quite lost the dirty tobacco hue left over from her parents' smoking days, not until it had been destroyed in the flood. Jen's house had always felt . . . smarter, somehow, more sophisticated, or sophisticated at all, really, full stop. The kind of place where people drank dark red wine and talked about Kierkegaard. By contrast, her house was *People* magazine and her mother's sweet, iced Chablis. By contrast, her mother's living room—enormous overstuffed plaid couch, chipped mirrored coffee table, rounded oak country hutch stiffly peopled with her dead grandmother's Hummels—everything angled toward the television console (from which a plasma-screen TV now sprouted on its single, plastic leg) as if in veneration to it. But here at Jen's was austere and intellectually rigorous discomfort, the straight hard lines of the academic bourgeois, complete with cat hair and scattered back issues of the *New Yorker*. Stevie hated herself a little for loving it so much. But if, as a child, she'd seen it as a model for taste, now as she moved through it, she felt pangs of nostalgia. There was the same overstuffed footstool on which she and Jen had crouched with bananas halfway down their throats. That, the dining table upon which Stevie had spread a piece of the found treasure of her parents' pornographic magazine stash over which she and Jen had gasped and giggled and sat in awed silence in front of a double-penetration pictorial that was difficult to associate with anything human—the plucked poultry bulge of the woman's rear, cocks nozzling out of her like hoses. It was the house in which she'd begun to understand the mechanics of desire in all their tawdry and beautiful manifestations.

A growing crowd perched and flapped around the house. Sam and Stevie moved silently toward the buffet table outside of the kitchen and hovered above the oversalted casseroles and congealing roasts, food like the dead themselves—earthly shell, spirit departed. Stevie stabbed at a cube of white and yellow Colby with a toothpick. It looked diseased and tasted like the plastic in which the entire platter had been wrapped, but she took another, and another. The fat fought the alcohol, revived her. Sam, who had not said anything since announcing himself to Jen's parents, worked on a chicken wing and managed, somehow, to avoid his mustache entirely as two vaguely familiar, unseasonably tan women waded toward them.

Sam smiled. Charm then disarm. Mission: datamine. Ellie and Carrie were lifetime Taylorites, members of their high school's inexplicably popular show-choir set. He could see them now in the blue lamé wrap dresses, the high teased hair, the nude dance heels. They used to get high on life and give their boyfriends belabored handjobs under blankets in the bus on the way home from choir competitions. He was sure they wouldn't know anything, were probably just here for the gossip of it, but as of right now his leads numbered zilch. Might as well practice his moves; he might just accidentally learn something.

The heavier one (Ellie?) tilted her head so far to the side, she looked like she would tip over. "Sam and Stevie," a long sigh. "So good to see you two." Carrie frowned at her and Ellie put a hand over her mouth. "I mean. Not good." She blushed.

"This is just all so sudden," Carrie said and stepped up to hug him, but stepped back quickly, the ghost of her perfume lingering where she did not. They shot each other looks and he made a note of it. Who had said, "at a funeral, everyone looks suspicious"? They were at Stevie now, who stiffly acquiesced into their open arms. She caught his eye over their heads and he saw she had no idea who they were.

"Ellie," he said and the smaller one looked up—whoops—"and Carrie. It's been a long time." Relief on Stevie's face. Recognition. He felt the shape of the moleskin in his front jacket pocket. He'd bought it earlier that day when he'd stumbled into Patti's Paper before the funeral, already drunk, thinking it might help him organize his thoughts and keep track of clues. If this were a real interrogation he'd probably recount this conversation like so: Carrie, heavy-set blond, wedding ring but no husband present—home with the kids? Possibly the silent, unsupportive type—follower of Ellie, better looking, queen bee, unmarried. Pointed croc pumps and a plunging-v wrap dress: repurposed date outfit, no kids. Carrie's frayed cardigan, short bob and sensible flats said otherwise. Test the theory.

"How are your kids, Carrie?"

Carrie beamed and dug in her purse. Photos all around, appreciative murmurs.

"How's Doug? How's the business?"

"You mean Chad? He's in Kabul right now—active duty." Carrie looked puzzled, took a step away from him and scanned the room. Stevie shot him a look. Too many questions; stop being weird.

"This is all so sad," he said and put a hand over his eyes. The smell of Ellie again, the heat of her at his side.

"I'm so sorry, Sam. I know you and Jen were . . . very close," a pause, a stammer. He looked up and Carrie was glaring at Ellie. She twitched her head toward Stevie then pretended to look for something in her purse. "Oh, right. I forgot—it was you two who dated? You and Stevie?" Now it was Ellie's turn to blush. "Sorry, I always remember you and Jen together.

Like at assemblies, you were always sitting together and. I don't know. That's just the picture I have. You and Jen."

Me too, he thought.

Stevie, dear Stevie, looked hurt.

There was an awkward silence and the women excused themselves to get water.

Sam went to the bathroom—giant poppies wallpaper, the strong smell of cinnamon from a diffuser vase atop the toilet—and sucked down the rest of his jacket flask. After that, the evening began to break itself into bits and pieces: tiled echo of the kitchen, a glass of something red and the fizz and chill of the soda water Stevie dabbed him with. The distressed face of a stranger above a speckled black sports coat. A mule-gray cat batting at his untied shoelace. The stomachey sound of someone sobbing. Tall linen-shaded lamp in the corner and the shadows of mourners. Terrific wind in the spring trees, slight curve in the window glass. The front door green on the inside same as the out and the smell of that wind—fishy worm rot and promise of warmth, of sun and life—obscene, given the circumstances. The quiet shelter of his car again. The sobbing man was him.

Sam startled, came to, clutched at his pants and saw the stain on his striped oxford—wine?—where the paunch was just beginning to push out. His tears had made ugly splotches on his spring wool pants. As Stevie drove, she fumbled around his console for something and came up with a piece of Orbitz and palmed it into her mouth as she turned right onto a county road. Where were they? The night was an oil slick out his window.

The investigation was clearly not going well. For one, the crying. He sensed he'd made a scene but could not find a shit to give. Sam knew he would feel ashamed and humiliated by all of this tomorrow, but for right now let them see, let them see. He'd lost the person he had loved the most if not the best and she was gone and it was the fault of someone. Someone somewhere. But who? He refilled the flask with the mostly empty handle he kept tucked up under his seat. Where again? Where were they—

He tried to ask this, aloud, but all that came out was mush-mouth noise. Still too drunk. He wanted to ask her to stop. He wanted to ask her to let him out, he would walk home. Home. He flipped open his phone and saw that he had five new voicemails. He visualized a heavy black curtain made of a dense, stiff velvet and heard the noise it made when it fell onto the stage separating one part of his life from another part and then he put his phone away and took another draw from the flask—sweet metal, like blood, and this thought made him laugh and put on his best Count Dracula voice and lean over to Stevie and mumble, "I vant to suck your blahd," and bite, ever so gently, at that strained and sticky neck, that salty neck that smelled of evaporated alcohol and Stevie's skin which somehow smelled exactly that same as it did when they were teenagers. Not a smell he could compare to anything else. It came to him as color and movement: a light green, a sort of slow-motion refractive effect, like the reflection of light in water.

Stevie gave a short cry and shrugged him away. "Sam! If we get pulled over I am going to jail and you're spending the night here."

He cupped her shoulder like a pal. "Sorry, Stevie. I'm such an asshole." This is what he meant to say, but it all ran together. Like water, he thought. Like the gulf at the delta's end. Everything mixed all together in the end, everything one. Like how the glaciers were melting and the seas were rising and would soon engulf the land and everything on it. The end of the world: he would be there and so would she and there would be no difference between any of them, all equal in God's eyes, like that night in the basement, the night of the flood, where his body was not just his but theirs too, a common body. He remembered touching a leg in a sexy way and not realizing for a moment it was his own. He wanted to be there now with them, with her. All together and mixed up and one like that.

"I want my leg for your leg," he said and threw up against the inside of the passenger door.

It was with a little trilling shiver that Stevie sneaked Sam into her mother's house, shushing him, an arm under his unsteady shoulder and across his broad back. She was in high school again, hiding from her parents, though it was not quite the same house since her father—distant, enigmatic, spuriously angry—had left. The boy on her arm was the same one, and just to think of him as a boy made her feel home and safe in a way she never felt in New York, which was, in some ways, the antithesis of both. She saw them stumble onto the stage of the linoleum as if watching the movie of her own life. There they were, lumbering shushingly up the split-level stair to the kitchen, gasping through tall glasses of water, stumbling across the great Midwestern desert of beige deep-pile, down the hallway, past the bathroom and its scented-tissue smell. A moment's fumble at the huge faux-brass doorknob and the weightless cardboard-core door open, and shut with hardly a sound, barely a quiver in the paper reaches of her mother's rancher and down onto the bed, which squeaked away from the wall under the propulsion of their combined weight. Sam's body pinned her arm and he turned toward her so that when she rolled over to come to some sort of equilibrium their noses touched. His mouth opened and he looked at her for what seemed like the first time all day. He smoothed a pinch of her hair with his thumb and swallowed hard, which was probably a side effect of his violent retching in the car but which, here and now and in the amber light of the sodium street lamp outside, was also disarming. And if whose lips led neither could later say, and if the wrenchings of their adult clothes by their larger and inflexible adult bodies was somewhat awkward, and if one of them whispered the name of that disappeared friend more than once in a drink-and-grief-choked fog, consider: What isn't forgivable, in the end?

The good thing about being hungover was that it dampened his panic and opened up into a painful, flat calm which gave him the room to contemplate his next move. This morning Sam knew two things: One, Jen was still dead and her killer was still at large. Two, he'd finally cheated on his wife, but with Stevie instead of Jen. Except for the ever-present ache in his hollows for Jen and everything she had been or promised to be to him, he wasn't sure how he felt about this. Stevie was familiar and strange at the same time, which was exciting. Somewhere to the left of the Jen ache, was a breathtaking reservoir of guilt for what he'd done, which, if he was really being honest, was not so much cheat on his wife with his old high-school girlfriend as have hallucinatory goodbye sex with his recently deceased soul mate. Then there was the thing he didn't know: the question of what had transpired yesterday between arriving at the wake and falling into Stevie's bed. His stomach dropped off another cliff and Sam rolled out of that bed and made it to the bathroom with one eye closed, damp and bleary and feeling oddly disembodied by the pain in his head and gut. He vomited and blubbered through his heaves like a toddler, snot and tears and hot whiskey bile all streaming out of him until he was sure he felt his soul slide out and into the toilet and he coughed and flushed and washed his face with cold water and left the bathroom a man who could face the world without blinking, like a man without a soul.

The bed was empty when he got back to the bedroom and he dressed and tried to ignore the breakfast making itself known to his nose. But Stevie met him at the end of the hallway with a plate of scrambled eggs and wheat toast. There would be no quick goodbye.

"Morning," she smiled a small, hopeful smile.

"Stevie," he stood there holding the plate at his chest. His guilt split and became many guilts. A hydra of guilt. "What happened yesterday?"

"What's the last thing you remember?"

Cinnamon, poppies.

"We were talking to Ellie and Carrie and I went to the bathroom."

Stevie nodded and led them into the kitchen. "I wandered around and said hi to a couple of people. Kaycee and Evan were there—do you remember them?" Table, fork, coffee. "Anyway, I lost track of you for a little bit, but then Carrie found me and told me you needed help. I guess you'd been going up to people and asking them where they were when Jen died. When I found you in the kitchen, you were talking to an older man. You were putting together a theory—that's how you said it, 'I'm putting together a theory. Where were you on March 27, at ten p.m.?

Sam coughed out a bit of egg. "Oh no."

"Which what is that? Is that when Jen died?"

Sam nodded.

"How do you know that?"

Sam shook his head, unable to speak. His old friend shame.

"And you were kind of loud. Like you weren't using your inside voice."

"I'm so—" He took a deep breath, half sorry, half checking his pocket for his moleskine. Still there. He would check it when he got home. Had he written something useful down, even in the depths of his blackout? Only, as it turned out, the lyrics to "Piano Man."

"You didn't actually say the word 'murder' though. If that makes you feel better."

She did look lovely in the morning—he remembered that about her. Her hair tousled well. She had a bit of egg on her own upper lip. "I'm sorry, Stevie." Poor Stevie.

She swatted his apology away. "Sam, when were you most happy? Like in your whole life?"

He shifted his gaze to the living room, away from her. The wall-to-wall was old and ratty but the bones of the house were good—the original wood trim hadn't been painted over, the bay window looked out onto an ancient oak in the front yard. The wallpaper was unfortunately bouqueted, but this was an easy fix. It was a classic '60's raised ranch, and if someone with an eye were to do it up, get rid of the grandmotherly decor, it could be a real mover, especially in this neighborhood, these schools. He'd been a realtor for so long that this assessment was swift, automatic, and almost subconscious, and a sense of unease followed it. He'd been a realtor for a very long time, true, but how long had it been since he'd had a sale? His wife's stiff face frowned from a distant pocket of his brain. What had come before all this?

He saw Jen's ghost and she was telling him she got into Northwestern. That she was getting out of this podunk cowtown shithole. The way she'd laughed when he'd blurted out the marriage proposal, either thinking or pretending to think it a joke, to spare them both the humiliation of taking it seriously. It had all gotten complicated at the end—the other guys he could never really confront her about because they were never actually together, the secrecy. He had loved her so much but the last year she'd lived in Iowa had felt like a slow disintegration. What had come before that?

"That summer," he said. "The flood summer."

"Me too," Stevie replied with something like triumph on her face. "It's like nothing in my life has been as real or as good since then. I got fired from my job. In New York," she shook her head. "But I'm having a hard time feeling sad—feeling anything—about it. Maybe this whole terrible thing is giving me some perspective," she lowered her head at him and he saw the old sparkle—the way she used to swallow him with her eyes. "Or maybe it was you—us—our old energy."

Sam was starting to sweat. Soon he would be in need of a beer. And now that Jen was in the ground, he had to begin, right away, with his investigation. For real this time. Just because he was maybe a drunk didn't mean he couldn't do something right and true for his friend. There were people to interview. Businessmen in Chicago—shady finance guys, her parents maybe, if they could bear such a thing. No more booze.

In his heart he hadn't cheated, that was the important thing. In his heart, it had always been him and Jen.

"That summer is why I need to do this. Why I need to find her killer."

Stevie's face fell. "That's not really what I meant." She looked disappointed. In him? Join the club, he wanted to say. Instead, he got up from the table and put a hand on her shoulder, squeezed. There was a six-pack in his trunk. The beer would be warm but he'd put it over ice at home. Regroup. God. Home. What was happening at home? What would he be walking into? His skin crawled and his heart thudded painfully behind his left eye.

"Stevie, I have to go. I'm sorry. I don't . . . I don't feel well." He flapped at himself—watch wallet keys cell—and strode down the stairs to the tiny foyer to stand in front of the sunburst window in the front door. The day outside was so sunny the world seemed flat. He wanted to drive a hole right through it.

Stevie had to jump up from the table to catch him. She hugged him. He kissed at her—got her cheek—fumbled with the door, then the deadbolt and the door again. Then he was floating free into the bright, prickly day. The sun was heavy leverage; it pried at his pulsing skull, and his car was overwarm and smelled like vomit. He did not even wait for the frosty glass or the ice. He would have been a danger on the road without the beer and whatever was waiting for him in the house was certainly worthy of two more. In just a few swallows, his headache began to recede. A few more and he felt like the pull of gravity upon him was less lopsided. He could sit up straight again, no vertigo, as though the natural metals in his head that had been dragging him toward the center of the earth were now oppositely charged. He felt buoyant. He felt like going for a drive.

Stevie padded back to her old bedroom. Sam had left his tie on the floor. It was a lovely, pale pink silk she somehow hadn't noticed before. It reminded her of the old pictures of her father. She flung it around her neck like a scarf and lay down on her back in bed and began to mentally undress the room around her. The lilac basket wallpaper border would have to go and maybe she'd sand down the orange-peel finish on the walls. A light gray or a buttercream yellow might be nice in here. Maybe a few area rugs over the top of the cheap, synthetic wall-to-wall. Her mother, oh her mother would be so happy.

She understood, intellectually, that she must be feeling a certain level of disappointment in Sam's hung-over flight, but she was so enamored of her hatchling plan that it was difficult to hold onto that disappointment with any level of gravity. In fact, she felt slightly ecstatic, as though she were moving faster through the world than everyone else, like a dog off its leash.

It had come to her last night. After the sex, the grief that taking care of Sam had displaced had come roaring in. She sat up with a sob stuck in her throat, a vision of Jen: denim jacket, black pants, those ever-present gray Chucks. In the vision, Jen's hand had been out but Stevie couldn't tell if she was beckoning or warning away. The desire to embrace her was overwhelming and the ache was an actual physical pain that woke her up. Sam snored beside her and she lay on her saggy old bed next to him and breathed through yet another veil of tears, tears that rolled down into the cupped palms of her ears and made her shiver. It felt like there was something big and dreadful rising up to meet her and all she could do was lie there, be puny, and wait for it to surface. She didn't want to think, anymore, about Jen's death. Nor did she want to think about what she was going to do now without the job that had kept her frozen in place for so long like Han Solo in carbonite. The sweat and blindness that would come with the thaw, the giant worm with a million teeth. She didn't want any of it and as long as she lay here, next to Sam, it felt possible to pretend none of it was happening. Being with Sam was making her heart bigger, somehow, and she wanted to feel this feeling for a little while longer, before the morning arrived and everything went back to normal—whatever that was right now. And the book. The agent. The news seemed like it should be a good thing, but she felt as though she'd already failed, just like she'd failed at everything else in her life, thus far.

This house had once been the limits of her world. Had she been happier then? Lying flopped out on the floor, next to her brother, watching *The Fresh Prince of Bel Air*, her parents on the couch? Retreating to the basement to play Nintendo when the fighting got too loud? All four of them sitting at the kitchen table—she remembered laughter. If happiness was a thing you forged yourself, was she happy in New York? Or was happiness something (as the word itself seemed to imply) that happened to you, or that you made happen, an atmosphere, a sense of being enveloped—something that could be invisible for years until, one day, it was gone? She listened to the soft sigh of Sam at her side. When they were teenagers it was as if they had run full speed at each other, and maybe, together, at the world. Stevie missed this. Being an adult meant sidling up to things, pretending desire was an ancillary to existence. To want something too much, as an adult, meant you were obsessive, unstable. It meant you were a nerd, hard up, pitiful. Being adult meant having feelings about your feelings instead of just feeling them. Being forever once removed from yourself. Stevie didn't want it anymore. What she wanted, instead, was to feel alive and excited and like anything could happen.

As she lay there, wrung out from grief but newly full of something else, rain made itself known at the windows and the night felt bigger and more important than it had before. The big thing was still coming but now she thought she could see the edges and maybe it was not a thing to dread but to welcome.

Home. That was it. Stevie would move home. The thought opened like a moonflower in the dark and immediately seeded others. Not just move home. She would make it all like it was, when she was happy, when she felt like a complete and desiring beast moving forward through the world. She would get her old job at the pool back. She would win Sam. Maybe she could even find her brother and get him to join in her experiment. Make repairs, rebuild their fractured, scattered family. Somehow it would be both romantic and comfortable, exciting and familiar. This is what she would write about. This was her blog, her book, her gimmick, her thing. Amanda Collins would go for it, she knew it. And it would fill the space inside her that all those years in New York had not, give movement to the thing inside her that had been at a standstill for so many years. She had ascribed the word "homesick" to this space, this inertia so often, but its obvious cure had never occurred to her until this moment. She would do it for Jen, to keep the fading memory of their former friendship alive.

This had been what she'd wanted to talk about with Sam, over breakfast—her plan. But he'd left too fast and she'd tried not to feel disappointed. She understood—he'd been hungover, overwhelmed, in mourning. Stevie held the narrow of the tie up to her face. That was the true smell of her adolescent happiness. Last night, after she'd cried and cried and then had her thought, she'd fallen back asleep by tucking her nose into the softness of the back of Sam's neck and felt so safe she'd almost cried again. The rain on the windows dappled the carpet in her room, the white particle-board princess-set furniture, the light blue duvet they'd wrestled with. The shadow the streetlight cast through the rain ran down her bare shoulders, like she was underwater and had just surfaced.

When the garage door opened, he was unsure how long he'd been sitting in his own driveway, or how he'd gotten there. All he could say, for sure, was that he was in his car, in front of his house and the garage door was opening. End of story. Had he opened it? He glanced up at the opener clipped to the visor as if willing it to speak. There were empty cans all over the passenger-side floor. The six-pack was kicked and there were more empties yet. Somehow. And now, here was Bonnie, emerging from the cave of his garage like a super villain, now standing in front of his car, squinting at him through his filmy windshield with the ferocity of a wife of six years, elbows crossed and hips tilted in a contentious contrapposto. His stomach was full of knives. They looked at each other for a long time, before she turned around and went back inside.

It seemed like no more than a moment had passed when he came to again, this time to the symphony of smashing glass. He'd barely opened his eyes, when the pain closed them again, and in that moment what did he see? A shadow? A man? Did he see or imagine, in a kind of phantasmagoric, half-dreaming state, the way the glass dust sparkled in the air like Christmas and the thick hair on the knuckles of the man who'd made it as they grabbed at him before the darkness, that old Labrador, had swum up to meet him again?

PART II

Chapter 3

Is This Heaven?

In an astounding turn of events, I am bursting with corn to tell you that I up and moved out of the Big City and now hail from the land of beer and bacon. It's all amber waves of grain out here. There are so many fields with so many dreams. Or so many dreams in so many fields? What I mean to say is: I live in Iowa now. This dispatch goes out to you from my childhood bedroom. I am sitting on my childhood bed. I am wearing a Vuarnet T-shirt and Umbro shorts which, while wrinkled, seem to have no idea how old they are. Not a fray.

"But *why* Iowa?" you ask.

I realize I've been too radio silent for too long and to fill in all the holes here would take a serious chunk of screen and I know you have some Gawker Stalker to read and the Go Fug Yourself Oscars feature that you keep opening to read then clicking out of when your boss swoops by and forgetting to open back up, so I will try to make the world wide web digest version for you here.

I got canned. This we know. By my ex-boyfriend. Oof. Then my old best friend died. This is not the Spring of Stevie, I think we can all agree. The funeral, though, brought some things into focus for me. Like that where I was and what I was doing was not really taking me anywhere. Like that torso ache I've been feeling for years now is not a burgeoning ulcer but something much worse: homesickness. I've always prided myself on being independent. Hell, I've been independent for all of my adult life. But for what? Where has it gotten me? Why do I think I should ignore the voice that reminds me that home is where I felt most myself, where I *became* myself, the place that makes me strong? Why do we think it's some measure of strength or character to plaster over the flyover yokel inside of us with double cheek kisses and all-black wardrobes?

Maybe Iowa is what I am and where I belong. Maybe that's not bad. The only thing I really want to do anyway is write, and while everyone wants to convince you that New York is the writing capital of the world, like nearly everything else about New York, that is actually only true if you are rich.

Also, I can't afford to be unemployed in NYC. Like not even for a week.

So I did it, I moved. It had been so long since I'd driven a long distance. That part felt the most like escaping. Like I was actively thrusting myself toward something better. Or something familiar but different?

I have a plan, you see. There's going to be a redo, a do-over, an ironic retelling of my own story that will lay like the thinnest piece of paper, over the top of my actual life.

I mean, I'm going to start my entire adulthood over, and see if I can do better this time around. First, I need a job. More on that soon. And I need to reconnect with old friends.

So now I'm here and it's time to begin to execute my plan. The first step is I have to get recertified in lifeguard training. That starts next week. The next step is I have to get a job as a lifeguard. Harder. Third step is something I can't share yet (after the funeral, I may or may not have encountered an old friend in a meaningful way if you get my drift and that is all I shall say about that for now). The fourth and fifth steps I guess I'll figure out as I put my feet to them.

So here I go. Doing it over like I did it back then.

I hope you'll come with me.

Stevie scanned the post, unsure about it. She looked up at Jim Morrison, who had probably never been unsure about anything in his life. Back in the day, she'd watched the Oliver Stone movie so many times with Jen and Sam and various stoner recruits. What was it about being an artist, a man? You could just say you were an artist and poof you were fucking Meg Ryan off Parisian balconies, performing Satanic blood rites with journalist witches. Stevie had once marveled aloud to Jen about how awful he'd been to everyone around him, at least in the movie version of his life, which meant in reality he'd most likely been much worse. Jen had been taking a hit of skunk weed their annoying companion Albert had brought around with him that night. "It's not hard," Jen's eyes, marbled by the purple light of the screen, had traveled somewhere beyond the damp and stanky chill of Stevie's basement. "All you have to do is destroy everything in your path." Then she blinked and her usual eyes were back and they zeroed in on Albert, who had fallen asleep between them. "What would Jim Morrison do?" she'd whispered slyly and glanced back up at Stevie.

Something hot had throbbed through Stevie. "Kill him," she hissed and for a beat there was a silence wherein both girls casually contemplated the kind of murder that occurs to every teenager at some point, and then they began to giggle and then laugh when Albert woke up from his stupor, just as Meg Ryan beheld Val Klimer's freshly shaven, beatifically dead face in a bathtub in Paris.

Jen would not have doubted herself, she knew. But Stevie felt herself hardly daring to exist in relation to the white, man-child colony known as American literature. *Steady, baby*, she said to herself. *This is just the beginning. You're not even in the game yet.*

During her last week in New York, at lunch at Aquavit, Amanda Collins had gone hard for the homecoming idea when Stevie had pitched it to her over their first glass of Pouilly-Fuissé. Amanda's eyes got big and she'd pumped her hands to the ceiling. Raise the roof. "Yes, girl! I love it. Moving home to Ohio! It's so Kevin Spacey in *American Beauty*! But with feminine shame and no murder at the end. Wait—that was set in Ohio too, right? Or was it Illinois? I get them confused."

"Chicago suburbs I think?" The post-Hughes angst of Thora Birch. "But I'm moving to Iowa."

She'd had some time upon her return, after the funeral, when her plan was still brand new, still just an idea, to reflect on what it would be like to stay in New York instead of moving home. Most of the time living in New York felt like living in a big, dirty, expensive city, which it was, but sometimes it felt like living in a movie. You couldn't make these times happen, though people tried (why else had the bars been full of young women drinking oversweet Cosmo varietals for half a decade?). They had to happen to you, and then there you were, watching yourself in a movie that was actually your life. These times could never be predicted. This morning, for instance, Stevie realized the cereal box she'd been eating out of since her return had a mouse-hole chewed in the bottom of it. Sometimes the movie you were in was a comedy. (Sometimes it was horror—the feeling she got when she'd realized the debris falling out of the windows of the first tower wasn't debris at all but people jumping out.) But then sometimes it was perfect. Like today. Besides watching lower Manhattan smolder and getting chlamydia from her boss, a comped lunch with a literary agent was the most New York thing that had ever happened to her. She almost wondered what would happen if she stayed. But then, she couldn't stay and write a book about moving home. And there was the mouse-hole and the elevated threat levels and the cops on the subways with semi-automatics. And her joblessness. She could find another precarious low-level white-collar job. She could temp, could recruit, could executively assist, but for what. Anyway, the pull that tugged her westward was much stronger, much wilder, than the quiet, organized thoughts of uploading her resume onto Monster.com.

Amanda put her hand up before she took a bite of her gravlax, as if to call for silence in the room. "Fuck, this is so good," she moaned and drained her glass, holding it aloft until a waiter resentfully swept it away. "Well, it doesn't really matter exactly where anyway. The point is you move home, you do teenage you, you what—work in a grocery store?"

"Lifeguard. I train first, you know, then get a job when the season starts." Somehow. And fingers crossed her severance would hold out that long. She thought it would if she were careful. Anderson had been merciful in that respect, at least.

"Okay, you lifeguard. Maybe, you know," Amanda Collins appraised her. "Get to the gym a bit. I'll send you a diet bundle—*Skinny Bitch in the Kitch, How to Eat like a Hot Chick*. You know. Okay. Great. Hot. You said there's a love interest?"

"Ex-boyfriend," Stevie felt her pulse jump a little when she thought of Sam.

"God, yes, so good. It's perfect. But, like I said, you don't want to come off like this is all just for a book. You want it to seem natural. I mean, it's a plan, but don't go all reality-TV with it. You know what I mean? Don't talk about the book on your blog—people lose interest if they think you're doing something because you got a book deal." A book *deal* was a stretch—technically, they just had interest. ("Intense interest,"—Amanda, on the phone earlier in the week. "They've basically written the contact already," then a low hiss "Eff ess gee" and Stevie had not asked for details, afraid if she did, the spell would be broken).

"And for fuck's sake don't make it up. Every editor is still so scared about memoir. Thanks to that epic fail that goes by the name of James Fucking Frey I can't even call it memoir anymore, I have to call it Blog Lit. No memoir please, they say, but give us some more of those Blog Lit books. Blog Lit and wizard bedtime stories and vampire romances for the Twi-Hards is all anybody wants right now." The displeasure that spread across the lightly Botoxed face of Amanda Collins was one of slight disgust and well-trod regret. For this she had graduated *summa* from Vassar, had passed up a slot at Carey Law. For vampires and wizards and bloggers. Stevie tried not to take the look personally. She understood what it was like to open doors you would never walk through yourself. "Thirty-something mid-life crisis Blog Lit," said Amanda Collins with what may have been choking fury or just a sip of wine gone down the wrong pipe. "So hot right now."

And Stevie had nodded and let Amanda Collins do most of the rest of the talking as the trout meunière melted in her mouth. She was savoring it all—the hope in her heart and one last fancy lunch before it was time to pack up and head off to Iowa, where there was plenty of trout but little meunière.

These hopes would keep her company as she finished packing up her clothes and dishes. The few, studio-sized pieces of furniture she'd been able to drag home from flea markets and Bed Bath and Beyond and cram into her tiny apartment weren't worth taking. In the end, the ease with which she would uproot, cut ties, fly the coop—it was as if her entire life had been held in place by a single tack. With minimal discomfort or even emotion (though she'd get a little misty at a goodbye dinner later that night, with three friends from work—blame the cheap beer—and when her elderly Polish landlord, Viktor, gifted her a lovely wooden box that had belonged to his mother, and warned her against marrying a farmer—"Farm boy, they all fuck pig.") she would suddenly be in the wind, plowing down I-80 in a rented U-Haul van, winging through America's vast and boring heartland with her own heart in her mouth and the welcome stench of manure worming into her nostrils. Going home, going home. She would roll down her window and scream it to a bloody deer carcass gathering flies on the shoulder of the interstate outside of Youngstown: "I'm going home!"

The deer carcass would not shout back.

When she'd arrived home, the weightless feeling had lasted for several days. It had been there as she'd driven around in her mom's CRV, those first nights, past her old haunts (Ollie's, where she and Melinda had once snuck in with terrible fake IDs and been rubbed up on by mammalian frat guys who sloshed pitchers of beer into their hair; the big houses behind Taylor High—now finished developments, but just mountains of soil back then—where they'd committed all manner of light felonies in their cars) and past the houses and neighborhoods where her friends had grown up. How strange to realize now that the bungalows down the road didn't just belong to Julie's family and Russell's mom anymore but to people like Julie and Russell themselves. People Stevie's age! Sometimes they had kids! Melinda and Doug's McMansion. The middle-classness of it all was exotic to her after so many years of grinding in a city where ownership was for the elite. The comfort and ease of Iowa seemed unbelievable—how you could just kind of wind up middle-class almost by accident. Was it possible that her grinding, all the work to set herself apart and make something different out of her life beyond the trap of family and the wide denuded prairies, had resulted in . . . absolutely nothing? This was the feeling that finally grounded her and it had lasted. Now, almost two weeks home, she found herself wavering.

Trying to roll all this up into a blog post, Stevie found her words felt wrong and forced. Too certain. She was about as far from certain as a person could be. She went into her dashboard and deleted the post she had written and began again.

The Next Big Thing

I moved home. I'm going to try to be myself again, like I was back when I knew what that was. I'm lonely and homesick and I don't have what other people my age seem to find so easily: love, a family, a rewarding career. I have thirteen years of hustling and scraping by but no job. I have no house. I have this blog where I write my thoughts. I have some nice second-hand designer clothes. I know where most of Manhattan's secret bars are. I know what the sun looks like when it's shining across the avenues at just the right hour at the right time of year so that the shadows of the buildings loom monumentally, dramatically—Manhattanhenge. It's enough to make anyone love New York.

A moment of love for New York can last years. Long enough to hold you spellbound and blind you to the life you aren't leading. What's so terrible about driving a car to the grocery store anyway? What is so great about soup from a sidewalk cart?

Stevie thought of the people she knew who had stayed too long in New York, who seemed curdled in some essential way. Who developed weird habits, like collecting vintage lunchboxes or only dating twenty-three-year-olds. But those who left also had unimaginable lives: they'd found people who made money enough to marry them away. She thought of her work friends, Brenda and Kim. How they used to meet in her neighborhood every Sunday for brunch—for months!—at Sidewalk or Niagara or Two of Cups until, within a few weeks of each other's banquet-hall weddings, they both moved to Long Island and she never saw them again.

The truth was that sidewalk-cart soup was actually really delicious but also that the constant emptying out made it hard to forge deep connections.

The rain—would it ever end?—flung itself at the windows and the house of her youth seemed to hold its breath around her. In the corner of her room, the stacks of unpacked boxes loomed in ways that would frighten her when she woke up in the middle of the night, confused about where she was.

So anyway, like I said, I moved home. I'll let you know what happens next.

She wished, for the hundredth time in the weeks since she'd returned, that Sam would call her back.

Sam squinted at the screen. "Jen Siegel is never gonna give you up, never gonna let you down, never gonna tell a lie and hurt you." There it was, next to a photo of her—big sunglasses, smirk, something neon hanging overhead, the kind of photo someone takes of you when you're all about a half hour from last call: impish, wild. Of course her last status update would be a fucking Rick roll.

This was her public Facebook wall but he couldn't shake the feeling he was doing something wrong by visiting. His heart was pounding like the time he'd found a porno tape in his parents' bedroom VCR when he was eleven and just figuring out how to jerk off. It felt like he was doing something perverted, a feeling which intensified with every message he read on the screen. The first few at the top of her wall were treacly post-death performance pieces that felt hollow and suspicious. "You'll be missed. See you in heaven," and "Love you forever, sister." Yearbook of the dead. Below that, a strata of concerned curiosity: "I called five times—did you lose your phone?" "Where u @?" and below that, most chillingly, normal stuff. Updates from Jen that were mostly song lyrics ("Jen Siegel is all shackles and bows") and flirty abstractions ("Jen Siegel loves it when you do that thing you do. You know the thing."). Something about the third-person made the posts into haunted houses. Sam tried to read between their lines and could not, though conflict twitched at their edges ("Jen Siegel is the bigger man"). He took a sip from the tumbler beside him. For courage, for strength. Unlike some men, for whom drinking was a way to make themselves have feelings, drinking dulled his. He could not have waded through the disaster that was the end of her life without a Bulleit neat. Even so, he felt the pain at his throat that meant tears were imminent and so was relieved—though not without the squirmy feeling of being caught—when a notification dinged across his wall that his former office assistant and two-time Taylor Butter Queen Melody Fitch had "poked" him. Melody, whose hair had scented the entire office with vanilla, even hours after she'd left. He'd never eaten so much cake in his life as during her tenure. He clicked on Melody's name and there was a photo of her in a tiered pale pink ball gown, standing next to the Iowa State Fair Butter Cow from 1999. With her name on his wall (what was a poke?), he felt not just caught out snooping on Jen but sheepish about his own blank profile. He'd grown up in the '90s and so he understood that to be successful on Facebook he must adopt an ironic stance but he didn't do irony well. It had always made him uncomfortable. It had been one of the things Jen, M.C. of ironies performative and otherwise, had claimed to love about him many times. Even years after they'd gone back to just being friends, she'd sometimes ruffle his head and pull it into her scant bosom, cradling it there and crooning to him in a Natasha from *Rocky & Bullwinkle* accent, "American boy, so sincere!"

He felt bad for himself about Jen, and then bad for himself as he pictured Melody looking at the profile picture he'd hastily uploaded from an old office brochure they'd had professionally produced four years ago. Somehow it managed to look like a flat replication of itself. Like he was looking at a photo someone had taken of a brochure, instead of at a headshot JPEG. He looked like a man wearing a mask of his own face, which was honestly how he felt much of the time in his life these days. Looking at it produced in him a chord of something hard to define. As though the insides were, for once, matching the outsides. Uncanny valley. He wondered, vaguely, if Facebook was somehow devouring his soul, the way old National Geographic photographers used to talk about how their indigenous subjects reacted to their cameras. Notably, he would fail to wonder this when it became a more accurate take in the era of third-party app datamining.

But no, it wasn't Facebook. He'd felt this way since the funeral. It had surprised Sam, and, if he was being really honest, somewhat disappointed him that the day after Jen's funeral, the day after the thing with Stevie (this was how he thought of it now, "the thing," another placeholder until he could think with a little more of a distance) that he hadn't woken up in an abandoned warehouse or the trunk of a Cadillac, that his hands weren't handcuffed to anything, including each other. That the heavy shadow of a silencer did not fall across his stoic face. In fact, he had woken up, drooling and alone, face down on his own driveway, in a little pile of glass from his car window. He'd gotten up off the sandy rough of his driveway, unsure if the thug he'd seen had been real or a hallucination. His chin was hurt. It was broad daylight; he had no idea how long he'd been out—minutes? Hours? Where had the goon gone who'd punched out his window and then him? Or had he dreamed it all, some Dick Tracy nightmare? It had seemed so real. There was blood on his face.

He'd stumbled into his house to the sound of his blood pattering onto the laminate flooring. Bonnie was unloading the dishwasher and when she'd looked up, half bent over, he thought he'd cry from the sheer pleasure of seeing the worry on her face.

"Jesus Christ, Sam," she'd rushed to him, dishtowel already held up toward his wounded face. He jerked back a little as she gingerly pressed it to his cheek and, with her tiny little exclamation point of a body, led him to the bathroom by the shoulders.

"There was a guy," Sam's face throbbed as he sat on the toilet. "In the driveway. Attacked me in the car."

"What?" Bonnie's face seemed not be able to decide whether to be angry or worried. She bent down to rummage around under the sink for the first aid kit and when she came back up he could see she'd settled on angry. "You don't need to lie to me, Sam. I saw you passed out in your car. Did you spend the night there?"

"No," said Sam absently. She stood up fully, cotton-ball in hand, and he realized his mistake.

"Uh, then, where the fuck were you all night?"

Her voice made Sam's pain worse, somehow. His words were garbled and he felt a tightness where his jaw was certainly swelling. "I'm telling you someone attacked me, I'm bleeding on the floor in front of you, and you're interrogating me?"

Bonnie took a step back now and crossed her arms. "I did not see a man attacking you. Why would someone do that? In your own driveway?"

"Because I know about the murder."

Bonnie put a hand over her mouth and he couldn't read her expression. "You mean your friend?" This seemed to awaken some nodule of empathy inside her. The tightness fell out of her body and she rubbed her whole hand over her face. "Sam, I'm sorry about your friend. I don't even give a shit where you were last night, okay? I'm not even going to ask. But there was no murder. Okay? She . . . did it to herself. She was clearly a troubled person."

"How would you know?" Sam's anger was a sun flare—molten, noxious—and Bonnie stepped back, surprised. Maybe a little scared.

"Brenda told me. I guess there was a history of depression? And that she'd always been a little different."

Sam turned away from her and looked out the window above the toilet. The Martha Stewart cotton eyelet café curtains framed the view: a wide, mower-striped field, bounded on the far side by a neighbor's chain-link fence. Land that had once been open prairie—clover, phlox, feverfew—and before that, an antediluvian sea. It had seen wooly mammoth and bison, the Ho-Chunk and the Otoes, the newly arriving Potawatomi. The great Ioway leader No Heart of Fear, who had bargained for territory against the powerful Santee Dakota and lost. On the other side of the fence, their neighbor's dirty white bichon barked incessantly at nothing.

It seemed to Sam there were two possibilities here, neither of them very pleasant: one, someone had gotten wind of his investigation into Jen's death and was trying to shut him up or scare him away. Two: he'd hallucinated the whole thing, which meant his drinking was even worse than he'd realized. Either way, he was in trouble.

"Fuck you. You don't know anything about her," he said to Bonnie with frost in his voice.

The empathy left her. Her body stiffened. She took a deep breath and looked up to the ceiling. "I've barely seen you for a month—you're like a ghost here. And then I hear this friend's dead, this girl you used to know, in high school, right? And then when you *are* here, you're drunk. And now this. Someone attacks you in our driveway? Or you're just lying to me about it and you were with . . . I don't even know . . . but you were somewhere last night. And when was the last time you had a showing? Do you even still go into the office?" She took a long breath and raised shaking arms toward the semi-flushmount above her. "What the fuck is going on?" She screamed with brass in her lungs—the sound of a marriage shattering.

He didn't actually remember how this conversation had ended, just that her screaming—of which there was more—had driven him into himself. He'd become entranced by the extremely satisfying way the tiny rubies of his blood contrasted with the white of the bathroom tile. The tile had been one of their first fights in their new house. She'd wanted white quarter-rounds, he, marble herringbone. White would get dirty, too much upkeep. But look at it now, he'd wanted to say: his blood like a bouquet of roses at his own feet, his love for Jen made manifest. His love for Bonnie, too. He could almost feel it in there, a dull little wire snapped to attention way down deep. Still a little juice in it. They had said other things to each other like all the things they'd already said at some point or another, the words in slightly different order, louder. Blah, blah, blah, remembers Sam. Blah, blah, blah, and then, sometime around noon, Bonnie had slammed the front door behind her, and he'd crawled out of the bathroom and onto the gray sleeper sofa in the guest room without bothering to convert it from couch to bed. It had been that way, mostly, since.

So no, there would be no poking back of Melody. What a mess this all was already. What was he even looking for? Did he think someone was going to come on her wall and confess murdering her? This was just one funerary banality after another until you came to the stuff she'd posted, which cut him because of how little he understood it. All inside jokes and innuendo among friends. It felt like watching a party he hadn't been invited to through a window in the dark.

But then there *he* was—starting back in the fall, some asshole named Jerry Kowalski had thrown a ghost at Jen Siegel maybe twenty times and unlike the friendly provocations from other people on her wall, to which she responded in kind, his ghosts went unanswered.

Sam clicked on Kowalski's profile and hummed—his privacy settings were tight but Kowalski did list Satchel Ferry, Jen's employer, as a network. A colleague? Did throwing a ghost at someone over and over again count as an unwanted advance? Kowalski's profile picture was taken from a distance. Someone's disarticulated hand lay on his shoulder as if in congratulations. He wore a suit and his forehead shone back the light of the camera flash. His wall, inaccessible to Sam, lay like a blanket of snow over the truth of him. Peoplefinder wasn't much more helpful but Google gave a few hits. There was a bunch of banking stuff. A headshot on an investment group's Q&A page and a bunch of unsatisfying market jargon Sam skimmed. Old cached links that led nowhere. Then, on the second search page, the jackpot: a PDF of a schedule for a mortgage lender's conference in Chicago over Memorial Day weekend. Kowalski was in the program to do a panel on reverse mortgages. Sam, who'd had almost no religion growing up and who trucked with no particular belief system, felt something like fate slide into place. This conference was his destiny.

Kowalski knew something, he was sure of it. The slimy, rich look of him. A boy who'd always been given what he wanted and had grown into an entitled man. What if what he'd wanted was Jen? How would a man like that react to a brush-off or a turndown? How many ghosts was one too many? A notification popped up from Melody who had invited him to play Farmville. Her hot pink lipstick winked at him from her profile. Was this what they had come to then? Two lonely adults plowing land together in a cartoon simulation while the pastureland around them was cleared to make way for the hog lots of the C.A.F.O.s cemented over the top of the family farms that had made the state what it used to be. The charm of a teenage butter queen, curdled. Feeling again slightly repulsed by the entire endeavor of Facebook, Sam ignored Melody's request, but typed a promise of sorts to Jen and to himself before he logged out: Sam Sullivan is . . . on the case.

There. Let that be a mystery for anyone who cared to take it up.

Three days later, he called in sick to work and drove east. Balancing his business Visa on the steering wheel as he drove, he read off the numbers to the administrative assistant and he was registered for the conference at the end of the month.

He was excited—this conference had the potential to be a breakthrough in his case. Kowalski, he felt, may have answers about Jen's death. And if not Kowalski, then someone. It had been a sunny morning in Taylor—one of the few nice days this spring, it seemed—and everything shone damp and golden, like a revelation, in the sun. Days like this made the rain seem apocalyptic. He recalled the meaning of apocalypse from his college poetry class, which had struck itself into his memory: an unveiling. The rain had been bad this season and there was already worry in the air about getting the crops in on time. A day like today with its birds and its wet greenery felt post-apocalyptic. He could almost believe the worst of the world had already been revealed. But now, as he closed in on Chicago, he drove straight into the light rain that seemed to never cease to fall there.

Though he had called in sick to work, there was little work to be done. No new listings, no contingents. He hadn't exactly planned to drive to Chicago, but being at home was no good these days, and he couldn't stop thinking about Jen, about the conference. He felt the first glimmer of hope in weeks. He couldn't wait until the end of May. He took a nip from the flask under his seat and felt the promise of the weeks before him.

The car slipped down the Ike past the dark soldier of the Sears Tower (forever the Sears Tower to Sam, none of this Willis bullshit), whose white antlers were invisible above the cloud cover, and Sam exited onto the Loop.

The parking structure on Madison looked like every other; it loomed beige and featureless as if the sidewalk had birthed it. There was a Popeye's and a CVS on its ground floor, which felt heartachingly monotonous and dreary, though he knew from the *Tribune* article he'd found online that its official name was the Poetry Garage, and indeed, as he entered, he saw that instead of just a color or a number, each level was assigned a poet: Sandberg, Dybek, Brooks. He had no idea from which level she'd fallen, so he drove up to the top level and pulled into a stall in the far northwest corner.

Sam got out of the car. The wind pressed the door back against him, as if to warn him away from danger. The Loop spread out before him, above him, the patterns and heights of its buildings making him dizzy. Though he'd been on the famed Architectural River Tours many times, Sam was unfamiliar with the street-facing buildings of the Loop, and so he had no idea that the shiny and thoroughly uninteresting skyscrapers in view now from the Jean Valentine level of the Poetry Garage comprised the financial center of the entire Midwest. There was Deloitte and UBS, the new Merc—global derivatives marketplace giant, a far cry from the old Merc, a nonprofit agricultural commodities exchange. There was Barclays and Drexel Hamilton and a corner away, keeping track of the massive depository of wealth, with its army of briefcased and calculatored accountants, was Price Waterhouse Coopers. The only building Sam recognized by sight from ten stories up was the Lyric Opera where, one frigid December, a lifetime ago, he'd been bundled into a little three-piece suit and taken to see the Joffrey Ballet perform the Nutcracker. It was one of the few times he'd seen his mother drink—intermission champagne—and though his father was sullen and distant, as usual, his mother's delight at the beauty of the lobby and the performance space inside had delighted him in turn, itchy and tight as his jacket had been. He remembered the way the Christmas tree on stage had grown and grown until Clara and the Prince seemed to be mouse-sized in comparison, and the terror he'd felt at the canon fire when the Mouse King attacked with his army.

He looked away and, recalling his purpose now, stuck out his head out beyond the edge of the concrete structure. He felt dizzy as the wet sidewalk spread out below him in all directions. Was that where she'd landed, ten floors below? Was it possible she had accidentally fallen? No, the concrete exterior wall of the building came up past his hip.

Surely he was imagining the shadow he thought he saw, the place where she'd bled the rest of her life onto the sidewalk. What a fucking waste. He spit into the wind and was able to follow the loogie for a moment before it dissolved in an updraft and became just another part of the clammy atmosphere.

Had she thought of him before she'd gone over? Had she closed her eyes on the way down? How had she hit?

He'd read something online once by accident, some awful pop-up that had wormed past his blocker. "SUICIDE VIDS III: Head First Plunge! Jumper's Spine Shoots Out Rectum!" It was one of those things the internet gifted you with every once in a while, something you wished you could unsee or scrub right out of your brain, but it was there, stuck there now, forever. Sam tried not to imagine this happening to Jen and found, thankfully, that this was not difficult, that it would have taken an act of sincere concentration and a better understanding of human anatomy than he had to be able to visualize this at all. Which was the other side of the coin, of course: that video would always be out there, waiting for him to be driven crazy with curiosity.

Fucking internet. Fucking brain.

Just stop, he thought to himself. Stop wasting your time. Think about Jen and her death and her life and make it mean something, right now.

Sam walked back to his car and retrieved the gas station bouquet of daffodils and baby's breath from the passenger seat of his car. He tore off its cellophane sleeve and plant-food packet and terrible neon green ribbon, which seemed to exist solely to sour the beauty of the flowers.

Jean Valentine judged him from a concrete post. *What are you afraid of? What will happen. All this leaving. And meetings, yes. But death.*

How was it that she was dead but he was still alive?

What do you dread?

Sam's throat closed as he understood, again, how very gone she truly was. How uninhabitable her world was. He only had what he had of her. There would never be anything else. No future—not the one he had imagined for them over and over and over again for most of his life, but no other, either. How would he find the thread and follow it back to life? He choked and the towering banks of the Midwest shimmered like a mirage in his wet eyes.

He had a sense he should say a prayer, but he didn't know how to pray in a way that felt genuine. Instead he leaned over the concrete wall of the building and picked the petals off of each daffodil. She loves me. She loves me not. He ran out of petals on the negative and plucked a leaf from the baby's breath to end right. She loves me, she loves me, she loves me. It was a prayer of sorts. If you believed in love, that it could transform, that it could save. Which he did, kind of. Or had. The petals, heavier at their centers, spiraled down to the street, where they looked festive, like the remnants of some jubilant celebration in the middle of the exhaust fumes and the indifference of the great city. They lay, vivid and bright on its dreary, damp sidewalks, like something burst apart ages ago by a long-departed sun.

Chapter 4

Sunk at the bottom of the deep end of the club pool was an ugly, heavy drain grate which attracted swim sticks and spongey Nerf balls. Once, shortly before their sweet summer night together, their last real night together, the night of the flood, Jen, who didn't get in often but made it count when she did, had somehow done a double off the old floppy diving board at the club. The centrifugal force made a long, bent beak of her hair and watching her, it was easy to get the sense that she was some thing, some beautiful object being twirled before you, instead of a real person. Red hair, black suit, white, white, beyond-white skin. She looked like something being majestically rolled away. Stevie had been on break from her shift, but was watching from the deck like a proud parent. Everyone was watching. That's just how Jen was. But then she didn't come up and didn't come up and the guard on duty, a lanky, bossy boy named Ralph, blew his whistle then jumped in the water. When he came up he had one arm around Jen, like they were on a date. The other hand clutched the fine rope of her hair, a chunk of which, it turned out, had somehow become wrapped around the drain, trapping Jen at the bottom until someone came and yanked her out, like the pool was a stage and she, the rabbit in the hat of a magician. It all took less than a minute, but there was a fuss, which seemed only to annoy Jen, who was fine. After Ralph had returned to his post and the concerned and hovering mothers of the other children had reassured themselves and gone back to their issues of *Glamour* and white-wine spritzers, Stevie said to Jen, "You could have died," and Jen looked puzzled, as if this were not something that had occurred to her while her lips went cyanotic at the bottom of the pool.

"But you were here. You would have saved me eventually. Ralphie just got excited, that's all," said Jen, and readjusted her towel over the thick, sticky blades of the vinyl lounger. Then she laid down on her stomach and hooked her thumbs around the bottom edges of her suit and pulled them out—a quick, robotic wrist flick that every pool girl did almost unconsciously. "Miller," she'd laughed and closed her eyes to bask.

The memory came to Stevie as she sputtered water nine feet above the drain in the indoor rec center pool where she was training to be a lifeguard. The ten-pound brick she held with both hands, which was now sinking down between her legs, might as well have been a boulder. Chase, her swim instructor, yelled at her from the side of the pool. From this angle, from below, he looked like a young hero—all muscle and shaved head, an immortal, standing above her with his arms crossed. "Nine minutes, Miller. You're almost there. Keep your chin above water or I can't pass you."

She could hear the soft roar of the pool all around her, the movement of the water into and out of her ears, the mechanics of its delivery and filtration systems, the drippy echo of the huge hangar-sized room, her own breathing as it became choppy and panicked, the body reacting on instinct, voluntarily close to drowning. Her legs jerked up and down and her torso seemed held aloft in the water by little else than the thought that her feet were stepping down on something slightly denser than air.

This kept happening, these fleeting thoughts of Jen, these moments of emotional ambush. A smell, a familiar street corner, a particular quality of the light on a sunny day and she was back in her old life, her old new life, with Jen or Sam, sometimes James, or, occasionally, a random fallen-away friend she had not thought of in years. Coming home meant dream-walking through a kind of fourth dimension where scenes of her youth played themselves out to her as she moved through the landscape she had once known so well. There was a special kind of nostalgia that came from moving away from a place and then moving back. It was the nostalgia for the life all around you but that you didn't have because it had already happened.

Even here, in the pool, the brick dragging her under, she had hit some Jen-shaped wormhole that made it difficult to stay focused on her present task. She looked up and realized she was watching Chase shake his head at her through a scrim of water that was quickly closing over her head. Every previously sharp sound softened. She was underwater. She dropped the brick, briefly watching its descent to the bottom of the pool, and then scissor-kicked herself back to the surface.

"Fail, Miller. A nine-minute-thirty-second fail."

"Can't you just pass me?"

"No."

"I was so close though."

"No."

"But I—"

"Stop wasting my time."

Chase was younger than Stevie by several years but his crew cut, demeanor, and granite abs gave him away as some brand of young soldier. Impenetrable and pitiless, he did not acknowledge Stevie's unusual age, but instead treated all his trainees as though they were freshly enlisted at boot camp. He would see them drown if he thought it would teach them a lesson. But a lesson about what? Stevie wasn't sure and she thought Chase wasn't either. Sometimes behind the emergent trill of his lollipop-bright whistle, she thought his eyes had the faraway look of someone who had just woken up and didn't recognize his surroundings.

Stevie cut through the water and made it to the coping of the pool in two clean strokes. She coughed to clear her throat then tried to look up at Chase, to make meaningful eye contact, but was blinded by one of the industrial fluorescent lamps that hung over the pool and seemed to halo Chase's granite head.

"I have to pass. I have to get a job."

"Yeah I know, you've said it before. You and everyone else, Miller."

"No, you don't understand, I need this job."

"Like I said—"

"Not 'a job,' *this* job. A lifeguarding job. It's the reason I'm here. I mean, it's part of a *plan*." She didn't mention the book—she sensed this would be a mistake—but even this statement was not even slightly intriguing to Chase, who seemed to have no curiosity about other people, at least not his students in this class.

"You have a week to get your time up. I'm not cutting anyone slack on the brick. If you find yourself in a life-threatening situation, you'll be glad I was tough on you."

"Chase, this is Iowa."

He put his whistle back in his mouth and moved toward the head of the pool where other students were doing laps.

"Nobody drowns in Iowa."

He spit out the whistle and yelled over his shoulder. "Not when my recruits are on the job, you bet your ass. Reardon! Brick! You're up!" Chase pointed at the heads of two girls, huddled together conspiratorially in a practice lane. "Stephanie says she can't do the brick today, Mr. Chase." He crouched down toward the heads and their voices became watery murmurs. Finally, Reardon emerged from the water, pout-faced and teenaged. She stomped over toward the deep end where Stevie was still catching her breath. Reardon was a swimmer on the Taylor High swim team. She had told them this when they'd all suffered through the requisite icebreaker on the first day. And her older brother, who had broken three state records in the butterfly, was head lifeguard at City Park. Iowa pool royalty it seemed. Reardon's shoulders were muscley and bunched below her ears in a perpetual swimmer's shrug. Whenever they were about to start for the day, she shook her arms out and hopped, as if warming up for a meet. Wet, her skin had the rubbery buoyancy of a harp seal's. She was dating one of the silent, acneic boys in the class. Stevie couldn't tell them apart in their caps—their Adam's apples all bobbed nervously, their waists all narrowed waspishly in the same direction. All of them were competitive swimmers except for Stevie, who'd lied and said she'd been one of them too, back in the day. She didn't specify which day that might have been, and in general was counting on the teenagers' inability to read adult ages, hoping they mistook her for a college student.

As soon as she'd told the lie, she wished it were true. Though high school had been painful in the way it always was, she'd felt so certain of herself at the time. Swimming was not for her; neither was debate or theatre or band. Newspaper had been her thing. But why? What had made the others not? She found, the more she thought about it, she wished she could redo so much more. Maybe if she'd had more friends with different interests, she would have a completely different life right now instead of a collection of experiences that felt largely accidental. What was it about her youth that had made her feel like she knew what she was doing? Was it that time had seemed so vast and unending, so epic, the future so filled with mystery and promise, like something dreamed that would never arrive?

Back then she measured each half-hour on the lifeguard's stand by the assembly-line-like progression of the kids up the ladder of the high dive—their horsing and joking petering off as they crawled closer to the top—and the quick vulnerable plunge, each diver hung, bent and still in the air for an endless moment, over and over and over again. And then after every shift, meeting up with Sam, rolling his hand-me-down Corolla into every forgotten farm pasture in the county, fucking in the sleeping bag he kept in his back seat, constellations of lightning bugs spread out for fallow acres beyond the cracked and fogged glass of his windshield, the humid chlorine smell of her filling the car as he peeled off her clothes. Then, a drive to pick up Jen after her shift, a party at the off-campus apartment of some recently graduated classmate, all halogen torchiere light and pot smoke. What about it had seemed so eternal? She made a note to remember all of this for this book. These were the thoughts that kept her company now. Instead of brainstorming editors to cold call at Condé Nast, she was sunk deep into the mire of her past.

Now, she spent the mornings feeling nostalgic, indulgently haunting old spots—the diner downtown that still served plate-sized pork-tenderloin sandwiches, the book store with the coffee shop, where you could sit all day and read the new releases with a refillable dollar mug, the kind of place that could not possibly be profitable and yet never went out of business—and afternoons humping through the water, practicing spine-stabilizing deep-water carries, distance swimming and breath work.

After a couple of weeks of this, she could barely lift her arms above her shoulders. She'd been a regular gym goer in New York, and even swam some lunch hours at the tiny, tepid Y near work, but this was something else entirely. Thank god she'd quit smoking two years ago. Still, she wasn't at the bottom of the class. One of the skinny boys was slow, despite his build, and there was Jelissa, an anorexic girl whose musculature seemed to sag between the huge knobs of her joints. She made Stevie so sad, it was hard to look at her, and she'd resisted any attempts at overt friendliness, as had they all. Which was fine with Stevie. The tensions that ran through the group of kids and shadowed every one of their interactions with each other were painful. These were children in bodies become unfamiliar and they stole furtive looks at each other, even from behind their masks of boredom. It was funny to think Stevie had been nervous about squeezing into her suit, about the width of her thighs or the new ridges of cellulite that had just started to surface there because to the kids her body was invisible in the same way that their mothers' cushy mammalian bodies were. Had Stevie ever been as uncomfortable with her body as they seemed to be? It must have been so, but when she thought of the way she and Sam had wrestled together like cubs, she couldn't remember any shyness or fear.

Chase's whistle tore into her ears. "Deep end for corpse float!" he yelled and Stevie left the wall to paddle out below the high-rise diving board, really a huge, moveable staircase that culminated in a short platform twenty feet above the water. Her favorite, everyone's favorite, was the corpse float where they all lay face-down in the water like victims of some nautical disaster, lifting their heads to breathe only when absolutely necessary. Despite its name, the point of a corpse float was to survive, and the singularity of this goal combined with the easy, relaxed motions of the stroke (which could hardly be called a stroke at all since the idea was to minimize movement and conserve energy and body heat) made Stevie so comfortable that she could see, for the first time, how easy it would be to give in to the elemental force of the water around her, to sort of disappear into it. Had it been that way for Jen? How much more difficult to step out into the thin, frigid March wind?

And there she was again. Jen. Was Stevie haunted now? Was Sam haunted too? She wanted, no, needed to ask him this but . . . where was he? And please god let her not have given him chlamydia.

She put her face in the water and spread her arms and legs, far enough away here, in the far corner of the pool, to be out of the way of the kids, who were sinewy and prone to sinking. The bubbles from her nose and mouth made her feel carbonated, buoyant.

Sam. *Where was he,* she wondered again? She had left how many messages at this point? He'd left her exactly one. But that one message, which gave nothing, revealed nothing, said nothing ("Tag, you're it. Um. It's Sam.") was enough to keep her calling back. And this, too, was part of the life she had chased back to Iowa—she remembered now, not just those sultry cornfield nights, but the nights when Sam just . . . wasn't there. Nights spent under Jim Morrison wondering what he was doing, why he wasn't calling, what she'd done wrong. Nights the glow of nostalgia had all but erased. But now instead of waiting by the phone like her high-school self, the phone waited with her, flush to her hip, her ribs, in pockets and purses, held close to places where she could still feel Sam's hands, if she concentrated, trembling and callused, making tiny white scratches on her soft, dry skin. The problem was she hadn't told him, exactly, that she was moving here because she was afraid of spooking him. Sam had a tendency to disappear into his own holes when presented with an excess of emotion or desire. Things always had to happen, or seem like they were happening, sideways with Sam. Still. The night of the funeral had moved them both. Had moved her, literally, back home. Her plan included Sam. She needed him. Her do-over wouldn't work without him. It was time to declare her position and out herself as someone who would very much like to place as much of her flesh as possible into the care of his cruel hands.

Chase called out the halfway mark and Stevie opened her eyes under the water. The limbs of her classmates hung down from their still torsos, greened by the water. They looked like a tragedy, like a public-service announcement about water safety or drunk boating. *Nobody drowns in Iowa* is what she had said to Chase, but here they were, these tired corpses. They conjured in her silly feelings of regret, as if she really were the victim of some tragedy-in-progress, trying to survive in deep and open water.

She tried not to think about what would happen to her project, to her whole book, if she couldn't get buy-in from Sam, if she couldn't get certified as a lifeguard. There were so many variables. Would someone hire an old lifeguard or would they write her off as a weirdo or a meth-head? What would she write about otherwise? In truth, there really wasn't much to *do* in Taylor. One *could* sit in the bookstore coffee shop all day with a dollar refill mug, but *should* one? And while she loved her mother, was she already feeling a little claustrophobic in her old room, no matter how much she rearranged and packed away, integrated the new with the old? These weren't doubts exactly, not yet, but like the itch that still sometimes plagued her even though the infection was gone, Stevie sometimes felt the stab of her old life shattering the new one. The old New York life was there, its failures and hollows, but so was the old-old Iowa life, punching up through the layers of time to either eerily match up with or vertiginously diverge from her Iowa present. The result was disorienting in about fifteen different ways. If she could just get in touch with Sam, she would feel more grounded. Less like the truth, which was that she had no idea what she was doing or what would happen or how this book would get written or her new life get lived and then what would be next after all that was over? She needed to talk to Sam and she needed to make it to Memorial Day. Once she was through the rainy spring drear, through the intensive training and first aid classes, once she had pushed through to the glorious golden Midwestern summer, everything would fall into place. It had to.

Chase called time with another long shriek of the whistle and when Stevie straightened up in the water she saw there was a stranger standing next to him, a shorter boy whose hair stuck out in regular clumps all over his head. As Stevie neared she saw they were pigtails. Little boy-length pigtails wrapped in neon elastics. His hair and his thick, dark eyebrows made him look mischievous, a modern-day Puck in Toms slip-ons and a white deep-V t-shirt which framed his curly black chest hair. Besides Jen, he was the palest person she had ever seen.

Chase yelled them out of the pool and announced they'd be doing some pool safety maintenance training with the city pools manager. Over at the bleachers, Stevie toweled off her shoulders, hooked the towel around her waist and was shrugging on her hoodie when the boy sprite appeared beside her.

"Hey, how's it going?" On the pool deck, one of the scrawny boys was giving another a snake bite. The bit boy screamed, his voice sliding down into the throaty, warbling whine of someone just entering puberty. "Jesus, I feel like I'm babysitting here, man." Up close, Stevie could see that the sprite was much shorter and at least five years younger than she but not nearly as young as he'd appeared from across the pool. He put out his hand, "I'm Elvis."

Stevie's eyebrow shot up and she smiled. "Elvis?"

But Elvis did not seem to be interested in further conversation about his name and before she could introduce herself he was talking again. His snappy staccato reminded her of New York. No wide vowels on him. "Listen, I have to run a safety demo outside and it seems some asshole has run off with our Annie's head. Can I use you? You have a head, and I need someone who's not going to giggle through the first aid stuff and you look . . . mature."

Stevie felt her face go red. "Sure."

Elvis clapped her on a fleecy shoulder. "Thanks, man," he said.

"Outside though? It can't be more than sixty, and it's raining."

Elvis grinned and turned to walk away from their reanimated corpses, "Chase thought you were all getting too comfortable inside," and he winked at her and something inside of her churned.

It felt like a long time she lay shivering on her back, rain collecting in the corners of her closed eyes. Finally, she heard the group approaching.

"What do you do when you come across a situation like this?"

"Her lips are blue." This was the chalky voice of a mysteriously tan girl in their class, Kelsie, known to Chase as Kirkpatrick. "Is that part of it? Or is it just because she's cold? Because I am so freaking cold."

"Survey the scene—where have you found her?"

"On the ground?" There was a beat in which Stevie could actually hear some of the other kids rolling their eyes at Kelsie.

"Yes, but where on the ground?"

Silence.

Elvis again, much closer. She could sense him squatting beside her, "She's outside of the pump room. Notice the open door there. What does that tell you?"

"Chlorine gas!" a boy yelled.

"Could be," said Elvis and she shivered toward the warmth of him. "So you've assessed the situation, made sure you're not putting yourself in danger—especially if there's a chemical leak. Don't go into the pump room if you think that could be what happened. Get help. Call an ambulance or send someone to call. She's unresponsive so we're going to check her ABCs." Two fingers at her carotid. She peeked and his eyes were just inches from hers. He winked and grinned. "She's got a pulse but she's not breathing. What do you do?"

"Make sure her airway is clear."

"Good. Then?"

"Begin rescue breathing."

And then he was roughly tilting back her head, one hand on her forehead, and then her nose was pinched shut and her mouth popped open and then his mouth was there. The space created between their two mouths felt cavernous and his breath tasted like pot and spearmint gum. Her chest expanded as her lungs filled with his breath. Twice, three times. It was a strange but not entirely unpleasant sensation. She lifted her tongue a little and found the tip of his. He lifted his lips off of hers. "Chlorine-gas poisoning is very rare, but you need to be careful when you enter a pump room. Always go with someone, and have them stand behind you and wait for a moment after opening the door before going in. That way, if there's been some kind of gas leak, you give it a chance to disperse a little."

The warmth was gone and she knew he'd stood up. She shivered again and wished his body back to hers but he was already moving on, explaining a few more things about titration and how to check chlorine and pH levels of the water, then he was moving the group back inside. She knew she should get up, that her not getting up would very shortly become weird, but she was tired. The ground beneath her felt, not neutral, but like a force pressing back against her weight. Was it bad luck to play a corpse twice in a day? It felt like bad luck. It felt like an invitation. When she couldn't hear Elvis's voice anymore, Stevie stood up and headed for the womb-like humidity of the indoor pool.

After class, Elvis was waiting for her outside the women's locker room. He thumped her hard on the shoulder with the back of his hand. "Thanks for being my victim," he said. "I forget your name." He was equal parts impolite and charming.

"I'm Stevie Miller." She passed through the turn-style and he followed.

"Stevie Miller. Like Steve Miller? Like 'Some people call me the space cowboy?'"

"That's the one," she said.

"So I'm not the only one with idiots for parents?"

"No, you are not." She wondered if he would say anything about the tongue touch. Was it possible he hadn't noticed?

It was nearly dark and the rain made the parking lot smell like an oil slick.

"Chase said you're a good trainee—well, he said 'recruit' but, anyway, he said you were good and that you've been stressing about finding a job."

"I wouldn't be putting myself through this if I wasn't."

"He said you're not the strongest swimmer, but no one else takes it as serious as you do."

"Well, I'm not a kid."

"Obviously."

"Thanks."

"What? It's a compliment."

Stevie flushed despite herself. His confidence was incredibly irritating—she had no doubt it worked on the twenty-something girls he probably took home whenever he pleased—but she was also flattered that he might not automatically consider her too old to flirt with.

"So, Stevie, are you cool?"

She stopped and turned toward him. He wore a long fleece-lined swimmer's overcoat even though he hadn't been in the water. She could see the invitation in his eyes, but there was also something more calculating there. As if he was trying to figure something out about her.

"Yeah," she said, non-committal.

"Are you a midnight toker?" he raised one of those hellion eyebrows.

"Maybe."

"Follow me," he said and they walked to the far end of the lot where his black BMW gleamed under the parking lot lights, a solitary liquid shadow. The thing was fully tricked out inside: camel-colored leather, DVD player with a drop-down screen. Even at the lowest volume, his bass cannon pounded in her like a second heart. His weed was superpowered, hallucinogenic. One hit and her heart was racing, patterns spiraling out on the sky visible through his windshield. Immediately, she knew she'd made a mistake. This wasn't the old ditch weed she'd smoked in high school and college, the stuff that made you giggly and hungry. This was a different thing completely. She wouldn't be able to drive for hours. Plus, she was sitting here with a total stranger in a car that looked like it belonged to a drug dealer.

"Oh," said Stevie.

"Let's fuck," said Elvis.

"You're a drug dealer, aren't you?"

"I'm the Taylor Iowa regional pools and recreation manager," he said and smiled. He put a hand up her sweatshirt and her nipple stiffened under her damp swimsuit.

"How old are you?" she asked.

"Do you want to work for me?"

"What?" Their conversation was sand slipping through Stevie's fingers.

"I got this country club I need some help with."

Stevie felt a small joy begin to creep over her. Elvis put his lips on her neck. He was spidery. Strong, thin, hairy. There was something insectile about the way he moved over her, as if he were rolling her up in a cocoon for later consumption instead of slipping a hand inside her swimsuit in the front seat of his car. For one small, clenched, brilliant moment she was seventeen again.

“The Willows?” she asked, hardly daring to believe her luck.

“The one and only,” he said. “You’ll be my special employee for a very special job. I need someone I can trust. Someone mature.” She felt the word again, this time on her skin and his lips found her ear, her jaw, her neck. The hand in her suit moved slow and soft.

Stevie wanted to know more but she knew she wasn’t supposed to ask. That would ruin this part of the story and she didn’t want to ruin it. She wanted it to keep going. “When can you tell me more?” she asked. The shadow of the rain on the windshield and the blue LED lights of his stereo display flashed across his forehead in an alien morse code. “When you need to know more. Now come here.” And Stevie closed her eyes and floated away.

The common corridor of the loft had no smell and no discernible color (was it gray? Green? A very conservative blue?) as was the style of the time. Exposed vent work ran along the ceiling above Sam as if to say, “You see? This building and the life that occurs inside it is all business.” Its inhabitants Bikramed and cycled their bodies into lean deal-making machines. They wore slim-cut ankle-hem suits and had very expensive haircuts. They looked alike and ate very similar chopped salads, a lot of grilled salmon, kale. Every morning, their doormen set out generic paper cups and free Starbucks coffee in air-pump carafes, which most of them ignored on their way out the lobby and across the street, where they stood in line at an actual Starbucks and paid four dollars for the same coffee in branded cups, their names spelled incorrectly on the sleeves. Sure, on the weekends they wore slightly uncool, below-their-paygrade jeans and drank too much beer and maybe accepted a few bumps of super-stepped-on cocaine from their VC buddies and took terrible shits or vomited the next day after eggy brunches at the Bongo Room. Sure, maybe they fucked someone two floors down who they would forever have to take pains to avoid every weekday morning until one of them got laid off or pussily gave in to the allure of a craftsman in Oak Park. But mostly they were machines. They got the job done. The young urban professionals that lived in these buildings, below these ducts, did not have time for anything superfluous, including drywall.

Sam found the door then found he couldn't go in. The key seemed to scorch his hand when he touched it inside his pocket. He swayed, unsteady on his feet and felt an overwhelming urge to kneel in front of the burnished silver, ultra-modern, sans serifed numbers.

After the death site, after the flowers, Sam had thought of little but the trip. Sleeping downstairs from Bonnie, in his office, he'd thought and wished and Googled and drank and then, last week, he'd screwed up his courage, stopped by Barney's Bagels and brought breakfast to the Siegels. They were still muzzy in their grief but heartened Sam by complaining about the bagels.

"These things," said Jen's father as he took the bag from Sam, slid out an everything and knocked it against the kitchen counter where it made a dry, hollow sound and shed poppyseeds onto the butcher block. "Like plaster."

Jen's mother had come in from the bedroom, clutching a tissue and wild-headed, as if she'd been roused from sleep by Sam's arrival. "Say thank you at least, Ben."

"Thank you at least," said Ben, their once-cheery routine old and dry as the bagel.

Sam hadn't known what he was going to ask exactly until he was there with them inside this spiritual bifurcation of their domestic space. There was the liveliness of the two of them, friends and arguers for many decades now, but the liveliness was cut many times, over and over, by the stillness of their mourning. Someone would mention grabbing a mug for Sam's coffee ("you can't drink a proper cuppa out of that *paper* thing") or ask him how he was doing, but the attention to these hosting energies waned quickly and Sam continued to sip noisily out of his hot cardboard cup. They were like houseplants that had wilted and were turning yellow.

"I've got a conference in Chicago next week," he said, and Marcia's eyes seemed to sink deeper into their sockets. "And I imagine," Sam cleared his throat, nervous. "I wonder if you have been to her apartment yet."

Looking at them, it was hard to imagine they'd left the house, much less traveled to Chicago to sort through their dead daughter's things. "And if you haven't, I thought I'd offer to . . . check it out for you first. Tidy it up. Get it ready for you." No one, including Sam, knew exactly what he was saying but his dimple made it seem like a perfectly rational idea. "I could even pack it up for you if that's what you wanted."

The three of them stood in silence for some time before Ben nodded slowly. "Thanks, Sam. Yes, I think. That sounds like a good idea. Doesn't it, Marcia?" He turned to Marcia, who looked as though she were trying to remember something very important. She was staring vacantly at the Toulouse-Latrec *Ambassadeurs* print on their wall. They'd chosen the kitchen red (cayenne) to match the scarf exactly and the entire room seemed to Sam to throb, like the chamber of a heart.

Ben prompted her again and Marcia got up and began to rummage aimlessly through a drawer below the butcher block. Aimless until, after what seemed like a very long time: "Here," she held up a set of keys which she then threw at him with no warning and he surprised himself by catching them—the reflex sharp from a career's worth of the move at work. "Don't pack it up yet just . . . bring me something."

"What—"

"I don't care. Anything. I don't know if I can do this yet but if you bring me something of hers, maybe then I'll know."

He nodded but something in him churned. He had known them for fifteen years. Their daughter was dead. How could he lie to them like this? And yet here he was.

But it wasn't lying exactly. He really was worried about them, wanted to do something for them in all this mess, though his desire to be inside her apartment felt not helpful and virtuous, but dark and erotic, bordering on the pornographic.

If he'd been paying attention, he would not have been surprised to find himself half-erect as he stood in the hallway before Jen's numbered, industrial door.

Of course, if he could figure out an angle, if he could talk to the right people, starting with Kowalski and maybe some other Satchel Ferry colleagues, then the thing he was *really* doing for them was solving Jen's murder. He hadn't gotten that far yet, but he trusted that instincts would kick in at some point.

And now here he was. Though check-in would begin in a few hours, the conference didn't officially start until tomorrow; this gave him time to comb through Jen's place for—for what he didn't know, though, of course, like the way Kowalski's aggressive Facebook ghosts had set off alarm bells in him, he'd know it when he saw it. He'd look around carefully, then claim his room at the conference hotel. There was the small but pressing fantasy of the fresh king linens, of in-room coffee first thing in the morning, and light sleuthing around the breakfast chafing dishes—sausage links or patties, eggs with cheese or without. Satchel Ferry was a major sponsor and he figured they'd have people everywhere. Bonnie would be expecting a call from his bedside dial phone. Or, maybe not. Maybe things weren't going smoothly enough between them anymore for a call. Ironically, his deception somewhat depended upon a certain level of marital stability. If anyone had bothered to ask, Bonnie would not have been able to tell them the name of the hotel or the fake title of the fake presentation Sam was giving at the Heartland Tri-State Annual Mortgage Conference on Lending, Servicing, and Regulation Compliance ("Two to Tango or Tangle? The Importance of Strong Realtor Relationships"), or even anything really about the conference itself. She did not even remember the fake reason he was there, but she might have intuited, without really understanding, the real one. That's how things had been between them lately. It was something that always surprised him about marriage: it just kept going, like some perpetual motion machine. One of them would have to do something to make it stop. Sam knew this was a bad thing, but it comforted him anyway.

So, here he stood, in front of Jen's door, feeling the kneeling urge for a long time until there was a sound in the hall and, panicked, he shoved the key into the lock and barged into Jen's silent apartment, heart wild in his throat.

One brick wall, polished wood floors, tiny galley kitchen with sleek black cabinets and a Baltic Brown granite countertop. The ceiling was high and featured more of that ductwork. The smell of old garbage and dirty sink. At first he'd been disappointed by the generic feel of her space. The furniture might have belonged to any busy, single adult—mostly Ikea and a few out-of-place vintage pieces. A couple of artsy indie band show prints framed but not hung, leaned against the walls in places (tasteful, middle class, twee: Death Cab for Cutie, Grizzly Bear, Iron and Wine). As if death had come for her here, had startled her out of her nesting chores. He didn't recognize these things, but then: the clowns in the drawer. Then: pinned to the fridge, a crinkled birth announcement from two of their high school friends, Doug and Melinda. It was old—they'd had at least another kid since that first one, he knew.

A memory struck him: the four of them in a fallow Iowa field, perched atop someone's old Dodge Omni hatchback. All those shooting stars. That summer: Jen's bare leg and arched foot anchoring her to the porch while on the swing her body shifted and swayed inside the taut cotton of her sundress.

Numb, he took a step and fell to his knees on the striped Ikea runner and then he was crawling—below the photos of her still-youthful parents in their happy, early middle-age, below the hall mirror and the mail-strewn faceted mirror console table below it, and then he was sobbing into the thirsty finish of the slate kitchen floor, then down the hallway, running his face across the sharp sisal of her bedroom floor rug, where, in the grit and rubber, he detected a whiff of the other thing his life could have been.

Chapter 5

Smoke from Sam's cigarette leaked out the cracked-open kitchen window, beyond which lay the gray and inscrutable, big-shouldered city. A mason jar half-full of butts sat on the table in front of him, an incongruous Formica-and-aluminum Googie thing. Next to the jar sat a small stack—two composition notebooks and a photo album. Next to those, a vintage pair of salt and pepper shaker clowns that Sam had found in one of the junk drawers in the kitchen while searching for . . . in his mind he called them clues, and they were, but not ones that would help him solve a murder. They were clues that would help him, finally, know Jen and, in the case of the salt and pepper shakers, know himself to her.

The shakers were a shock. Something live and dangerous. Stronger and sharper than the yawning ache in him as he inched his way around the dark museum her small one-bedroom had become.

He'd been with Jen when she'd bought them at the Iowa State Fair, both of them swollen with cheap beer and fried ham balls. The clowns were each bent at an angle, so that they either bent towards or away from each other, depending on placement, their mouths and eyes wide in what was supposed to be joy or mirth but fell far short. Jen had said about them that they were either screaming in horror or one is giving the other a rim job. And so she'd bought them, delighted by her own darkness.

After he'd entered her apartment, face down, and after he'd stopped crying and looked up from her bedroom floor, he'd found himself in front of a bookshelf. She'd always been particular about what she read and he imagined she'd tucked the books away so that her casual guests did not find out too much—or assume they understood something—about her. Though what would they learn there was unclear. A bright pink copy of *The Valley of the Dolls* was stuffed next to a biography of RFK and a Dover Edition of Wordsworth she'd probably bought in college for a dollar. "Rolled round in earth's diurnal course/With rocks, and stones, and trees." The line from the Wordsworth poem had been sneaking into his head with some regularity since the funeral. He couldn't remember the title of the poem, which he'd read in a freshman year literature survey. He remembered, though, that the poem was about a dead girl and this was most likely what had caused the excavation in the first place. The line had taken on a life of its own, and was now rolling round his stuffy head, echoing off the walls of Jen's tasteful greige walls. In place of memory or thought, the line bounced around Sam's head at lunatic velocity, a kind of internal echolalia. Sometimes just the word "diurnal" would wax and wane in the muddy slush of his brain.

Still on his knees, he opened the Dover Edition and found the poem.

A slumber did my spirit seal;
I had no human fears:
She seemed a thing that could not feel
The touch of earthly years.

No motion has she now, no force;
She neither hears nor sees;
Rolled round in earth's diurnal course,
With rocks, and stones, and trees.

Jen, or some studious undergrad before her, had marked out each iamb. Unstressed, stressed. But then here *was* something in Jen's hand—he recognized it still—"Poor Lucy The Thing," she'd written in the margin below the poem. "We're all things. Maybe I'm a tree?"

Maybe I'm a tree. Oh lovesick Sam, how long you could wallow in the obscurity of this utterance. Thankfully, instead of filling the rest of our story with this poet's metaphor, Sam's bent head (*maybe I'm a tree maybe I'm a tree maybe I'm a tree*) noticed a stringy black spine on the bottom of her bookcase, shoved to one side, held in place by a faded floral photo album before the shelf broke into books again (*Moby-Dick*, *The Corrections*, *Beloved*, *Speedboat*, *Ariel*). He'd held his breath and pulled out the album out and the book with the black binding came with it. A composition notebook. The tree turned to paper.

Of course she had a journal. Didn't all girls? Scraps of themselves laid out on the page like a problem to solve. Like a recipe or a blueprint; won't someone come and figure me out, make me. He'd pulled the journal and photos from the bookshelf and stacked them on the table, then turned back to search the rest of the apartment. The feeling of anticipation was almost too much to bear. The "almost" tipped over into the actual when he found the shakers. He'd taken them out too, along with a little whiskey from the bar cart, the ice cubes stale and freezer burned. Everything seemed to glow in front of him like sacred artifacts.

He picked up the photo album first, ran his finger over the faded pastel cover, the word *Memories* in a grandmotherly font, surrounded by blobby, completely uninsectile butterflies. How strange to find his actual memories here. He opened it.

Which was more wrenching? The poorly lit 4x6 glossies—Passover Seders and junior high hallways, college frat parties (a long-haired, red-eyed Jen, held aloft horizontally by two sneering boys, one with his tongue out and held toward her delighted elven head, as if preparing her to receive some sort of Satanic sacrament. Both the boys wore different Pearl Jam t-shirts), and, for some reason, photo after photo of the sky, some aching depths of blue, some flat and gray, hardly pictures at all, unlabeled—or the way the handwriting changed from journal to journal. Bubbly, round, and cherubic, leaning into the sharp scrawl he had not seen for so many years but still recognized.

Then, there it was. He slid it out from its cellophane sheath. They had called it their album cover. Sam leaned, cross legged and windblown against his Corolla, black Members Only jacket hunched over his shoulders, arm around Stevie, who wore a huge plaid flannel that almost completely covered her stringy cut-off shorts, making her girl legs look even more fragile. She was in the middle of exhaling a cloud of smoke. Her arms were crossed, her smoking hand cocked at the elbow, cigarette pointing off stage left, toward whatever it was they'd be coming up on soon (sex, flood, the complications of school and their own friendship, divorce, break-ups, eventually: death). They were in a parking lot—school he thought, or Hy-Vee, where they sometimes met after his shifts to exchange intel on parties or plans for the night. Jen crouched in the foreground of the shot, red hair falling sideways over her face. She had on her tortoiseshell Raybans—he had forgotten about these but now that he saw them, he remembered her face in them in various settings—the front seat of his car, against a plastic white chaise at the pool, standing on the wide front steps of their high school—and her brow was furrowed. She'd been messing with the settings on her mom's Minolta, thought she could set its timer and run back to the car to get a shot of the three of them, but she'd accidentally taken a picture instead. Her lips were turned up, her mouth slightly open, as if she'd just said something to the kids at the car. Her skin was porcelain in the print, but a slight sheen of brown freckles shone through on her forehead and the top of her nose. It looked like she was about to ask you a question or tell you a secret.

Sam held the photograph up close to his face. He held his breath and wished he could crawl inside it.

He jumped when his phone rang. It seemed impossible, a message from the universe. Though he'd been avoiding her for weeks, he answered it. "Steve."

She was pissed and he didn't blame her. But she was worried too. Was he okay? What was going on? A pause and then: Had he heard? She'd moved back to Iowa.

"You what?"

"I got laid off at work, because of my blog which is maybe going to be a book?" She was talking a mile a minute and her voice was too high; something wasn't right with her. "I'm back at the Willows! Which is"—her harsh bark turned into a cough—"weird. And anyway, I thought you might want to hang out? Sometime?" Only later would he understand how much she had left out. "I've been calling but. . . . Where are you?"

Sam looked around and could not begin to say. The album, the journal, tugged at him. He'd needed to talk to her just a minute ago, and now he couldn't get off the line fast enough. "Chicago. For a conference. I'll be back home soon though. I'll call you then." He cringed at his own callousness, added, "Steve, are you okay?"

Silence and he thought she'd hung up on him. Then, "Yeah. Yes. I'm fine. I just thought. . . . We'll talk when you get back." And then she was gone and he reversed himself again and wished she were here. He flipped his phone open to call her back, but the pull of the notebook was stronger. He couldn't wait.

She had not been a good journaler. The notebook was spotty with entries, with a lot of pages given over to scribbled desk notes. Grocery lists. Errands. For a time, he read through each of these, spellbound by the mundane. They both fed and negated his burning for her and dulled the creeping dread that had once been a hallmark of his hangovers, but which now seemed to be with him all the time. Reading them, he was her Toto, poking out from her bike basket, receiver of the dull and enchanting language of her everyday life. *TP - tamps - samn - spinach - egg - chix. PO send back Loft skirt - party wine - call Frank - intercom/sink.* Sam imagined that this was how religious people felt reading the Bible. Something holy seemed to be rising up as he pawed through the scraps of her life. He tried to pay attention so that he might catch a clue or intuit something important, but he just kept seeing her going about her daily life, all alone. He read these lists first, thinking of them as appetizers, and then he returned to the more substantial entries.

The first was from college.

5/09/99

4th interview today. Graduation's in a month. Wonder if they can see the spinning daisies in my eyes. I am in no way ready for this. For the world. For a job. Is there something inferior that I transmit, somehow? All these plastic men making plastic money. I didn't think they'd care if

I seemed plastic too, but I seem to give them a vibe. I smell sincere and they're not sure they can trust that. One of them asked me where I saw myself in ten years and I said "rich or dead," and I could tell he liked that, the way his eyes narrowed and moved over me, but still no offer. I don't get what genre I'm supposed be playing here. Smart and naïve co-ed? Wicked Gecko protégé? Data nerd? And not only do I not know what category of person they're looking for, I don't know what they're reading off of me either. How do you fit yourself into a culture? It was always easy with men: just be what they want. Doesn't seem like finding a job should be all that different. It is so weird when you think about it though—how do I know what I'm supposed to be? It's not even like you get to try on all these costumes. You just pick something and then you are that. That seems both simple and hard.

But she had done it, he knew. One of those interviews had worked out and she'd become an analyst, first at Goldman Sachs, where she'd done a rookie year, then on to Satchel Ferry after that. When she'd become a banker after college, Sam had felt shocked. At Northwestern, she'd majored in philosophy with a minor in anthro, which at the time meant one of two directions: Peace Corps, or grad school. When he'd talked to her, sporadically through most of college, but then a bit more at the end of it, when all the unknowns seemed to loom so large for her, she'd never told him she was even considering it, much less going on interviews.

"It must be nice to be an & Son," she'd said unspitefully over the phone one night deep in the sunless cave of the January of their senior year. "I'm here pounding my brains out about what I'm going to be when I grow up and your most difficult decision is what kind of beer should I get drunk on with my frat brothers this weekend."

Okay maybe there had been a little spite. But it was true, he'd conceded. He knew what he'd be doing and whether he was suited to it or not was of little interest to him. The trouble was, as he'd find out in due time, he would not be good at it, at least not at first, and not for some time after. He would get and be good at his job, eventually, for a while, but even those gains would be eroded over time by the vicissitudes of the market and his burgeoning alcoholism. That fall he'd begun formal training with his dad. It was the slow season and there was plenty of studying to be done. His father wanted him to have his license by March so he could really help out. And he'd been dutiful, studying for his license while juggling his business and English classes. But when it came time to sell homes, he was a miserable salesman. His father, a professionally affable but domestically withdrawn man who'd cleared a million in home sales the prior year, could not understand it.

"They don't know what they want!" his father had Alec Baldwinned at him after yet another client had fallen through. "You have to tell them what they want! And why! You have to be able to translate their stupid ideas into houses for them! Home is a magical place! You have to be a magician!"

But back then, on the phone with Jen, in the winter of their discontented senior year of college, with their futures breathing down their necks—so near and yet still so unimaginable—it had not yet even occurred to Sam to wonder if he'd be good at the role he was stepping into. The possibility of being bad at one's chosen career was not a conversation anyone was having in college.

"Maybe I'll travel," sighed Jen. "Do the backpacking Europe thing. How much do you think that costs? Could I make it waiting tables at Gino's over the summer?"

When he'd finally got up the courage, years later, to ask her why she'd gone into finance, she'd told him it was the only clear path. That nothing else was like that. There was no one else telling you do this, get a job, make six figures except banks, tech, and consulting firms. "It's like those were the only jobs available. Bain or Goldman. No one was saying to me, 'Here's something less soul sucking you could do.' It was the most obvious thing. I mean, they sent recruiters to us like the Army or something."

Thinking about that time now—the way they'd fallen into conversation as if five months hadn't gone by. A single conversation could tether them together over months then years. The tether was a chord of affection that included no one else, not even Stevie. That intimacy you only get with a handful of people in your entire life. Over the years he'd asked questions about her job and she'd explained, at length, the deals she put together, the asshole associates she worked for, but it all seemed so abstract compared to the orderly and tangible process of selling houses. Even when she'd gotten into the mortgage side of things, it was mortgage as an abstraction—a single piece of capital to be bundled and sold with countless other pieces. He had never asked her if she liked what she did. This seemed, now, on the other side of her life, like a terrible error.

Out the kitchen window was the requisite view of the Sears Tower in case one was given to forgetting where they lived. Most of Chicago was so flat, the high rises didn't have to be very high to ensure a view. Sam knew he was supposed to derive some sense of Midwestern identity and pride from the very fact of Chicago. Iowans spoke of it with reverence. It was their New York, their San Francisco, a marvel, a wonder, but he was always surprised by how ordinary and ugly it was once you were out of the Loop. Just a few blocks north was Alinea—which in two more years would be the only Chicago restaurant with three Michelin stars—housed in an offensively concrete gray modern building with no defining features, tucked in among the Public Storage and PNC Bank storefronts that ran along Halsted. A little farther was the Steppenwolf theatre, another cultural landmark, and ugly in a different though just as perfunctory way evoking brutalism without fully embracing it. You could develop an eye for the hard lines of Chicago, especially on the river, and near the lake, where the water seemed to balance something in the concrete slabbery of the city. One might even come to tolerate the 1980s townhouses with bay windows, and find the modernist juxtapositions interesting, but Sam could never find it beautiful. In this way, it was a very Midwestern place. Unassuming, practical, without use for ornament. Jen had loved this about it. "It's miles of short beige buildings and then all of a sudden there's, like, an enormous three-story Picasso sculpture in front of you. It's the best city for art, because the whole place is a canvas." Sam couldn't help but feel this was Jen's relationship to Chicago as well—she'd been the brilliant surprise here.

In her journal, there were several pages of what appeared to be apartment listings and her notes about them (*studio in boystown, 897-1435, tuesday 6/18—dead flies windowsill, fish smell. 1 br townhouse wicker prk openhs tomorrow—30 fucking ppl ahead of me*) but the next true entry began the day after 9/11 and the entries that followed were sporadic.

September 12, 2001

It all looks like a movie. That's the first thing I said and it's the first thing everyone says about it when you talk to them. If I think that does it mean I think this didn't happen? Work is still closed and no one knows how long the L will be out of service. Everyone is scared. Bill sent this email to everyone. It said, "even in this time of great crisis, I want us to be thinking about how we can turn current events toward our favor. Think of swimming with the tide, not against it. Stay strong in America!"

September 23, 2001

Feels like people are being nicer out there. On the L & out on the street, the bars, people have dropped their city faces. "Except if you're Muslim," Asma said. We were all standing around waiting to see how bad the market close was going to be. Half watching because who really wanted to know. And Asma said someone spit in front of her on the street and called her a towelhead. "But the guy was black," said Asma, eyes locked on the screen, hair perfect, Calvin Klein suit perfect. One eyebrow, immaculately threaded by a group of Indian women in Lakeview, cocked. "So I was just, like, dude. No. We should be colluding. We should be working together to get rid of the White Menace in the Loop." Asma turned around and pointed her angular brown hands at us, riddled us with bullets, blew across the tips of both pointer fingers. She's not that much older than us and already a VP. Apparently they used to call her the Titty Outta Citi—only woman in her cohort and she smoked them all. Setting up to retire at 40.

After she shoots us she tells me to get her an Americano from downstairs and when I come back up she's on the phone. She says "Thanks, white girl" and winks at me and then does a deal for an upstream Hongkonger oil company, even though the world is on fire. Basically, I mean, she's magic.

He'd already been at work on 9/11, no TV, and the office had such slow internet, he only used it to check email and post new listings. Bonnie had called and he'd run across the street to the café where everyone was turned toward the old tube TV in the corner above the lunch counter, mouths and eyes agape like a row of Munchs. The waves of surreality and helplessness surged and receded in turn. After a long time, among those who hadn't been called off to pick up kids from school or meet their frightened spouses at home, talk turned quietly to cousins and grandkids in the city, and then, as the full horrors kept unfolding (Not an accident. A commercial not a private plane.) to family and friends in the military, for surely they would be called up. Everyone knew someone who lived in New York, or D.C., and maybe even someone who worked at the Pentagon or for air-traffic control somewhere. Sam had always felt it was a true American tragedy—not just because of lives lost but because of the paths that radiated outward and reached deep into every corner of the country, even rural ones, like his. And these reverberations gave birth to more: ongoing war abroad, but even here—the militarization of the police, the expanded power of a president to declare Martial Law. He'd also shuddered at the way everyone seemed to want to claim a piece of that tragedy, even as it was still unfolding. Even as he drank his coffee (or had it been beer? Surely he'd have moved on by then) he'd thought of Jen and prayed for Chicago, and wondered in the naive midland way of his, what those bankers had done to deserve this.

Sam turned back to the journal, his stomach sour. Already he'd gone through half of the entries and at least four fingers of whiskey. He was trying to conserve it, to not to read it all at once and be done. He opened it again, intending to flip through it to gauge how much was left when a folded piece of paper slid out of it and onto the table. It was a page from a composition notebook, like this one, folded in half. He skimmed it and saw his name, and the words fell out of focus for a moment. He held his breath. It was an entry from high school.

9/31/93

I know it's not really, but this whole day has felt so unreal. This is like a love scalene. No equal sides. Or maybe like a trapezoid. I do feel trapped. But it's my own fault, again. Mrs. Mitchell has this quote poster up above the blackboard. It's some fucking ship or something, a tall ship, like a pirate would steal, and it says, "You are the hero of your own story. —Joseph Campbell" and I just stare at that poster all class period and I think how fucking wrong it is. I'm not the hero of my own story. I'm the villain of someone else's story and the tawdry love interest of another's. Maybe I'm the hero of, like, Sam's story. Or Stevie's. For now, all for now. When they find out. When I finally have to tell them. . . .

They'll make me walk the plank.

Fuck, that sounds so stupid. But it's easier to write than what will really happen. Because really, in real life, they're gonna be hurt and they won't want to have anything to do with me, anymore. How can I love them and then also be doing all this to them? They're going to think, "Well, that's it, Jen is a skank bitch and I can't believe I thought she was my best friend" and then they'll have commitment issues until they're at least 30, and probably end up divorced a few times. And it will be my fault. And still. I can't stop. Proof that something is really wrong with me.

I know S & S will be over soon. Since M and I broke up, Sam has really been hanging around. I don't even know how he found out since I didn't tell him, but it's obvious he knows.

He can't possibly have any time left for Stevie. I think he loves me and I thought for a minute I felt the same way about him, but now I just miss Stevie. Which sucks because you basically broke up with her last summer after the break-in. Which, yes, totally weird but also don't you get it on some level? Wanting to be inside a space that isn't yours but isn't not yours either.

But, so, I can't see her when he's coming over every night. Not even if I knew the first thing to say. And the other thing is still happening. The Very Bad Thing I wrote about before. It's all collapsing. So even if I could get up the courage to do any number of things I should do, I couldn't. Just because of that.

So anyway, this made-up day. The Very Bad Thing called 4 times today and LEFT MESSAGES ON OUR MACHINE EVERY TIME. My dad checks it every night! If I'd gotten home after him. If I'd played it while someone—anyone—was in the room. Death.

TVBT does not understand boundaries or the natural and circumscribed limitations of the habitat of the teenage girl. And I don't understand his. Not even for all the time I spent at his house.

So there are like five people at least whose lives if they heard those messages would just be instantly ruined in an obliterating and echoing kind of way. So that's something.

Oct. Today.

-Can you stop?

-I don't think so.

-Why not?

-I don't know. I just know I'm not the hero here. I don't even think I'm the author.

**this notebook will self-destruct in 5, 4, 3, 2 . . .*

His whiskey was out again. Sam stood up and everything on the table jumped as he knocked into it. He felt hot and lurched unsteadily back toward the bar cart, willing his brain to process what he was reading. He was getting that feeling again, the one that filled the grief hole that had opened in him with plots and suppositions. Or maybe, this time it showed up to pave over the shame.

I thought for a minute I felt the same way.

The Very Bad Thing.

What had she done? Sam's hand trembled as he poured, skipping the ice this time.

Collect yourself. Maybe The Very Bad Thing is a clue.

Without noticing he'd done so, he brought the bottle back with him to the table.

He lay the loose paper over top of the notebook pages. They matched.

He inspected the foot of the book, where the pages met the binding, and found no evidence of anything torn out. There was, or had been, another journal.

Out the window, the sky at dusk had cleared and in the orange and purples of twilight, the lights had begun to blink on all over the city. It was the moment of the day that cities were the most beautiful. And even now, clamoring as he was, Sam was arrested for a moment by the sight. A city at dusk was a special place—a place of both possibility and rootedness. He loved how people in apartment buildings often didn't draw their blinds and you could just walk down the street, looking in at them eating dinner and watching TV and once in a while fucking or fighting. The things people had to do to make themselves right in the city before it was time to leave home and meet the world and whatever the night would bring. He was sure Jen had sat here and looked down into the apartments across from hers—in one, right now, a woman stood in front of a row of blond oak cabinets, opening and then closing them, looking for something. In another, a cat lounged on the back of a couch, framed by tropical plants, dreaming itself into a jaguar. Next door to it, a row of treadmills whirred in the big second-story window of a Crunch Fitness—all those people running nowhere. How many times had Jen stopped just here on her way to something else and looked?

He found no other notebooks. Even after he'd taken all the books off the shelf, then moved the bookcase itself when he didn't find another. He'd looked under her bed, into the bins full of gym clothes and ratty old pajama bottoms. It was not in a shoebox full of dead batteries and a neon-pink dildo on a shelf in her closet. It was not in her bedside table, next to the condoms and the pens, and the hair ties, wound round with strands of her fine red hair. Not in any of the cabinets in the TV console, not in the bathroom or shoved into the stack of fashion magazines that made a table by the bathtub, upon which stood a lighter, a Diptyque candle (Tam Dao scent) and a cherry Chapstick, which he opened and put on his own lips before pocketing. It was not under the sink, beneath her purple Conair hairdryer or the plastic tubs of tampons and cotton balls.

Dizzy, he sat down hard on the dirty marble tile.

Who was The Very Bad Thing and what had Jen done to everyone?

Something had not been right—he'd always known it. Had always wanted more of her than he sensed she would ever offer or give. Their last time together. The last time they were more than high school friends or booze-cheery, slightly distant adults. It was the night of graduation and there was a bonfire out in the woods north of the school. The property belonged to some huge farm family that seemed to have a kid in each of Taylor's graduating high-school classes for a decade. Every year they bought kegs and made a fire and the small-city kids of Taylor would drink and fight with the country cousins—angry man-boys with patchy mustaches and mullets. He'd picked her up at her house. She'd been distant since winter break and now she was leaving. Northwestern on scholarship. The night has always come back to him in slices of light and noise, like walking along the perimeter of a fence. Everyone is drinking, laughing, pink fire-glow faces. Then Jen is kissing one of the country cousins, and everyone's clapping. There's a game of spin-the-bottle. Then just the two of them, someone shouting. It's him, he's shouting. "I love you, don't you love me? I don't want anyone but you. I don't want to do anything in my life but be with you." The worst thing is the look on her face. She feels bad for him. There is nothing returned. She's shaking her head, putting out her hand—*there, there*—and then they're on the ground and she's trying to push him off. It's so cold over here, away from the life of the fire. He's not conscious of wanting anything from her, but he is so, so, so fucking sad. And somehow, in his sadness, he's ended up on top of her, on the ground, and she's panting but not saying anything and she's so small in this way he never noticed before. He can tell she's pushing against him with all of her force and it feels like nothing.

And then she's zooming out—a camera trick, but in real life. Someone has him, is dragging him off her. He shouts and tries to get free. Two swim-team guys have their hands on him. They are deeply, deeply stoned. "Hey man, chill," says one. Jen is already standing, shivering. "Are you okay?" asks the other and she nods. One of them puts an arm around him, turns him about-face and begins to walk them back to the fire (oh, there it is). He puts his one-hitter to Sam's mouth. Makes flame. "Here, man.

Just be cool." And after Sam exhales his plume of pot smoke, he turns his head to find her but she's gone.

The rage he felt later, after she'd left the party without him, after he'd stumbled into someone's van and taken a whippet and spun away for a minute—galactic star-trail—after all that he was fucking angry. So strong it was a taste on his tongue.

Instead of anger now, there was just shame, gigantic and crushing, opaque. And an anxiety that something had not been right all along, and he'd missed it.

His glass was empty and when he got back to the kitchen, he saw that the whiskey bottle was too. Vermouth it was, then.

The journal entries were sparse for years, turning back to lists and notes, as if she had only had time to live her life, and no time to reflect upon it. There was a list that pulled at Sam. It looked, at first, like a random list of clothing, but three items caught his eye:

red dress, gold gladiators, pink pashmina

And he remembered. Jason Dolan's wedding in a refurbished barn in Solon, Iowa, it must have been in 2003 or 2004. That year, everyone was getting married in barns. Catered barbecue, Pabst Blue Ribbon. The wedding barns were not like the barns of their grandparents, barns they'd spent years and years of weekends in growing up, learning how to milk cows and goats (harder than it looked), shearing sheep, chasing the chickens and holding their soft, fragile bodies close to yours, cluck more vibration than sound, the articulate reptilian gleam of their feet; the crushing sadness later at dinner as you first understood the provenance of the Shake 'n Bake drumsticks on your plate. Grandpa's fucking jokes about it.

The wedding barns were clean, hay bales neat and stacked around the sides of the building at seat height, fairy lights twinkling from rafters. There was no squeaking of mice, no visible shit, no rusting implements left out or buried under dust and feed to be tripped on and punctured by.

But the wedding barn's proximity to these things conjured them anyway and at Jason's wedding, like all the rest, Sam kept checking his shoes, sure with a whiff he'd just stepped in manure.

The red dress she'd worn, with the little cloth buttons at the top, kimono-like. As if someone had sewn her into it. They'd played that fucking song, like they always did at every wedding since 1986, and he'd gone looking for her, wanted her to remember—it had been their song. They'd always danced to it together at the high-school dances where they sulked with friends in corners, pretending to be there ironically while enjoying the sanctioned touching, the heightened emotional drama of it all. He'd tried to find her, but her date (Gordon? Geoff?) had already cleared a little spot on the dance floor and was making a big show of twirling her around, dipping her, singing the chorus at her through tender, half-moon eyes, rubbing his face up to hers when Chris de Burgh sang the line, "The lady in red is dancing with me, cheek to cheek." Wedding guests whistled and clapped, and the DJ pointed his little spotlight at them. Sam had pathetically tried and failed to make eye contact with her as the song wore on. He expected her to lock eyes with him and smirk, but her eyes were closed, and the pleasure on her face was sincere. When she opened them, a minute later, she did see him. She winked and his heart did its thing, but the wink was disappointing, automatic. A quick reaction, no nostalgia in it at all. And then her date was dragging her off the dance floor, and one of the bridesmaids nearby was fanning herself with her own hand, performing for the coterie of maids around her, whose raised eyebrows and oohing mouths made it clear that they expected Jen's date was taking her away somewhere to fuck her and indeed he didn't see her again that night, not even when the high-school crew moved the celebration to a local bar Jen loved, known for its toaster-oven cheeseburgers. That night too, he'd reached for her and found himself clawing the air. This was how it was with her, how it always had been. She came to him as absence as much as presence. He had always wanted something from her, some tangible evidence of his existence in her eyes, and she had always given him whatever existed between nothing and something.

More shame washed over him. What did he want? Did he wonder what his life would have been like if she'd loved him like he'd loved her? Did he wish he'd married her? He could not seem to move beyond his failure to her, but how had he failed her exactly? Perhaps he'd failed her by not being very important to her. Certainly by not seeing the shadow that seemed to always be creeping up behind her.

He paged on to where the journal entries began again.

11/13/06

Lunch with Asma. Thought she might try to recruit me but no. She's worried. The longer this goes on, the worse the end will be. "Total collapse," she says over a neat green field salad. "Lehman is maybe the worst off. They're basically a mortgage hedge fund now instead of a bank. I mean, they're killing it, currently, but it's musical chairs. Or is it hot potato? What's the one where when the music stops and tens of thousands of people end up jobless and homeless? That game. That's the one they're playing and now that prices are starting to head downward, I'd say it's time to take a chair. Bear too. All those subprimes they acquired. Have you heard anything inside? Is this nihilism writ large or are people really this stupid?" I said I thought it was probably both.

She's got a healthtech hedge now, making money making money making money making money. You can just keep saying it like that and it keeps making sense. It's money all the way down. I got what she was saying. I'd asked about it at work. What did The Overlord say? "Think of it like a hot bag of flaming shit. You don't hold on to it. You toss it over to whoever's got their hands out and you don't stop tossing until the music's stopped." These fucking bankers and their musical chairs. We go to very expensive colleges and get BAs in micro and macro and MBAs at Kellogg to be told, basically, that the whole thing is just a second-grader's birthday party. I told him he was confusing ding-dong ditch with musical chairs and the way he looked at me. It was like I had just confirmed some suspicion for him. He told me to go big or go home. So I went home and later he called me yelling because he needed some info on the Ahab CDO and why wasn't I at my desk. I told him I was at home, being unable to go big, currently. He hung up on me mid-sentence. I probably shouldn't write it here because EVIDENCE but the shit J has us doing lately. It's not not legal? But . . . the word came down a few months ago—commands from the top: more sub-primes, more Alt-A, more securities, more sales. Make it happen. Okay cool. I can bundle and sell with the best of them, but I need more product to slip into those bundles. So I call Des Moines of course, mortgage branch, talk to Tim. Give me more loans motherfucker. And he laughs but only for a second and then he gets quiet. And I ask him what they told him to do because how can you make more people buy houses—expensive ones—short of some awesome commie thing like universal income. And his throat clicks when tries to swallow and he says "stated income loans." And that's when I understand that we—I mean the whole country and possibly the world—are in very deep trouble. I say, just to make sure that I am understanding this colossally terrible, world-ending idea, "You mean, the lenders ask how much money they make, and the borrowers just tell them," and Tim says yes, and then I say, "and then no one checks on whether or not they are telling the truth," and Tim says nothing.

I don't mean to be all dramatic but what have I done? It's all fake. Money is this fake thing. Obviously, I mean, of course, but it's not just that I've built my whole life around it. It's that I'm building other people's lives around it too. When Asma asked if we knew or we were trying to fuck everything on purpose, I felt really excited. Total collapse. The way she said it. I imagined myself like Cillian Murphy in 28 Days Later, *wandering around a burnt-out Wicker Park, Fiore: destroyed. Urban Outfitters: looted. Me in white rags. It felt like something to look forward to. But after I talked to Tim, I got scared. I'm still scared. But I'm also still going to work. Still selling securities. I didn't realize the apocalypse would just be me going to work.*

Sam held his breath. Something *had* been going on at work. The apocalypse? Was Kowalski The Overlord? Was he J? Had she learned something he didn't want her to know?

1/1/07

Remember that Doors song? This is the end, beautiful friend, the end. It will never not remind me of that hilariously bad movie, and S, stoned in the basement, tears running down her face, me telling myself don't laugh don't laugh. *But also, I can't get it out of my head today—feeling it. Ever since 2000 came in on the top of that roof in San Fran, rolling on E and waiting for the planes to fall out of the sky, every New Year's feels like a tiny apocalypse. Maybe this year will make good on that feeling.*

I found out today that S has a blog. She's funny. I mean I always knew that but now everybody else gets to know it too. You know how they say, "read it and weep"? I did that.

When I think back on what I've missed . . .

My beautiful friend.

A blog? Sam wondered. A funny blog?

When Sam imagined blogs, he imagined the Coldwell Banker newsletter, which was delivered quarterly by email. He had not, at this point in his life, ever read an actual blog. He would read Stevie's blog, eventually, after everything shook out the way it did, thinking he might find some clue, though by then the concept of clues would have lost their murderous gloss for him, and he would do it, merely, as a way to understand Stevie better.

6/28/07

Someone should tell Bill Gross that his name suits him, I don't care if he's a genius. It's an insult to tramps everywhere, comparing us to CDOs. I like "subslime" better. Or maybe that's an insult to slime. I guess that makes me mother of slime. In any case, I don't think this all ends with these lenders declaring bankruptcy. That number he quoted, the one from Bank of America: half a trillion in ARMs, all headed up up up right now, about to explode over our heads. Here comes W's shock and awe after all. The bombs bursting in air. And that's just the ARMs. I think I was wrong about 2007. The world's not ending yet, the world is winding up to end. It's a big world with a long arm (haha pun intended). This is all just the beginning.

Aug 13 07

This city is gigantic and so, so small. I ran into J today. How could I have forgotten what I'd done to him? I guess I thought all this time he didn't know about what I'd done. But he did. And I think he's suffered greatly because of it. But I realized something else and that's: I hurt him either way. All those years, pushing it down. I had already hurt him whether he knew it (which he did) or not. Her too. My true blue. My girl. I still miss you. Maybe I'm the coming apocalypse. Maybe I'm the thing that blows everything else down.

Sam's chest tightened. Who was this J? Kowalski again? It didn't seem like it. This entry felt more personal. Was J an old friend? Sam raced ahead, wondering if this finally was something that might help him make sense of everything that had happened.

8/17/07

American Home last week. Countrywide crashing this week. The sky is falling over and over again. The train is off the tracks now. All those really terrible securities we packaged. People are going to look back and say, "It was obviously too good to be true, how could they not know?" But the truth is, we did know. The truth is, I knew. Even before the stated income loans. When those turds from Honeycomb Mortgage showed up at the office that day in their shiny suits and their loud voices, I suddenly understood we were part of a huge scam. Maybe the biggest ever done. How humiliating that I had to literally meet the lenders to get the drift, the grift. It was so easy to imagine them convincing a client to take an ARM ("Listen, you want this place right? If you can flip it before the rate goes up then it's all profit for you, no risk."). And then that was it. They made the deals and we sliced and shrink-wrapped them and sold all the banks our lunch meat which was really people. Legal money laundering. And so what if I didn't say it to myself, I knew it even back then. It's like Asma said. We're in the game where tens of thousands of people lose everything and it's the fourth quarter. There's no stopping it now. And it's my fault.

Somewhere in his depths, Sam's deep alarm began to sound. She was talking about total financial collapse. True, he knew, the housing bubble had burst in a lot of places, which might account for more than some of his slowdown, but surely the banks weren't actually selling garbage? Had she known something and been killed for it? But instead of answering him, the journal hurried on.

Aug 24 07

Asked J to move in with me. He won't use the word "homeless" and I'm sure would cringe at the suggestion, but I really don't think he has anywhere to stay. It doesn't feel like penance—I like having him around. But it makes me sad too. What I did to them. I think that in a fucked-up way, I did what I did out of love. Like I just loved her, loved them. Then that night I stopped by and it was just . . . you know. Home alone. And I don't know what happened, but something was there between us. It was like another presence. Like an extra person, full of frustrated desire. This other person was totally embarrassing, but it was impossible not to notice her there. And then what happened happened and here I am trying to pay for it still.

J has track marks under those tats. I think I might have ruined him.

So, in the months before her death, she'd not only been involved in something sketchy at work, she'd also taken in someone off the street. A friend, possibly a drug addict. Someone she had wronged. Someone who might have a reason to push her off a parking structure when they found out what she'd done. Someone *also* called J.

He sighed, frustrated at her coyness in journal form. She wrote to obscure identities, as if she expected someone else to read these entries some day, which was in keeping with the gentle narcissism he had always found exciting in her. It was so un-Iowan and it marked her as different.

Now, though, he just wished she'd write out the names of the people whose lives she had messed up so he could figure out if and how they were implicated in her death.

The last entry was dated five days before her death. Six days before the last open house Sam would host. A week before the point at which his life split into two halves, before and after.

3/10/08

Got a phone call this week. I've never spoken to a Fed before. He had a soothing voice, a little twangy. In my mind he looked like Tommy Lee Jones from Men in Black. *I'm supposed to get some documents together for them. DSM and Chicago offices. In exchange, they might not send me to jail. No promises though. I told J I was leaving for the Iowa office for a while and he got all squinty on me. Sometimes the way he looks at me . . . exactly halfway between fuck and kill. But with a big question mark at the end. I shouldn't have said anything and just gone but now he's breathing down my neck. Says he wants to go with me. Trying to horn in on my trip which could make the corporate espionage very difficult. Worried that he knows. But not that worried. When the world is on the brink of economic collapse it's difficult to be worried about much. Even the Feds.*

So that was it: she was working with the FBI and so had definitely been involved in something. The trip to Des Moines must have been the trip she'd called Sam about and never taken.

Jesus Christ.

That provided plenty motive for her murderer. And if only she'd made it out of Chicago, maybe she would have confided in him. Maybe he could have helped her.

But who, *who*, was J? Had he killed her for what she knew or what she was planning to tell the FBI? Sam lifted his right ass cheek lightly off his seat and pulled the tiny moleskin from his back pocket, wrote the letter J and underlined it twice. Jerry Kowalski could be J, who might have reason to hush her up. But surely Kowalski wasn't the unhoused J, the one with track marks and tattoos. So maybe there were two Js, the home J and the work one. Sam wrote the number 2 beside the J and circled it. He felt sludgy with liquor and uneasy.

He had known—everyone knew—that it had been easier to sell homes in the last few years than it should have been, at least it was before his listings had started to dry up. Houses had been getting more expensive while, improbably, people had kept qualifying for loans to buy them. That this was a bubble was so understood in real estate no one needed to say it. And when they didn't say it, they also didn't have to confront questions about what the consequences would be when it burst. Even all the mortgage lender bankruptcies this year had barely qualified for watercooler talk. Good riddance to shady practices. It wasn't his job to advise his clients to buy cheaper homes, and if they were getting approved for big ones, well that wasn't his job either. But if you slowed down for a minute, rolled down your window, you could begin to smell the stink rolling in like a rotten tide. Already, there was talk of foreclosures in some of the biggest, hottest markets: Las Vegas, Phoenix. The lenders their office kept on call seemed to pay no mind. Sam's friend Brian had told him as long as their office was meeting quotas, that everything was just fine. He'd told Sam not to worry about it and then he'd offered him monster truck show tickets. Sam knew what Bonnie would say and turned them down, wishing for a moment he could ask Brian to go with him, knowing sadly that in the stoic economy of Iowan masculinity, he could not. It occurred to him now, but would not when he was sober, that maybe he should have asked Brian a few more questions about the kinds of loans they were giving out and to whom. More than once in the last two years Sam had been surprised—a young couple—T-shirts and jeans—closing on a half-a-million dollar, 2,500 square foot "starter home," a single mom who had the same job bagging groceries at Hy-Vee that Sam had worked at seventeen, signing on her second home. Then her third. But Sam figured that looks could be deceiving, and anyway it wasn't his business, it was the bank's.

So he did, he recognized that creeping feeling of knowing something wasn't quite right while everyone else acted like it was. But that was a just a feeling, an intuition. Jen's journal entries made it sound like she'd understood something concrete. Something frightening. Unease gave way to fear. Sam thought of Cassandra, Priam's most beautiful daughter, always right, never believed.

Sam closed the notebook and stood up, feeling the booze reach his feet. He lurched toward the bedroom, then thought twice, and pawed the notebook off of the kitchen table, taking it with him to bed, before crashing face down into Jen's pillow, still fully dressed. He did not hear the pepper shaker, which had shimmied to the edge of the kitchen table, smash onto the slate floor in the middle of the night, but in the morning, on his way to make coffee, he would catch a shard of it in the bottom of his foot, and he would feel like crying, and then he would cry. Something else lost.

Sam paced Monroe, smoking a Marlboro Light. They were chick cigarettes. They went with the black pants and little backpacks of Jen's college years at Northwestern. He'd been down here with her for a weekend once. Ecstasy and warehouse clubs and the uptight costumes of the wealthy daughters of Chicago and the rural girls who emulated them. They all smoked Marlboro Lights and ordered fruity martinis. Sam had never felt so Iowan.

The lights of the Palmer House glowed like Christmas on the otherwise chilly block. The buildings here seemed to rise, uninterrupted from the sidewalks, everything made of the same gray concrete. It was an east-west street and looked like the alley behind some more important thoroughfare. The lake was only a few blocks away, but from this vantage point the city seemed to end. There was no hint of the Palladian arches and bronze lions of the Art Institute or the new Tiffany-bean UFO in Millennium Park

He really wanted a drink. *Wanted* maybe wasn't the right word. It felt like a rodent was clawing its way up his esophagus. His foot throbbed where the clown shaker shard had pierced it and he felt another pang. *Ham balls*, he thought. *Iowa State Fair*. And then, unbidden, her words floated to him: *The Very Bad Thing.*

His Very Bad Thing tugged at him so hard that he felt he could suck down the entire pack of cigarettes and not feel the end of his need. He resisted, trying to tamp down his alarm at the size of his desire for a beer this early in the day. He needed to stay clear. To focus.

It was always like this in the mornings: regret and fear, promises, resolutions. In the aftermath of the funeral, the fight with Bonnie, he'd allowed a little honesty to permeate his haze. Yes, he had a problem. But, who didn't in these early days of the new millennium, when the world had shattered into a million tiny pieces called the internet, called Al-Qaeda, called "social media" whatever that was. You could have a thousand friends now. You could borrow more money than you had ever made in your life. You could offer yourself up for recruitment into a many-tentacled terror organization. You could leave your life and walk into a war that wasn't yours. The possibilities for expansion seemed endless, the outgrowth, the way the market, the world, would just keep getting bigger and bigger, forever, like the universe. This made many people excited but Sam felt acutely, without being fully aware of or able to articulate it, that these possibilities atomized the self. There was something about drinking that made him feel solid and present, one piece, complete. The new way of the world and all its exciting possibilities masked the losses that one was forever accumulating. This latest loss being nearly unbearable, the worst yet. So he was here, on a slick street in Chicago, shaking a little as he tried to stick his cigarette butt into the hole in the Smoker's Station. One for courage.

He headed inside and checked himself in at the registration booth on the second floor. The woman behind the table greeted him by name, and handed him a name badge and a flimsy branded tote bag full of shiny brochures from the sponsoring banks and mortgage agencies in the tristate area. He threw away the lanyard and tried to tuck his name badge into the interior pocket of his rumpled Kenneth Cole, but the shaking was worse now, and he had to stop, and put down the terrible tote in order to accomplish the task. In doing so he caught sight of his armpit—already damp. His heart was pounding him a headache. If he didn't have a drink, he realized, he might flub this whole thing up, and badly. He took the conference schedule but abandoned the tote on an empty table a little ways down the hall, and nearly ran down the escalator back to the lobby. With an enormous sense of relief, Sam immediately found an inconspicuous side table in the Gilded Age lobby bar—the beauty of the bar diluted by the boring suits of the bankers and realtors, the yoga pants of the tourists—ordered a Stella, and tried to look unconcerned as he waited, flipping through the schedule. Sam wondered what Jen would think of Kowalski's talk, "Go Backward to Move Forward: Reverse Mortgages in the Post-Subprime Age," and he wished suddenly and fiercely, that she were here, sharing a beer with him so he could tell her about all the incredible things that he'd been learning. Of course, she'd already known them all, which was why someone had killed her, but still. He just wanted to talk to her. Hadn't that been the thing he'd been looking forward to most about her visit? The chance to just sit with her and ask her questions about her life. Impossible to think he'd never do that again. She'd never get that smile when she saw him—the under the eyebrows one, the one he thought of as her get-over-here-you-big-lunk smile. The one he'd searched for and missed at Jason Dolan's wedding.

He peered around the room, incognito in his small-town realtor disguise. The turnout seemed small—there were barely any more conferees than regular guests, judging by the lanyards and the tote bags. It had been a bad year for mortgage lenders. Maybe there were fewer of them. Maybe there wasn't much reason to commune. He finished his beer, edges smoothed, and took the stairs up to the Wabash Room, where he found the easel announcing the potentially murderous Kowalski's talk.

He took a seat near the back of the banquety conference room suite, near but not next to a conferee in a taupe three-piece suit with a big floppy mustache that made Sam feel self-conscious. He ran his thumb and forefinger over each wing of his own and wished to run into the bathroom right then and shave it off. But some unseen helper dimmed the lights and Kowalski stood up from his seat behind the podium, cleared his throat. A bar graph appeared on the screen behind him, a multi-colored cityscape, like something out of Willy Wonka.

Kowalski was smaller than Sam would have guessed and he had a kind of jittery energy that didn't square with his VP title. He seemed more like a real estate agent, Sam thought. Like someone who was forever trying to sell you something. No wonder Jen hadn't liked him enough to throw a ghost at him. There was a smarminess that you could practically smell.

Sam tried to concentrate on the gist of the talk but the first graph was replaced by a second, then a third, and Sam found himself unable to pay attention to what Kowalski was saying. Instead he imagined Jen, trussed up in a navy blue skirt suit, heels flashing, knocking a beer back with Kowalski after work one day in one of the plague of Irish pubs on these streets. Or maybe a sports bar, The Billy Goat. A glass of pinot noir at Michael Jordan's, she, facing the window, the business-class bustle of Michigan Ave., Kowalski, pointed inward, at her, his fidgety hands always too close to her waist, her knees. Always pressing another drink on her. Put it on the Black AmEx, the same one he uses for his Thursday afternoon prostitute, the thrill of that financial proximity. Sam imagined Kowalski indulging in that certain low-level sexual harassment that his universe (in the guise of his undergraduate fraternity and Kellstadt MBA) had taught him to come to expect was owed him by his female subordinates. Perhaps he had crossed a line. Maybe Jen had confronted him. His gaping vowels, that flat Great Lakes honk of an accent, all spoken too loud, too fast. An accent evolved for yelling at ball games and bartenders, his pursed lips, the face youngish but the veins already old. He was not a man people said no to. And Jen was not a woman who put up with much. Had he killed her for it?

Sam gave up trying to follow the mortgage and investment charts and instead looked at Kowalski's hands as his Power Point slides made the shadows in the room shimmer and spin. Was he changing the slides or was it the unseen helper? The hands were at least partially obscured by the mic, the light, and the podium, so it was difficult to say. Which was maybe why Sam woke up to the mood of the room too late, missed the stirrings of discontent until they had already grown loud. Until, suddenly (it seemed to Sam) two men had stood up and were pointing, indeed actually shouting, at Kowalski, who looked not the least bit concerned or surprised at their outbursts.

"I can't believe you're really trying to sell this horseshit here. To the actual horses," said one of the standing men. Even in the relative dark of the room, Sam could see he was young and wore jeans and a blazer, instead of a suit.

On the other side of the room, another man, older, his suit blue, waited his turn then leveled his thunder at Kowalski, “So let me get this straight: the economy is in freefall, half of our colleagues aren’t here this year because their companies have imploded, all because of subprimes, and you’re advising us to give out bad loans to vulnerable populations. Again. I mean, on top of the bad ones we already made, let’s be honest here. How can you honestly stand up there and shovel this shit? This is larceny.”

“Hey guys,” Kowalski stuck his hands out in front of him like *trust me, I’m harmless*, which of course had the exact opposite effect of making him look like the charlatan he was. “You all wanted to know what’s going to take the place of the ARMs and NINAs you were happy to hand out left and right for years. Well, here it is. Reverse mortgages to seniors looking to have a little fun before they kick the bucket. What’s the risk? We do a bunch of these and maybe the economy starts looking a little more stable. This is good news.”

“You think you’re some kind of hero then? Ripping off old people who don’t understand how these things work? Bear’s corpse isn’t cold and we might still lose banks. This is just the beginning. And you want to keep doing it. Business as usual.”

“That was bad luck for Bear but these things are still getting made, they’re still being traded. Everybody knows what’s in them now. No one is getting ripped off here, and the earning potential is off the charts. Make ’em and pass ’em. Fast as you can.” Kowalski chuckled.

The man in jeans appeared to be on the verge of some spasm of involuntary violence. “You’re crazy. A bulge has already gone down for this. We’re looking at the end of the world and you’re . . . what . . . investing in it? People are losing their homes. People are losing their jobs. And this is your attitude—more grist for the mill?”

The floppy-mustache guy next to Sam muttered, “That’s how you make money, kid,” and the guy on the other side of him smirked.

As if by magic, the lights popped back on and Kowalski’s mask was affixed in that same self-satisfied twist. “You might not like it, but I have news for you: this is how this world has been working for some time now. That’s a nice coat, fancy jeans—you look like you’re doing well. What do you think you and all your buddies have been getting rich on these last few years? That dream market you been blessed with in whatever shit burg you're hawking blocks? That's not an accident. That's made. In rooms like this one."

The older man in the back had apparently sat down because now he struggled to his feet again and put his hands to his mouth, "So that's how you want to play? Insults? This isn't *Glengarry Glen Ross*, you fucking yuppie Polak. You'll answer to somebody. You're all going to answer to somebody." Here, the old man looked around the room. If he'd had a cane, he would have pointed it. He tried to meet the eyes of everyone in the room but most wouldn't look at him, cowed by the shared discomfort of a public showdown. When his eyes settled on Sam, he hissed, "You'll be sorry," and Sam felt his body contract. If he'd had the courage to run, he would have, but he felt rooted to the spot by the old guy's glary prophet eye.

Kowalski forced a laugh and shook his head. "I tell you guys how to print money and you want to run me out. That's fine. But I'll leave a stack of cards, in case any of you want to hear more, privately." Kowalski slid sideways out of the room, a snake in silks. A few of the guys turned to each other and started to argue in the aisles. Sam snagged a card from the podium and ducked out to trail Kowalski, who seemed to have decided to set up a mortgage-fraud-advice-booth at the lobby bar. Sam—not sure what he'd say until he said it—took a stool beside Kowalski as the bartender set his drink in front of him.

"Interesting presentation in there. You really think these loans are a good idea?"

Kowalski looked sideways at him, his eyes flicking down then up, checking for a name tag. He didn't smile. "Fuck if I know. I hear the talk, blah, blah, blah the world's ending, subprime Titanic, but I'm still rich and I wanna get richer. It's not my business if nobody else wants to pick up the money that's laying on the ground in front of them. Who're you?"

"Sam Sullivan. Coldwell Banker in Taylor, Iowa."

Kowalski blinked. "Where?"

"Taylor. Iowa." Sam annunciated it as if speaking to a slow child. He'd been to enough of these conferences to expect this. The big city guys always wanted to out-dick the small-towners. At least at realtor conferences, Sam could shame them for their ignorance ("Taylor, Iowa, fastest growing tech corridor in the region. Surprised you don't know it.") The guy was apparently doing business with the Satchel Ferry mortgage branch in Des Moines. He knew Iowa. But Sam could tell Kowalski was a Chicago purist. The world ended at Humboldt Park. You had to be either very rich or pretty poor to take this stance. In college, the real Chicago kids were always calling out the suburban kids for claiming to be from Chicago. As an undergrad, Sam had seen more than one bar fight start over this distinction or lack of it. They were the worst, all of them, real and imposters. And, in college anyway, they were always rich. When the poor Chicagoans began to move into the area a few years after Sam graduated, looking to start over, looking to get their kids away from the city, but wanting to remain close to their families and support systems, no one cared to parse the cultural borders of Cook County with them. Instead, there was a low hum of fear surrounding the brown menace showing up in their schools, settling in new developments on the south side of the city. Suddenly, being "from Chicago" became code for being working class and Black in a place that superficially celebrated diversity as long as it looked like success—doctors, college professors, writers. It was the thing Sam disliked most about his job—when he'd had active listings, anyway—the white code people used to suss out the unofficial redlines in the neighborhoods they weren't familiar with. *How are the schools? That big apartment complex a couple blocks away, my friend heard it was mostly families from Chicago.*

Sam shook his head. Time to dive right in then. "I'm from Taylor and so was my friend, Jen Siegel."

Kowalski frowned, squinted at something in the distance, looked away. "Oh, yeah. Taylor." He downed his drink and signed in the air to the bartender for the check. "Sorry about your friend."

"Wait," said Sam. "What are you having? We'll have two more."

Kowalski hesitated, looked out across the field of industry professionals crowding the low brown lobby furniture, sighed and turned back to Sam. "Negroni." Kowalski sat there, silently, obstinately, tearing his wet bar napkin to shreds.

"I need to know what happened to her."

Kowalski put his hands out and shook his head. "She jumped off that parking garage in the Loop."

Dick.

The bartender, a young woman whose youth was blunted by her over-bleached hair and the black vest that was part of her work uniform, set their cocktails in front of them.

"Listen, Jerry, I've got some inside information that makes me wonder if her death really was a suicide at all."

"Oh, yeah?" Kowalski looked somehow bored and distracted at the same time.

"Do you want to know what information?"

Kowalski looked straight at Sam for the first time since he'd sat down, "Not really, bro."

"I have reason to believe she was being investigated by the FBI at the time of her death."

Kowalski kept looking at Sam and Sam had the sensation of looking into an empty house. Sam used to think he could read people like a detective could read a clutch of clues. He'd thought he could read people, and that this explained his successes over the years, past though they seemed now to be. He knew when to smile and frown, and how to squint his eyes and move his brows to show warmth, affection, sincerity, concern, shared frustration. But Kowalski, the man who would refinance seniors right out of their homes—Sam found he could not read Kowalski very well at all.

"Why?"

"I thought maybe you could tell me," said Sam. "I think maybe she was doing something at work that was about to get her in trouble."

Kowalski laughed a dry bark into the air between them. "Jen Siegel was the Scary at Satchel Ferry. She knew how to make money. So good it was scary. So, sure. It's possible she was into something she shouldn't've been."

"What about you. You were her direct supervisor, weren't you?"

Kowalski's blank face belied the intensity of his voice. "Did you know the tranches were her idea? A few years ago. That's how she got into Mortgage. She'd been fucking with a guy from Lehman and he told her how to package them. Who to sell 'em to. Everybody wanted her product. Sounded boring as shit to me. Wave of the future, she said."

"By ripping off people who can't afford to be homeowners."

"Yeah, well. She didn't ask too many questions about where the loans came from, you know? You don't want to spend any time at the sausage factory. This is Chicago. Everybody knows how their sausage is made. Anybody who claims they don't is a liar or a fucking idiot. So some slumlords lose a few grand on a bad flip. I'm supposed to be sad about that?"

Sam shook his head, "That's not the sense I got from—" Keep it close to the chest. "She seemed to be worried."

Kowalski shrugged, "Maybe. I mean, after the whole thing slid into a bear market and it became, like, clear what was happening. Maybe she had some regrets. After that, I always told her: don't feel bad to take what you earned. This whole system is stacked. It's like a game: if you find a way through, you deserve the prize." Kowalski slid off of his stool and dropped two twenties on the bar. He looked like a man who had never felt a moment of culpability in his life. He looked dangerous.

"She was a pretty titty, but I always thought she was a little fucking nuts, too. Good luck, Dan." Kowalski didn't make eye contact again as he sauntered off and Sam thought, for a moment, of following him. He had a flash of Kowalski in a dark alley off Monroe. Of the blow he would like to deal him there. He could almost feel the weight of the bottle in his hand. The pipe. The wrench. *Colonel Mustard, in the alleyway, with the candlestick* Sam thought wildly. He could see the smashed-in head of the man and feel the power it would take to do such a thing gather in his biceps. Optimistically, full of rage, he took a step away from the bar and immediately felt the liquor spread through him like an epidural. He swayed a little in place and sat back down hard. Fuck.

Kowalski was already gone anyway. Or at least Sam couldn't pick out his shiny Joseph Aboud from all the others oozing through the lobby at that moment.

Sam tried to think through his anger, to be a good detective. *Concentrate*, he hissed to himself. Had that been something like a confession? The words Kowalski had spoken were already getting a little jumbled, the memory not quite a solid thing. Wispy, drifting, the smoke of a dream. Could Kowalski have killed Jen? Did he know who did?

Sam fished his tiny Moleskin out of his inside breast pocket and chicken scratched as many of Kowalski words as he could remember, though the order already seemed shifty and wrong. He certainly seemed like the right type of sociopath to push someone from the top of a parking garage. But had he?

Time stuttered and the angry young guy from Kowalski's presentation had come up to the bar. Sam wondered if he might know something about Kowalski.

"Hey," Sam said, "can I talk to you for a minute?" Time skipped and Sam was looking at the guy's shoes. The guy was talking about his shoes. "Blackspots," he said.

"No, I'm fine," said Sam, a little mush-mouthed now.

The guy laughed, "No, the sneakers. They're AdBusters. Like, fuck the corporations! I had to stand in line five hours to get a pair."

Another flicker and the guy was yelling "Go Hawks!" as he handed Sam a drink. And Sam yelled back. And then there were a bunch of people around them and they were all singing the University of Iowa fight song. Let the walls and rafters ring. More rounds. The warmth of simple masculine intimacy, the ease of a new young friend. But then.

He must have been talking about Jen. Talking about her murder. The other Hawks had dispersed and the warmth and ease in the young guy's face had dried up. His smile stretched unnaturally, held in place by the glue of Midwestern politeness. His eyes looked past Sam, more interested in who he might know in the conference crowd.

Another gap and Sam was outside smoking a cigarette—a Camel Light. He was surprised to notice the tan filter and was wondering where it had come from when he heard a familiar voice and the landscape seemed to snap into focus in front of him. Here was Sam, lurking behind a potted shrub at the hotel entrance, on the other side of the building from where he'd come in, and there was Kowalski, standing in the shadows just beyond the reach of the marquee bulbs. He was speaking to two other men, also in shadow. Sam could only make out Kowalski's side of the conversation.

"Obama Hussein," he said and laughed. "I mean, what is he, eggplant or babaganoush?" The laughter of the two men was loud and flat.

Sam shivered and realized he was cold in a bone-deep way—he'd been out here for a while in the damp and the chill. Had he followed Kowalski from the lobby in order to spy? Or had their paths crossed inadvertently? It would be the height of irony if he'd decided, in his browned-out twilight state, to spy on the man.

Another choice piece from Kowalski drifted over on the frigid evening wind. "Just a life-support system for a cunt," he laughed. Smoke billowed from his nose like the bull he liked to pretend to be.

Sam's rage was enormous and complete, seemed to eclipse not just his thoughts and confusion, but his entire consciousness. Without thinking about it, he took a step toward Kowalski, who was stepping on his cigarette and saying his goodbyes to his audience and Sam followed him out into the night, which had begun to spit rain. Kowalski was moving quickly, faster than Sam, who was still just coming out of his stupor.

And then a roaring, and the bright drag of the streetlights brought him snorting back, awake now to the terror of finding himself stumbling down a quiet city street. He felt clouded in pain. Had he hit his head? He touched the back of his skull and found a tender knot. Jesus, he had. The hands explored further and found fresh blood under his eye, the sting of an open wound. The city had a dirty urinal glow this time of night and it was hard to see, but he could tell something was wrong with his hands. He stopped walking and squinted at them. They were swollen and sore, and covered in dark flecks that he could not make out clearly in the dark of the night. Perhaps influenced by the stink of road construction in the air, his scrambled brain suggested that he'd fallen and stained them with tar. He sniffed them, then bent over and heaved onto the pavement. The smell of Campari wafted up and overtook the stink of blood on his hands. The panic that had been scratching lightly at him now began to pound furiously. Where the fuck was he? What had happened to him?

There was a construction sign: I-90 detour ahead. Okay, that was a start. He walked another two-hundred feet to the end of the block he was on, shadowed on both sides by abandoned storefronts, but there were no street signs on this block. He stopped walking and spun around, panicky, then startled when a voice echoed out of the darkness toward him.

"Hey, man."

Approaching him was a young Black man in a half-tucked Obey-style Obama T-shirt, green pinstriped boxers peeking over the top of the waistband of his baggy black jeans and a bandana knotted sideways around his head. Sam had never been mugged before. He felt two equally charged currents of fear and shame as the man approached and he fought the urge to run away from him into the darkness.

For the first time in his life, at least in his life as a voter, a Black man was running for president, and the talk was that, if nominated, he might even have a shot at winning. Barack Obama's fresh-faced campaign babies had been swarming the small towns and college campuses of Eastern Iowa for months now, with the fervor rising to a fever pitch in January, during the caucuses. Sam had been a lifelong independent and felt it was his duty to maintain the appearance of political equilibrium as a way of better serving his clients, but even he had to admit the guy was exciting. Something about the cadence of his voice. Though McCain—who knew—he wasn't such a bad choice either.

As the man neared, Sam pushed down the urge to tell him he didn't have any cash.

"You lost?" said the man, who paused now and looked concerned and wary.

Sam opened his mouth to speak and found that his throat was hoarse, as if he'd been shouting. "I'm looking for Halsted."

The guy pointed back the way Sam had come. "Missed it. This Pilsen. Halsted back there."

Sam thanked him, shame blooming afresh (was he really so racist as all that? It seemed so. And would he approach a stranger covered in blood on a dark block alone to offer him help?) and did an about-face as the man continued down the sidewalk and crossed to the other side of the street.

He stumbled down Halsted for a bit, then hailed a cab, which took him the rest of the way back to Jen's. He had his keys, which meant that he'd gotten his car out of valet at the Palmer House. But where was his car? It was this problem he was puzzling over but promptly forgot when he turned on the light in Jen's bathroom and saw his face the mirror. It looked like he'd smeared himself with fake tanner, but the slip, the smell . . . it became stronger in the confines of her bathroom. Clearly blood. Blood darkening the friendly lines of his face, blood in his crow's feet, his laugh lines. Blood crusted in his mustache. There was a fresh cut on his cheek. It was small—about an inch or so in length—and not that deep, though he gagged a little as he caught a white flash of fat in the subcutaneous layer as he pressed the mouth of the wound open and it began to throb and bleed anew. It wasn't a cut so much as a split. As if he'd hit his face against something. And it couldn't possibly have made so much blood—enough to coat his face and stain his hands? He fished in his pockets for his phone. Maybe he'd made a phone call or sent a text that contained a clue.

There, stuck in the clamshell of his cell, was Jerry Kowalski's business card.

A flash and he could see Kowalski's face beneath his hands, feel his hair, the way it slipped from his grip, so he grabbed it again, harder this time and with it, began to pound Kowalski's head against the ground. They were on the pavement, Sam straddling him like a lover.

Oh fuck.

Was this a memory or a dream? Sam seemed to feel the dull thud of a head in his hands and the satisfying, sickening way the impact reverberated back up his arms.

Had he killed Kowalski?

He sat down on the floor and began to cry, and would have stayed there all night, if the stink of himself had not made him gag again.

He crawled into the tub and turned on the tap, which is why he didn't hear the front door open, or see the figure in the doorway until I made myself known by gasping his name.

Chapter 6

Opening week was wet and cold. Stevie sat in the manager's gazebo near the tennis courts, and checked in the occasional guest. Though the pool was newly opened, her official first day of work had been a couple of weeks ago, when Elvis had given her and the five guards she was to manage an orientation.

When she'd arrived that first day, she was surprised at how little the club had changed over the years. The Willows was exactly like she remembered it, when she and Jen had haunted its bleachy corners, eating rocket pops and sneaking Everclear into their snack bar lemonades. The main pool was small and kidney shaped, only big enough for one actual lifeguard stand near the low board at the deep end. She supposed that the other two guards on duty still sat in folding beach chairs, one at the shallow end and one at the baby pool, just like it had been in Stevie's day. The pool itself was painted a cool blue and the deck was pebbled concrete that was supposed to look like river stone. It backed up to the dining room, which looked out over the pool: the farm country interpretation of a coastal ideal—seaside dining. Not all that fancy for something calling itself a club, but expensive enough to be exclusive. The troop of them had gathered in front of the gazebo where Stevie now sat, bored in the late May gloom, all of them too shy and polite to introduce themselves. Then Elvis had arrived, opened the padlocked gate to the pool deck and marched them down to the deck to meet each other: Melissa and Pedro,

Daria, Ashley, Jeremy. And Stevie, assistant manager. Stevie smiled and gave a small wave at them and two of the girls waved back. It was stupid, but Stevie felt happy to be working, to be in charge of something again, even if it was just a handful of teenagers.

As he spoke, Elvis chewed his gum and twirled his guard whistle, which he had with him even though the pool would not be open for two more weeks. He seemed both completely at ease and completely in charge. There were no ice breakers, thankfully, he simply showed them the place and they followed him like ducklings as he walked them around the grounds.

At first, Stevie had felt that breathless feeling, being near Elvis again but, as the orientation wore on—as they inspected the bathrooms, and he showed them the time clock where they would punch in, as they filled out W-9s on the benches in the women's locker room, as she watched him arrange his face around his dark, guarded eyes—she realized there was nothing good or sweet about her feelings. They were one part horniness, two parts unease. Elvis was intensely charismatic. He knew when to lock eyes with her. How to look her up and down so that she felt like she was the only one in the room. He knew how to be buddies with the two guys, and which of the girls he could touch lightly on the shoulders and which of them this would make jealous. With a growing sense of uncertainty, she watched him manipulate the six of them gently as they moved from pool to snack bar, kitchen to restaurant. It was nearly imperceptible, but she'd seen it in at media industry events with Britely clients, heard it in their voices. He was used to getting his way, like they were. Used to people doing what he wanted.

Before orientation day, the last time she'd seen him had been the day she finished training and was awarded her lifeguarding certificate. He'd come to distribute them to all the graduates, signing his name with a flourish at the front desk of the rec center pool before he handed them out, like an author signing books, thought Stevie. When he gave Stevie hers, she saw he'd scribbled something on it. *Parking lot ten minutes.*

She'd slid into his BMW and he'd said, "happy graduation, Miller," and tossed her a joint and they'd rolled out into the night. Through Taylor. Past the empty mall parking lot, and the Hy-Vee where Jen had worked.

They drove out to the reservoir, through the open gates that read *Road Closes 10pm*, even though by then it was already later than that. Their conversation was one-sided. "I still want you for the Willows" he said, and because the weed had slowed her down, her dumb heart skipped a little at the first four words and she almost told him she wanted him too before she heard the rest of the sentence.

"But I need to know I can trust you," he said. "Can I trust you?"

"Sure," she said.

"But how do I know?" he asked.

She laughed and the laugh came out too big, a little wrong, stoned. "You don't know me, but we've already fucked and you've promised me a job. I should probably ask why I should trust you." The night swam by slower, slower. She realized the car was stopping. He rolled down the window and the car filled with an enormous rushing sound and the stink of fish. They were at the dam spillway.

"I found your blog," he said. "I like it. You seem kind of pissed off. And you're not all networked up with the idiot townies around here. You don't know anybody and you don't have anything to lose. And you're smart." He undid his seatbelt and was on her so fast, his hand encircled her jaw and clutched it. "I need one person who's not a fucking idiot working for me." His fingers were squeezing her jaw now. She opened her mouth to speak, and he put his own mouth over hers hard and without hesitation. Tongue in her mouth, hands everywhere. He was on her so fast, too fast for her to consent but she found she didn't care. Liked it this way, actually. Some part of her was appalled at him, at his presumption. Another part of her though—perhaps it was the part that doubted that real harm could befall her in her hometown, or maybe it was the part of her that had always responded to power and will with her own desire—thrummed on.

"From now on, you're mine," he said and bit her lip.

She both did and did not want this and while she would come to regret it much later, in the moment, she came hard almost immediately.

She'd heard somewhere once that every human had their own internal clock, not as a metaphor but literally. That each person's body bent time differently, and that civilization was a matter of agreeing to sync our clocks, as much as was possible. In the front seat of his car, getting fucked by Elvis, she felt as though her clock was ticking slowly, steadily, while Elvis's raced around itself. Like in old movies, the cheesy special effect that shows time passing. That was Elvis's clock. She could not quite articulate the question that hovered slightly beyond her consciousness then, and anytime they were together thereafter, which was, more or less, "How did I get here and what do you want from me?"

"Listen," he'd said after, as if in response to something she'd said, though she was only listening to the oceanic sound of the water as it surged through the spillway somewhere out there in the dark beyond, "I'm not going to get into it right now, and really, the less you know the better, but I scheduled orientation—it's in a couple of weeks. I hired some high school students for you to boss around, if you still want the job." Apparently, giving her the barest explanation about the circumstances surrounding her hire while he pulled up his cargo shorts and she lay dripping against the tan leather interior, the warmth of him still all over her, was as much as he figured he owed her. And something told her Elvis always knew who was owed what.

"Come meet the kids and I'll explain everything."

This was the moment when she could have—probably should have—said "no thanks, I've changed my mind." She knew that whatever was coming would be nothing but bad news, and yet, she was curious and she found herself wondering if it—whatever was coming—would make a good story.

So she had arrived at the orientation, ready for something though she could not have said what.

Stevie's employees—the kids—were generically attractive and polite: taut skin, more smile than face. After orientation, over the course of the first weeks of the season, they would do little to differentiate themselves in her mind and possessed the sort of affectlessness of teenagers trying to be invisible to adults. Their eyes were vague and uninterested when they looked at her, but crystalline for each other.

Eventually, after this first day, they would come to differentiate themselves. Pedro and his muscles, the way he twisted his arms up under his T-shirts to hide his chaffing teenage nipples. Ashley: tiny and blond, blessed Queen Bee and Daria her opposite, body bunching out beyond the confines of her suit, eyes punching hard into everything they saw. Jeremy and his A.D.D. "You'll be on first shift Tuesday and Thursday," she might say to him as they all gathered around her perch at the gazebo for a staff meeting.

Ten minutes later, his hand would go up (he was the only one who raised his hand before he spoke to her), angry curl in his voice: "But Mrs. Miller, why didn't I get any hours this week?" Mrs. Miller. Too Midwestern, too young, to use the correct address. She had told them all to call her Stevie on that first day but none of them ever would. How did teachers do it? Her antipathy to them, to their bored faces and restless bodies, must have been palpable.

They would come alive when Elvis stopped by—his charisma, his maleness, spoke of true authority to them. "Daria, if you're late again, you're fired," he said, and her brown skin had almost seemed to pulse with shame, and she'd shown up to work ten minutes early every day after. One day became another and the rhythm of the place, the sameness of each day, allowed her to sink further into herself. Very quickly, she felt the scrim of this new old life lay itself gently over her old old life. New York receded in her rearview. A place she'd visited once, but a life that belonged to someone else.

Later, through the early weeks of summer, as the rain continued and they struggled to keep the pool open and the world seemed to be stuck in some perpetual spring, she would wonder things about them. Where did they go at night? Did they take long car rides under the scudding clouds of their wide-open rural sky? Did they follow the tractor paths, banked in gravel, off the backroads, turn off their headlights and creep through unknown fields? Did they stop and drop their seats back as far as they would go and mount each other, the bend of their limbs accommodating dash, wheel, shift box, parking brake, seatbelt heads. Did they hand-crank their moon roofs open and hoist themselves through, let the dusty fingers of the night comb back their hair, and wonder about what would happen to them when their lives finally began?

For all of them this was their first, or almost their first job. Daria and Jeremy had spent one or two summers detasseling corn. Hard labor under the August Iowan sun. Now, they were ready for ease. They wanted to be tan all over, not just on their forearms and ear tops. Their fingers were still sore from last year. Though they were rural, Midwestern children, and so would never say it themselves or anyone else, they wanted to meet other lifeguards from other schools and towns and fuck them in the back of flatbeds, on plaid blankets in fallow fields, stars like breathing holes punched in the top of some enclosure they were trying to escape. The big old bug jar of their lives. They played together after hours when the pool closed, dunked and chased, sat on each other's shoulders for chicken. Sometimes they got serious and practiced stabilizing carries on each other, practiced heaving each other out of the water, one handed, an excuse to touch each other. Pedro, especially, like to goad Ashley into these activities. "Hey Ash," he'd call as he lifted a leaking bag of garbage from a can, "bet you can't lift me out of the water." This was always met with an eyeroll from Ashley, but then he'd get in the pool and splash her until she whined, "Stop," stretching it out into two syllables, and then relented, diving in without a splash and hauling him to the side of the pool, stacking his limp arms on top of each other, rolling him out. They did this while Stevie watched from the shadows of the concrete block bathroom, and stopped when she emerged to tell them it was time to punch out.

Watching them goof around, Stevie remembered a time, back during that summer when she was still a kid, before everything had fallen apart, when the regular pool manager had been out with mono and she'd been tasked with closing up. One night, she had snuck in Jen and Sam after the G.M. had gone home. They'd turned out the lights and eaten mushrooms and laid on the white plastic lounge chairs asking each other questions about the world that none of them could answer. They had burned the tips of their fingers, firing up the huge metal slab of the snack bar grill and eaten gooey grilled cheese, sitting nipple deep in the baby pool. Jen had asked them if they would get married and they had both laughed, but

Sam's sounded hollow. The shrooms made it easy to hear everything in that laugh, and she was glad that the dark hid her humiliation. Maybe it was there, then, that Sam had started to pull away. Maybe he was already in love with Jen. Because certainly that's what had happened. Stevie had always known it a little bit. Then Jen had shushed them and told them to listen to the sound of the water sloshing against their bodies. The world was enormous then, and they felt timeless and eternal, bodies polished by moontides, primordial, part of some ancient secret. Sitting in the lukewarm baby pool in the dark, under the hallucinated cruciforms of patterned light that partitioned the night sky, breadcrumbs dotting their clavicles, they felt wise, which was exactly how you knew that they were sixteen-year-olds, high on drugs.

Near the end of their orientation, after the tour of the facilities and the paperwork, Elvis had taken them through all of it: the chemical mix, the tests each hour, sign-in sheet for members, cashier's box for their guests. Headboard for accidents, lost and found, the tornado and storm warning system, bathroom duty. He'd dismissed them with a lazy salute—"Stevie will call you with your schedules next week. See you when we open, *muchachos*,"—and they'd walked out the front door of the country club restaurant in a line, like baby ducks.

Then he'd cocked an eyebrow at her, beckoned with a finger, *you come with me*, and they'd walked back down the hallway to the men's locker room, back to the pool deck and into the pump room.

Pump room, she thought to herself, and her crotch began to ache.

"Assistant Manager Miller," he'd said as he closed the door behind her and pulled the chain on the bare bulb above them. It flickered and swung and gave the concrete room a noir-ish cast as it made their shadows dance. He leaned his body against the wall of the pump room that wasn't covered in pipes and tubes, boxing her into the corner near a large plastic cylinder she would later find out was the sand filter. "Here are the real terms of this job offer." He put his head near hers and again, she felt that dull heat between her legs. "You," he whispered, "sell for me" and then his body was against hers, but instead of embracing her he was straining past her, reaching behind the sand filter, and pulling out a large, locked metal cashbox. He set it on the ground and knelt down to unlock it with a key on a chain pulled from the dark tufts of chest hair framed by the deep V neck of his T-shirt. He laid the box open and stood up again.

All she saw was a bunch of old diving sticks.

"You want me to sell pool toys?"

"Come on, Miller," Elvis sounded disappointed. He picked up a blue one and put it in her palm, as if this were a relay race and he was passing the baton.

Her stomach flipped and the horniness turned into something more expansive. This was it, she thought, though what exactly "it" was, was as-yet unclear.

She popped off the nippled cap of the diving stick and turned it upside down. A tiny baggy of ivory powder fell out into her palm. *Sand*, she thought stupidly, though only for a moment.

"Coke?" she said as he took a bag from her hand and opened it so that it gaped like a little mouth. He stuck the lockbox key into the mouth and held the mound of powder to her.

"Bump?" he asked.

"How much coke is this?" she asked, ignoring the key. He put it to his nose and sniffed, pinched his nostrils together, grinned.

"The blue sticks have eight-balls. All the rest are just a gram each. One twenty for the other colors. Three seventy-five for the blues—we reward for buying in bulk."

"I mean, how much is in the whole box?"

"That's for me to know," he said. "What you need to know is this: members and only members can buy any time they want by asking to purchase a weekly guest pass *special*—the special part is key. And you collect cash or card info. You tell them you have to move the cash and receipts down to the lockbox and they'll ask if there are any diving sticks in the lost and found. You say you'll check. Come down here, put the cash in the envelope, take the sticks back up. They daily limit is one blue, and three of any other color."

When Stevie was growing up, the local lore was that if you ordered double oregano on your large cheese pizza from Spot's Pizza, you'd get your pizza delivered with a kine bud nestled in the box. An order of double parm got you a meth rock. This was widely known, and seemed simple enough but for some reason, they'd never tried it, even on those nights when no one was holding and the convenience stores carded. Maybe it was because, deep down they'd known it was just an urban legend and they didn't want to jeopardize its existence in the world. It was one of those things, the belief in which made life more exciting. But now, as Elvis explained to her the ins and outs of the operation he was running out of a private country club and possibly the other municipal pools he managed as well, she wondered if it had been true about Spot's after all.

"Do you really think you're going to sell this much coke to the upper-middle-class moms of the Willows?"

"Oh yeah. I know I am. Why do you think they gave me this job, Miller? Demand is demonstrably there."

"What demand? Whose? And what about the guest pass?"

"There isn't any guest pass," he said, ignoring her first question. "It's a front."

"No, I get it," she said, "but what if someone's hanging around. Someone who isn't trying to buy a nightclub's worth of drugs. Someone who actually wants a guest pass?"

"Assuming they don't ask for the special, you put it in the books as a guest pass under their member number so there's a record. Just like their membership—they don't show cards to get in, they write their number. Same thing here."

Elvis dipped into the open bag again and offered her another bump. This time she bent close to his hand and took it. Stevie snorted lightly, then began to giggle.

"What?"

"This is completely ridiculous."

He took a step away from her. "I thought it was a good idea."

"It was your idea?" Stevie laughed harder. She put a hand to her face to stop herself but couldn't. The coke was thrumming through her now and the power differential between the two of them seemed to disappear. This hadn't been a surprise, exactly. She'd been waiting for just such a set up when they'd made their deal that first night in his car. But this? This was too funny; hilarious, really. Like that TV show *Weeds* that she'd seen a couple of times at Anderson's apartment, having never been able to afford cable herself, but crazier. The *Miami Vice* version. She hadn't done coke since the S&M night with Siobhán, she remembered now, and once again appreciated the way it whizzed through her. She wiggled her jaw and still could not stop smiling. The elation of it—this was just the kind of thing that would make perfect book material. What was better than yuppie drug dealing in America's heartland? She'd do the job and write the book and wait for a spot on the *Times* bestseller list to open up and grant her a new life. Jay McInerney, eat your heart out.

"You know in New York people just call a phone number and get it delivered? Like lunch."

Elvis stepped closer to her again and he was smiling but his voice was chilly. Her hair was in a ponytail down her back and he pulled it lightly. R*re-establishing his dominance*, said a voice in her head that sounded like the narrator of a nature documentary. He put his lips on her throat and the coke seemed to all rush down to her crotch. "You're going to do this for me," he bit at her neck and pulled her hair a little harder, "right, Miller? And you're going to make a lot of money doing it. A lot." She swallowed and nodded, soaking and hot and frightened and thrilled at all once. He pushed her against the wall. It was cold and damp and smelled of a quarter century's worth of mildew. He bit her neck again. Something inside of her raced with terror and joy. Then he unbuttoned her Levi's cut-offs with a quick rip, and oriented her the rest of the way.

The memory gave Stevie a chill in the damp shade of the gazebo. Elvis had not been part of her plan, but there was something about him that she couldn't stay away from. It was the part of her that had always been drawn to the thing you shouldn't touch. He was a copperhead sunning itself on a rock, a downed electrical wire, a bottle marked poison. He was the high ledge that beckoned. *L'appel du vide*, the call of the void. Stevie wondered if this is what had happened to Jen. If the void had indeed called and instead of ignoring it, Jen had answered.

She had asked Elvis more questions, after the pump room. And he had opened up a bit. The operation at the club *had* been his idea and he was eager to explain just how good of an idea it was. He'd started dealing in college—a cousin from the skeevy end of Buffalo Grove was his hook-up. But he hadn't intended to make it part of the job—that had been an accident. He was actively dealing when he'd gotten the front desk job at the rec center. His friends and their friends, friends-of-friends, and finally strangers, they'd just show up, mostly wanting weed, but eventually his cousin made in-roads with a guy who knew a guy from Jalisco and then they'd been able to get whatever they wanted. Cocaine was the most profitable, and the least likely to attract the kinds of addicts that would blow his cover, though he still sold a little weed here and there.

And then, at the same time, he'd just kept working for the consortium of local public pools, revitalizing them, raising money for repairs and improvements, bringing in new money. He was actually good at both things: running the pools and dealing drugs. Then, last winter, the director of the Willows had hired him as a consultant for the club, which was losing members left and right. And now here he was. He'd stayed at a dead-end job long enough that the boulder of reality had rolled away to reveal a cave, a path, a new way.

He'd said he couldn't do much about the restaurant of course, which still served Crab Louie and Jello salad desserts, though there *was* a way to make that hip and young, to lean into, instead of away from, the Midwestern supper-club aesthetic. He had ideas for making more out of their memberships—members, people who were used to charitable giving, liked to feel that they had some control over the rank order of their importance. Elvis invented different levels of membership (starfish, seahorse, dolphin, shark), plans that came with a particular number of meals and pool admissions per month. He visited a University of Iowa tennis clinic and hired two Adonis-like college students as pros, then emailed their photos to the club mailing list. Small things, like this. Then big things, like the coke. It all began to add up.

Orientation day was a Monday, and the dining room was closed so they'd sat on the ledge of the empty pool, smoking cigarettes.

"I want to expand eventually," said Elvis, and blew a perfect smoke ring as his jaw clicked softly. Jen would have been impressed. "Black Hawk County, maybe. Decorah. College towns are good."

She'd had so many questions—*how do you build a drug client list? How do you convince someone to give you managerial authority over the town pools even though you have no bachelor's degree or administrative experience whatsoever?*—but no idea how to ask them. And he'd never asked anything of her. Except if she was a midnight toker. Which, she never really had been before, at least not since high school. But she was home now and maybe that's why it all felt okay.

Stevie gazed limpidly toward the red-clay tennis courts, feeling vaguely sorry for herself. What had seemed thrilling (if a little silly) in theory had already grown monotonous, five days into the season. The weather sucked and the only members so far had been moms desperate to leave the house with their little kids, kids who would jump into the pool gamely only to retreat to towels minutes later, their lips blue, their bodies shivering. Stevie kept wondering if one of those moms would be her first sale. They all looked so tired and puffy—they could use it—but it was hard to imagine them lining up for a stick. And she was basically chained to the gazebo. Elvis had told the guards that if a member wanted to buy a weekly guest pass, he had to speak with Stevie, no exceptions. But Elvis was worried that too many people asking for such a thing would begin to seem suspicious, so Stevie was only to leave the gazebo when absolutely necessary. It wasn't like the old days, when she'd check in her friends under other member's names. She'd sat on the tower that hulked over the deep-end and had felt the eyes on her: kids from school, middle-aged dads, the fear of the children who asked her permission to go off the board. This collective gaze glowed on her skin like heat, like solar radiation. She'd been tall and lithe and the chlorine tousled and bleached her hair. No inch of her wasn't young and beautiful. Here, she felt like the Midwesterner approaching middle age that she was. Except when Elvis found her alone and then the scary thing that came alive between them was there and she was someone else. Maybe that was it. Why she kept letting him and why she kept wanting it.

She sighed and looked at her phone. No Sam.

A tall man with a pocked nose, skinny legs and board shorts to the knees approached. He had a towel over his shoulder and a floppy demeanor, like a family dog. The smile he flashed her was winning. "Here for the guest's pass." The guy's accent was Swedish, she thought.

Was this going to be her first sale? "You want a guest pass?" she repeated, unsure of how to clarify the situation.

"Yah. I mean I want—" he paused for a moment and thought about it, "the weekly guest pass special," he said, then he winked at her. *Jesus Christ.* Stevie pushed the sign-up sheet toward him. "Guest name here please."

He looked skeptical. "My real name?"

"You're a member of the club, right?"

"Yes, but. . . ."

"Check the box there for the weekly guest pass special," Stevie was so nervous, she was afraid her voice would shake if she said more. Though the day was gloomy she was glad to be wearing sunglasses. "Cash or card?"

"Card," he gave her his debit card and she hauled out the old manual credit-card stamper—*knuckle busters* the retail kids used to call them. She awkwardly rolled the press over the card and handed it back to him. "One minute, uh," she glanced at the sign-in sheet. "Karl."

He winked again and began to whistle as she wandered down the pathway, onto the pool deck and into the pump room. She chose a yellow stick for Karl, the color of the Swedish flag, and waved at Pedro on the lifeguard stand, padding below him, as he lazily wound his whistle around one finger in big swinging loops, then unwound it and wound it again.

I'm doing it! She thought. *I'm operating a drug front!*

Karl's eyes lit up when she handed him the diving stick. "There you are my little friend," he said and Stevie wasn't sure if he was talking to her or the stick. "You are . . . ?" He put out his hand to her and she startled a little.

"Stevie," said Stevie and shook his hand.

"Stevie," said Karl. "I like that name. It's like, sassy?" Karl had gray, upswept hair but his accent and its upspeak made him sound a little like a teenage girl, not unsassy himself. He gave her a big smile, then looked around and shook his head. "You Americans, so uptight around this thing!

Now, I am a criminal." His teeth were glacial and he clicked them at her, like a horse. "I am a professor though, so, this is all low down yeah? Between us? You and me?" Everything he said sounded like a friendly question. He was very close to her face and though the sun had yet to make an appearance today, she could smell his sunscreen—bananas.

"Nothing to worry about here, Karl." She slid past him and back into her station in the gazebo. "Enjoy your guest."

He stuck the stick into the pocket of his board shorts and walked through the turnstile down toward the water, sounds of horseplay echoing up toward them as if in response.

"*Tack*, Stevie! Happy Memories Day!" he called without turning around.

Stevie shivered again. Just like that, her life of crime had begun.

Stevie left a cryptic message on Elvis's cell phone from the burner he'd given her to report the sale and drove the two miles into town to the Gringos parking lot to meet her mom for dinner.

Her car was a used black Jetta, courtesy of her severance package. It was a lot like the beater she'd driven in high school. She'd been so long in the world without a car, she hadn't yet readjusted. It still felt funny—the freedom of being able to cover distances in mere minutes on a whim—and, compared to the subway, lonely.

The dinner was a belated homecoming, a celebration. With Stevie first in training, then newly managing the pool and her mom on third shift in the E.R. most days, they'd seen surprisingly little of each other since Stevie's move. Which was okay—Stevie was in no hurry to reproduce the shared-space dramas that had kept them at each other until the day she'd finally moved out. But then, a family newly shattered by divorce was a different beast than a single mom and her adult daughter. And James had still been around back then, just starting to get into trouble, which had added a layer of strain to everything.

Her mother was tiny in the big vinyl booth in the corner, but the margaritas, when they came, were head-sized and glowing a deep chartreuse.

They looked like a movie prop: poison. Stevie had ordered hers with salt but now she saw why her mother had skipped it—the glasses were too heavy to properly lift. There would be no rough salt on her tongue, transformed into fire by the liquor. There would, instead, be very long, thick straws and a lot of pre-made sour mix. While Stevie's mouth cried, her mother made a pleased smacking sound. "These are my favorite."

"I can see why."

The walls of the restaurant stretched up three stories into an open atrium and were painted a deep orange. On the sound system, the music of a Norteño band polkaed up the balconies that overlooked the main floor. Stevie and Viv sat on the second balcony like spectators of something, though neither knew exactly what. That the restaurant was called Gringos seemed to offend exactly no one, especially because it was run by two, a tan couple in their forties whose love of cocaine and hot tub parties in the eighties had finally started to show on them. She wondered if they were club members.

The server arrived and Stevie ordered the seafood chimichanga, as she always did, which she loved all the more for being prepared primarily with sour cream and those tiny frozen shrimp pet stores sold as lizard food.

"I just wanted to say welcome home, babe! Cheers!" Her mother did indeed lift her margarita with both hands and Stevie struggled hers up too, both of them sloshing a bit onto the salt-strewn black tabletop. Her mom wore a linen cardigan over a broomstick skirt. As she grew older, it seemed to Stevie that something in her seemed to lean backwards toward the days of her youthful hippiedom. When Stevie was growing up, she'd been business casual—the square-shouldered blazers and white commuter sneakers of the '80s, of *Working Girl*—now she wore more jewelry, more scarves, her Danskos red suede and a metallic leather. Maybe it was genetic, all this nostalgia.

"Are you doing okay so far? I'm supposed to be moving back to second shift next week, but I haven't seen the new schedule yet. We'll see if that b-word Alison remembered. How's lifeguarding? Is it everything you'd thought it would be and more?" Her mom was razzing her a little. She was still so clearly and newly pleased to have Stevie home, even her initial confusion over the job could not dampen her pleasure ("Tell me again? About the job?) Though that would obviously change if she knew the whole story.

"Well, first of all, I'm *assistant managing* a pool now," Stevie said with mock pretension. Her mom laughed. "It's okay. I mean, cold and rainy this week, but there's not much to get the hang of. The kids are funny. They're babies. It's been a while since I've been around people that young. I can't believe that was me, the last time I lived here." *Then there's the fact that I'm dealing coke to Swedish college professors because I can't say no to my boss due to the state of being dickstruck by and also kind of scared of him.*

"Well, I still think of you as a baby, but I know what you mean. You and your friends, you were colts. But really, if you can believe it, your dad and I were younger than you are now when we had you. And only a couple years older than you are now when we had your brother." Here was the requisite wince that Viv always made when she mentioned James, a quirk of the lip, a tic of the eye. Stevie was certain she had no idea she did it.

It seemed impossible that she could ever be as old but also so young and lovely as the ghost of her thirty-two-year-old mom. "God. You were married with kids for years already. Look at me—struggling toward seasonal employment with a bunch of sixteen-year-olds." Now it was Stevie's turn to wince—she'd meant that to be a joke but it was too true not to fall flat.

"Don't think of it like that. You have the book. That's your real work. And you left New York because it wasn't really your home. You're following your heart in a way I never did. You're so much braver than I was, leaving for the big city so young and then starting over again, now."

"I don't think I'm braver. Or maybe I was brave once but I'm not anymore. And look, we've ended up in the same place." Had that sounded bitter? Snotty? She hadn't meant it to.

Stevie thought about her last week in New York. She'd stopped by the dog park on West 81st and watched—for a long time—a lone greyhound curl anxiously around the perimeter of the fence.

That's what it felt like, living in New York. Your lean, anxiety-diet self slinking around the perimeters of places. Imposter, sideliner. There was also the threat of real danger that had eventually sunk into the depths of the subconscious but which was ever present. After 9/11, no one had ever truly relaxed again. It felt to Stevie like the city had dug deeper into its parties, its scenes, but the anxiety floated over the top of it all like a stink. And in fact, there had been a stink. The so-called "maple syrup event" in which the city stank of syrup for days in October of 2005, frightening people and setting off a chain of humorously unnerved conspiracy-theory blog posts on *Gawker* and the *Gothamist* about chemical warfare and weapons testing. Years later, when the smell reappeared, the 311 system (perhaps one of the very best and most underrated things about the city) along with the EPA and Emergency Management, would track it to a factory in New Jersey that processed fenugreek seeds. But it was telling that in 2005, the first best guess on everyone's mind—after ascertaining that they had not, in fact, picked up a smear of someone's waffle breakfast from the subway—was terrorism.

When she'd looked up from the pacing greyhound, the lights of the Rose Center planetarium had glowed blue behind the park, looking from the outside like a small, simple moon, but promising a view of the whole universe inside. And this too was a metaphor for the way Stevie lived adjacent to the cosmos of the city, but never really inside it. She didn't have the money for that, nor the insider friends. Somehow she'd been here for nearly fourteen years and was leaving, still a transplant. Anderson Anderson and his Montauk weekends had never really belonged to her.

"Having a husband and children seems brave to me. Brave and confusing and difficult. How can something that everybody does feel so impossible?" Stevie thought of that night with Sam and the thought plucked a taut wire deep inside. But then instead of Sam's face, sunk in the frilly barge of her teenage bed, she saw Elvis, who gave her his swarthy wink.

"It's just what people did back then. You got married after college—there wasn't much to think about, it's just what happened next on the timeline. I don't think it's brave to do what everyone else is doing. I hated it, but I was also so glad when you left for New York because I knew then you would always do what you wanted."

"It was brave to get a divorce."

This her mother acknowledged with a wince and a long sip from her straw. "It was not brave. It was ugly. It was vanity. I'm happier now, but if I could have seen how awful that whole process would be, I don't know that I would have asked your dad for a divorce in the first place. James is still so damaged from everything. I mean, I assume he is. The way he still never talks to me."

"What made you do it?" Stevie was equally surprised she had never asked this simple question, and that the information had never been offered. At the time, there had been a sort of forced narrative from her parents, the language of which never changed no matter who was reciting it or when: just don't get along anymore, not your fault, still love you very much, mom gets custody. Stevie simply assumed she knew why her parents divorced but when she opened that file in her brain and tried to look beyond their pre-loaded language, there was nothing.

Closed eyes. Blossoms high in her mother's cheeks.

"You father and I had an open marriage."

Stevie gasped and immediately coughed. The margarita mix burned up her nostrils. "What?"

Her mother closed her eyes and moved her lips silently.

"What're you doing?"

"What?"

"Who are you talking to?"

"Higher power. It looks like Grandma, but it's less Republican. I'm just asking it for strength and asking that you continue to love me and not go back to New York."

It was Stevie's turn to blush. She ran a finger around the rim of her glass and sucked at the salt that stuck to it. "What do you mean about an open marriage?"

"For the last ten years of our marriage, we had an open relationship agreement. So if one of us went away for a conference, for example, and we told the other and we were safe. I mean we took . . . precautions. An open marriage."

Stevie could not move farther forward in this conversation, but neither could she drop it. It was currently happening and there was nothing she could do to change that. She was in quicksand.

"Conferences. Like, did Dad . . . meet people at insurance conferences?" There seemed to be no way to process this information. No way at all.

"Yes. And I had two relationships at nursing conferences. I don't want you to judge us. It started in the eighties. Our friends were having key parties and everybody was trying new stuff. And things were not going well after the first five years."

"What do you mean?"

Viv took a long pull of her margarita. "At first it was all Fleetwood Mac shows and nights at the disco, but then you came along and everything changed. We bought a house and it was expensive. There was all this stuff to fight about, all of a sudden." She sighed and twisted a ring on her finger—a ruby set in twisty pewter sculpted to look like something vegetal or animal. A tree or a dragon or a tendril. "Even before that, though, it never really felt right. The day your dad proposed to me, I was going to break up with him. But then he got down on one knee. He was wearing this beautiful gray suit." Stevie knew it: the one from her photo, the photo of her parents and their young, entwined hands. Later, she would take the photo out of the album where she kept it and looked at her father's acne-scarred, freshly shaven cheek, into her mother's deep-set eyes. Did they look more hooded, a little frightened? Was there something she'd never noticed before? Later still, the photo would be destroyed and Stevie would eventually forget it had ever existed at all.

"But an open marriage is a hard thing to keep control of. It stopped being just conferences or out-of-town . . . rendezvous. He was seeing someone here. I never found out who, but I could tell."

"That's why you got divorced."

"That was the moment, but it had been coming for a long time. It might even have been okay with me, but he was sneaking out of our motel room, after the flood. I thought you and James would find out. I felt like. . . ." she took a breath. "It seemed like we should all be together just then, and here he was, leaving and coming back when he thought I was asleep. I thought we had rules, but then, suddenly, we didn't anymore."

"No wonder I'm so fucked up."

Her mother nodded and put a rough, nurse's hand over Stevie's. "That is exactly why you're so fucked up."

A lone trumpet sounded and a man sang back in sorrowful Spanish. Below them, the enormous old oak bar was beginning to fill up with college students. There was a plastic blackboard behind the bar, and a tattooed girl in braids and a rolled-up flannel shirt wrote on it in neon dry erase, *Hora feliz—$2 Usted Lo Llama. Antes se coge al embustero que al cojo.*

"Has Sam called you back yet?" Her mother had, of course, noted his car in the driveway the day after the funeral. Stevie got the sense she didn't want to hex it by asking too many questions aloud but she knew Stevie was waiting and so she was waiting too. She wanted to know where they stood. For her part, Stevie had been avoiding the topic because she couldn't bear to hear her mother's response, which would be something on the continuum of "Oh well, he's an idiot then" and "I'm sure he'll come around soon." The kinds of things mothers have been telling their lonely daughters forever. But here they were after all. Stevie was surprised to find her head filling with mist.

"We talked but" it was her turn to wince now, remembering her coke-fueled yammering, "he couldn't get off the phone fast enough. And I haven't heard anything since. I keep wondering if I did something wrong or maybe I felt something that wasn't there. It felt *there*, though. You know?"

The look on her mom's face was unbearable.

"I thought. . . ." *Oh god, what a fool she had been.* "I thought he was, like, really into me."

And here were the mothering words, and the pats and the shush and the warmth of her mother's body, her first true love, the first place she'd called home.

"He'll call you, baby. He will. Just give him some time. He's probably surprised you're here."

Stevie nodded, uncomforted, and a single tear dropped into her margarita.

"Maybe you need to make a big to-do. What we used to call a grand gesture," said her mom, taking a deep drag off her straw. "You know like Carl Borak?"

Stevie nodded. She knew of Carl—he'd been a boyfriend of her mom's in college before she met Stevie's dad. She'd met him once and that was enough to get the impression that he had never really stopped wanting to date her mom. "He and his friends stole your parked Bug and moved it to Veteran's fountain in the middle of town."

"And spray-painted 'WILL U GO 2 HOMECOMING VIV?' on it."

"Spray-painted? I don't remember that part."

Viv waved her hand. "Yeah, he painted the whole car for me later. Matte black."

"I don't remember that part of the story. So you drove around in a matte black Beetle because some guy destroyed the paint job asking you out?"

"It was the '60s. And it wasn't some guy. It was Carl."

"I see."

"The point is: it got my attention. You need something like that."

"To end up in jail for vandalism and destruction of private property?"

"Sam is asleep. Most men are. He probably doesn't understand what you mean to him. The right grand gesture will snap him awake."

Stevie was meek now. "Do you think that will work?"

"Yes, I do. But you have to help him understand what you mean to each other. Find him. Tell him how you feel. How could he say no to *you*?" More sweet mom-talk. But maybe she had a point. And Stevie did feel hopeful, even as she knew with whatever small piece of her brain remained untouched by nostalgia, horniness, and drugs, that a grand gesture might be a bad and counterproductive idea. But the rest of her brain was not untouched. The rest of her brain was touched all over, and those parts agreed with her mom. In any case, it would make a great book chapter. Why not take its next piece of advice?

"Sometimes I think that's all I needed when things started to fall apart for us. A grand gesture." Her mom looked down into the glowing toxic bowl of her heavy margarita glass. This regret was new and Stevie wasn't sure what to do with it. Being far away for so long had afforded her a certain distance from the family drama, but now she was home and here it was, this indigestible and uncomfortable fact. Something occurred to her.

"Did you still love him?"

Viv seemed to dismiss this question but answered in the affirmative anyway. "I guess. Kind of. He's not the same person I married. He changed while we were together. It wasn't even the open-marriage stuff. It's like he got colder or something. Raising you and James wasn't easy for us. Especially James. I think we could have loved each other more—I wanted us to—but we got distracted. We just thought the other person would always be there. And then, one night I rolled over and he was gone. I don't want that to happen to you. I mean, I'm glad it hasn't happened to you."

Was it better to have lost something or to never have had it? Stevie realized she'd been hoping Sam would simply show up at her door with a bottle of wine, his hair a little out of place, that dimple where it always was and then. . . .

And then what?

She'd never gotten that far. And that was the problem. With Sam, and maybe, she'd begun to fear, with the whole endeavor. Somehow it had come as a surprise to her to find she was not just the narrator of her own story, but its author. She had assumed, her entire life, that she was always stepping into a story whose beginning, middle, and ending had already been written. At least, it felt that way. Every failure, every decision, a plot point along an ordained arc. She kept wondering when this life would feel like something she had done instead of something that had been done to her. And now, here she was, rewriting it—actually being told to back up and redo, erase, try again, but this time make it weird and funny. This time be its metaphorical and literal author. Make it the kind of life you'd buy in hardcover with a 20% off member discount. Stevie felt panic begin to crawl up her throat and she ate a tortilla chip to push it back down.

Her mom peered down onto the mezzanine below them and when she looked up again, her face was different. Stevie's panic returned.

They both started to speak at once.

"What—"

"I have news—"

Her mom had that tone and that look that meant she was about to say something difficult. Stevie sat back and shook her head and braced herself for whatever was on its way. Cancer? New boyfriend? James sick again? James dead?

“I’m losing the house.”

“What do you mean?”

“I’ve missed some payments and they’re threatening foreclosure.”

“I don’t understand. Who is ‘they’?”

Viv sighed. “The bank, honey. It’s my fault. I took out a huge loan and it was shady. I knew it was shady but I needed the money.”

“Okay, back up. What loan? Why did you need the money? How big?”

Viv gazed down again and didn’t meet Stevie’s eyes. “You’re my daughter. Some things I won’t burden you with. But it was a lot. And I didn’t realize, at the time, that the interest rate was adjustable. For a while I could afford it, but then the payments kept going up and up. And I needed to keep taking out money. Then, they cut my shifts at work.”

“Who in the what now?” On her way to fear, Stevie was often waylaid at anger first, something she’d picked up from her dad. She closed her eyes and tried to summon patience; the fear would find its way in no matter. “And you took out a huge loan against your house? Our house? Why? When?”

To her credit, Viv’s tone remained steady and maternal. “Last year. Your brother needed rehab. And I sent him. I kept sending him. I didn’t want him to be sick anymore and I knew if I let him get away it could be years before I saw him again, or never. He did ninety days in-patient. At first it was only going to be thirty, but the doctors kept telling me more in-patient was the surest road to recovery. And I’d been in our house so long, but after the flood—we were only partially insured, you know. We just didn’t think we’d . . . and anyway, the payments were still pretty high since I’d bought your father out but I could manage them. I thought it would be hard but doable. Then with the extra months of rehab and work shifts drying up. . . .” Viv trailed off.

“You didn’t tell me.”

“I knew how much you were struggling. I didn’t want to add to it. And James begged me not to tell you. You know how he is. He’s so independent, so wild.”

“Did he ask you for the money?” Stevie would kill him. If he’d taken money off their mother claiming it was for rehab she would find him and murder him.

"No. I had to pick him up from jail. In Utah. Heroin and pills. It was terrifying. He was like another person. Like some of the people who come into the hospital late night. Mindless when he was high and mean when he wasn't. And so sick. He was going to die. I could see it in his eyes. He'd gotten into oxy—an injury of some kind, his back I think—and then he just couldn't get off of it. Pretty soon, it was too expensive and the heroin was easier. That's what he told me, anyway. I basically had to cut and run at work to get him. I missed a few shifts they couldn't cover and I've been paying for it since." Viv was not a crier. She was, as the expression went, tougher than wang leather. She had been raised on a small and unprofitable ranch in the western wing of the state by poor Evangelicals and had learned to do for herself because of it. So, when she wiped her eyes Stevie felt a sense of dislocation. She wished she could comfort her mom but realized she had no idea how to do such a thing. "I didn't want any relapses. I didn't want to have to I.D. his dead, overdosed body. I've seen too many of those. It's hard enough when it's other people's kids. So I sent him to the best place I could find for the longest they would take him. And I'm glad I spent the money."

Stevie opened her mouth to fight this new information she didn't want and instead of saying anything else, she surprised herself by bursting into loud, unlovely tears. Soon she was sobbing. She didn't know who she felt worse for: her mom, her brother, or herself. She cried for them all. For the sacrifices it seemed her mother would never be done making, for the heretofore unknown extent to which her brother had fucked up his off-the-beaten-path life, for the bad decisions *she* continued to make, moving home being one of them, working for Elvis another, and fucking him yet another. When you don't live at home, it's easy to pretend that your family's problems aren't your problems too. When you live in a big city, it's easy and maybe even necessary to be taken up completely with the question of your own survival. But move home and you soon find your own life richly and painfully complicated by and entwined with the problems of the people you love. This community included Jen, too, who did not live at home, but who had lived close enough to still belong to it, in Stevie's mind. Maybe if she had just checked in with her once in a while. . . .

Ignoring the curious eyes of the waitstaff, who began, suddenly, to bus clean tables nearby, Viv let Stevie cry. When she seemed to be finishing up, she again took Stevie's soft hand in her smaller, ropier, practical hand—short, square fingernails, knuckles just beginning to gnarl with a touch of arthritis—and kissed it, patted it. "It's okay. It'll be okay."

Stevie sniffed. "Mom, no. You're not going to lose the house. I have some severance money from Britely. And then I can help you out with the mortgage."

Viv shook her head. "It's not your problem and I don't expect you to fix it. Besides, what are you making—ten bucks an hour? Until September? It's not enough."

This was a typical stubborn hard line from her mom. She would have to work around it, though she wasn't about to explain to her mom why she was making a lot more than ten bucks an hour doing pool work.

"Can you sell it?"

"I'm underwater. That's what the bank said. 'You're underwater on the mortgage—you owe more than the house is worth.'" Viv barked, "I said, 'That's twice now it's been underwater.'"

"How did that happen?"

"Stevie, I don't know. The guy at the bank said the market's shrinking. Do I know what that means in practical terms? No. I just know what the bank tells me."

"My book, Mom. I'm writing this book, right? If I can get it out and get it under contract—my agent says there's already interest—then maybe I can help you." And she thought but didn't say, *there is always the drug dealing, too.* Viv began to pull back but Stevie held her hands tight. "Mom, I'm going to help you. You're going to take the rest of my severance and then I'm going to pay you rent and when the book sells, we'll put the rest toward the mortgage. We'll get caught up."

"Stevie, it's your money, your life. You didn't come home to give it all away to someone else."

"You're not someone else, you're Mom. Anyway, it's my house too. Where am I supposed to live if you lose it?" There was something in Viv's pinched face—a tiny flutter of hope, maybe. "Come on, I should be paying you rent anyway."

Her mom gave a small laugh. "I don't know, Stevie. I never wanted to make my problems yours. That's a thing I always told myself about my kids."

"It's not your problem. It's James's. Or, I don't know, maybe he's everyone's problem. You did a good thing helping him. You shouldn't have to stand by and lose your house as reward. Let me help you."

Let me drug deal us back into a single mortgage.

And then: "I'm sorry I left, Mom. I'm sorry I left you and James. I'm sorry I left you alone." She didn't think she'd ever said it before and now she wasn't sure why.

Viv looked smaller, older. Stevie understood, for the first time, that some day, in the natural order of things, she would watch her mom die.

"I'm not. I'm glad you got out of here and found a life. I didn't want you to get stuck here with us and all our problems. Now though. You've seen the world and it's returned you to me." She smiled. "All this sad talk. Why? My baby's home!" Her mother stood up a little uncertainly from her seat and leaned over their balcony. "My baby's home!" she yelled, arms outstretched like a Latin dictator. A few of the college students below raised their glasses and yelled back. The noise filled the hollow of the restaurant. It filled something in Stevie. And she remembered the pull that had brought her back home—the cottony memories of her youth, when she was young enough to still be inoculated against real sadness, though she didn't know it then; when the rest of her life lay ahead of her, that hazy fade-to-white, cashmere ever-after.

Chapter 7

This was how the start of the season went: Stevie managed the pool and sold a little bit of cocaine to a handful of its members. So far they numbered Karl, and two frat-gone-to-fat dad types who both said something about a weekend with the boys and whose Oakleys had identically reflected her polarized, rainbow tinted self back to her. Once there had been a girl, quiet and skinny—she reminded Stevie of Jelissa from her lifeguarding class, all knobby joints and sadness—and Stevie had refused politely. The girl had gone away without a word, and some time later, Elvis had called the gazebo. "Rich college students are our bread and butter. You can't just tell them no."

"She's in college?"

"Of course she's in college. Dude, rich college students are gonna be like our main demographic. You know?"

And the girl had come back, definitely not a college student, just as silent as before, and handed Stevie her cash with a smirk.

And that had been it. There wasn't a lot of business—for one, it would not stop raining. Greg, the Club's G.M. did not like to pay pool employees to sit around. She knew Elvis had a plan to deal him in eventually, but he needed to get business up first. Meanwhile, Greg was always closing the pool due to weather as a way to save on employee wages. A classic money-laundering chicken-and-egg scenario, she supposed.

Though Elvis was the drug dealer, Greg always struck her as the slimier of the two. She'd met him in person once, to approve her hire. They'd sat there, alone, behind the closed door of his office, which stank of the industrial cleaning products of the restaurant and the pool. He wore fancy tasseled loafers and looked her up and down and asked if she had any experience in the hospitality industry. "Hos-pi-TAL-i-ty" he'd said and raised an eyebrow on its penultimate syllable and Stevie got the clear impression of a double entendre but had no idea what it might be. When he called now—it seemed like every other day—to close the pool early—she always knew it was him from the seconds-long mouth-breathing that preceded their conversations.

On days the pool was open, she spent a few minutes with the lifeguards who were usually hungover and otherwise uninterested in her companionship and then haunted the gazebo for the rest of each shift. She watched Paul the tan, long-haired pro adjust the hips of the tennis mothers in their shiny purple Under Armour skirts and wondered what she was going to do with her life. Wondered what it was she had already done. She tried to will herself to think about her book, but she seemed unable to settle her brain into productive or creative thought patterns. Instead, she kept a kind of paralyzed witness as memories long past surfaced and surfaced beside more recent failures. Where was the joy she had felt all those years ago? Had it really been there or was she projecting backward? What made her unlovable and someone else lovable? How had she arrived here? Had the last fifteen years of her life counted for anything? If so, what? Where was Sam? It was as though she could not process the present moment at all, here on this mildewed plastic chair, whistle around her neck, squinting against the light reflected off of the silver European sports cars in the parking lot.

At night she came home before her mother, and showered off the pool stink and the sunscreen, collapsed into sweats, and watched TV as she and her mother ate through their bachelorette dinners. Salmon resting atop bagged salad, buttered noodles, crackers and cheese when they didn't feel like cooking, a glass of wine for each. Conversation a comfortable loop of track they loped together. *You'll never believe this guy they brought into work today: methhead, bone through skin. Have you heard from Sam yet?*

Don't let it get you down. What about your other friends? Who's still here? I'm so glad you're home (a little cautious here, don't push, don't scare away this parakeet of a daughter, so lightly alit on the sofa. She is unhappy, yes, you can see that the winds that blew her back home might just as quickly arrow her away from you, maybe forever. That tension between wanting the best for your children, and wanting them always within the distance of your grasping arms). Once: *How is the book going?* The silence that made the mother look up. (Still there. How far to push? She had a vague feeling it was not going well but she wondered if this was just because she was a pessimist by nature, her days full of needles and charts, rounds and the stink of bleach, bodies, vomit and wounds; all the bad decisions and luck the four counties could cough up. It's okay. Don't push. Let it go.)

For her part, Stevie would, indeed, pad her way back to her bedroom every night to sit at her old white particleboard desk, in the heavy old office chair she'd found hulking in the basement and stare at her computer screen. But the pathetic truths of her life kept planting themselves in front of her. She was thirty-two and what did she have to show for it? The job in New York had been a stop-gap, just something to pay the bills, but it had somehow gone on for nearly a decade. She'd had no real friends when she left. Drinking acquaintances from work. A succession of skittish boyfriends who all came complete with a set of fun and adorable college friends who became her friends, then disappeared forever when the skittishness turned to panic and the boys dumped her.

"The tribes of New York," her work friend Tovah had said to her once. They'd both been deeply, irresponsibly drunk on a Tuesday night following, for both, the dissolution of another relationship, which meant, for Stevie, the loss of another set of friends. Tovah's ex had been stifling: couples cooking classes. Maclaren strollers already picked out. But Tovah was not the designer-stroller type. She sang heavy-metal karaoke at Arlene Grocery on Wednesday nights. Tovah was loud and funny, slightly older than Stevie, and very, very cool. Stevie wanted to be friends with Tovah, but would never be cool enough. She'd auditioned for a permanent-friend role once—had gone with Tovah to a friend's party in a Tribeca loft (more money): a sweaty night, a live DJ, beautiful theatre people who talked about themselves incessantly, who asked Stevie nothing. One of them had plucked at her pilled work cardigan and raised an eyebrow. The shame. Stevie would never be a part of this crowd, it was obvious. But Tovah seemed to like her company in times of crisis and so had called her.

"Job, college, prep school, suburb. Everybody's tribes come from one of those."

Stevie recognized this truth as soon as she'd heard it. A little late to the party, Stevie had begun to realize how many of her acquaintances had money. She had no savings and lived paycheck to paycheck, and it embarrassed her to realize how long she'd stupidly believed this to be true of everyone she knew who was her age in New York. How naive of her not to have realized earlier: they had their own east coast vocabulary, an in-group code of places and private jokes that came from the network of private schools, ivies (large and small) and Seven Sisters colleges that made up their interconnecting webs of social groups and work acquaintances (in the foreign parlances of these webs she had learned of eating clubs, Head of the Charles, the Jitney; of Elm and Key; the Fuck Truck) and their own shared set of experiences that seemed to be more or less the same whether they were from Wesleyan or Princeton, Trinity or Smith. They all had nicknames, especially the men, and some of them had jerseys with these nicknames printed on them, though they weren't athletes and the jerseys were worn only on special occasions that usually involved drinking to the point of senselessness, though you would have been wrong to call them bros, or jocks, or stupid. This was a way of speaking that was the opposite of Midwestern: secretive, wry, insider-y. A language made by people who would one day have a say in the ways language was woven through the culture. They would be ad execs and screenwriters and the first generation of start-up geniuses to decide what the internet would be for.

Years later, in a different job, long after this boyfriend (Tattooed Dave was it?) and this drunken night with Tovah, she'd recognize the wealth of Anderson Anderson right away and feel equally repelled by and attracted to it. There was the way he said "tom-ah-to" instead of tomato; the withering look one of his friends had given her when she spoke excitedly of her corporate museum card, which gave her free admission to the Met and the MoMA; the way they were always going away to stay with distant friends on summer weekends; how they used "summer" as a verb. Everything was tasteful: the cute brick ranch with the saltwater pool in Southampton, the Tudor in Connecticut, the two-floor condo on Cape May, the renovated eighteenth-century farmhouse in the Berkshires. Nothing you could call a mansion. But then she'd notice, say, a little Warhol in the downstairs powder room (even the term *powder room*). Or the fact that the hand soap in that powder room was sixty dollars a bottle. She'd remember: these were second homes. How did one even keep a second home? Who looked after it when you weren't there? Who kept its fridges full of mineral water and pinot grigio? Just thinking about it stressed her out.

Last summer, Anderson's friends had had a particularly robust wedding season. Their wedding announcements showed up in *The New York Times* and, weekend after weekend, Stevie and Anderson put on their fancy clothes (he: a black floral Thom Browne suit and Stubbs and Wootton skull smoking slippers, she: a Ralph Lauren fishtail evening dress she'd found in a Filene's basement for 80% off its original price and metallic leather-look PU heels) and twirled through the private oaky ballrooms of the members-only clubs that dotted the city. On-site sushi chefs. R&B bands studded with lesser-known Motown alumni. His female friends threw spendy bachelorettes—CentroFly rented out; bottle service and a personalized drag show at Lucky Cheng's—that she was invited to by default. It was the closest she would come to a Cinderella story, the closest she would come to being rich. She understood then why people embezzled and lied and stole. She began to cling too tightly. This clinging caused Anderson to see her, as if for the first time. He told her one night, as they cruised the rooftop of the Met for a private fundraiser, that she was talking too loudly. Another night, he'd looked at the leopard-print camisole she'd put on for drinks at Dorian's with his friends and wondered if she might want to wear something "less trashy." He'd started to ask her to split more dinners out and stopped picking up the tabs at bars. He'd told her, thoughtfully, somehow managing to sound and appear kindly as he said it, that she wasn't beautiful or graceful, or even that pretty, but that there was, after all, something about her. This was the last "compliment" he would ever give her.

The chlamydia, the intern—none of it had surprised her, in hindsight.

And anyway, wasn't it what she deserved? She'd understood he was boring and of middling intelligence long before Eugenia had arrived on the scene. It was the money that had been interesting to her. Anthropologically, she'd told herself. Because it was so different than her own experience. But when it was gone, she knew that this had also been a lie. She wanted to be rich, just like everyone else. He'd tried to be nice, in his own way. He'd taken her out to eat at Sushi Samba, which was loud and flashy—hard to make a scene, and she knew right away from the look on his face what he was about to do. She'd looked around at the tasteful paper chandeliers, the glittering columns and the beautiful people around her and said goodbye to them. She said goodbye to their rude and poreless server and the voluptuous cabernet with its dung-and-leather undertones suspended at the top of its crystal stem like a giant purple blossom. She said goodbye to all the shoes on all the feet in the dining room, most of which were more expensive than her rent, whose owners had no idea how much money they had in their checking accounts right now, if they even had checking accounts.

She didn't really care what he was saying to her. It sounded like some poorly written dialogue from the beginning of a romantic comedy where the heroine is dumped by the terrible cardboard person she is dating, paving the way for her to meet and fall in love with her soul mate. As his mouth moved at her regretfully, she made up her own dialogue. *It's not you, it's me,* said the false Anderson Anderson. *But it's not even really me. It's the disappearing middle class and the fucked up late capitalist divide that keeps us trapped in our own little castes—my stock rallying forever, yours plunging off a cliff. Plus, that leopard-print camisole made you look like an extra on Dynasty.*

She imagined flinging her cabernet right in his face and storming out of this beautiful restaurant forever.

But no, instead, she heard and forgot his dumb excuses for breaking up with her almost immediately, finished the wine, and let him give her a final hug as he hailed himself a cab and left her on Barrow Street alone. A week later, she would find him and Eugenia licking each other in a crusty corner of Niagara, and a week after *that* she'd be fired, diagnosed with chlamydia and given the awful news about Jen, all in a single day.

"What's your tribe?" Stevie had asked Tovah, slightly hopeful that she might become a part of it. Maybe already was, somehow without knowing.

"Combo: Bard-High-School-slash-CUNY-Jew. We hate all those Dalton and Dartmouth assholes. Except, of course, for marriage. Obviously. What's yours?"

"What?" said Stevie.

"Your tribe."

"Oh, me? I don't have one."

And this had still been the state of affairs when she'd left New York—no boyfriend, no friends, no job, no tribe. She had framed it as a choice, but in reality, she had flunked New York. And that's why she was here in this ancient squeaky chair, at the desk where she used to write editorials for the high-school newspaper about potholes in the Taylor High parking lot, heart pounding hard, thinking about her life and its indecisive, haphazard shape, missing the city she had grown to hate, feeling sorry for herself.

Up until her mother had dropped the bomb about the foreclosure, she'd been able to convince herself that she was still adjusting, that she was, indeed and actually this time, an anthropologist, studying the contours of her own upended and brand-new life. Collecting observations, making field reports, watching from a distance and that all this would come seamlessly pouring out once she'd made the decision to sit down and write. But every time she made the decision to begin her book, she felt paralyzed. The book had become a much bigger piece of the puzzle than she'd thought it would be.

She'd approached Elvis after the Gringos dinner when her mother had announced the foreclosure and asked him for an advance. He kept an office at the Taylor Rec Center, where she'd done her lifeguarding training, and she'd gone down there one rainy day, when Greg had oozed over the phone to order her, once again, to close the club pool early.

She'd found Elvis whistling tunelessly to himself in a janitor's closet, and she'd been charmed but when he'd emerged and she'd said hi, his face had fallen and the whistling had stopped abruptly. She'd felt an apology at her lips but had no idea why.

"Miller," he said, "I wasn't expecting you." And he'd looked around as though he were worried about being seen with her, then he'd ushered her into an office and shut the door, despite the fact that there was no guard on duty. An elderly woman breast-stroked slowly across the pool.

"Hey," she said, swallowing the apology. "I was wondering about. . . ." She was nervous. She realized it made her more nervous to talk to him than to fuck him. "Something's come up with my family. It looks like my mom is going to lose her house. Our house. I guess it's in foreclosure or something? I'm not really sure." She swallowed. "I know you said there'd be a lot of" and here she dropped her voice to a whisper, "money. Coming out of. You know. The thing."

He snorted at her from behind the faux-wood desk. "The office isn't bugged, Miller." He leaned back in his chair and looked at her for a long minute, doing some sort of calculus. "I can't do it. Sorry. I'm sorry for your mom, but I'm paying you based on what we sell, and. . . ." he'd shrugged. "You haven't sold that much yet, so. . . ."

Stevie reddened. "It's not my fault the weather's been lousy and Greg keeps closing us down."

Elvis narrowed his eyes and stood up. He came around to her and put his hands on her shoulders and gently squeezed. "You're good at persuading people to do things, Miller. Maybe you could persuade Greg not to close so often."

She tried hard not to understand what, if anything, he was getting at. She struggled to look at him over a shoulder. "Shouldn't that be your job?" she said.

He sighed and took his hands off of her, then walked over to his office door and opened it. The woman in the pool was now on a kickboard, and she breathed rhythmically into the water in front of the kickboard.

"Good to see you, Miller. I'll see what I can do, okay?"

But he hadn't sounded all that sincere.

And so now the pressure was on. In what she presumed was a lie, she'd accidentally told her mother the truth. The fate of her family's home really was now pinned to what seemed to Stevie like a long shot—publishing a book that didn't yet exist—and this was not turning out to be helpful in terms of generating pages. There was too much riding on the book. But also: how could she possibly write down this—let's be honest—record of her failures, and expect someone to publish it? What was she supposed to be writing about? Her dead, estranged friend, who was maybe, as it turned out, her last true friend? The old boyfriend whose grief-stricken horniness she had mistaken for rekindling? The truth that it was the dead estranged friend he'd really, probably, been after all along? How could it be that the friends who had broken her heart in high school, the ones she had left behind, would be the people she wanted now? And how had things spun so far, so fast, out of Stevie's control?

Suddenly she felt like she had absolutely nothing to say, and what had seemed like a good idea a couple of months ago, now seemed like a colossal mistake. The only hope was if she could somehow write about the drugs, but if she did that, she certainly wouldn't be able to keep selling them. It was a quandary.

The experience of her brain chewing through her already ravaged sense of self was, by now, familiar. Every night when she sat down to write, this tickertape of grievances began. The deluge of doubt and negative self-talk had become something like a wall between her and the book. Was this writer's block? It was how she felt: arrested and disordered by the spew of thoughts that blocked out all semblance of narrative. She thought of these privately and awfully as "Reasons to Kill Yourself: An Ode to Jen."

A little while after the dinner at Gringos, she had written a blog post from the depths of these nightly failures.

Does This Deserve a Title?

The thing about moving home is you are moving home. Deep, right? I mean home is this box full of old stuff, and some of it's fun and you get it out and turn it around in your hands and wind it up and it dances, and something in you melts a little and returns to itself. But there are other things in the box too—broken things that have always been broken, but that you forgot were in there, broken things that were whole the last time you checked but now have chunks missing and jagged, cutting edges.

I'm glad to be home. It feels like the right place. But it's a haunted place. Haunted by Jen, for sure, but also, surprisingly, the ghosts are of people who are still alive—the men who have left this house and refused to return—my dad, my brother. They aren't here, but somehow their leaving is still hurting us.

I left too, I guess. But not so irrevocably. Maybe that's why I came back—because someone had to.

The things I can't say are beginning to stack up. Not to worry. I'm fine. But it may be a little while until I figure out how to say what needs to be said about it all.

Her readership, which seemed to have shrunk from small to tiny since her move, had clucked a little in the comments. A blogger named Sammy who wrote her own blog, Office Cult., told her to hang in there. Someone reading this post in the future might have thought of the word "vaguebooking," which would be coined the following year, to describe the practice of writing melodramatic yet unspecific Facebook posts in an attempt to get people to respond to you with care and concern. But more likely they would not have read the post at all, as the practice of blogging and its foray into book publishing was about to come crashing down on the heads of every witty white twenty-something writer with a Wordpress or Livejournal account.

Now, a few days later, Amanda Collins (who would be ruffled by this tiny cultural disaster but pivot quickly and successfully to baby-food cookbooks) was calling Stevie, interrupting her nightly desk-fugue state to find out what the fuck was going on.

"What the fuck is going on?" the agent had demanded.

"What?" said Stevie. She could hear the outro music to *Dancing with the Stars* in the living room, where her mom had propped herself, feet up. The cursor in her Word doc blinked dumbly and Stevie wondered if she could sync up her heartbeat to it if she concentrated hard.

"Your latest blog post. It sounds like you're quitting."

"Quitting?" Stevie wondered if it were possible to quit something that had so far earned her nothing.

"Listen, a book is different from a blog, I know that. But the blog is the content that draws them into the book. If you don't keep writing about whatever shit you're going through at home on the blog, then how will anyone know that they want to read your book? Also, please, you need to tell me what's going on. Why all the mystery? How far are you in the book now anyway?"

Stevie wanted to hang up on Amanda Collins and never speak to her again. But instead she told the lie that writers have always told agents and editors.

"A few chapters in. It's going pretty good." Stevie pretended to forget Amanda Collins's other questions, and Amanda Collins, mollified by the lie (which she knew was a lie), pretended to forget she had asked them. Like any successful agent, she knew getting a book out of a writer was a little like giving a hand job—you had to know when to squeeze and when to stroke.

"Well, good," said Amanda brusquely. "Just don't stop writing your blog. What's going on out there, anyway? You're lifeguarding right?"

"Just running a drug front out of a local country club pool."

Amanda barked her laugh. "Girl, don't tease me like that! What a book that would be."

Stevie's pulse quickened. "Yeah, but I'd end up in jail."

"Worth it! Anyway, I'd love to see a couple chapters in the next few weeks. But first, write me a proposal. Get it to me next week. It's not likely anyone will bite for a debut, but you never know."

She was still stewing-slash-panicking about this new development when her phone rang again—this time a local number she didn't know.

"Stevie? It's Melinda. Fitzpatrick?" Melinda Fitzpatrick, wife of Doug, haver of two small children, former Marlborough Light enthusiast, current dental hygienist. "I heard you moved back. After the funeral."

"Melinda, it's so good to hear from you. I've been meaning—" Stevie heard the fumbly thud of a dropped phone and when Melinda put the phone back to her mouth, she was already speaking again, "—call *you*, but I'm elbow-deep in bath-time right now—it's always something over here—so I thought I'd see if you wanted to come over tomorrow night. Doug's cooking dinner."

Stevie brightened. After weeks of chasing Sam, Stevie hadn't felt like calling other old friends, like risking more rejection. It was interesting to *her* that she had moved home, she had realized, but not to anyone else. Stevie's sudden appearance on the scene did not make a difference in their lives, which had been developing and deepening in Taylor without her for a decade and a half by that point. At once, she felt the weight of her own loneliness.

"Yes," she said. "Yes, I'd love to."

Somewhere in the distant soundscape of Melinda's house there was another thud followed by a thin, alarming howl. "Oh my god, gotta go. I'll text you directions and time and stuff."

Stevie turned onto the treeless subdivision north of town. Mel's text just said Elm Park, but as she puttered past a beige stucco McMansion whose owner was edging his lawn and frowning suspiciously at her old Jetta, she came to a fork. Elm Park Drive or Elm Park Court? She bore right and passed Elm Park Lane as well, and here, before she could make up her mind, she found herself turning right again, as though compelled by some force outside herself. The street had sidewalks now, and twenty years of growth, both natural and unnatural. The windows in the three-story homes were so big as to resist curtaining, and each house was set surprisingly close to its neighbor—but this was unmistakably their old hang-out spot, Mars. Stevie followed the road until it terminated in those same, familiar, reflective yellow signs. Back then it had been all clay dunes that lined the road, piled up from the earth movers that seemed to be forever breaking new ground. They had watched from their hotboxed hand-me-down cars as the trees and pasture of the old farmland disappeared and sprouted, instead, a road, then houses that looked out over the fallow fields that the farmer or, more likely, his children, still held onto, to be sold for even more money at a later date, until the land had given up the last of its topsoil or the lease ran out and there was no one left to farm it anymore.

This was it: where they'd come to smoke weed and ride out the rest of their googly-eyed acid trips and drink the two-dollar forties their friend Sean, who had a man-thick beard at sixteen, would pick up for them at the convenience stores near the college. They fucked out here, in cars, or on unzipped sleeping bags on the weedy undergrowth, and got bit by chiggers, and painted the bites with clear nail lacquer, like you were supposed to. They laid on the warm tarry road in late July and looked up at the stars—which made them feel small—and felt the drugs thrum and ebb inside their heads, which made them feel big, and they sighed up into those firefly-lit nights, trying to feel the whole world at once but feeling only the slippage of it instead. *These are the days to hold onto*, they said to themselves, to each other, quoting Billy Joel, because this was something they knew they were supposed to say, but they didn't know why, not really, not yet.

Stevie's phone rang. "Is that your black VW down at the end of the drive?" It was Melinda. Stevie checked her rearview and saw a distant figure on a porch, waving.

"You bought a house on Mars?"

"I know, right? Who would ever have thought." Melinda laughed.

Stevie wondered wryly if all those times at Mars, bumming lighters and rolling jays from leftover McDonald's bags and humping in the shadow troughs made by car headlights and the hair-holding and the trying not to fly off the face of the earth, maybe Doug and Melinda had just been thinking of all the sweet real estate.

In fact, Melinda *had* planned to own a house on Mars for as long as it had existed. When she was little, her family had done their time in the trailer parks on the edge of Taylor. At age thirteen—old enough to know what she didn't want out of life—the smaller towns emptied their students into one of two junior high schools in the county and she met the boy who would become her husband. He spoke at length and with pride about his father's construction company and she would—largely unconsciously—begin to plan her future fiefdom.

This was what you could do when you stayed where you'd been planted. You could plan for the future in some substantial way. You knew the contours of everything intimately, there was no learning curve, so it was easier to make achievable goals for yourself. No accident in any of it.

And it *was* sweet. It was one thing to drive by one of the huge faux-

Gothic boxes, to see it from afar, like it was on TV, like a photo in a listing. It was quite another to be inside. To really see the giant red handblown glass chandelier that hung, like a threat, over their heads as they all hugged hello, new baby sandwiched between them; over the hardwood of Doug and Melinda's rich, dark floors, and the impossibly colored foams of their Crocs (hers an urpy, Pepto pink and his Kelly green); over the secrets of their finished basement: a carpet-walled room where he watched porn nightly on a projection-screen TV—the genitals on screen, enormous and slightly too dark; over the sewing room on the other side of that carpeted wall, where Melinda secretly ripped the seams of his work pants and stitched the crotches back up too high, so that they pinched and chafed the tender skin of his balls.

The baby squawked inside the hug and Stevie let go of Melinda, who held the baby and who now acquiesced to the smacking sounds it had begun to make by casually unbuttoning her shirt.

"You want a tour of the place? Doug?"

Doug nodded and made a beckoning motion toward Stevie. A younger boy had appeared from somewhere, a shy shadow behind him. He followed them quiet as a cat as Doug showed her the cold duplicitous basement, and upstairs the puffy king-sized bed under the vaulted ceiling, the Jacuzzi bathtub, the Jack and Jill sinks. He toured her out to their chocolate-stained cedar deck, past the covered jacuzzi and the view: east and west out over the fiefdoms of backyards, each rolled out behind its house like the train of a furry green gown. The groupings of iron patio furniture and grill carts, Sunbrellas and bright plastic lawn toys (here a bright green turtle sandbox mounded up from the earth, there a red pedal car with huge bulging eyes for headlights sat askew on a paved patio in front of a walk-out basement) huddled near each home. It was all very grand, but somehow seemed a little fragile too, like any wolf could come along and blow it down.

And in fact, in five months three of their neighbors (including one next door) would be foreclosed upon. And they would not be able to sell this house, which would be worth less than they owed on it, which was way over a quarter of a million dollars. And they would be stuck waiting for the market to recover, watching the neighborhood empty out, and it would begin to reclaim the desolate, planetary feel it had when they were teenage interlopers.

Right now, though, the high ceilings and recessed lights, the deep prairie of the colorless carpet, was nearly intoxicating. The entire house smelled new and sterile, as if it had just been unwrapped, whole, from miles of heavy plastic. Stevie wished it were hers.

After the tour, Stevie perched in the new kitchen on a metal stool with a slat in its middle—something made to look industrial and vintage but which, judging by the perfect powdered metal finish of it, was certainly newly made and probably very expensive—and noticed not one grease stain anywhere. The older kid—who could have been anywhere between five and eight, Stevie had no idea about these things—stared at her from behind Doug's legs and she felt like she always did around kids: awkward and seen-through.

"I had an IUD," Melinda whispered as she plopped the now-full and wiggly baby into her green, jungle-themed Excersaucer. "She was a total surprise." Stevie hadn't seen Melinda in a decade but she looked essentially the same beneath her makeup and expensive boot-cut yoga pants which somehow, maybe because they were black, or because she had paired them with a faux-fur hoodie-vest, seemed more formal than their genre would seem to imply. Stevie, in her Umbros and sweatshirt—she never seemed to be able to put on anything that required more effort than this, these days—felt sloppy by comparison. "I had such bad PPD with that one," Melinda pointed accusatorily toward Doug's legs. "I just wasn't totally ready. But, you know what they say about God and plans."

As Melinda spoke, the kid headbutted Doug's ass. Doug tapped him hard on the head, "Stop" he mouthed, while picking furtively at his crotch. Stevie closed her eyes hard for a moment, and when she opened them Melinda was setting a glass of white wine on the island in front of her. "Guess what? It's wine o'clock," she said, and pointed to a clock that hung above their kitchen sink where, indeed, in place of numbers, each hour read "wine o'clock" in looping script.

Doug took his hand from his pants and set it on his son's head once again, disengaging the boy from his legs, then disappeared out the sliding glass doors to the porch where he fiddled with their enormous, shiny grill.

"He hates when I tell people, but it's the truth! He also hates when I tell people I had C-sections so I could keep my ladygirl tight, but that's the truth too. People should know what they're getting into when they have kids." While Melinda talked about her vagina, she grabbed an enormous bag of pre-shredded salad out of their Sub-Zero, tossed it into a large bowl and dumped in half a bottle of Paul Newman brand Italian dressing.

"So what was New York like? That must have been crazy! What were you doing again? Some kind of recruiting?"

"Mid-level creatives. Magazine editors, ad people, PR that sort of thing."

"So you got them jobs and that was your job?"

"Yep. Pretty boring."

"Did you ever get, like—oh who's the *Vogue* editor, the *Devil Wears Prada* chick?"

"Anna Wintour."

"Yeah did you ever get Anna Wintour a job?"

"No, she's still the editor of *Vogue*."

"Anyone famous?"

"No, it was mostly mid-career people."

"Did you ever try to get yourself a job like theirs? You used to be in drama or on the newspaper or something, right? Didn't you want a job like that?"

Yes of course. She had been insanely jealous of her clients.

"I couldn't. I didn't have any of those skills. My only skill was getting people with those skills jobs."

After waitressing her way through a bachelor degree's worth of night classes at Marymount, she'd first picked up a job at a smaller tech recruiter, then, when the industry contracted overnight and her client list disappeared, taking their shady "stock options" with them, she'd lucked into Britely, where she'd been able to contract with more artsy clientele—Nerve, Penguin Group, *BOMB* Magazine—only to be eventually seduced by stupid fucking Anderson Anderson and his snobby patrician-hipster charm. For some reason, she assumed that working to put creatives (how she hated the nouning of that adjective) into jobs would somehow help her get a job like that someday too. Or no, she didn't really assume that. She just saw herself in one of their jobs at some undefined point in the future and never bothered to question this assumption or take the simplest steps toward actually making it happen, like getting an assistant job in a field, instead of recruiting adjacently. Mostly, her job was to sort clients into job slots and so that's what she did. Watched the talent accumulate from her side of the glass. It was the same feeling she got during college, waitressing at Pepe's, a pan-European bistro in Midtown, when she'd decant something vintage and delicious—a fizzy Dom, say—the wine *in* her hands but always moving *away* from her, into the crystal, onto the table of her customers, through their MAC'ed lips, down the taut, severe mechanics of their throats, past the wealthy juttings of clavicle and rib. The world-sized valley between them: server and served.

Mel was silent for a minute, working the salad hard. Then she said, "You came home though." People always wanted to hear how amazing New York was and how great your life there was, but they also wanted to hear that Iowa was better. She looked at Stevie sideways, and Stevie understood that she was asking how she'd failed.

This was the hardest part to explain, because even after all that trying, there was still the city. The glorious, exhausting, soul-crushingly expensive city and the way it had competed, for so long, with an agonizing homesickness that had never gone away. She knew if she told Melinda she'd been laid off, Melinda would think she understood. It made sense to move home—especially under those circumstances—but that wasn't it at all. It's that her soul had a homing device planted in it and try as she might, she couldn't fight the magnet that drew her here, toward Taylor, toward Sam, even toward Jen, even though she was gone. It was like a magnet drawing her back into the past from the present. To the pool, to those epic days that stretched into humid, smoky nights when she had and would always live forever. Stevie didn't know how to explain it to someone who'd never left. So she didn't. And forget mentioning the book.

Half the time it didn't even occur to Stevie to mention it to people. And that probably said something in and of itself about her investment and attitude toward the project. Luckily, Melinda found a different conversational stream in which to eddy.

"I mean, I get it. Personally, I would have moved back after 9/11." Mel laughed, "Personally, I never would have moved at all, I guess. I don't know how you did it. Were you there for that? For 9/11?"

Stevie was relieved to be moving on from personal catastrophes to larger, national ones. "I was there. I mean, I wasn't *there* but. It was pretty awful. Everyone was scared for a long time." And even after that, though the fear dissipated into something difficult to touch and farther away. Something like a cloud they all moved through and under. "Everybody was softer for a while. More polite." This too was hard to explain so Stevie stopped trying.

"What about stars? Did you see the stars?"

"No, you can't see the stars. Except for that night, the night of the blackout four years ago. I went up onto the roof of my apartment building and you could see them all. All the stars. That was amazing, actually. At first everyone thought it was another terror attack. I walked from midtown to the Upper West Side because they shut the subway down. You'd get the radio reports from the cabs sitting in the gridlock as you walked. And the radios reported that it wasn't an attack, and then the whole thing turned into a block party. Grocery stores were giving away steaks and people were like, cooking out and playing music on their stoops."

Mel laughed, "No honey, I meant like celebrities. Woody Allen and Seinfeld."

Stevie smiled, embarrassed. "Oh. Not really. I saw Willem Dafoe carrying a TV out of Best Buy once."

"Willem Dafoe. . . ."

"*Shadow of the Vampire. Once Upon a Time in Mexico*." Mel was a blank. "Um, *Spiderman*? The bad guy."

"Riiiight. William Dafoe. Knowing you, I would think you'd have some crazy hook-up stories with some famous band guys or something."

Stevie laughed. The closest she'd come was a Lower East Side glam rocker who called himself Lucky and had given her HPV. This was in college, when she was still in thrall to the bartender/artist tribe. The dancer-turned-bartender. The record-label-VP-turned-bartender. The teacher-turned-bartender. At the time, the men, before she got to know them, seemed vaguely ennobled by their failures. Afterwards, she'd make herself feel better by holding these failures against them. Then on to her corporate days and attendant shift to the Ivy League tribe, the gristmill finance bros so proud of their time-shares in Southampton, eventually, chlamydia. She thought of Elvis and wondered whether he considered himself part of a tribe. Probably not—he was too predatory to be properly part of anything. What STD would accompany this current mistake? Her stomach lurched.

"Come on, Stevie. You used to be such a slut," Melinda gamefully jostled her with an elbow, eyebrow up and Stevie laughed again and tried not to hear the slightly smug note in her voice. She was relieved when Doug came back in to get the pre-made patties from the fridge and Melinda reminded him about the buns and poured herself a second glass of wine. She swung the bottle toward Stevie, but Stevie's glass was still nearly full. Melinda moved the salad to the island between them where it sat under the gray enamel pendant lamps like a criminal, oily and wilting. The baby smacked something on its Excersaucer which made an electronic croaking noise. Mel seemed not to hear it, but instead gazed blankly past Stevie at Doug conjuring fire like an oracle, with great effort and some peril.

"Listen, Stevie, don't do it."

"Don't do what, Mel?" Stevie asked, lightly, but she already knew.

"Any of it. Husband, kids. I am so fucking tired and Doug, he masturbates all the time."

Stevie tries to smile, "Mel—"

"No, I'm serious. Like *all* the time."

Then she smiled wide and Stevie heard the hiss of the slider opening.

"Mel, take him? I'm grilling, not babysitting." Doug was palming the boy's head again, pushing him into the kitchen, toward the women.

Mel smiled too-big at her tousled son, standing there like something lost, at Doug's busy form bending over the grill.

"Babysitter," Mel muttered into her wine glass. "How can you babysit your own kids?"

Stevie's burger was cold on one side, her bun burnt. Dinner was mostly spent trying to coax the children to eat *their* dinners, which shared no components with the adults' or each other's. Finally, after the baby had spit out her fourth straight mouthful of sweet potatoes and had begun to cry, Melinda gathered her up and plopped her into Stevie's lap. "Let me do the dishes quick."

Stevie, who had been examining the cold end of her burger for a more well-done section, was surprised and had to clutch herself to the baby to keep them both from sliding off her chair. When she looked down, the baby was smiling up at her through a film of orange puree and yellow-green snot. The baby was heavier than she'd imagined it would be and there was something alarmingly comforting about its weight on her lap. It patted her cheek with one sticky hand. Stevie felt an unaccountable urge to bite the hand hard, and in fact was moving her mouth toward the hand almost unconsciously when Melinda interrupted, swiping the baby's hand and face with a damp washcloth. The baby began to cry again. Stevie bounced a leg, shushed it. She was bemused by how much she was enjoying hosting this fussy stranger in the crook of her body. The way everything inside her seemed to bend toward it. The baby's flour-sack-bottomed heaviness.

Stevie had always told herself she didn't want kids—their inconvenience and neediness was inconceivable to her. When she thought about them, an abyss yawned open in her mind and she knew, if she had a kid, that all her love and time and money would flow into it for the rest of her life. She had told herself that this wasn't for her. That the freedom that she had reached for and won as a teenager, the freedom of moving to New York and starting a brand new life and sleeping in shifts with Siobhán and fucking her boss and never having to speak to her family if she didn't want to, and now, the freedom to do bad things with and for Elvis, that this freedom was somehow better than having a child, because it was a freedom over which she presided with complete control (or at least this is what she told herself as she lay each night below Jim Morrison), though admittedly when she thought about it that way, made it seem a little less free and a little more rigid. The pleasures of these freedoms were complicated, fraught. The baby on her lap hinted at something simpler, elemental. Satisfying. She felt the poke of an icy finger—had she been making the wrong decisions all her adult life? Holding something at arm's length that she actually wanted? There was the terror that lurked behind such a decision, and this was the terror of loss. Of the possibility of losing something so monumental that the self was lost with it. Self-annihilation through procreation. She put her nose on the baby's wispy head. Yes, probably. She'd been doing everything else wrong, it seemed. Why not this too.

The doorbell rang.

"Shit," said Melinda from the sink. "Doug? Could you get it? It's the girls—I forgot I told them to come over a little early, to welcome Stevie to town."

"Hmm?" said Stevie, baby trance momentarily broken.

Melinda took Stevie's wine glass and walked it over to the part of the open-plan space that was designated as the living room. She sat it on the coffee table and patted the couch. "Bring that peanut over here and take a seat! It's book club night."

It was Ellie, whom she hadn't seen since the funeral, and someone else she didn't recognize. Like Ellie, the stranger was also taut and blond, but seemed more fragile. As if some internal force was holding her together, but barely. The two women arrived at the kitchen island to receive their chardonnays.

"Stevie, you remember Ellie and Bonnie right?"

"Hi, Ellie," Stevie gave a little wave from the couch and the baby grabbed her thumb, "but I don't think we've met."

"Oh," Melinda looked surprised then troubled for a moment. "Bonnie is Sam's wife. I guess I thought you'd know each other."

There was a pinwheeling out of the room and then a sound of surprise that she realized, a little too late was her own. Stevie felt herself blush, ordered herself to stop blushing, blushed even more. The baby began to squirm and fuss in her lap like a dog before a tornado and Stevie was glad that this gave her something to do with her hands. As her heart beat out of her chest (was it actually visible to Bonnie?), she kissed the baby's head and beeped its nose, unable to look at Bonnie as she said, "I didn't know Sam was married. He didn't say anything at the funeral." Nope—too defensive. Stevie tried not to actually cringe. Why had she said something about the funeral? What if his wife knew about their fucking? Probably she did. This was obviously the reason he hadn't returned Stevie's calls. And below the panic, a voice that she recognized, the same one that always surfaced, the part of her that could still be surprised by people. A wife? That asshole. What about her book? What about her plan? And then, below that another, lower, smaller voice: *You knew.* Some part of you knew all along. Both that Sam, handsome charming Sam, wouldn't be a single thirty-something, not in a place like Taylor and also that she had been kidding herself all this time that he'd felt the same way she did after the funeral. God, he'd been so drunk—she'd heard him retching in the bathroom while she was cooking them morning eggs like some kind of sucker. Of course he hadn't felt the same way. Hadn't he called her Jen in the dark that night, more than once, no matter how much she had tried to pretend she hadn't heard? It had always been about Jen for him. Even when they were together, it had been about Jen. She was the glue that had held them together. Without her, there was no them. Stevie pushed all this down so fast and hard she nearly leapt up off the couch.

Bonnie nodded her head at Stevie, corners of her mouth turned under, nostrils flaring in disgust. She tried to make her voice light but she avoided Stevie's eyes and instead stared at the baby in her lap. "Apparently, he was so drunk at the funeral, I'm not sure he could have told you his own name, much less mine." It was an attempt at a joke and Bonnie forced an awkward laugh at the end of it, but Melinda and Ellie didn't join in. Stevie watched them exchange quick looks. "You were good friends with her too, weren't you? He always used to refer to you as Steve and for a long time I'd thought you were a guy. Steve, Sam, and Jen. Just two bros and their hot girl friend."

Stevie felt a spike of anger at the erasure, which poked through the pathetic scrim of her self-pity. It hadn't really ever been about her. She felt her face getting hot again.

Then, Jen's voice in her head. *Stevie. You must chill.*

"They were totally in love with each other," Melinda giggled and Stevie could suddenly hear the drunk in it, something let loose and out of control. "Jen and Sam I mean. You were already gone I think, but right before you left there was that juicy rumor, for a while, that you broke up with Sam to be with Jen, but then you went to New York and ruined that," Melinda made a sound with her mouth like all the air going out of a tire. "Then it was just Sam and Jen, Sam and Jen. Do you remember?" she said to no one in particular, "He followed her around *everywhere*."

Stevie and Bonnie locked eyes though Stevie wasn't sure what it was that was being communicated between them.

"It was weird though, like they were always together but they weren't really together?"

Why did Stevie tremble? Why did her mouth go numb and why did the thin skin pound over the curve in her ears?

"Like he was stalking her or something? We'd be sitting in the commons trying to finish trig homework or something and Sam would be there, with his back to us, by himself. Obviously listening but pretending not to. Or remember how Jen was in show choir? Jen told me once Sam went to all their shows, even their dress rehearsals. He sat in the back with everyone's parents and watched them. Remember those gold and blue lamè wrap dresses they had? Oh my god. Terrible. And he like, he gave her rides home from school and then just sat in his car on her street for like a half hour. She used to tell me all about it. But she, you know, she liked it kind of. Holy booty call, Bat—"

"Okay, Mel, how about some water?" Ellie appeared at Melinda's side with a glass. Then there was a silence in which Melinda seemed to realize what she'd done. Her mouth gaped, carp-like, and she seemed to be drowning in the air in front of them. "Ancient history, though right? And then he met Bonnie and she was the best thing that ever happened to him!" Melinda raised her water glass and took a deep drink. "Anyway, Doug and I were in Cancun and missed the funeral."

Ellie looked at Melinda for another long moment, then turned to Bonnie, "How's Sam, Bon?"

At least, thought Stevie, Melinda had taken the heat off of her for the moment.

Bonnie kept smiling at them, but her body seemed to vibrate on another frequency. If she'd been a drawing in a comic book, she would have been surrounded by tension lines. She was like something plucked—both instrument and bird—twanging and naked in front of them.

"I don't know. He hasn't been home in two weeks."

Ellie gasped and this seemed to startle Bonnie into movement. She walked unsteadily from the kitchen island and perched lightly on the arm of the couch, next to Stevie. She set her wine glass on the coffee table and rubbed her hands over her face. "He left for a conference, some realtor's thing, no big deal. But that was the weekend before Memorial Day. I haven't heard from him since. I think maybe he left me."

Stevie was now panicking in multiple directions—Bonnie's sudden proximity, whether or not she knew or would suss out the infidelity on her, and now the news about Sam missing. When had they spoken? She tried to remember the day but they were all blurring together lately. Had it already been two weeks ago?

"What conference? Where?" Melinda gasped between gulps of water as she and Ellie moved to the couch across from them.

The baby reached toward Bonnie, who looked down at it, grimaced slightly, and looked back up to Melinda, leaving Stevie to feel somewhat insulted on the baby's behalf.

"Chicago," said Bonnie, "Some mortgage thing I think?" and Stevie moved carefully, attempting nonchalance by softly scratching the baby's nearly bald head. It could have been a coincidence of course, that Jen lived in Chicago. That the last time she'd seen Sam, he'd been convinced of Jen's murder, seemed not to be able to give the idea a rest, seemed so convinced, she'd had to drag him out of Jen's parents' house when he'd attempted to interrogate one of her uncles while blind drunk. It could have been a coincidence, but that was doubtful.

Melinda was consoling Bonnie, who nodded that yes, she had called all the hospitals. Who noted that yes, they had indeed had a big blow-up fight—actually a series of fights—in the weeks leading up to the conference. And no, she hadn't yet called his parents, but she would tomorrow.

"Bonnie," Melinda gave her a look as if she'd caught her lying about going over her Weight Watchers points.

"I will, I really will," Bonnie sighed. "I just wanted one more night of feeling like things are still kind of normal."

It's been two weeks! Stevie's alarm bell rang out. *Definitely not normal!*

Melinda nodded and came over to embrace Bonnie, as did Ellie. The three of them stood there, old friends in a time of need, as Bonnie wept a little and Stevie sat nearby, making faces at the baby and awkwardly trying to disappear.

After some time, Ellie pulled back. "Why don't we do book club next week?"

Bonnie shook her head. "I've been home alone with this for so long. I'd rather think about something else for a change."

Melinda nodded and reached down under the coffee table and pulled out a book. "Well, let's get your mind off of it by talking about how amazing this book is. I forgot to ask, but obviously, Stevie, you've read *Eat, Pray, Love.*" Stevie became aware that her legs were wet and looked down to see a runny green substance dripping from her thigh onto Melinda's carpet. She was immediately relieved to have a reason to excuse herself. *Thanks, baby,* she telepathed to her shit-covered new friend as she handed her off to Melinda and made her way to the bathroom, and shortly after that, the front door, the car, and, in the car, to the nearby Taylor High parking lot. She parked her car and gazed out across the rolling grounds in front of the nondescript building, where a band of her peers had once burned the billboard-sized missive "420 4EVER" onto the lawn with weedkiller, and she began to hyperventilate.

Her vision blackened at the periphery and something thundered through her, huge, heavy and she let out a howl and rested her forehead against the steering wheel. She howled for Sam and what she couldn't have, for her lost friends, for the way her life seemed to be shrinking away to nothing at all and how she stood on it, dumb and doomed, floating out to sea like a penguin on an iceberg; for the missing weight of the baby on her lap. And underneath it all, a terrifying drumbeat of anxiety: where is he, where is he, where is he.

She was still anxious when she knocked on Bonnie's door later that week.

Chapter 8

Their bedroom was Ballet Slipper, the kitchen Goldenrod. Here in the dining room she had wanted a bright peacock but Sam had objected and so they'd settled on Twilight which, while a blue, actually tended toward a dark gray in the daylight. Bonnie sat at their beeswax-rubbed Danish walnut dining table and wondered, with ever-increasing alarm, where her husband was.

The Goldenrod had looked nice in chip and even in a footlong wash on the wall, but it had quickly become oppressive. Every time she walked into the kitchen she tasted mustard. It was too midcentury. That was a common mistake people made: they got into the midcentury stuff and then they wanted it all to be midcentury, down to the mustard walls and the shag carpet, and their houses became museums, like the All-Electric House outside of Kansas City, where she and Sam had traveled for a long weekend some years ago, before the bad times. The All-Electric House was a relic from the '50's, constructed by Kansas City Power and Light and outfitted with all the latest domestic gadgetry of the times. It had automated curtains and, over the fireplace, a kitschy painting of the sea breaking majestically against a rock formation, which slid back to reveal a hidden TV. Most vividly though, she remembered the out-of-season aluminum Christmas tree, which shone a frosty pink, spotlit through a cellophane color wheel. "Jetsonsesque" was how Sam had described it. To her, the house felt optimistic, a dream made material. Was there once a time when people's dreams had been so simple? Hers certainly had been: a husband, a house—a beautiful house—a time ago she'd thought, maybe a couple of babies growing up beneath doorjamb pencil marks. That was what people did when they got to a certain point. When they got settled and bored enough. When they'd figured out all the paint colors. Now though, the way things were going. . . .

As usual, the doorway was just a silent, pristine doorway, no children screaming through, no marks. Bonnie looked at her fingernails. They were East Hampton Cottage—just the barest breath of pink—and chipped from where she'd been gnawing on the tips. Before she'd had dreams, she'd been a nailbiter with an overbite and thick eyebrows that shook hands in the middle, the ghost of a mustache, a vast tumbleweed of pubic hair, back fat. Thank god for science. Thank god for good orthodontics and licensed estheticians and yoga instructors. Bonnie in her late thirties would be unrecognizable to Bonnie in her late teens and thank god, thank god for that.

The house too—they'd bought it for a song. Originally built in the sixties, the kitchen had never been updated and so everything went, even cabinets and flooring. $35,000. Under the appalling carpet: merely subfloors. New hardwoods throughout had been another, what, $15,000? The admittedly peevish scraping of the ceiling popcorn, the new porch and trellis, the finishing of the basement and subsequent claiming by Sam (that Cro-Magnon dictum of the new millennium: every man must have his cave), the asbestos removal. How many issues of *House Beautiful* and *Dwell* and *Better Homes and Gardens* had she mutilated and collaged onto the wall of her home office, alongside the swatches and chips and samples?

A few years later, while interval training at a gym many miles from Taylor, Iowa, Bonnie would stumble across an episode of *Hip Flip* while channel surfing the tiny TV on her treadmill and witness the demolition of this very kitchen. Of two sledges breaking, synchronized, through the mustard-colored walls, which she had never gotten around to repainting, through the white subway tile which had looked so modern when installed and now seemed dated and cheap. She would let out a small cry when the beefcake contractors, thighs and biceps flexing together, hooked their crowbars onto the white cabinet uppers and yanked them from their privileged elevation into the swirling dust below, like the toppling of the statue of a beloved dictator. "Look how open this space is now," huffed the contractor bohunk, who was covered in a light drywall dust, though his hair was still perfect.

Bonnie would come home from the gym that night and run her hands along the walls of every room in her significantly larger house and kiss her significantly wealthier husband on the top of his bald head as he sat in his study (no man cave here), and she would float into her walk-in closet, painted a warm Swiss Coffee white, past the marble-topped island littered with ring trees and clangy bangles, to the far side of it. She would grab her sturdiest kitten heel from the built-in bookshelf that held not books but shoes, sink to her knees and with a few sharp taps, put a small hole in the wall behind her row of hanging athleisure-wear, and then, a few inches further down the wall, another hole, and another. She would kneel there on the natural-fiber shag for some time, the shoe in one hand, the other holding her up as she tried to look directly into the holes. What was back there, anyway? She wondered this despite the fact that they had built the house themselves, that no one else had ever lived here in the space before them, and that, in fact, the space had not existed before they had visited the weedy plot with her new husband's architect friend and he had made a box with his hands and pointed it vaguely at the horizon and said, "Right here! Perfection." This house, which began as a space no bigger than the curved palms of the architect, had never had mustard walls or linoleum floors or speckled laminate countertops. But for a few minutes outside of time on the Moroccan wool shag, Bonnie will put her eye to the holes she's made in the wall and expect to see, somehow, into that old life: Sam blowing his mustache off his lips as he hand-washes the red Le Crueset casserole, a wedding gift from a gourmand uncle of Sam's; that old faucet with the spray head on a hose that would never stay fully retracted, but hung down from the curved spine of the spout. What had Sam called it? The elephant dick. Bonnie will sit on her very expensive wall-to-wall and follow the hollow tug of grief down the wormhole of a memory.

*

The problem with sitting in her dining room—her back so straight it was slightly arched toward the double sliders that looked out onto the house-length porch, which perched above a yard that fell dramatically away into a ravine filled with trees and brambles below (she could imagine throwing him over the railing and watching as he rolled away into this ravine and out of her life, forever)—and waiting for her husband to get home from wherever it was he'd gone, was that it felt like punishment, like he was punishing her for something, even though he was technically the one who deserved to be punished. And how she wanted to punish him. The scenarios spun through her mind so vividly they made her heart beat faster. She could punish with silence—freeze him out, thicken the atmosphere with her resentment—or with fury. She might scream and throw whatever was at hand at him for the satisfaction of watching him cower and duck. Sam was affable, a chatter. He would probably crumble under a regime of silence. But right now she was waiting, half in quiet desperation for all that she would do and say to him when he returned, half in worry—how did she know he hadn't smashed up on I-80, dead from drunk driving, or in jail for the same? Although maybe if she was being extremely truthful, she was really more like three-quarters angry, one-quarter worry. It did not escape her that she worried about him much less these days, as his behavior grew more erratic and strange. Like the thing with the driveway attack. She was nearly certain now he had punched out his own car window. The more confusing thing was that he was not, historically, a great liar, and as far as she could tell, when he told her he'd been attacked, he had not, strictly, been telling her a lie. He seemed to be suffering from some sort of paranoid tough-guy fantasy, which had been escalating, along with his drinking, since his friend's funeral, which had also been one of those nights he hadn't come home, a red flag she had missed. It had all been getting bad for a while. He always seemed to be walking around in a weird little daze, like he was always just waking up from a long, dreamy nap. The thing in the driveway may not have seemed like a lie, but his cover story certainly had. In the middle of the week (or was it three weeks ago now? Her concept of time seemed to be getting a little funny) apropos of nothing, he'd announced that he'd be driving to that conference in Chicago for the weekend. Before she could sigh deeply enough to protest, he'd waved a few printouts in front of her face. "I'm going to be on a panel about the realtor-lender relationship," he'd said but when she'd held out her hand for the papers, he'd triple folded them and stuffed them in his back pocket, like a bookie with his race results. "Anyway, I shouldn't be more than a couple of days." That right there. She kept coming back to it. It was so vague. "I shouldn't be more than a couple of days" also meant that he might be more than a couple of days. Why the uncertainty? Had he been telling her then he was leaving?

"What if I go with you?" she'd asked then, more to see if he would squirm than honest desire. He obliged her: "Bon, I mean, it's gonna be crazy. I probably won't even have a chance to leave the hotel. What about if we plan something for the fall? Maybe see the Cubbies play?"

When she had turned and walked away from him in response, it felt as though she was finishing something. There was an almost audible sense of this—a needle lifting off a staticky record—and she knew she and Sam were over, maybe not right then, but soon. She had a distinct sensation of setting something down she would not pick up again.

They had been so happy once, that was the worst part. They'd met at a friend's party shortly after college, and she'd been immediately taken with him. That face. She'd been a temp at the time, working the front desk at a local financial consulting firm, and she had come home from working late, dressed in her awkward work clothes—bulky cardigan for the cranked-up air-conditioning, mandated high heels and pantyhose. In his pink broadcloth button-down and teal Dockers, he'd looked like a demented Kennedy and she'd felt utterly self-conscious around him. They'd spent a few hours at that party talking about—was it poetry? It was poetry, but via Monica Lewinsky. And then at the end of the night, he'd quoted Walt Whitman to her, "I celebrate myself, and sing myself,/ And what I assume you shall assume,/For every atom belonging to me as good belongs to you." And how could she help but melt? The first time she'd spent the night with him, she'd been a virgin, and though she hadn't told him, he'd seem to have known anyway, and he had been gentle and funny with her and looked at her, afterwards, with the kind of cinematic ardor she would remember all her life and never truly experience again.

"Your back," he'd said, tracing it with a finger. "It looks like you have wings."

How had they gotten so far away from that?

She had no idea and she knew perfectly well in equal measure. It was both the booze and not. She had not felt it back in the early heady days, but it had entered their relationship sometime not long after the wedding. A presence she'd always felt. Like he was always half looking over her shoulder at someone behind her.

Still, she wanted him to be safe. She needed him to be here so she could tell him it was over. And she had no real idea how that was going to happen, but he was long overdue to be back and this inconvenient fact was complicating everything.

When she heard the car sweep into the driveway, she clenched her fists and sat there, a held breath. The next sound should have been the intestinal rumbling of the garage door, but it did not come. Instead there was a knock on the door, almost too quiet to carry into the kitchen.

The front door, too, had been a fight. Sam had wanted a more traditional red, but Bonnie thought the red paint with the red brick would make the place look like a firehouse. He'd been at work when she'd painted it a modern charcoal. It had taken him a few days to even notice, which made his complaints when he did notice seem disingenuous. She'd accused him of picking just to pick and he'd accused her of decorating him right out of their house and she'd told him that he could be part of the interior-design process when he got better taste. This daisy chain of bickering would go on into the night and next day, when he debuted the phantom of a hideous new mustache that grew undiscussed, like a smell, between them.

It was That Woman. Not the one who had been haunting her marriage for years and had possibly, in death, finally ruined it, but the other one. The one who had fucked her husband after the funeral of the first one. God, her dad had been right: Trash likes trash and you couldn't, not ever, escape entropy.

She hadn't been sure—hadn't even had an inkling really—until she'd met Stevie at Melinda's and then she just knew. It was in the woman's body language. The way she had curled in on herself, on that baby, as Bonnie spoke. Now, seeing her through the door, Bonnie noticed with some satisfaction that she was pretty, but not in particularly good shape. There was a discernable belly pooch, a certain widening at the hips. Bonnie felt as though, through some magic in her stronger, smaller body, that she had power over this woman.

Bonnie opened the inside door but not the screen. She stood there with her arms crossed. She would not mistakenly be nice to her again.

"I think I know where Sam is," said Stevie through the screen. And this was a surprise, but it was painful too. Bonnie didn't say anything but begrudgingly pushed upon the screen and beckoned her in.

They walked into the kitchen together and Bonnie tapped the walnut table. "Sit."

Stevie sat.

"Coffee? Tea?"

"No, thanks," said Stevie. Bonnie plopped a mint tea bag into a mug of water, nuked it, brought it over to Stevie, throwing out a coaster as she did. Oh, the tension.

Stevie opened her mouth to say something and Bonnie said, "I know it was you. After the funeral. I figured it out after Melinda's that day."

Stevie said nothing for a moment, then, "Sam's in Chicago."

"No shit, Sherlock."

"I think he's at Jen's apartment."

Bonnie sighed, stood up, filled a mug with tap water and opened her freezer, pulled out a pack of Camels, rummaged for the lighter in the junk drawer. "Smoke?" she said over her shoulder. When she turned around, she saw that Stevie had laid a joint on the table between them. Trash likes trash.

"I didn't say anything at Melinda's but I've seen you at the club. Just once. I went with a friend and you were there."

Bonnie sat back down and dropped her cigarette next to the joint. She picked up the joint instead and lit it, puffed at it, exhaled thoughtfully from her prettily pursed lips, as if she was blowing fluff from a dandelion, a bubble through a wand.

"My friend said they call you O.A."

"O.A? Who's they?"

"Old ass. Because of your cellulite. At the start of the season, I guess everybody was like 'Who's that grown-up lady messin' around at the pool with the kids?" Bonnie took another drag and did not pass it to Stevie. She had always been a secret smoker. Even Sam didn't know. In college, whenever a roommate or a friend would offer her a cigarette or a hit off a bong, she'd wrinkle her nose and call it ditch weed. This earned her a reputation for being snooty, too good for it, which she cultivated because it made her look more like the kind of person who would belong to a sorority and marry the son of the most successful realtor in town, and not the person she was, Bonnie Abernathy, daughter of Cindy, who had run off to Wyoming with a mechanic when she was two; daughter of Dwayne who kept a small farm spread near Dubuque where the land was rockier and so not as easy to cultivate, but cheaper too, and so Dwayne kept a scraggly field of silage corn which he mostly fed to his animals—a few dairy cows, some sheep, ducks and a handful of pigs. It was enough to keep him in a farm stand all spring and summer, and to supply to restaurants over the winter; enough to keep him in booze every night; not enough to keep him and Bonnie out of poverty. She'd started making Dwayne's rollies for him when she was in sixth grade and had smoked since seventh, though almost never in front of anyone. Farms were dirty work and Bonnie learned that no matter how often she did the laundry or how many showers she took every day, the stink of those animals on her dad's small, pitiful spread and the weed he sold when times were tight followed her all through school. Look at her now in her renovated house in the good school district with her stupid son-of-a-bitch husband. This time she took a huge hit and held it until her lungs convulsed and she coughed and coughed. Stevie stood up and got her a glass of water from her own fucking sink.

When she could talk again, her throat was tight. "Was he drunk when you fucked him? Because, well, I mean, he's been mostly drunk for the last two years, but also, he can't actually get an erection now without half a bottle in him." She smirked then caught her own reflection in the windows, visible now that night had tucked itself into the neighborhood. She was small and taut in her black Gap Body wear, not a hair or a muscle out of place. She looked like something premade and packaged. Her bloodshot eyes sagged, even as she smiled. She was not smizing, as Tyra would have said. She frowned, could feel the tears coming and let them. Bonnie knew she was a lovely crier. A boyfriend in college had once told her he got hard whenever she cried. She had taken it as a compliment—in those days when boys were still learning how to be adults, one took most of the creepy things they said as compliments. How else to survive among them? To realize the dream?—and had felt a strange pride over her crying face ever since. She appreciated her tears. They seemed to be proof not just of her goodness, but also of Stevie's badness.

"I swear I didn't know," Stevie said. "That he was married."

"This is Taylor. Every man over twenty-five is married, unless he's inbred or in jail. And even then."

Joint in hand, Stevie stood up and skinned a paper towel from the roll with her thumb and ring finger, and handed it to Bonnie.

Bonnie pressed it to her eyes. "Stop fucking touching my things. Please."

Stevie sat back down. "I'm sorry," she said and sheepishly pulled on the jay.

Bonnie softened, sighed. "So you think he's at Jen's."

"I do. I mean, I don't know for sure. It's a hunch, but it would make sense."

"How did he get into your friend's apartment? What's he doing there?"

"I have no idea."

"Okay, well." Bonnie examined the roach she now held for a very long time. "Will you go? I don't think I can deal with whatever is going on there." Something had been wrong. Even before the funeral. One night, Bonnie had heard him on the phone with someone, planning to meet in Des Moines. He'd been whispering. Later, she'd checked the phone bill, called the number and was sent to Jen's voicemail. And there'd been other stuff. He was slipping at work, she knew. Bonnie didn't know if he was stepping out to see someone, but when she called just to say hi, like spouses sometimes did, and he wasn't there but they also couldn't tell her exactly where he was, she wondered. Then, sometimes they could tell her where he was. She didn't think he'd been selling houses because he'd stopped talking about selling them. There had been a time—boring and sweet—when he'd told her about each sale, each family, every house. And maybe she should have recognized the thing in his voice then, the thing that said "this could be us, this is what I want," but she'd missed it and to be honest, she thought he'd missed it too, both of them unaware of how he felt or even that he was drifting away until one day he was gone. And then there were the empty airplane liquor bottles she'd found shoved here and there in the strangest places—in his sock drawer, out in the garage, behind a stand of old paint cans, under the couch pushed back so deep she'd only seen it because at that point she'd begun to look for them.

But then, there was also something else tugging at her, the shadow of real violence: What *if* Sam had gotten mixed up in something out of his depth? What if Jen *had* been murdered? What if Sam really did get attacked by people who wanted to hush him up? There was something enticing about this idea because it meant that Sam hadn't completely lied to her, had allowed her some dignity. Then the darkest questions: What if he'd gone off the same roof Jen did? What if he's dead in Chicago for any of the reasons above?

The questions and fears inside Bonnie paralyzed her. "I just. I can't do it."

Stevie said nothing, but Bonnie saw she would go and relief flooded through her.

Later, she lay in bed and wondered if she was a coward, but by that point, she'd been husked out by the weed, the visit. She fell asleep without answering her own question and slept all night, without waking.

The girl, who was nearly in college, looked younger from this distance at this angle, as she squinted up at him and bobbed up and down on his dick, like something mechanized. She gagged and squeezed at his thigh and he slowed down his hips, rolled his eyes away from her, a hand nestled in her hair. The walls and floor of the janitor's closet were damp concrete and from where Elvis stood, beyond the bleach-stink shadows of mops and industrial-sized vats of cleaning fluids, he could see out of the tiny window to the pool deck and the guard stand. In order to serve the pool and locker rooms at once, the closet had two doors and he'd snuck them in through the back one—a locked door in the men's locker only he had the key for—and had kept the light off. He could see Chase who had no idea he was there, standing at the pool's edge with a rescue tube draped around him like a sash, like an extra from fucking *Baywatch*.

Suddenly, someone stepped into his line of sight. It was Sherry, he saw, and she wasn't looking at the pool, she was looking right at him, or where his face would appear to her if the light of the closet were to suddenly come on.

His first impulse was to keep eye contact with Sherry while he came in Emily's mouth, but no he couldn't keep his eyes open and when he groaned and fluttered them open again, Sherry was gone from view. His stomach cramped.

"Get up," he yanked the top of the girl's suit back up over her little breasts—one nipple stuck up over the top in the gloom of the closet, an accusing eye—then took her arm to lift her up off the kickboard on which she'd been kneeling. Too rough. Her expression bruised and he sensed she was about to argue. She wiped her face with the back of a hand and coughed thick and phlegmy. He moved close to her and smiled, adjusted her swimsuit, tucked the wandering nipple away. "What are you now? Nineteen?"

She didn't like the manhandle, was wary of him now, "Eighteen."

He squeezed past her, toward a can on a shelf behind a mop bucket. "Whoa baby! All grown up and barely legal." He fished around inside the can, then brought out an orange pill bottle with a big sticky bud inside. "Thanks, Em—I'll get you back on the schedule starting next week. Don't smoke it all in one place."

Her eyes went wide and she bit her lip, slung her Jansport around both shoulders. She didn't say anything but she moved to kiss him and he gave her his cheek as she shimmied past him through the door frame and out onto the pool deck. Wrong door. He cursed himself and his cum-slow brain. When he walked out of the locker room and came around the corner and onto the pool deck, Sherry was standing there against the painted cement brick wall with a scowl on her face. He walked across the pool deck quickly without acknowledging her, catching one last glimpse of Emily's sweet ass in cut-offs before she made it through the turnstile and around the corner into the greater hallways of the Taylor Recreation Center.

Chase, who stood at attention, eagle-eyed, at the other end of the pool, now noticed him. "Hey El," he yelled. Great. A whole blow-job audience.

Sherry followed behind him, flip-flopped feet turned out like a ballerina's and slapping the floor, big Le Sportsac duffle weighing heavy on her left shoulder. It came naturally to him to imagine the puffy brown nipples on *her* breasts, to wonder, almost without real thought, if he was up for a second go. He pushed open the glass door to the pool manager's office—his office, he still felt some pride at that— and flicked on the overhead fluorescents, held the door for her. He sometimes thought if he ever ended up going to jail, he might not mind it that much, he was so used to the institutional stench of the pool. The human stink of it. Damp crotch and foot.

"You're a disgusting townie loser, you know that?"

"Thank you," he said and finally turned toward her angry face. He actually liked the word *townie.* It made him feel proud inside even though people mostly used it dismissively. He had gone to two years of college but found it uninspiring, a waste of money. Found the TAs who taught his freshman classes to be unhelpful, frightened people, and the professors of his sophomore year bloated with their own importance, dismissive of the area and quick to treat their students like the rubes they believed them to be. One of them began so many sentences with "When I was at Princeton," that it seemed like a tic. A snob was kind of the worst thing a person could be, when you thought about it, and practically everyone at the university thought they were better than the people around them, the people of Taylor, just because they happened not to be born here, which was nothing to feel proud about at all, since you didn't get any say about that. Elvis, himself, had not been born in Taylor, but in a paved western suburb of Chicago, which was maybe why he was so sensitive to the attitude at college. And if it wasn't the professors, it was the students, many of whom were from actual Chicago and whose eyes became haughty when they asked where he was from and he said Schaumburg. To the people of Taylor, though, he was a city kid and not to be trusted. And so three semesters of college was enough to teach him that it was a place for the smaller minded, and that what he really needed was to lie about his home town (which he now did regularly, claiming to be from an empty rural nape just west of Taylor) and to make a lot of money so no one would again mistake him for someone who could be patronized. However it might occur, metaphorically or literally, his top career goal could best be described as benevolent dictator.

That benevolence, actually, seemed to be kind of a problem for him lately.

"What do you want?" The trick was to be chilly with the young ones.

"I want you to start cutting me in like you said you were going to. Or was that a lie too?" After he'd given Sherry the assistant manager job at this pool, he'd started coming in odd hours in order to avoid her. He tried to keep fresh on the schedule, but he'd messed up today. Let his excitement over a nooner with a teener in his office mess him up. He'd started scheduling Sherry odd hours when it had become clear that she was not going to let this go, but she must have switched with whomever he'd scheduled for this shift specifically so she could corner him on her break.

"It wasn't a lie at the time. But I found someone else."

Sherry's face was a little puffy, as if she'd been out drinking last night, and now he saw her eyes were red.

"Why?" Her face softened, "What did I do wrong?"

Now he moved to her. The trick was also to be warm. "Hey, hey. You didn't do anything wrong. I just needed to keep you here. You're important to me here. Plus you're fucking hot. There's no way I could send you to the club, babe, all the way across town like that."

They were trading: soft and hard. It was her turn, "Then I want a cut of what's coming in here. You gave my job to an old lady, you know? What's she, like, forty?"

"Thirty."

"Is there a difference? I'm not going to be able to afford next semester, El."

"I'll think about it. And don't worry about school. I'll pick up next semester for you, okay?"

Sherry nodded, grim, angry, hurt and in the possession of a testimony that could, if not put him away, then at least cause a lot of expensive legal trouble for him. It's not that he didn't like her. Sherry was technically smart and pretty tough for a girl—she *was* a nursing major—but she also wanted sole and unlimited access to his dick, which would never do.

In the midst of a run of fucking last spring, he'd made the mistake of taking her to see the new Tarantino film, *Grindhouse*, and afterwards she'd begun to refer to them as El Wray and Cherry, delighted by the phonetic similarities of their names. Maybe he'd even been off his head a little. Somewhat into her. He didn't know what that meant or felt like anymore, though, so he did the easiest thing, which was nothing—no more movie dates, no phone calls after hours, only a little fucking in his office after a shift—until, eventually, he'd lifted her away from him like a claw-stuck kitten. It was always better to keep looking ahead, keep moving ahead, he'd finally told her. And she agreed, but while her ahead included him, as did his, only one of theirs included her. There was quite a lot of shit-flinging until, at last, he'd placated her with the promise of her own operation at the country club, the job he would end up giving to Stevie.

When his desk phone rang they were standing like gunslingers, hands at their hips, a standoff. He was reluctant to take his eyes off her, as if she might maul him once he broke eye contact. He moved to the phone with a finger up, commanding silence, and heard Sherry's gasp of disgust, felt her flap the air with frustration, watched her huff out the door as he put the phone to his face and let whomever it was on the other line explain themselves.

"Uh, hello? Is this . . . Mr. . . . Elvis?" He could practically hear the acne on the kid. It was one of his baby seals from the club, the high school students he hired for cheap—like Emily—and who, if he liked them, once the school year began, ran weed into the schools. The trustworthy ones, he promoted. He usually had a good eye for who would work out—they couldn't be too confident or too smart. The quiet kids were the secret keepers. The pussies. The cutters. This kid though, Pedro, had turned out to be a mouthy pussy—one of those kids who seemed like they'd have no game whatsoever and then turned out to be the life of the party. Elvis didn't like him, didn't like even hearing his own name in this scrub's mouth.

"What do you want?"

"Hey my man, how's it going. Listen, hey, there's a problem down here? At the pool?"

"Is that a question or a statement?"

"Uh . . . what?"

"Jesus, don't leave me in suspense—what's going on?"

Pedro's voice cracked, "The mix," he coughed. "The mix is off. I don't know what happened. We went on break and then we came back and now some of the people here are having, like, allergic reactions? To the water? Like someone shocked the pool?"

Elvis could hear someone yelling directions in the background, all official like, and felt his balls fall to the floor.

"Did you call 911? Who's there? Cops?" He did not need any first responders, or god forbid, cops, poking around in his pump room. "No," said Pedro, "no cops." But he sounded nervous, like this was something he might be wrong about, and Elvis hung up on him, already carefully jogging the slick pool deck, past Sherry who refused give him the satisfaction of asking what was going on, past Chase who was saying something after him that he now completely ignored. He redlined the Beemer to the club, dialing and redialing Stevie on his cell, wondering where the fuck she was and why she wouldn't pick up her goddamned phone.

As he made the turn from the gazebo into the pool area, he saw a collapsible gurney and first-aid kits on the deck. There were a few people gazing gape-mouthed at the paramedics, who were bent over a couple of kids, one younger and one older and bigger. They were shiny and pink—like they'd been badly sunburnt, but it had been cloudy all day. He almost expected to see steam rising from their splotchy hides, but they were shivering in their wet swim trunks. They sat on two chaise loungers on the far, deep-end side of the pool. The chairs were the new ones he'd convinced Greg to splurge on—a nice neutral stone-colored Sunbrella fabric suspended over a heavy iron skeleton. They were heavy fuckers so they didn't get dragged all over the place and kids couldn't use them to build forts. The towel-wrapped crowd standing and sitting near (but not too near) the loungers looked frightened and puzzled as they watched the two paramedics, one on at each chaise, the first gently turning over the screaming pink wrist of the little kid (a scrawny eight year old, if Elvis had to guess, though he knew shit-all about kids and their ages) as if he were looking for something taped to the other side. The second paramedic had a stethoscope and was making the older kid, a beetle-browed teenager in red board shorts, breathe slowly in and slowly out as she patted it over different areas of his chest and back.

Ashley and Pedro came out of the pump room, both wearing thick yellow kitchen gloves just as he passed the eight-foot stencil on the coping.

"What happened?"

Ashley spoke woodenly as if she had been rehearsing the answer to this question. "I called break and everything was fine. After I whistled that break was over, these guys jumped in and basically turned red. That one," she pointed to the bigger kid in the red board shorts, "he couldn't breathe. Like, his face and throat were all puffy. Jeremy got him out. It's like, the water did something to them."

Elvis shushed her and backed them toward the pump room. "Shut your fucking mouth. You don't know the water did this to him—you're not a chemist or a doctor. If those kids have parents here, we're sued. It's bad enough you called the paramedics."

"But he couldn't brea—"

"Unless someone is having a heart attack or bleeding out. . . . Next time, call me before you call 911. Where's Stevie?"

The two bewildered teenagers shook their heads, wide-eyed. Pedro swallowed and spoke. "She called this morning and told us to open."

Elvis clenched his jaw. "If there's no manager here when you come in, you do not open. Get it? You call me."

Pedro wouldn't take the hit like a man. "But she told us to," he whined.

"You're fired." Elvis turned to Ashley. "What about you? Do you want to keep your job?" Ashley nodded and he took in her smooth tan shoulders, huge eyes, weak chin. She looked like one of those horse-loving girls. Like she'd never had a cock in her mouth—not even the word. "Okay, then. Tell everyone the pool is closed. Get them to stop gawking. Then close it up for the day. Put a sign out, 'Temporarily closed for repairs.'"

Before she could make a move, one of the paramedics came over. "You're the manager?" she said. Elvis nodded. "Something's not right with your water. One kid has chemical burns and the other one needed an EpiPen."

Elvis ran his hands over his face. What the hell was this? He turned back to Ashley. "This only happened after the break?"

She nodded. "Before that people were swimming and everything seemed normal."

"But you left the deck, you and Pedro both."

She nodded again.

"For how long?"

Her lip was quivering now. "Ten minutes?"

A guest approached, a tall guy with a pockmarked face. When he spoke, he sounded like the Swedish Chef. "I saw something," he said. "When the kids were away and the pool was paused. I saw another girl go into the pump room. I thought she worked here, you know, I thought she was starting a shift and was testing the water or something. Then she walked out of the pump room. And her bag was, how do I say it, empty going in and full coming out?" The man seemed to be looking at Elvis intently, though it was hard to tell through his sunglasses. "I think maybe it was full of the . . . pool toys?"

Elvis did not know that Karl would have been able to identify Stevie on sight. He had actually been working up the courage to ask her out the next time he saw her, coke dealer or not. That it was Sherry who had sabotaged him, even before she'd given him one last chance to make amends with her. Sherry who had felt completely vindicated to have caught Elvis with a new conquest, while her gym duffle was stuffed with thousands in cash and thousands more in cocaine.

Fuck. Elvis left the group and tried not to break into a run as he made his way to the pump room.

The pump room with its old feet smell always made him horny, even now, even in the middle of whatever lake of shit he'd just waded into it. He'd lost his virginity in a pump room. The first year he'd had a job, age fifteen. She'd been the G.M. of the pool, not a college student, older, married to a small-time pro football player from Arizona who lived in Iowa half the year. She was finishing a master's degree in something. Sports management? She'd seduced him one night when they were closing. Had made him her bitch, basically. Ordered him around. Made him do whatever she wanted. And though he'd liked it, doing whatever she told him to do, he liked better the idea that he could do this too, and get other people to do what *he* wanted. It was like a whole new world had opened up to him.

She had taken him out with her that night to the strip of bars that oozed students until two a.m. And this was another horizon. There were sports bars and dance clubs, and an underground bar with wall-to-wall carpeting and a huge fish tank. So many bars packed into a few square blocks. It was famous, this strip, and famously well patrolled by local bully cops so he usually steered clear but he could see why she loved it. One-dollar blowjob shots, every place damp from the pitchers of cheap beer the college students sloshed from the bar to dark corners, girls younger than him in tube tops with sticky lips, farm girls whose arrival in Taylor had been marked by the purchase of five-inch heels and an Entropy tanning package at Body Electric. For all its rural feel, for two square blocks, just east of the main campus, Iowa's own Las Vegas roiled and puked every Wednesday through Saturday night. He had seen, then, how he could make a living off of this energy, this binging, puking desire for attention and annihilation. Probably forever.

But not, of course, if someone was trying to sabotage his pool.

He fumbled in the dark before he found the flashlight that hung from a hook on the rough, damp wall. The stash box lay on the floor, deep in the corner behind the sand filter, away from the light of the summer day that slunk around the doorway but didn't enter. It was flung wide open and empty of both cash and sticks. Fuck.

"You two," he summoned the remaining guards who were herding the guests toward the pool gates, "were you messing around in the back of the pump room for any reason?"

They shared the same look of confusion.

"Okay, look, bring me your bags."

More confusion.

"Right now!"

"Our bags?" Jeremy croaked, scared now, that he was about to be fired too.

"Bags, backpacks, wherever you stash your street clothes when you get to work. Bring them to me. Now."

They brought them down to the pool deck from the gazebo. Jeremy's lame square Reebok gym bag, Ashley's giant string-knot purse in a beige chino color—the purse of a middle-aged woman. They both stunk—Jeremy's of old socks and Ashley's of a grandmotherly perfume—but no coke. Nothing but towels, old receipts, sunscreen and rolled T-shirts. Ashley's makeup bag was a holographic mylar color and had a big-eyed unicorn on it. It was full of Lip Smackers and glittery nail polish. He would definitely hire her back next year and make sport of trying to fuck her.

Well, what had he expected. Someone had come in and done this to his pool then taken his stash. There had to have been something like five grand in there. He was kicking himself for not picking it up sooner. He called and texted and called and texted, getting angrier by the minute. Stevie still didn't answer. She had said she needed more money, hadn't she. And he'd told her no. Which had maybe not been a great move on his part, but what was he supposed to do? The business wasn't doing as well as he'd wanted or hoped. There had been too many forced closures on the rainy and stormy days, a problem Elvis hadn't foreseen when drafting this business model—a huge and stupid oversight: he'd worked inside for too long. And why wouldn't Greg order them to close? It was cheaper for him to send all the staff home than to have them sit around guarding no one. Stevie had been right: he should have been working on Greg with the closures. In the end, wasn't everyone just trying to protect their investments, including Elvis?

But this was too much. Had he really misjudged her that badly? If so, this made everything partly his fault too. Maybe he hadn't been right about her after all, about her neediness and desire to be cool, and the ways in which these traits could be manipulated by him. He had picked her because she really had been kind of cool, and kind of sexy and also bored with her whole dumb life, ready for an adventure. He would get to know these things about her officially but he could sense them about her when they were still strangers. That was his gift. But there were complications, too, weren't there. He hadn't anticipated the foreclosure. And that obviously that wasn't his fault or his problem. It was hers. Her fucking fault, or her dumbfuck mother's. And if she thought she could do him like this. Well. She was going to need a correction.

He gave Ashley back her unicorn bag and stood up.

"Get everyone out of here," he said and walked back out the gate. He would deal with the water later, right now, he needed to deal with Stevie.

Viv did not hear the first knock, she was *just* awake, the old dream fading. Baby Stevie, and anachronistically, baby James, swept away by the river as it raged, their huge baby heads bobbing cartoonishly above the churning green water. The image was bad enough but it was the wrenching feeling of loss that echoed through her body as she climbed back to consciousness that always brought the tears. One thing about children that no one really prepared you for was the crushing heartache. When nothing was going wrong, it was there in the darkness, waiting. So that when the bad thing hit, whatever it was—SIDS, tumor, mass shooter, and later: mental illness, drugs—its revelation felt familiar, if not comfortable. *Oh*, she would think to herself, to the darkness. *I've been expecting you.*

When James had first left (and here the haunting word *runaway* still rose unbidden fifteen years later, though she would never say it on purpose, even to herself. It was always in the voice of Del Shannon, that ghostly falsetto), before he'd called collect from Sioux City ("Where are you going?" she'd asked. "West," he'd said, sounding like a man for the very first time, and she'd known he would never really come home again), the sustained panic had made her levitate. She'd felt flayed. For a week she was a bird in flight, unable to alight, to take rest anywhere. She had kicked out her boyfriend Harry, when he'd been mush-mouthed about the last time he'd seen James and she sensed in him, for the first time, the kind of evasiveness that had spelled the end of her marriage, but instead of being evasive about another woman, Harry had trouble looking her in the eye when she'd asked about her son. This was the moment the bird of her panic had truly taken flight. The police would arrive before she'd even thought to call them, care of the neighbors and the holy glory of her screams.

(And here, another wince—it would be years before James told her about Harry's night-time visits to his bedroom, years before he either trusted her enough or got up the nerve to hurt her back. This, too, felt like something she'd known all along.)

The knock came again and lifted the needle from the decades-old groove of her maternal self-loathing. It made her unreasonably angry, even though it was well into the afternoon. She was on third shift this month and had not yet gotten used to the rhythms of it—she felt hopelessly scrambled every time she awoke at two p.m. from a fitful six or seven hours, never sure if the melatonin helped or hurt—and it seemed as though someone was always knocking. She was sure it was the Obama canvassers. Kids—most of them younger than Stevie and James—were constantly dropping by and leaving brochures, stickers, buttons. She had told them, all of them, many times, that she would certainly caucus for him (though privately she also liked Hilary Clinton, felt a kinship with the cuckolded woman) thinking this would take her off some list, but they continued to arrive at her doorstep, young and sweet and so full of honest purpose.

By the third knock and she was throwing on her robe, then she was at the door, almost against her will.

A sprite stood there. No, she corrected herself, it was Puck. She blinked against the memory of the klieg lights as she stood on stage, a diaphanous Titania, Carl Borak in leaves and brambles next to her. And here was Carl Borak? Or certainly not Carl, who would be nearly sixty by now, but maybe his son? She opened the door and felt as though she'd walked into her own distant youth.

The boy—young man, really—smiled as she opened the door but she didn't notice the strained quality of it until he spoke. "Stevie's mom, right?" His eyes swept the house behind her. "I need to speak with her immediately. It's . . ." he looked down and bounced on his toes. "It's urgent."

The bird chirped, jumped from its branch. "What's going on?" *Do you know Carl Borak?* she wanted to ask but realized this would just confuse the situation. "Did you tell me your name?"

"Ron," said the sprite. "I work with Stevie at the pool. She hasn't shown up for work in a couple of days and the boss can't get her on her phone. He's pissed. Is she here? Everyone is so worried."

Later, talking to the police, Viv would feel ashamed at how easily she'd fallen for the lie—like most nurses, she had always considered herself unbullshittable, so what happened next came as a surprise to her.

Later, after giving her report, she would not recall the face of the officer who had helped her, but she remembered his buffed black boots and the shuttered look of her own face in the hospital bathroom mirror as she cursed Carl Borak, wherever he was, and the vanity of her own nostalgia.

But here, now, charmed, she moved aside and invited Elvis into her house.

"She left for Chicago earlier. I think it was unplanned—maybe a friend of hers was in trouble? She probably just forgot to call about it."

Elvis moved confidently up the stairs and into the kitchen where Viv expected he'd stop, but he kept moving, instead, down the hall, tilting his head into each doorway as though looking for something. Or someone? Did he think she was lying?

"Ron?" No response. She cleared her throat, "Sorry, Ron? What's . . . can I help you? Stevie is definitely not here." Her laugh was nervous when she meant it to be strong. "I promise."

Now he had disappeared into Stevie's bedroom and was not coming out. Viv gave up the hope of coaxing him back into the hall by standing there and calling his name, like a dog, and followed him into Stevie's room.

It had taken Viv *years* to train herself not to jump every time she walked into Stevie's room. The Doors poster always spooked her, looked, out of the corner of her eye, like a man standing there on Stevie's bed. Now, though, she saw how very Christ-like Jim Morrison looked. Arms outstretched, leather pants nearly falling off his skinny hips. Instead of reminding her of a hazy pot-fogged youth, he looked like a religious icon, like a witness or some apotropaic vision.

Elvis pawed at scraps of paper on Stevie's white particleboard desk. "Did she leave a note or anything saying where she was going?" He picked up each scrap of paper with thin, dexterous fingers. The fingers gave her a chill. They looked insectile, the way they crawled across the landscape of the desk.

"No, I told you. She's in Chicago with a friend."

Stevie had, in fact, left a note, scribbled, as their family notes always were, on the white board stuck to the fridge, but she wasn't about to tell him that. A dark feeling had bloomed in her gut.

"Can I get you a drink? Maybe some lemonade? Or a beer?" Viv moved with purpose back out of the room and down the hall to the fridge, hoping he would stay put, cringing slightly when she heard his voice right behind her.

"Sure, sure. How about both. Arnold Palmer."

Viv tried to laugh but it barked out all wrong. "That's tea. Arnold Palmer has tea." The carpet turned to linoleum and she counted each tile as she crossed it. Thirteen to the fridge. When James was a toddler, she'd taught him to count this way. No stepping twice in one tile. No stepping on cracks. The mother's back, unbroken, bent over the toddler's grasping fingers, the wavering legs, so chubby and round, they looked hopeless, like toy legs. Like someone's bad drawing of legs. James had to take huge monster steps on those bowed sausages to get from one tile to the next. Every time he made it, tile after tile, to the fridge, he roared. His mom had roared with him, her voice low and gravelly and his high and scrapey. Love in the tumbled sonic bits between them.

She reached up to swipe the address off the white board. He caught her arm from behind. She swung her other one wildly. It felt like a club, instead of something that was biologically part of her, and she managed to obliterate most of the street number, the dust of the dry erase blacking the side of her hand. She could feel him bobbing behind her. He was short—maybe he hadn't seen.

Then he had her other arm. Then she was down on the linoleum. She had an absurd image of her arms popping off her body, the way Stevie used to do to her Barbies. There had been so much disarticulation, in fact, that she and Dan had, for a time, referred to the basement playroom as the graveyard. The graveyard. She blinked and willed herself back into the kitchen, into her body.

The sprite's knee dug into her back. A bit of old food dried to sharpness bit into her cheek.

"What's the street number?" Her shoulders strained the bounds of their sockets and she moaned. "Your daughter stole something from me. Do you understand? She's not a good person. You need to give me the address so I can help her."

The logic confused her and she almost answered him. Help her. Stevie needed help.

Viv put her forehead to the tile and breathed in slowly.

When Stevie was born, Viv hadn't let them take her to the nursery. Hadn't let the nurses give her the formula they brandished. She'd sent everyone out of the room, even Dan, and she had run her hands over every bit of Stevie. The purple, pruned hands, the curly fuzz on her bloody coned head, the furious red stork bite between her eyebrows, which seemed to rise up from her forehead like flame, the perfect shell of her ears. Most astoundingly, the tiny, creased feet. Stevie had latched, sweet and sharp, and Viv had made her a promise. Had simply said, "I promise" and let the hushed silence of the world fill the room.

If she was going to die, she would die back in that room, on that day of pain and wonder, when she'd first become a mother. She closed her eyes and tried to feel the weight of her baby in her arms.

"The number. What's the number. What's the number, Viv. The number." His voice had gone flat. He knew he wasn't going to get it from her. However this was going to end, it would end soon.

There was a muffled sound as her right shoulder dislocated, something like the cracking of a knuckle. Then: lightning. She screamed and the weight on her lightened. She felt as though she might float to the ceiling. Thunder followed, a ringing. More pain. The whole world was underwater and she remembered her dream. Moved back into it. But Stevie and James weren't babies anymore. And this was sad. She missed their baby selves, thought of their baby selves as separate people, really. She hoarded any time she got to spend with them. Still, she was glad to see them. She'd been so worried about Stevie lately. Especially lately, for some reason. But she couldn't remember why. Now Stevie looked healthy and grown. Nothing to worry about here. She held a riverboat pole. She was a ferryman. James sat on the flat-bottomed boat beside her. All the things from their house were piled on the boat behind them. Her refrigerator, her washer and dryer. She felt a tinge of annoyance. What did they need with all that? She opened her mouth to ask them but they were already further down the river. Too far to catch them now. What was she going to do? She couldn't afford all new appliances. She found the sandy footpath on the riverbank and followed it, jogging first, just enough to keep the boat in view, then running, running, and yes, she had enough momentum now she could do it—she took a huge, bounding step and jumped far up into the air. The ground raced below her and she seemed to hang there for a moment in the air. She reached the zenith of her flight and began to sink again but propelled herself back up when her foot hit earth. As always, she thought it hilarious that she could do this—could leap so high she could fly, essentially, in her dreams—it just took a little momentum. And, as always, she was grateful to have remembered how.

The pain in her shoulder lassoed her, woke her up and brought the linoleum back into focus. He was gone, she knew. The house seemed lighter without him in it. Oh god, she had to call Stevie. Viv rolled over to her side and reached around herself with her good arm. Fumbled the stupid thing out of her pocket. It took a few tries because of how badly her hands were shaking. Voicemail. Viv's message was broken and nonsensical. Watch out. A man. Had she stolen something? Come home. No, don't. Just run.

She hung up and tried to stand, but found she couldn't. Christ. He may have broken her shoulder, and her head—did she have a concussion as well? She lay on the floor for some time, trying to gather her strength. In the end, she didn't remember calling 911, but at some point she must have because then the ambulance was there, and then she was on a stretcher, bouncing toward the threshold of her home. The momentary relief she felt in not recognizing the medics from her hospital gave way to another panic. Oh god, the neighbors. The older ones, the stay-at-homers. Mrs. Ferrer, the Tansey-Pauls. As her gurney exited the house she'd lived in for over thirty years—nearly half her life—a home which she was now on the cusp of losing, here they were, gaping on the sidewalk or rustling silently as their curtains parted. She tried to wave at them. Mr. Tansey-Paul's frown looked as though it would eat his face. Look, I'm fine her wave tried to say. But no one waved back as a police officer crawled into the ambulance with her. When had the cops arrived and why? What had she said to them. Oh, Stevie.

"Where are we going?"

"The hospital," he said. He was young, but his uniform was big and bulky and the bulk made her feel safe.

"Which one?"

The cop yelled up to the front, "Where we goin'?"

"Lutheran," yelled one of the EMTs, the kind Hispanic one who had brushed the floor bits off of her face where they were embedded, and handled her sagging arm with remarkable delicacy.

No. Her coworkers. She shook her head. "Tell them Saint Joe's instead."

He did and the ambulance made a couple of left-hand turns. She was grateful for the extra moments to compose herself. To consider her options regarding how much to say to this cop about her daughter. Not that she knew anything, and this is exactly what scared her. Stevie, Stevie, what have you gotten yourself into? Maybe she shouldn't have said anything about the open marriage. Was it still possible to traumatize your child when she was thirty-two?

"Mrs. Miller?" said the cop. He looked a little like Sam. Was Sam behind this, somehow? "Ms." She said automatically.

"Sorry, Ms. Miller, you said back there, this guy was looking for your daughter. Do you know why?"

"Did I? I can't remember. I'm sorry, I'm a little confused."

"You reported to dispatch that someone had come into your home and attacked you and that he was looking for your daughter."

Good going, Viv. She thought fast.

"He was a stalker." She paused and watched him nod and make a note. He had not and would not register her lie. She elaborated. "He was a co-worker. He's obsessed." This part, at least, might be somewhat true.

"And where does she work, your daughter?"

"The Willows Country Club. She's a lifeguard."

He looked concerned, "And how old is your daughter?"

She told him, and here she saw the thing pass across his face. The thing she'd seen when she'd told her friends, her coworkers, that her daughter was moving home. An interest at this obviously good news, but there was an edge too—contempt, maybe? Smugness? She'd been telling them for years that her daughter lived in New York. To their ears this simple statement of fact was a brag. Now, their expressions seemed to say, you're just like us again, except (and she was sure the younger ones laughed about this over beers after work) your super-successful daughter will be doing the work of an athletic high schooler.

Fuck you, she thought, glad she had lied to him.

"I see. So, we're not talking about child endangerment here. And where is she right now?"

A fist inside of Viv squeezed hard. "I don't know."

"The address on the white board? You said she was headed to Chicago?" She also didn't remember telling him this detail. Everything was so hazy. How long had she been semi-conscious?

"A friend's house. I don't know if she's actually there or not." More and more it seemed likely not, but . . . maybe? "I tried to call her but. . . ." Viv shook her head.

"I can put a call into the Chicago precincts and ask them to keep an eye out, but that's about all I can do, until something happens."

"Something has happened. That asshole beat me up. I thought he was going to kill me." Fucking cops.

"To your daughter, I mean. I suggest you keep calling. I'll come talk to you again when you get settled in."

She should go to Chicago. To the address on the whiteboard. Though she hadn't paid it mind before, the attack had imprinted it. The ambulance jostled and her arm screamed. The pounding over her right eye told her a migraine was imminent. Maybe they'd give her some Imitrex at the hospital, but she doubted it. She was sure to get sedation while they reset her arm—nothing broken, just dislocated—which she would be foolish not to take. And they'd definitely want to monitor her for the head trauma. Either way, she wouldn't be clear enough to drive for hours, even if she discharged herself early against medical advice. Plus—and here she felt some shame, because it was possible the life of her daughter (her grown-ass adult daughter, she reminded herself) was at in danger—but, she, Viv, was scared. She didn't want to run into the guy again. She hadn't even been able to protect herself—how could she protect Stevie?

The ambulance pulled under the concrete canopy at the emergency entrance of Saint Joe's Mercy and the cop climbed out the back, dapping a medic he knew who was finishing a cigarette outside the doors, right in front of the no-smoking sign. While Viv waited to be wheeled into a hospital in which, with luck, she'd be a stranger, she flipped open her phone and called the one person in the world she knew with a gun who could maybe get to Chicago faster than she could.

Telephones don't work when you want them to. Not in horror movies, not in novels, not in real life. You'd think the cliché would have faded out a bit, after everyone began carrying their phones around with them, but it still works, because we all still find ourselves caught unprepared all the time, in a myriad of ways. In this way, the phone, even the cell phone or the smartphone, functions as both a metaphor and the literal truth.

Stevie did not yet have that dopamine machine, the iPhone, and neither did our mom. They wouldn't for a little while yet, as they and the rest of the world waited for the price to come down and for financing to be available, which it would—just had, actually—until everyone grew used to carrying one around, and became dependent on it, at which point, like any smart drug dealer, Apple would raise the price back up. And though they were used to talking to each other frequently, there was no dropping a pin, no sharing locations on social media apps, no FaceTime, no SnapChat, no maps. Stevie couldn't afford to text much and Mom didn't get how and so just ignored the feature on her own phone.

Stevie had a car charger, of course, and she had plugged into it when she set out for Chicago, a little frantic, worried about Sam, frightened that he had followed Jen into the abyss. She'd planned to call Elvis from the road to tell him she had put the kids in charge of opening that morning, but when she got beyond the Quad Cities and opened her phone to call, she saw the charger hadn't been charging and her phone was dead. When she got into city traffic, she felt like she couldn't stop as she was swept along the Dan Ryan like a blood cell in an artery, a little unsure of herself as a rusty driver fresh off her move from New York. During this cell outage, not only did she miss a panicked call from Pedro, two from Elvis, and three from our mother warning her about Elvis, but she also missed a downright maniacal message from Amanda Collins who had improbably sold her novel on proposal to a blog-obsessed editorial assistant at a Simon & Schuster imprint. It strains credulity, which is how you know it's true, but after everything settled down, she played them for me—the mumbling Pedro, the hissing Elvis, the crying mom and then, there was Beyoncé's "Single Ladies" played as if from a great distance, and Amanda Collins, her mouth too close to the receiver, singing off-key about liking it, putting a ring on it. ("She's crazy," I said, open-mouthed. "I know," said Stevie. "I didn't know she was going to do that. I don't even want to write this book now.")

When I buzzed her in, then opened Jen's door, Stevie looked frazzled, but not afraid for her life, like she should have been, like we all shortly would be. And then frazzled turned to puzzled as she tried to figure out what the hell she was seeing.

"James?"

"Hi, Sis." I gave her a big hug, but it was like hugging a statue. She was frozen in place by confusion.

"James?" She said again. "What?"

"It's good to see you too, Bella. How long has it been?"

Stevie smiled a little, despite herself and her confusion and the fact that she was still very, very mad at me for being the source of mom's impending foreclosure. She hugged me again, unstatued by sisterly love. "I don't understand. *What* is happening right now?"

"Sam's here," I said. "That's probably who you were hoping to find, right? Well, good job, you found him. He's napping on the couch."

Stevie followed me into the living room and gasped when she saw Sam. "He looks sick."

"He's detoxing," I said. "Actually, he is mostly now detoxed. Probably all the way. But I need to get him to eat more. He hasn't been good with that this week."

"Detox? Jesus. Shouldn't he be in a hospital?"

"Yeah, probably," I said, a little defensiveness creeping into my voice now. Big sisters have a way of making you feel like everything you do is wrong. "But, you know. We're squatting. We didn't want to attract any attention. Plus, if the cops came around. . . ."

"Why would the cops come around?"

"Because that's what cops do, Stevie. They come around and then bad things happen." I scratched the back of my head. Might as well tell her everything. "He thinks he might have killed someone."

"What?"

"Jen's old boss or something? I don't know. Ask him."

Sam was waking up from his nap and saw Stevie. He gave her that killer smile and I saw my sister melt a little, and felt a pang of sadness for her. This would always be their dynamic: Stevie reaching out for Sam, Sam, always stepping back. But today it didn't matter. The look of relief on Stevie's face made it clear she'd been thinking the worst, probably trying not to indulge in it, but being unable not to.

"Are you okay?" she asked Sam and I wandered out of the room as she knelt down and put her arms around him and he let her. "I'm okay," he said. "I'm sorry."

On June 6, 1944, Allied forces stormed the beach at Normandy. 209,000 Allied soldiers were killed. D-Day. The official military title of the thing was a dark chuckle: "Operation Overlord." The other mission, the fake one, the one they were feeding to the Germans with false dates and locations, was "Operation Bodyguard." Churchill gave it the name, breaking his own naming rules, set forth in 1943 ("Operations in which large numbers of men may lose their lives ought not to be described by code words which imply a boastful or overconfident sentiment. . . . Proper names are good in this field. The heroes of antiquity, figures from Greek and Roman mythology . . ."). Maybe in that sense it was a double fake out—meant to make anyone who discovered its true name doubt themselves.

Here I am both bodyguard and overlord, though we've moved a bit past June 6, 2008, on our story timeline (past, even, incidentally, June 9, the day the iPhone 3G hit the general market for $199). But what can I say, I like the metaphor.

Fiction is the lie through which we tell the truth. Camus said that. He's a good one to read if you want to feel better about the impoverishing and unorthodox life choices you have made. I'm sorry for pretending to be an omniscient narrator. I'm sorry for hiding my protagishness behind the supposedly free indirect discourse of others. I faked you out, but I'm telling you the truth now. And it's not because I wanted to storm your beaches. It's because I didn't know how else to do it. I'd never written a book before. I'd read a lot of them, but reading to escape your shit life is a different thing than writing to start a new one. Plus, I was working with a partial draft. Stevie had started the book when she moved back home, just like the story says. It was in first person, and it was supposedly nonfiction but it smacked of romance novel. Reading it, I could tell I was reading the life she had anticipated would await her after she left New York, rather than the truth of what was really going on (no mention of Elvis or the cocaine, just for starters). The story was supposed to be: Midwestern girl moves back home from the big city for a do-over, returns to her roots, falls back in with a rakish ex, finds true love in all the old places. But it wasn't working out that way, and Stevie struggled more and more to write it.

By the time I got to it, the narrative felt set, irreparable, if you think of narrative as a kind of rending, which I do now. I took what she gave me, what she'd abandoned, and I backed it up a bit, de-romanced it (sorry about the chlamydia, Stevie) and tried, for once in my life, to tell the truth about my family. It went from a blog-turned-book to a novel because I couldn't continue in a first person that was not myself but my estranged sister. That felt too much like actual lying. And though, yes, this is a work of fiction (kind of), and fiction tells stories, it should never lie.

The truth is, this story is only a little bit my story, just like Jen's apartment was only a little bit my home for a little while. Books are houses, after all, but ever since the mess at the first one, the house of my father, I've never wanted another. Or, I'm content with this one, such as it is, because I built it myself. Books and houses are big on boundaries, on closings. And while I'm no fan of happy endings (the biggest narrative lie of them all), I do want a little more light on my skin—even the scarred parts, even the burns and holes. Maybe those most of all.

Anyway, I didn't know how to fix the story, once I'd broken it with, well, me. But even that's more realistic. I'm always breaking things. Family trust. Mom's mortgage. My own one dear body. Or, at least, the old me did. So something about my authorial intrusion felt true despite the trickery.

I left it the book this way expecting Amanda Collins to tell me the deal was off. Instead, she called me drunk and possibly coked up one Friday night and said she loved it—Brilliant! Postmodern! Actually what she said was, "Fuckin' meta, James." And that was the last I heard about it. Frankly, I think she was desperate to prove to my editor that her insistence on letting me ghostwrite under Stevie's contract hadn't been a colossally bad idea. A delivered manuscript, even one poorly conceived and executed, was a win.

Don't worry—Stevie's alive. But by the time everything went down, was over and epilogued and cleaned up again, she had lost interest in writing the book. "I don't want to write about myself or my life or Taylor or Jen or you—no offense. And definitely not Elvis," is how she put it. The narrative she was expecting and trying to write fell apart and after that, she didn't know how to make a story out of all the pieces. Everything felt too pat or too sentimental or too simple. Life was a mess. Books can't be a mess. They have to be organized. Or at least, that's what Stevie thought. My whole life has been a disorganized mess, so I'm okay with a little bit of narrative chaos. And I don't blame her for not wanting that. She was upset about a lot of stuff that came out but, ultimately, she's a practical person—we Iowans are—and she didn't want a good book deal to go to waste. It was her way of helping me without actually sacrificing anything, and I respect and am thankful for that position. I talked to her a lot as I was writing the story and she gave me a ton of great insight into her own side of things. And Sam talked to me about his. Everyone was super helpful and I'm thankful to them. But anyway, this isn't the acknowledgments. Let's keep it rolling.

PART III

Chapter 9

If you want to know who killed Jen, it was me.

Not directly. I mean, like, not in the library with the lead pipe. But, I was bad for her and whatever else was going on with her. My presence in her life didn't help.

If you really want to hear about it, the first thing you'll probably want to know is where I was born, and what my lousy childhood was like. I don't feel like going into it but I will anyway, because you deserve as much and now, really, what choice do I have.

Thanks for reading this far.

When Stevie walked around Taylor, she was lost in a rainbow nostalgia daydream. When I walked around Taylor, all I wanted was to get out. All I saw was shit. It's another cliché of course, but all I remember from a young age was fighting. I don't want to sound ungrateful. I've met a lot of people in rehab whose parents did not do the basics or abused the shit out of them. It wasn't like that for us, but it hurt anyway. A five-year-old doesn't have the perspective to understand that he should be grateful that his parents, of which there are two, feed him food when he's hungry. He just sees the fighting. Feels it, really, deep in his body where it lives for the rest of his life. At least this is what therapists in recovery tell us. You do not need to medal in the suffering Olympics. You feel what you feel.

In my experience, in treatment, a lot of things become clear to you that had previously seemed complicated and a lot of things that had seemed knotted and twisted and strange suddenly became clear.

How much of my shitty life had I blamed on my father?

"Sure, he's an asshole," said Dr. Morris, "But so what?"

My friend Riley referred to this process as The Great Untangling.

We met when we came into the program together. She was younger than me, but we were both resort bums and we compared stories of the kitchens we'd cooked in, the spas we'd mopped.

"The Snowbird pool in a snowstorm," she said and closed her eyes blissfully.

"Better than H," I smiled and she'd laughed.

"Uh, no. But close. Close."

Riley and I liked to joke that she was Girl and I was Interrupted and someone would say, "What do you mean?" and Riley would say, "Well, it's because—" and I would cut her off and just start talking over her. That was it, that was the joke. We made it up one night at dinner when someone was telling the old Interrupting Cow knock-knock joke, a true dad joke if there ever was one, though I don't remember my father ever telling it. It wasn't very funny, but we both knew that, and somehow that made it come back around to being funny. We considered ourselves cleverer than everyone else, and that's because we were. But not that clever. We were both in rehab, after all, as we liked to remind each other.

I got clean because of Riley. Because I could feel her looking up to me in this way. With her, I got how it would feel to be someone's big brother. Somehow it made me understand Stevie better. I loved Riley but a small part of me was always trying to shake her off, too.

She gave us tiny hashmarks on our palms for every thirty days we spent sober. Little prison tattoos with my hard-time buddy. After the last one, we'd parted ways, promising to keep in touch. She'd flown back to her family in L.A. and I had bummed around Salt Lake for a while.

I almost used again after I got the call from Dr. Morris about her O.D. But then I didn't. These heart-wrenching fucking stories, common as dirt. That was ours. I kept making the hashmarks. I make them still.

So anyway, that's what I learned in rehab. That my parents were to blame for everything but that it also didn't matter. I want you to remember that while I tell you what I tell you next. Know that even if I haven't forgiven them, I think I at least understand them a little more. That my dad, while an asshole, was also trying in his own way. That my mom was kind to us but also often at work or fighting with dad. Plus, I was a surprise and I think by the time I came around, they'd used up all their good will and energy raising Stevie. All this fighting was mysterious to me until it wasn't. More on that shortly.

I didn't sleep well as a child, and Stevie, because she was much older, was fascinating to me. I followed her everywhere. I eavesdropped and spied so much that my spying gave the house a completely different texture. It had secrets and I kept them.

One night, sleepless and curious about Stevie as I often was, I wandered down from my room. I was restless, that was part of it, but I also had a weird sense that something important was happening or about to happen. I don't really believe in haunted houses or ghosts, but I do think houses have a kind of accumulated intelligence, certain fields of energy from the ways their inhabitants inhabit them. I followed the too-heavy silence of the house into the basement, where the energy beckoned me, and I witnessed the threesome that opens this book. I had not yet encountered porn—was still too young to have friends who brought it menacingly to school—and for the longest time I couldn't figure out quite what was happening. It seemed like something painful but then it seemed like the opposite of that. And it made something low in me quiver and grow hot, and the shame I felt was immediate and crushing. This was something I was never to have seen, that seemed, on some primal level, completely wrong, yet I couldn't look away. It was utterly terrifying.

But then Stevie threw up, and the basement began to flood, and I ducked back around the opposite corner of the stairwell and into my father's stereo room, a musty space with a dimmer on the light switch and carpeted walls to dampen the sound of the hi-fi. He'd play Stevie Wonder and Michael Jackson. Moon Martin, Frank Zappa. Leslie Gore, Kool and the Gang, Fleetwood Mac, Donna Summer, the Beach Boys. He'd crank it all as high as he could without damaging the speakers. It was a man-cave before man-caves were common. It was the way he separated himself from us—his little sonic cocoon. And in the room there was a large, cool cedar chest. I liked to lay in it sometimes, wrapped in my mother's wedding dress, smelling the forest around me and imagining myself a fawn, alone, ears flicking for any coming signs of danger.

After I watched Stevie, Jen, and Sam go outside and saw the river reaching toward us, I hid in the cedar chest, my calm place, thinking I might be born away safely in the coming tsunami. Thinking that probably I deserved to die for what I'd seen. But no tsunami came. The carpet took on water that night, but the real flooding would not begin in earnest until the dam gave way the next morning. That night, as I lay, my heart pounding against the cedar, I heard voices and cracked the lid. There was my father in his terrycloth robe and suede mule slippers in the stereo room. And there was Jen, looking nothing like a child next to him. Not the way Stevie did. Though of course she was.

The other thing was the way my father was looking at her. He looked hungry. He looked like the thing I imagined I was hiding from in the chest. "What were you doing down here?" he asked in the same voice he used when we were in trouble. I thought he might spank her. But Jen looked him right in the eye.

"I was licking your daughter, Dan."

He reached out for her then and she danced away a little. "You want a kiss? I probably still taste like her." He reached again, like an animal taking a swipe, and this time Jen let herself be caught. He didn't kiss her, but he put his hand on her crotch, those little cut-off shorts she had squirmed back into so quickly, and slipped a finger inside her, then caught his breath. "You're so wet." And like that they were on each other and I saw my father's penis for the first time, and it frightened me. Him on his knees, that piece of him reaching, straining for her and she straddling him, disappearing him inside her, his hand splayed over her whole ass, crab-walking them backwards until his back was against the far wall, and he popped the lock on the door and turned the dim light off and there was just the squicking of them together, like something stuck in river mud. And then it was over, their silence heavier and more complete than the anxious silence before the threesome, and from inside the cedar chest, I heard the sound of humans composing themselves and then the door opened and closed and neither one of them said a word to each other and I thought they would surely hear the sound of my heart breaking, which sounded to me like a distant, whining thud, the sound of a missile landing on the earth but not exploding. I stayed there for a long time, and when I came out, I heard my dad around the corner, slopping around on the carpet, starting up the wet/dry vac, and I ran back upstairs as lightly and quickly as I could.

In the upstairs hallway, the light was on under Stevie's door, but not my parents' and I hated my mother for being stupid enough to sleep while her house was coming down around her. I continued to feel that way for some time.

Stevie left the next summer. She'd been my lifeline, the only one in the world I knew I could still trust, though I never and could not have articulated this to her. And then she was gone without even asking me how I felt about it. And our parents were now officially split and that's when I started to see Taylor's true face.

You could look at Taylor and see a hip town with a lively bar scene and a lot of nice, hardworking Midwestern people being kind to each other, or you could see something else. You could see the look in their eyes when the kids in my junior high talked about fags. The murderous glee. The trailer parks. The way the pastureland and prairie shrank year by year. One day there, the next day a hill of dirt with a development sign on top. Like someone was waiting to be congratulated. I met some older men who were not picky about my age and they introduced me to weed, then meth, then the rest of it. You can say that I was their victim or you can say that they provided me the only paternal warmth I would feel as a teenager. Later, I told my mom I got addicted from prescription pills after an injury out West, but it was a lie. The truth was, I was curious and eager to be delivered from the hellscape of my life and I never said no, and, back in the happy, early days of oxy, it was cheap and easy to get.

Later, I would find the guys who drove around Omaha all day with packets of black tar heroin tucked into their cheeks like demented chipmunks. Later, I would keep moving West as far as I could and never find the end of the great opiate highway of America. This was after things got worse, after my mom started dating Harry. That's when I knew it was time to escape.

Now I know there is no escape.

I mean there is. Jen found it. But I'm a sunk-cost kind of person. I've been through too much shit to bail now.

Taylor is not a place I miss or like. But it is a very American place. I can say that as someone who has roamed the country trying to outrun myself and the horror is the same everywhere.

By the time I ran into Jen, I was clean. I had just done three months at the fancy place in Utah my mom paid for (which I'm hoping to pay her back for with the proceeds of this book—thank you for doing your part!). But I almost didn't see her.

When I walked into the apartment and found Sam in Jen's bathroom, I recognized him right away, even covered in blood. He has one of those sweet Midwestern faces. A real Aaron Eckhart. Enormous head, big eyes, dimples. Ageless. The girls had loved him, my sister and the rest—including a number of underclassmen after she graduated. His panty-dampening was so renowned that I encountered tales of it when *I* got to high school, even though it had been years since he'd graduated. Like an echo in a chamber, a fart in a car, his reputation as a hot dude hung around the way things could in a small town.

I only mention this because the first time I saw her, I didn't recognize Jen at all, though I'd spent way more time thinking about her in the intervening years than I had of Sam, or even my own sister. I mean, she looked familiar. I knew I knew her. But it took a while to figure it out.

I was at this cute little café up near DePaul. I liked to sit there and write and pretend to be a student. Sometimes, sitting there, I was visible. Some cute girl or guy would mistake my frayed hems and grease stains for fashion. I admit to cultivating a look, to the best of my abilities, and writing in longhand was a thing at the moment. My laptop lack, my yellow notebook—it could have been a choice instead of something thrust upon me by poverty. And my skin was clear and true. I was a beautiful lost boy. The illusion was nearly perfect when I'd had a shower at the Y, when my bruises were covered. But it never lasted long. There would be an invitation: a date, a meet-up, a park walk, whatever. Once in a while, I went. It was better when it was on the same day, so it wasn't odd that I was in the same clothes. So I had not yet accumulated the stink of another night outside, or in a shelter, or someone else's apartment. Once, this big boy, this cub, walked me into Lincoln Park and we ran into two of my friends from LPCS. Lager and Pete were high on something, calling out my real name and screeching like peacocks. Practically shitting themselves with mirth. And this cub, this new thing—that was all it took for the fuzzy outline of me to snap into focus. "Hey, James?" he'd growled and I knew then that it was coming and my hopes of a hook-up in all the ways that can mean, were dashed. "Are you like, homeless?"

There was no point in denying it. They only asked when they were totally sure. It wouldn't have mattered to a certain type, I knew, but that wasn't the type I wanted. I wanted cute students. I wanted dorm rooms and bad tattoos and leggings and youth dew. I tried to steer clear of the homeless students, who could offer me nothing but to blow up my spot and reveal me as a philistine. Whenever I met one at the shelter, I avoided it for a few days after.

Chicago is a city of many things, but it is not a place of limitless possibility. It is not a city wherein a young homeless man, no matter how pretty, can get his fuckfill of Blue Demons and Wildcats. The children of Chicago know their class. In Chicago, you grow up pinned to a nabe and that nabe is who you are. And an Englewood cannot make it to the organic moderne restaurants of Randolph Street, though they are less than ten miles apart and connected by train, though the good suburbanites of Crystal Lake and Arlington Heights sit on the Ike for hours on Friday nights to drive in for a meal, then drive back out. Chicago is a city designed to be divided and so it is. And all the seraphic DePaul ass, and all the Northwestern polymaths won't touch a homeless kid once they find out.

Or maybe I have that wrong. Maybe I'm being unfair to Chicago. I've been accused of being unpleasant and humorless before. Anyway, it didn't matter anymore after I ran into Jen one day at my café. I recognized her as someone I knew but I couldn't place who she was. I sensed she was from my deep past. Had I waited tables with her in Park City? Had I smoked meth with her one night after closing time, or both? Addicts in recovery always have to be careful about this. It took about twenty minutes and a lot of stolen glances to confirm her. But when I knew, I knew, and some mechanism in me clunked into place and the old feelings and fears started to crank up. I watched as she pursed her lips over her latte and read the contents of some sort of portfolio. I thought about not approaching her—that would ruin my spy, after all, and I knew that she figured much more in my childhood than I figured in hers. If I figured in hers at all. I might have left it at that if an old failure hadn't spotted me from across the room, and proclaimed, in that frattish way that is somehow simultaneously aggro and charming, "Miller! Hey, Miller!" and though I saw that she paid this no mind, when the bro added my first name, something flickered across her face, and she looked up. Right up at me.

She squinted as he dapped me ("the terrorist fist jab" as white conservative America would come to know it that summer thanks to Fox News). The bro was nice and eager to show there were no hard feelings on his part, though I still winced when I thought of the way he'd reddened then blanched, skinned of his shirt. The way he'd stepped back and kept stepping back, something about me suddenly so wrong he had sling-shotted away from me, leaving me alone and sober at the club.

I could feel her looking at me as he walked away, tilting toward me. And then she was there, at my table, in my light.

"You're James. You're Stevie Miller's little brother."

"Jen."

"You're a grown up."

"It happens to the worst of us."

"Only the good die young?"

"Obviously, right? We're still here."

She liked that—her eyes narrowed but a big smile lifted her face. The same face now that I had placed it. She had hardly aged at all—all that fair ginger skin. Fine porcelain still.

"Tell me everything about your life," she said, and she meant it. In a real way. Not like when you run into someone you went to high school with at the mall and you coo at each other about how wonderful and fulfilling your lives are before rushing off to whomever to report back about how fat, how old, how bald, how poorly dressed you'd found each other. Which is probably why I said what I said next.

"To be honest, it's been pretty shitty since you fucked my dad." I didn't say it out of spite, you see, but because she truly wanted to know. And this was the truth. My truth.

She put a soft hand on my wrist and gently tugged. "We need wine for this." And so we went downstairs, where the burble of the espresso machine gave way to a velvet-curtained wine bar, and she ordered a bottle of rosé, my favorite, which, I admit, disarmed me. I hadn't had a drink in a while, but drinking has never been my problem, and I accepted a glass. I needed something for this, too. Her insistence that I tell her my story also disarmed me. She never once tried to deny it or make excuses, even after I'd had it all out. She looked full of sympathy. It is not an easy thing to sustain a look of sympathy without it, at some point, appearing strained or insincere. And when I was done with my story, she said, "I'm sorry I hurt your family," and I believed her. But when I asked her why she'd done it—seduced my father and my sister (and I would later find out, Sam too, under my sister's nose, though it is not such a great feat to fool my sister), her face kind of emptied out.

"I don't know, Jay." No one had called me Jay since I was little and I liked it. "I want to think I'm a good person, but sometimes I do things that don't seem to support that thesis." And then she looked more worried than blank, and then somewhat alarmed—as if she'd just gotten a bad diagnosis—and then she was blank again. She bought us another bottle, though it was all her drinking by then, and she asked me what I was up to, and I felt pity for her because this line of questioning would make her feel even worse. But, besides pity, I also felt a groinal tingling at the prospect of continuing to make her feel uncomfortable.

"I'm homeless, which is also, in essence, my job."

She blanched—they all do, which is why I don't say a thing to the ones I want to fuck—then blushed. That fair skin of hers forever giving her away. "Why?"

"Most people don't view it as a choice," I said, allowing the chewy vowel sounds to crisp up into sarcasm.

"You did. Didn't you? Choose it?"

And here, I actually got mad. I became hissy, low voiced. "Do you know how it was in the house after the divorce? The divorce *you* caused? After we had a house again, which took a really long time? My mom was devastated, my dad and sister took off, and it was so quiet for years. For years, my mom just worked and made dinner. I'd go down to Florida once a year to see my dad and hang out with his new family—he had twin baby girls with that dumb Evangelical wife of his. I hated them all. Stevie never came home. Maybe once in awhile at Thanksgiving, but it started to feel like I'd dreamed a sister, like I'd made her up. But then, when I saw her, and I remembered how she'd just left me, left us, when I needed her, then I hated her, too. So that's how it was for a few years until things finally started to seem a little normal again, I guess because I just got used to it all. Then my mom's new boyfriend started creeping in on me. By that point I was fifteen. Old enough to know if I didn't get out, I'd probably get raped. So I mailed my mom a letter and went to Colorado on a bus."

Jen looked stricken. "I didn't realize. . . ."

"Oh yeah, ripple effect. Anyway, for a while, it wasn't like being homeless. It was just traveling. And there were the mountains. And in the winter I could usually get a ski resort job and those come with housing, so then I wasn't homeless. The housing ate up most of the paycheck but it was a place to live and food to eat. And then in the spring and summer I camped and worked at Home Depot. But eventually the work dried up. I was also deep into heroin by then."

Jen flinched and looked down at my arms, landed on the three solid triple bands of black ink encircling my forearm, the ones I'd put there to hide the scars.

"I got done with rehab, then I came here because I didn't know anyone who could get me heroin here." This was the Cliffs Notes. The longer version is that I had tried to stay in Utah, clinging and scared after Riley's death, thinking it would be the safer choice. I had even picked up a janitorial shift at Vivint Arena for a while and found a room share through that job but, wouldn't you know it, my roommate turned out to be a junkie. I didn't know if we emitted some kind of subconscious signal, some opioid pheromone to each other or what, but the night I found him passed out in our bathroom with his works scattered beside him, I knew I had to leave.

"So you came to *Chicago*?"

I shrugged. "These days sometimes the cities are cleaner than the towns, or at least they're not that much worse, if you don't know anyone. Plus it's about as near to Taylor as I'm willing to get. And I want to see my mom at some point."

"How long have you been clean?"

"Thirteen months." I opened my palm to her, to show her the hashmarks. The last was still scabby. I wouldn't tell her about Riley that night, but eventually, I would. It made sense—they reminded me of each other.

"Where are you staying tonight?"

"Lincoln Community, maybe." The truth was I hadn't decided yet because I'd hoped to make someone here and set it up.

"Let's go get your stuff—I want you to come home with me."

In the winters, when the inversion was upon the valley, the clean air of the Wasatch high above Salt Lake City felt like absolution. Who needs a home who has boughs and caves and the prickly embrace of the mountains and the high plains desert? The sound of water was always somewhere in the mountains, carving out rock, carving out a space for you when the snows began and the creeks iced over. I'd developed a taste for mountains on the Front Range, but left Colorado when I'd heard the mountains of Salt Lake were closer in, the heroin cheaper. A bus ride to get you up or down the mountain and into a righteous, gleaming city full of dope. Zion they called it, and it was.

Somewhere on the road, a copy of *Walden* had come into my possession and I kept it with me, always, though the book seemed written for a place wilder and more magical than exurban Massachusetts, even before it was an exurb. It made my homelessness feel like a project instead of a blight, though there were nights I shuddered myself to sleep wondering what the fuck I was doing, feeling carved out and desiccated, sick, sure I must have HIV. Sure I could feel it beginning to gnaw away at my kidneys, my liver. I felt enlarged in all the wrong places. I could go home. I could go home to my mother. I thought about it often. But I was not done punishing her for decisions other people had made for her. I was not done punishing her for Harry, whose long nails made soft scratching circles on my back through my school basketball jersey. Whose hand had once landed on my thigh, pinkie brushing my dick tip, dick reacting instinctively—a kind of boinging—followed by a more intellectual shriveling. The man was a walking After School Special, and I chalk it up to my mother's loneliness that she would ever tolerate such a creep. Mom who was wiry, small, hard. Whose bedside manner must have seemed reassuringly bullet proof. She was a fighter and she wanted other people to be fighters. My father could not be convinced and she had yelled him out of the house straight into Jen. The soft warmth of her giving so easily after all those hard scrabble scuffs at home. It must have been like sinking into a warm bath. It must have been like heroin. No thought, all sigh.

There was nothing more beautiful than the polluted mountains at sunset, straw up your nose or needle in vein, that soft desert wind that smelled like pine and cedar. The oranges and purples of that particulated sky. The way you were so much closer to it there, almost a mile up, even in the valley. Chicago was the ugliest place on earth by comparison, a trash heap of a city. Don't tell someone from the mountains about your mid-century International, your Bauhaus-inspired, your Prairie style. It was all yellow-brick garbage to me. Which is what I needed. Which is why I went there. I needed an anchor, some V-thread sunk deep in, to keep me from floating off into that velvet ether.

I slept on the pull-out couch in Jen's living room some nights. Some nights, I didn't come home. In some strange way, it felt more delicious to be out on the street after Jen gave me a bed, because then I really was choosing it. I felt an invisible umbilicus tethering me to that empty bed and I knew nothing would happen to me because of it. That's what it's like to have a home—you're fearless, bulletproof. To have a home is to always know where you should be. It meant you didn't have to worry too much about wherever you were because you knew where you were supposed to end up. A trip out was nothing more than a temporary absence.

My first couple of weeks in Jen's apartment, whenever I left it felt like wherever I went was incidental because I knew where I belonged. It's a very different feeling than when you're on the street, hoping for a bed, hoping not to get jacked for whatever you'd managed to scrounge for yourself especially in the winter—gloves, hand-warmer packets, cigarettes—but dreading it too because of all the bullshit that goes along with getting one. The good thing about the street, though, is you feel armored. You're always ready. After a couple of weeks at Jen's, I started to feel really vulnerable—kitten-like—when I left the house. Like any old thing could come murderously sailing into me. I was a soft-shell crab.

So I stopped staying there every night. Jen gave me a key, though, so I could come over when I wanted to, and even though I expected to disappoint her or cross some line, that never happened. Until, of course, it did.

That first night, though. We stayed up all night talking. Jen had gone to Northwestern and became a consultant right after. It was the late nineties, she told me. You either went into finance or became a consultant. There was so much money out there, waiting for people to come along and take it. Companies were pouring money into recruiting bright undergrads. There was still enough anxiety about computers to discourage a lot of kids, though Jen did invest some early money in Trilogy down in Austin. "Thrillogy" a classmate of hers called it and described working there as a Spring Break Mazatlan booze cruise for the smart kids. She lost her investment. It was an early lesson and why she moved from financial consulting into mortgage. There was something about a building. It was a thing; it existed. One could imagine any number of money-making moves happening inside it. One could imagine, as some of her colleagues did, an empty space with stacks of bills inside. Cash by the square foot. After the tech crash of 2000, this seemed like an even better bet. One that rested more squarely in the world of the concrete, sometimes literally. The Information Superhighway dream of the nineties had stalled, the World Wide Web was a place that was not really a place yet, which was something engineers knew—the engineers who negotiated seven-figure salaries and hundreds of thousands of stock points and bonuses if they went public. They went to their jobs and threw basketballs at tiny door hoops and had blue sky meetings and did not do much of anything because there wasn't much to do yet. They were ahead of their times, job-wise. They could build the back-end but when that was done, there wasn't much else to do but hire more people hot off their degrees in the hopes of finding one person who could tell them what the internet was for. They were building something whose shape and purpose was still a mystery. "Fuck that," said Jen. "I want material. I want bones." She said this with a mug of hot tea in both hands, cross-legged across from me on her couch. Her long sleeves went right up to her knuckles and she swam in her threadbare men's Brooks Brothers button down, soft and broken in. A tiny silver Tiffany bean winked from her collarbone. She cultivated the kind of sloppiness and chintz that comes with old money. The over-washed white Converse loose on her tan, pedicured feet. Though solidly middle class herself, she had studied class as her extracurricular and she knew it was essential to reflect richness back to rich people in such a way as to convince them to hand over large chunks of their money to you.

Though, in real estate, she explained, you were just as likely to be working with the great-grandchildren of mobsters and teamsters. "But after 9/11, everything just seemed so fragile. Those buildings. The planes looked like toys. The money started to dry up. I've just been hanging on and trying to do what I can, you know?"

That first night, both of us shrimped out on her couch, we talked about everything. It felt giddy and a little desperate—there was something gasping about the ways we reached out to each other. I think we were both so lonely. And I did. I fell for her. Technically, I wasn't interested in much of anything besides dick back then (and dope—it was never far from my thoughts). But Jen was enchanting. I had ideas about things. I had *Walden*. But I wasn't used to having conversations. Somehow the conversation with Jen, even though she was talking finance and corporate shit I didn't know anything about, was interesting. Sexy, actually. She had a way. I'm sure you've picked up on it by now. When you talked to her, you felt like she was holding you very close and there was a smell—not even a smell, but a suggestion of a smell—something creamy and fresh that gave way to a sandalwood growl. It seemed too abstract to be an actual smell, but I suppose it was some perfume or another. In any case, I definitely wanted to fuck her, like she'd fucked my sister and father. Maybe it was something in the Miller blood. Maybe it was the whiff of incest and the essential thing that's wrong inside of me. But I think it's why I felt somewhat tethered to the bed she offered. I had thoughts about literal bed tethers. I wanted to put as much of her body into my mouth as would fit. How can I describe it? She made me hungry.

We lived like that for a while. Me coming and going, her doing her best to redistribute the world's wealth to the top one percent. But one night, she found pills on the floor after I'd come home from some club or other. She confronted me, "Are you using again?" She was mad. I wasn't using—I'd been stashing and selling pills to college students for months at that point. Some kid would hand me a couple in a bathroom and I'd pretend to take them then sell them on Craigslist later. But she didn't believe me and then she kicked me out. To be fair, I wouldn't have believed me either, but we got into a huge fight. We said mean things, you know how it goes. At some point I blamed her for wrecking my entire life, and she broke down. "I know," she said, "I know I did. You're right." And I let her cry for a while before I went to her and we both cried. She told me that she knew that she was a piece of shit. She was a piece of shit, that was indisputable, she said. But she was a scared piece of shit. I didn't know what she meant but when I looked into her face, I could plainly see how scared she was and I wondered how I'd missed it before.

That's how she put it, scared. Not anxious or worried. She was scared. The world was so scary. The more she learned about it, the less she wanted to know. I asked her what she meant and she said she was looking into some shady stuff with the bank. I asked her which bank and she said, "All of them." And I asked her what she meant, and she told me a long story about securities and bad loans. About how she'd figured out their mortgage office was setting people up for foreclosure, not verifying employment, offering way too much capital even to people who were truthful about their income, and when she looked at the names on these loans: Leroy Johnson, Letitia Costa, Ramon Barrera, Destiny Jackson.

I didn't totally get all of what she was saying but I got this. "They're not white."

"Some of them are, but a lot of them aren't. And I guess it's possible that they're all totally middle class and able to pay their ARMs. But . . . it doesn't feel right to me. I'm going to go out to the mortgage office in Iowa next week and see for myself. I think the banks are giving bad loans to a lot of vulnerable people. Something very, very fucked is about to happen. Is already starting to happen, I think."

"What are you going to do?" I asked. She didn't know.

I spent one last night there, and then I never stayed there again. I went out the next day and got a job at a gas station and, a couple days later, I happened into a shitty, tiny studio apartment and paid three months down with the pill money. Though we'd made up, the fight loomed large in my mind, and so did Jen's talk of economic collapse. It had all spooked me—the idea that she might be making up conspiracy theories, the idea that she might not be, the growing emotional intimacy that the fight seemed to hint at and which made me deeply uncomfortable. I was not and still am not great at being close to people, for reasons familiar by now. To be honest, I also wanted to keep moving pills without someone breathing down my neck about it.

The owners of the gas station, Luis and Ana, gave me a steep employee discount and that helped my wages go farther too, though I ended up eating a lot of ramen and Doritos. They were a nice older Dominican couple and I'd come to find out they had a son my age who had moved to California. They hated working nights because they sometimes got robbed, so I worked nights for them. Sometimes the wife dropped off plates of plantains and beans when she showed up in the middle of my shift, picking up the cash and whisking it away. Once in a while some tweaker would walk in with a gun or a bat or a knife and I'd have jack shit to give him, and he'd tweak on out, almost relieved, it seemed to me, that he'd committed a lesser crime than the one he'd planned on. These nights unsettled me, but, how can I explain? I was never truly scared. You live out in the world long enough and you can tell when you're in the presence of a sociopath, someone who would truly like to hurt you, whether or not it benefits him directly. You develop a sense. I had a sense for the neighborhood assholes and I'd show them my empty cash drawer, and point to the sign that read NO HAY CAJA FUERTE AQUI/NO SAFE ON PREMISES but I didn't let them go empty-handed. They always got a box of Lemonheads or a Mars Bar for their troubles. For all its murderous corners, Chicago is a city of candy, and it amused me to give them the local stuff. Sometimes they laughed as they ran out the door.

I read about her in the paper, in the so-late-its-early hours at work, hot off the presses. It was something to do that made me feel tethered more securely to the world around me. Like Jen's keys. After years of bouncing around, it felt really good to be tied to something that way. I was ringing up a suit for a small coffee and a *Tribune* and there she was at the bottom of the front page. Flatland, 2-D. A news-bite curiosity. "Woman Jumps From 'Poetry' Garage." Film at 11. I almost didn't read it, but my eyes snagged on her name and I picked up the paper. My throat closed and the guy stood there with his coffee in one hand, trying to figure out why I wasn't handing him his newspaper. "Get another one," I said without looking up and he snarled at me but obeyed then left.

I couldn't believe it, but I could. I thought it must be someone else even while I knew it wasn't. I called her and called her and when I couldn't get her, I left work and ran to her house. I let myself in. I waited there all day and night, like that pitiful dog who walked itself to the commuter rail every day for years after its owner died. I sat vigil on the fold-out, my old bed when I wasn't in hers, now folded in, on its uncomfortable, tasteful beige cushions. I remember the city was so loud at night. I'd never noticed the noise before though I'd slept there, on and off, for months. It sounded like a conch shell held to the ear. It sounded like the street was asking me to join it. I saw myself curled on the sidewalk below like a fetal pig and I understood. For a minute it did seem like an option, no worse than any other. That's how I knew she'd done it. That moment. There had been no murder like Sam claimed, but I came to realize that my sudden absence may have played a roll. I sat very still after that, shifting only when my back began to hurt and I sat there until the morning. I stayed for a few days in more or less this state. Then I took her one plant, a pothos perched on the top of her refrigerator. The tendrils almost reached the floor and I threw them over my shoulders like the arms of a dance partner and left with it.

So, when I say I killed her, this is what I mean. You walk up to someone crouched on an invisible precipice and bump them and they fall. It's not murder, but it's not like you're an innocent bystander, either. Some part of me may have known something was wrong even before our fight, before I left. And looking back, I suppose I think she seemed smaller, diminished somehow in those last few weeks. But that may be my own projection. Her death masque projected over the top of her real face. Maybe I knew something was wrong, but I also didn't.

One of those last nights, which I didn't know at the time would be a last night, she had come to my bed. In my memory, the scene is constellated, each moment trapped within itself and next to but somehow not connected to the others. There is her hand under my t-shirt, my stomach tense. "I have never been in love," she said. "But people seem to fall in love with me."

There is the mumble of my mouth on her undulating animal throat, "There is something about you."

She is still but there's an energy coiled around her, like she is about to spring and bite. "I feel like the likable heroine in a romance novel. Or like a femme fatale. I feel like a character in someone else's novel. Like an astral projection. People put all their shit onto me and see themselves in me, and somehow I reflect something back to them that makes them happy. Do you ever feel like that? Like someone's flattened, empty pouch?"

I wrap her hair around my fist, pull back, round her neck backwards.

She tries to swallow and there is just a dry-clicking.

I tighten my grip.

What had I ever read as open about her? I look upside down into her eyes and they are hammered tin. Flat, dull.

"Fuck me," she says. "Fuck your fucked up divorced daddy dick dream of me."

I let her hair go and she wrapped a hand around my wrist. Her grip was bruise-strong.

To be honest and hypocritical, I do not think it is anyone's business what happened next.

I was there at the funeral, of course, in Iowa, more or less in disguise, my sister and Sam having not laid eyes on me for years and having, that night, only eyes for each other. I admit to taking some liberties with point of view. I admit to imagineering some sex scenes starring my sister. To which I say: Sometimes we do the things we do to keep the boundaries of ourselves in place.

In my more generous hours, I think that's all Sam and Stevie were trying to do: keep themselves in place. Stevie herself gave me that line about how her life in New York felt held in place by nothing more substantial than a thumb tack. She wanted more. She wanted something that felt like a real life, even if it meant reconstructing an old one.

And Sam. I guess Sam's problem in general was that he didn't know the boundaries of himself, and he found a kind of Dionysian oblivion in booze, in Jen. She mentioned him to me once, about how he was calling her a lot—more than usual. "What's usual?" I said.

She shrugged, "once a month."

I made a little noise, "For how long?"

"Like six years."

We didn't talk about it again after that.

Jen and I didn't talk about Sam, but Sam and I talked a lot about Jen.

Though I still had a key, I hadn't been back to the apartment since right after the funeral. I couldn't bear it. I had, in fact, taken a long time to psych myself up for my visit that night, unsure if I'd even be able to get in the door—perhaps the lock had been changed, maybe her parents had sold the place or put it on the market already, eager to be rid of it. There might be a realtor's box on the doorknob. That thought had panicked me so much that I knew I needed to visit one more time before the place was inevitably emptied.

To be honest with you, I did have a couple of O's in my pocket and while I hadn't planned on doing them, I also hadn't not planned on it. Jen would have been so pissed, I know. But I didn't. Do them I mean. For a minute, when I walked into that bathroom, I thought I was seeing my own dead body and it scared the shit out of me. Once I realized it was Sam in the tub, and that he wasn't dead, I flushed them. He saved me. I hope you *do* read that part, Sam. Thank you.

From the looks of it, he had been close to aspirating his own bathwater when I found him. One of Jen's old journals was bleeding its ink onto the bathroom floor, pages puffy and already dry. Like some good luck spell gone wrong. This made me angry—Jen was a proud person and would have been humiliated to know Sam had done this, had read her journals. I was sure the only reason they were still around is because she'd forgotten to pitch them. There were photos scattered in the kitchen, and the shards of something sharp and broken on the floor. There was an old sticky bottle of Malibu rum turned over on the kitchen counter, and more empties on the bar cart, which he'd wheeled into the hallway. I took this all in after I'd gotten him, prone and gasping and shivering, out of the tub.

The murder talk began almost right away "I killed a man," he said to me. Not hello or what the hell are you doing here or who are you.

"Haven't we all?" I said. "Sam, do you recognize me? It's James. Stevie's little brother." And Sam smiled and said, "No, you're an angel."

"Hardly," I said, but it pleased me to hear this.

After helping him into his clothes and heating up a frozen Amy's burrito from Jen's freezer, I gave Sam another bath. That might sound odd—it had taken all my strength to haul him out the first time and we were practically strangers to each other. But he was trembling and wrecked. The burrito had not revived or sobered him and he seemed cold still, though it was finally warming up a bit outside.

I remembered when he'd once done the same for me, that summer in the motel, when Mom and Dad were at each other and could hardly be bothered to feed us. I remember I stank—even I could smell myself, little though I was—and when Stevie insisted, I only demurred a little. I wanted Sam to do it I told her, aware even then of the small way that would slice her. This is the secret of children—their blunders are sometimes not blunders at all. What other way is there to assert power in a world that denies it to you? So Sam had bathed me gently, and at the end of the bath I lay on the bottom of the fiberglass insert, embraced by the echoing whoosh of an emptied tub and he put a towel on top of me and told me to close my eyes. I did and he told me a little story in which I was shooting through the universe on top of a dragon in flight. I was far away from the quarrels of my parents, and those damp brown motel bedrooms, the squeaky cot that smelled like my own piss.

At Sam's side at the bathtub, I gave him no dragon—he had clearly found his own—but I scrubbed him gently with something that smelled so poignantly of Jen that it choked me for a second. For a second I wished for those pills back. Then I got down to the business of detoxing Sam, which mainly meant flushing the rest of the alcohol in the apartment (of which there was very little left), feeding him, holding him when he had tremors, which weren't too bad, fetching blankets and making him drink water by the gallons. Talking him out of the idea that Jen had been murdered and that he had murdered another person.

"You said that before. Can you explain, please?" said Stevie when I got to that part. By then, night had arrived in Chicago and it was a perfect one—rare that summer. The streets giving up the heat of the day, the air kissing us through the open window screens.

"It's okay now," said Sam.

"I'm getting there," I said and kept talking.

Sam and I had squatted in Jen's apartment in Chicago for nearly two weeks, waiting for the electricity and water to be shut off, which never happened. He told me Jen's parents were still waiting for him, to bring something of hers home. I wondered if they would find us here someday, call the cops, but they never came. I found out later what he brought them: a hideous clown salt shaker. When he showed it to me I recoiled. "Sam, what the fuck?" I said. "You can't give that to them." He stroked it and slipped it back into his jacket pocket and told me the story of their day at the fair.

It took some time for him to get better. And it wasn't just detoxing. Kowalski had clearly beaten him badly, apparently when Sam was blacked out. He spent a few days gibbering about murdering the man, about seeing a body on the ground, about gouts of blood. He wouldn't let me take him to the hospital. He was terrified of seeing a cop.

That first week, Sam watched the news for hours and hours, steeling himself for a body, until finally one day I called Satchel Ferry on speakerphone and asked to speak with Kowalski myself. I hung up after the operator transferred me over and a gruff voice said, "What?"

"See?" I said to Sam. "Not murdered. In fact, he probably nearly killed you."

Sam took a deep breath, "That might have been him. But if he *is* alive, he's still my prime suspect."

"Sam!" I wondered, not for the first time, if he had permanent brain damage and whether it was from the alcohol or the beating. "No one murdered Jen." I picked up one of the bathwater-swollen composition notebooks that were still strewn around the apartment. "She was ill. Depressed. She felt responsible for this mess," I gestured to the television, which was now always on, as another beacon of doom ticked across the bottom of the screen. "Housing Market Apocalypse?" it read, under Wolf Blitzer's tightly groomed head. By July, the question mark would be gone.

I went to work at the gas station most days, and when I came back, Sam was always either sitting on the couch in front of the TV or re-reading Jen's journals, scouring them for some sign of her murderer, of her illness, of himself, of his importance to her. Whatever he found seemed to leave him unsatisfied.

It took another week to get him to let go of the notion that she had been murdered.

"But how do you *know*?" he asked a hundred times. "Jen and I, we were supposed to meet up again. Do our thing again."

"What's your thing?"

"We always loved each other. I think she was my one true, real love."

"Have you been listening? Everyone thought that about her."

Sam had shaved and we sat across from each other, clutching coffees, dwarfing the dinette set, even though neither of us was particularly large. His eyes wandered away from me, so I said it again. "Everyone thought that. But what was she left with, in the end? She was all alone."

"She wasn't alone," Sam shook his head. "She was with whoever did this. Whoever . . . killed her." And he looked at me hard and I put my hands up.

"No. We've already been over this. Come on."

"Maybe it was you. How do I know *you* didn't murder her?"

I looked away from him down onto the avenue, at the streetlights reflecting off the cars as they oozed like mercury into the twilit distance. "Because I loved her, too."

After that, we didn't talk about it anymore.

I came to my theory about Sam later, after all this went down and we were back in Taylor, for better or worse. That detail in the second chapter, about the mystery novels in his office, is true. He'd asked me to run in there to grab some files for him when he was in rehab, after Bonnie had left. It all made sense suddenly—his paranoid idea that someone had been trailing him, his insistence that Jen was murdered. I had chalked it all up to paranoid alcoholic delirium, and it was, but certainly it had been spurred on by the wall of detective novels in front of me. There they all were Nick and Nora, Marlowe, Mike Hammer, Sam Spade, of course, and quite a lot of writers I'd never heard of. I took a few home with me and later got to know Joe Pitt, Dante Mancuso, Inspector Borlu, and Cassie Maddox. Though I'd always been genre neutral, I saw how these books could feed an obsession. Especially if the person in question was already a bit unstable. Just like houses, books aren't always sound structures.

*

It's true that I left out some parts of this story when I was telling it to Stevie and Sam, reunited there in Jen's living room. I left out the part about Sam being obsessed with Jen to spare Stevie. I left out the details of the sex parts too, to spare both of them, though I had to tell them both about our dad, of course. About our dad and Jen.

Though my recitation to them, and later to my mother, was abridged, I have held back nothing from you, reader. Though I consulted them heavily in its writing, I've suggested to each of them that they not read this book, not because I have been unfair, but because I haven't been. Because I have finally, here, at last, told the whole entire truth as I know and experienced it.

If they do read it (and I suspect they will, at some point—once you get a taste for the truth, it is difficult to go back), I hope that they find freedom in these pages, alongside the pain.

Please know that I tried my hardest. For once I really did.

And know that I love you.

And that I'm sorry.

"You saw us?" said Stevie, finally, after I'd had it all—or most of it—out. I'll never forget the look on her face. Sam's too. Both were stricken. "In the basement? And Dad . . . Dad and Jen?"

I nodded. I felt bad, but also, to get it off my chest, finally, after all these years? The feeling was indescribable. I did what I could while they processed this new old news. I held her hair while she threw up. Sam sat on the tub beside us clenching and unclenching his jaw, murderously silent.

Stevie was still spitting when the thought occurred to her.

"Mom doesn't know. Oh my god James, you can't ever, ever tell her."

"Mom can handle more than you think, Stevie."

"Fucking Dad," she said, and here she retched a bit more, until Sam put a big hand on her back and her body calmed down again. "Have you talked to him about this? What does he have to say for himself?"

"No, I haven't talked to him."

"Well, we're going to. Do you have his. . . . Just let me. . . ." she wandered out of the bathroom and found her big tote bag on the floor near the couch for her phone, forgetting it was dead. "Is there a charger around here?"

"What do you have?" I asked.

"Nokia."

I shook my head. "There's a store a few blocks down the street, a Rite Aid I think? That way," I gestured north. "But listen, I don't want to call Dad. I never want to talk to Dad again, to be completely honest."

She nodded and looked out the windows into the halos made by the streetlamps, into those lit up rooms where other people were living their strange and complicated lives. "Okay, it's fine. I don't know what I'd say anyway. I do still need to charge my phone though. All I have is a car charger and I think it's broken."

Later, she would tell it like this: she was walking into the Rite Aid, nodding to the security guard, who was nodding back when she heard someone say, very distinctly, right by her ear, "Hey." It was so clear and so close that she immediately turned toward it, and there, across the store at the far cash register, in a Cubs hat and sunglasses, but unmistakable, was Elvis. And he was buying a lot of duct tape. Rolls and rolls. And then she heard the voice again, a voice she would later attribute to her own instinct or maybe even the security guard, but which I can't help but think of as Jen.

The voice said, "Run."

So she turned around and ran out the door, ran around the corner and back down the street parallel to Jen's until she found the alley to the parking lot. Then she zipped up the alley and, first peeking around the corner like a cartoon character, then determining the coast was clear, she slid into the doorway and buzzed the apartment like a maniac.

When she came back up, she was coughing with breathlessness.

"What happened?" I asked, worried.

When she could catch her breath, she said, "I saw someone. Someone I know. And I don't know why but I think it's bad that he's here." And then she told us what she'd been doing with her summer. I can't lie—some twisted, horrible part of me was glad that she had finally sunk to my level. Or at least, had begun her descent. There would have to be a lot of sinking yet to do before she caught up with me.

"How did he find you?" I asked, still thinking maybe the whole thing was a weird coincidence.

"That's just it, I don't know. I never had the chance to tell him I was leaving. The only person I told was—" her eyes grew wide and she gasped. "Call Mom, you've got to call Mom right now."

When she answered, it was immediately clear something was wrong.

"James?" Mom's mouth sounded like it was full of marbles. She sounded confused, as though she wasn't sure if she was imagining me.

"Mom," that old pang inside. "Hi, Mom. Listen, I'm here with Stevie—"

Viv groaned, "Stevie's in danger, you have to tell her." Then there was a shifting sound and I heard someone else's voice in the background.

"Mom, where are you?"

"Hospital. Saint Joe's. Wait, Stevie's there with you? Is this a dream?"

I panicked and handed the phone to Stevie.

"Mom, it's me—"

Silence

"The hospital? Oh Jesus. What's—"

Stevie listened for a long time, then put the phone down and covered her eyes with her hands. "Oh my god, oh my god."

Mom's voice trickled out of the receiver "Stevie? Are you there? Can you hear me now?"

Stevie picked the phone back up. "I hear you. Mom, I'm so sorry—" and she was cut off again. "You called *Dad*?" It was clearly a rhetorical question, and I felt my bowels tighten. "And he's on the way right now."

"Okay, I'm okay. No, I'm coming ho—" There was a shout from the line and Stevie jumped. "Okay, okay. We'll wait for Dad."

Pause.

"Yes. Right. Yes, I promise. Okay, get some rest. I—we love you."

Stevie put my phone down. "Elvis—the guy I saw downstairs at Rite Aid? He attacked Mom. She's in the hospital. She's okay, but they're keeping her overnight for observation to make sure she doesn't have anything wrong with her, with her—" Stevie began to cry. "With her brain. Right now, she's on painkillers so she's a little funny, but she says she's okay."

A little later, we will think to call and talk to a doctor on her floor and who will thankfully confirm this, along with Mom's prognosis for a full and total recovery.

"He's looking for me. Mom thinks he thinks I stole something."

"Stole what?" Sam asked.

"No idea," said Stevie, big-eyed.

I looked at them both, older than me but still such babies. "Well, there are two options: drugs or money?"

"Oh," she said. "Maybe both? I didn't, though. I didn't steal from him, I swear."

"And Dad is on his way? What's going on?" I said.

"Dad is coming. He's on a flight from Tallahassee right now. He has the address and he's bringing his Glock. Mom said to wait here for him and not to leave. I mean, obviously." Stevie put her face to the window. She couldn't see Elvis below but she knew he was out there, somewhere.

Sam, who had been watching all this silently, whispered hoarsely, "I'm going to kill that asshole."

We all looked at each other.

"So it's delivery then?" I joked, but no one laughed.

There was nothing to do but wait.

Chapter 10

We all sat on a home-made blanket bed on the floor, out of sight of the windows, shades drawn tight, TV turned up, half-empty Chinese containers scattered all around. Stevie chewed her nails as she laid on her belly and read Jen's journals, sometimes laughing, sometimes having to put them down and turn away from us for a while, though she would always turn back, sometimes teary, sometimes not, and begin to read again.

"She was so sad," Stevie said once, wiping her face on the chenille blanket that made up the part of the bed underneath her. "Why didn't we know how sad she was?"

"I don't think that anyone can comprehend the depth of someone else's sorrow," I said, and I meant Jen, but I meant me, too. And Sam. And Stevie herself.

Sam scooted his body next to mine where I sat watching the ending of another episode of *Buffy the Vampire Slayer*. I'd found the box set in a cabinet and we'd put it on, to make noise, but also for the company and as a kind of elegy for a childhood that had not only slipped past but that had never really existed in the first place. As Dark Willow shot green bolts from her hands and prepared to end the world, as Xander reminded her about the day they met, the first day of kindergarten, as he told her that he loved her, Sam put his arms around me and I let him hold me for a long, long time.

*

We startled awake, gasping, all of us tangled together in a heap when the buzzing began. It was still dark and someone had turned off the TV. I had no idea what time it was. Sam took his arm off of my chest and I bounded to the little screen in the front hallway, my blood pressure skyrocketing me out of sleep.

It was not Elvis, at least. But the arrival of my father, though a little more bent and balder than he had been when he'd left, did not make me feel any calmer. I buzzed him in and waited.

He was leathery and tan, which made him look older, although, it had been so long since I'd seen him, I suppose he would have looked older no matter what. He had on a Hawaiian shirt, and a gray mustache that made him look a little like Sam, though his eyes were not as kind. Beyond that, his face had a faint, over-bitten, rat-like look that I noticed in my own face when I was feeling less-than-kind to myself. Anyone who didn't know him would probably have said he was handsome. Cheesy, but handsome. The cheese was a new feature. It fit him.

I let him in and stepped back out of hugging range, though he didn't even attempt one.

"Hi Dan," I said.

"James!" He seemed glad to see me, and unsurprised that I was here. I wonder if Mom had called him again, after we'd spoken, or if he was just so out of the familial loop that he had no idea that it was strange I was here. He wore flip-flops and his holster bulged out at his hip, even under the Hawaiian shirt. He saw my eyes go to it and he patted the bulge. "This right here is my good-guy gun. That's a nine-millimeter. I understand Stevie's in a bit of trouble?" He had a drawl that he'd never had when he lived with us. When we had all lived under the same roof, he'd been distant, withdrawn; if anything he was slightly too formal. There had been no flip-flops and no Luger, not as far as I knew.

Stevie stepped forward. "Hi, Princess," he said and tried to draw her into the hug he'd skipped with me. "What seems to be the trouble?"

"Don't fucking touch me."

He looked confused, and I suppose he was. "What's going on? I get a crazy-ass call from your mom—no surprise there, I guess—but crazier than usual, and she says get your gun and get on the first flight to Chicago, someone's trying to hurt you. So here I am, no questions asked. Saving you. Only it don't look like that's what you want."

My god, even if he'd done nothing else but leave us, the drawl was a crime in itself.

"Do you even know whose apartment you're standing in right now?" Stevie asked.

Dan looked around like he'd only just noticed he was in a strange place. "It's nice I guess, in that city way." He looked at Sam. "Yours?"

Sam just stared back at him.

"Jen lived here," Stevie said. "My best friend, Jen Siegel? From high school?"

And Dan at least now had the good sense to start to look wary, but not nearly as wary as he should have. Was it possible he may even have forgotten what he'd done all those years and another lifetime ago?

"You know, the one you fucked?"

And now he looked stricken, went white. "Jen," he croaked.

Stevie nodded, matter-of-fact. "Yeah, Jen. She's dead, by the way."

He moved back toward the door, toward escape. And because Stevie and I were watching him, we didn't notice Sam until he was swinging and there was a great thud, meat colliding with meat, and a cracking sound that may have been spine or jaw or knuckles or nose, and then our dad was on the floor, blinking like a baby in wonderment of the world.

Where does one start the conversation? Why did you fuck my best friend? Who then killed herself, possibly, at least in part, because of the fucking of you? Which wrecked the rest of us, too, the rest of us who have not been able to build the lives we envisioned for ourselves because in the fucking of my friend—is fucking even the right word? Was it rape or just some gray area that exists so Republicans can keep marrying child-brides?—you took something away from all of us: her, me, James, our mom, even Sam, you selfish disgusting prick? And this emptiness, this lack, has landed us here, in this abject place, crouched on the floor, waiting for someone to punish us for our sins, both real and imagined? That coming here to do something, finally, at last, fifteen years too late to save Jen, and possibly us too is the very, very fucking least you could do? But not really because just the sight of you (the sound) makes us want to puke?

Stevie just stood there over him, thinking it all but too overwhelmed to say any of it. Then she bent over and took his gun out of its holster and trained it on him.

But, eventually, we did ask him those questions as he lay there. And he answered them, every one, lying on his back, blinking at us dumbly, with his hands at his shoulders in a posture that suggested both "Don't shoot!" and "Who, me?"

He had dropped the good-old-boy routine by this point, and resembled now the man who had walked out on our mother, on us, after fucking my sister's best friend. His eyes had gone dead and reptilian, and I felt like I was seeing his true form. He answered us in a resigned and half-sincere voice that occasionally broke into insipid excuses and victim-blaming. I don't need to recount it here—we all know what it sounds like.

At one point I looked up at Stevie, and it was clear she was thinking of shooting him. I managed to catch her eye and shook my head. He was an enormous piece of shit, but he was our dad, after all. And, more than that, not worth going to jail for. Still, I needed him to be sorry. Really sorry. And so I took the gun from Stevie and put it to his head and made him apologize until it sounded like he meant it. Until he was crying, blood and snot dripping from his nose, and he finally put those hands of his down and just laid there, trying to breathe through it all.

That's when Stevie gently took the gun back from me, no doubt afraid that I was now contemplating it the way she had been just a few minutes before.

"Get up," she said to him. And he rubbed his eyes with his fists, like an overgrown baby, and got up, cheek and eye grown dark and puffy where Sam's punch had landed. This time she didn't point the gun at him, but she didn't put it down either. "The bathroom's back there if you want to get cleaned up," she said. He nodded, something in him just done.

He was in there for a while and when he came back out there was something in his face that struggled toward contrition. At least he was trying. Sort of.

"I'm sorry," he said, absently touching his face and glancing fearfully at Sam, who stood near Stevie and me, our protector. Stevie still held the gun but it was at her side now and she looked at him intently, maybe wondering what I was: what did we need with this asshole, now that we had his gun? Or maybe, like me, she was just remembering all the things he already hadn't protected her from.

"I am. I'm sorry." Dan took a deep breath. "I . . . I loved Je—"

"Don't you say her name," growled Sam.

"I loved your friend. In my way. I did."

Sam tensed and stepped toward Dan and our dad put up his hands again, "Okay, okay. I'm sorry." He took a deep breath. "That's all. I'm just. Sorry."

Everyone in the room seemed to relax at this. We had all passed through some crucial moment. But we were not yet done. Having the sense to look chagrined, Dan asked quietly, "But, so what're y'all gonna do about this mess right here?"

We all looked at each other blankly. What *were* we going to do?

As if in answer to his own question, Dan walked into the living room and began to drag a beige sectional into the front hallway. There, he propped it on its arm and leaned it against the front door, then went over to the kitchen table and picked it up.

"Dad? What are you doing?" asked Stevie.

"What does it look like I'm doing, kiddo? I'm trying to keep this asshole out of the apartment. Where's the back door?" said Dan.

Sam shook his head, "There isn't one."

"Didn't this whole damn city burn up in a fire? What do you mean there's not a second exit?"

"This is a high rise," Sam shrugged.

"In that case, we should stay here, make him come to us," said Dan. You could tell he had a kind of Custer's-Last-Stand concept of what should happen next.

Stevie shook her head. "Absolutely not. We've got to get home. Mom's all alone at the hospital and she'll be even more alone when they discharge her." The guilt Stevie felt was crushing her. I saw the weight of her soul in her face. The bags under her eyes, the way she was aging in fast-motion in front of me, like the special effects in a movie. She could not believe the things she let that asshole to do her. She could not believe the price our mom had paid.

"But he could be out there right now," I said, pointing out the obvious.

She walked over to the window, leaning back from it slightly. "I still don't see him on the street."

"There's a lot of the street we can't see. Mom said he knows we're on Halsted and maybe one of the building numbers, but she doesn't think he got the whole thing, right? What would you do if you were him? How would you find us?"

"I would drive up and down the street," said Sam, glad to have an opportunity to show off his procedural acumen. "Stake it out, but without being too obvious."

"So assume he's sitting down there, somewhere, jacked up on coffee and coked out of his mind, waiting for Stevie to make a run for it. What's our move?"

It was fully dawn now but still too early to be very busy on the street. If we made a run for it now, it would be obvious. Sam turned the TV back on and found the weather channel.

"Look," he said, "a storm." Indeed, the radar showed a fleet of green blotches marching steadily over the city from the west, like an advancing army. The rainfall was predicted to be nearly an inch. It would be a bad one. "We should leave when this rain starts, in a couple of hours. It will be harder to identify us, and the traffic will be worse, which could hurt us, but it could help us, too."

The channels changed on the television, and they all looked at Dan who had picked up the remote off the kitchen counter and was flipping stations. He stopped at Fox News. A blond woman with a large, bouffant hairdo spoke from the bottom of her throat, "I think one way that people who are going to try to defeat Obama is to somehow prove he's other—he's not one of us. If they can't prove he's a Muslim, then let's prove his wife is an angry Black woman. I think it's going to get ugly. I don't think John McCain will sanction it. I think McCain will—it's my opinion he will generally try—"

A generic brunette white man cut her off, "But he won't be able to control it."

Another man jumped in, "Oh, I don't know. I'm kind of curious about Obama, where he lived, what he's done and what he believes. The birth certificate is out now, but is it enough?"

"I know that, speaking just for myself, I'd like to see the long form certificate."

"Dan?" Sam said, and then, when Dad did not look up: "Dan!" and he jumped and looked away from the TV screen and back at us.

"What!?" he sniped, before appearing to remember that he was in a room with a bunch of people who wanted to kick his ass. Already, in fact, had.

"Did you rent a car?"

"Yeah, of course," he said, quietly now, his gaze still locked on the television. "You can't trust these big city cab drivers. I'm in the garage around the corner."

"So we'll sneak out during the storm, run to the garage. . . ."

"Why doesn't Dan sneak out by himself and go get the car?"

Stevie held the gun up at us. "Because then we'd have to give him back this."

"Y'all think he's a U.S. citizen?" said Dan who seemed to be completely oblivious to the conversation at hand. Where *had* that infernal "y'all" come from?

No one answered. He continued, "I don't know if a Black man can be president. I don't know if we're ready for that." My father seemed to speak almost to himself. There was a station break and an ad for the local Fox affiliate came on. "More information today about the death of Aaren Gwinn in North Chicago last month. Gwinn was shot by police officers who were in the area, working on a drug investigation. . . ."

The affiliate ad continued.

"College media website Facebook is under investigation in Canada this week. University of Ottowa students claim the popular site sold their data to advertisers, violating Canadian privacy laws.

And, with the year only halfway over, 2008 is already the deadliest for tornadoes since 1998. We are on track for a record-breaking year. At least 110 people have died, including seven in Parkersburg, Iowa, last week. Tune in today for your midday report."

Stevie turned off the television.

Dan looked at her, and at his gun in her one hand and the remote in the other. "You know what's funny? I could probably shoot this guy in the street and I bet no one would blink an eye. I bet they would give me a medal."

"I'm not giving this back to you," she said. "Either of them." She still looked undecided about shooting him.

"Look," said Dan, struggling to regain control of the situation. "I looked at the map. Halsted is a long street. It's like a needle in a haystack if he doesn't have the building number. If you want to leave right now, odds are, he'd be miles away. Or, I could go alone—he doesn't know me—but I'm not leaving without my gun."

Just then, of course, the front door buzzed.

There, in the doorcam was Elvis. He held a white delivery bag. My feet went cold. He wore a baseball cap but it was obviously him—Cubs cap, sunglasses on a rainy day, plus who would have ordered takeout for breakfast? We watched as he pressed every buzzer at once, like an unattended child in an elevator. He shifted and the bag bulged. What was in there?

"How'd he find us?" Sam wondered and Stevie and I looked at each other.

"Where'd you park?" I said to Stevie.

"Garage. Where'd *you* park?" she asked Sam and he looked at me.

"No idea."

I closed my eyes. "Oh fuck."

Last week, I'd called around and we'd gotten Sam's car out of impound together. Sam had been tired out by the task though, and seemed kind of freaked at being out of the apartment, so I'd dropped him off in front of the building. There were no spaces, but I circled a couple of times and was rewarded with a miracle of a space.

"Fuck, fuck, fuck," I said, and covered my face with a hand. "I totally forgot but . . . Sam's basically parked directly in front of the building, on the other side of the street." And though Iowa plates were not uncommon in Chicago, plates from Taylor County would have been a dead give-away.

"I'm so sorry. I can't believe I didn't think of it. With everything else, I just. . . ."

"It's okay," whispered Stevie and put a hand on my shoulder.

Someone must have answered his buzz because Elvis was now clearly having a conversation over the intercom. Though everyone was silent now, I put my finger to my lips anyway and pressed the two-way button. Elvis's voice rang into the apartment, tinny and menacing. "Yeah they forgot to put her last name on the order? Do you have an apartment number?" There was an indistinct squawking and the door buzzed and he disappeared.

Later, when I was asking her questions about what had happened, trying to get my details straight, I'd ask my mom what had been written on the whiteboard when she'd erased it in the attack. She could still recite the building and apartment numbers, the street. But then I said, "Was there anything else?" and Mom thought about it for a second and then slowly nodded her head.

"Sure," she said, "I'd written her name," she blinked. "I'd written 'Jen.' As if Stevie was going to visit her. As if she was still alive."

"Well," said Dan, "Elvis has entered the building."

"We've got to go," said Stevie, quiet at first, then louder. "We've got to, we've got to go! We've got to get the fuck out of here."

The three of them dragged the sofa backwards away from the door, and we opened it carefully, first a crack, then, when Dan gave the all-clear, we tumbled out into the hallway. Empty, but for how long, God only knew.

"Elevator or stairs?" I asked.

Stevie thought for a second. "I don't know—have you seen cameras? Which has cameras?"

"The elevator definitely has a camera," said Sam. He'd noted it upon his arrival here, so many days ago, had turned his back to it just in case.

"He would have taken the stairs then."

We tiptoed across the hallway like the Scooby Gang. It would have been funny if we weren't so scared. It seemed to take an interminable amount of time to hear the stupid arrival ding of the elevator, but then there it was and then we were standing inside it. Stevie was pushing the close-door button repeatedly, frantically, when the door to the stairway flew open.

The elevator dinged again and Elvis swiveled toward us, hand going into his delivery bag for whatever was in that Styrofoam takeout box. Not Szechuan, I assumed. A single roll of duct tape fell out of the bag and for a second, I held my breath, sure it would roll right in and trip the elevator doors to open all the way again, but it rolled the other way instead and the elevator doors closed and then we were dropping, down, down, down toward our destiny.

We made a blind dive for the front door just as he skated out of the stairwell, heaving, gun drawn. Stevie turned around and fired hers and the sound made time stand still. It rolled like thunder, made a sound like the building was collapsing, like the building was being hit by airplanes. She missed by a wide margin, putting out a can-light in the ceiling, bullet presumably making its way into the floor of the apartment above, but the move had momentarily shocked Elvis into stillness. Stevie with a gun was the last thing he'd expected. He stood there and watched us run out the door. I did not look back again.

We made it to the garage, which felt a little safer, and followed Dan up the stairs to the second floor, and piled into his Ford Escape. He peeled it out of the spot and seemed to fly down to the entrance.

"Dad, slow down," Stevie yelled from the front seat, arm with the gun bouncing wildly.

Dan put his foot on the gas and went through the automated gate. The arm of it flew off in a piece and into the street and we all screamed then, sliding into morning traffic like we were in a movie.

This was not the way to blend in.

Sam turned around in the back seat where he was braced and still rocking from Dan's stunt driving. "What's he driving?" he yelled up to the front.

Stevie yelled back. "Black Beemer!"

"He's behind us."

I looked and there he was, swinging wide around a corner a block away and then righting himself out of the fishtail.

I know that car chases are exciting in the movies and probably in those detective novels Sam likes so much, but in real life, at least in my experience, they are monotonous, kind of boring. Our car chase didn't resemble so much a car chase as a friendly caravan to an agreed upon destination. We tried speeding up, but the traffic became thick and unyielding. We had a hard time weaving for the same reason, and every time we managed to change lanes, Elvis was right there behind us. Eventually we got on 88 heading back west and there he was, exiting with us. He didn't stand up through his sun roof and shoot at us; he couldn't drive us off the road in this traffic with so many witnesses and a traffic helicopter overhead. And what could we do? If we flagged down a cop and reported his plate, he'd be able to tell them we had shot at him. And then what? One of us was an employee in his drug syndicate and another of us her bodyguard, sent to hunt him down? On the other hand, was he going to kill us? He couldn't kill us all. He was, after all, just a small-town drug dealer. Murder would have been way worse and murdering four of us just this side of silly. It was hard to imagine and end game for either party. The only thing that was clear was that Elvis was waiting, would bide his time and follow us wherever we were going to go. Which, judging from Dan's fuel tank, was, sooner or later, going to be the gas station.

"Shit," he said when I pointed it out to him. "Those assholes at Alamo never fill the tank anymore. What ever happened to customer service?"

"I think we can make it." This was Stevie, who was still in the front, peering at the mileage left on the gas tank. "I mean, what are going to do? We can't stop." She had a point and so we drove on.

But, nature had other ideas. By the time we hit Davenport, the storm had started, earlier than predicted. It was the hard punishing rain of the denuded prairies, the kind that made it sound like someone was trying to hammer through your roof from above. We drove as fast as we safely could, thinking with luck we might drive out of it. That happened sometimes—you took a beating for ten minutes and then emerged to sunshine on the other side. But not today. After a while, the cars ahead disappeared and all we could see were their taillights as red smudges through our inundated windshield. Even Elvis had disappeared somewhere behind us. The car rocked and Dan turned on the radio. "This wind is bad. We'd better check for a tornado." There was nothing on the weather service but rain and more rain. A flash flood warning announced itself in robotic beeps. A thunderstorm warning followed. "Yeah, no shit, thanks," said Dan to the radio and turned it off.

The traffic had slowed so much it had nearly stopped at this point. We crawled westward, our chase now officially in slow motion, the rain never letting up except for the reprieve of overpasses. Suddenly, Dan turned off the lights and floored it, cutting hard to the right.

"What are you doing?" I yelled and hung onto the Oh Jesus bar as the Escape swung wildly onto the shoulder.

"There's an exit up here. I think Elvis is in a far lane—we might be able to shake him if we get off the highway."

I noted, with alarm, that the water on the shoulder was beginning to collect and spill out onto the highway, which meant it was deep, but you couldn't tell how deep just by looking.

"No, don't!" I yelled, but it was too late, and Dan wouldn't hear it anyway. We slammed through the water, thudded over something submerged on the shoulder and careened down the shoulder to the exit ramp doing at least sixty, somehow, huge gouts of water flying up on either side of us, like we were Moses parting the Red Sea. So much for going unnoticed. We followed the exit ramp right until it dumped us off onto a county road. More water. We fishtailed slightly as the SUV hydroplaned sideways. Dan revved it again as the road cut through a flooded corn field and we passed a little green sign that filled me with dread: Squirrel Creek

It seemed to happen both all at once and also in slow motion.

The SUV revved and revved but we slowed down. I opened my window and saw that somehow there was churning mud halfway up my door. If I opened it, the fish-stink waters would come roiling in. In front of us, water swallowed the road.

"Shit," said Dan as the car slowed.

"It's him!" yelled Sam, pointing, and there, sure enough, about a quarter mile behind us, were the goggle-like xenon headlights of Elvis's BMW. They were moving back and forth, like the car was slowly shaking its head.

Suddenly, our car was airborne. Or, that's what it felt like, like being lifted gently up and floated mildly through the air. Obviously it was not the air we were floating through but the swollen and flooding waters of Squirrel Creek, an eastern tributary of the Wapsi. Dan gripped the steering wheel and jerked it back in the direction of the road, but the car did not respond. The current had lifted us off the ground and was currently floating us backward toward Elvis. We watched in horror, as the BMW grew closer, until, abruptly, it began to float backwards too. Before it did, we got close enough to the car that Sam said later that he'd been able to see Elvis clearly through his windshield. To see the stunned look on his face. That dumb, uncomprehending surprise.

The ground was totally gone now. There were only trees and telephone poles to remind us that we weren't on a boat, and we whimpered as seconds dragged on and we were pulled inexorably toward our fate, and the cold churning of the water so close now, I could have reached down and touched it.

Behind us, Elvis's car had flipped around and seemed to tilt up, its back end stuck up into the air, like a swimmer, poised to start a race, and then, the next second, as if it had never been there at all, it was gone.

Stevie screamed and we churned backwards faster, closer to whatever culvert or bank Elvis had slipped off of.

"Where is he? Where'd he go?" she yelled and crawled back toward us, into the back seat, gun forgotten on the floor of the passenger-side front seat. She reached me and Sam and Sam clutched her tight. "Don't look," he said, but by then there was nothing left to look at.

"Should we jump out?" Dan asked as he unbuckled his seat belt. I shook my head and yelled to him, "No!" I knew from my time in the canyons out West that a flood was swifter than it looked, that it took only a few inches to knock a grown man off his feet and that people died under just such circumstances not infrequently, in floods slower and lesser than this.

The wind picked up and we slowly, slowly drifted off the course that

Elvis had taken, when he had slipped, nose first, over the horizon and off the edge of the world.

Eventually—probably mere minutes, but it felt much longer—and with a great squeaking and grinding of metal and wood, we lodged in a stand of trees in a pasture that ran along the road. Stuck fast and buffeted gently by the waves, we watched, helpless, as the world washed away around us.

We huddled there in our humid terror, bobbing, for some time. Dan called 911 and the local sheriff's office promised to send help but warned that it would be a while. They had several trapped motorists and not enough skiffs. They were waiting on more help from other counties.

The dark came. Dan fell asleep in the front of the car, all alone. The three of us were squished in the back seat, but no one tried to move back up front. Instead, Stevie and I each put a head on Sam's shoulder and he kissed us each on our frizzy, damp crowns, and we took turns telling each other the plots of our favorite movies to pass the time.

"Once upon a time," began Sam, "there was a famous cat burglar named Hudson Hawk who was looking forward to being paroled, when he suddenly found himself blackmailed by the Mario Brothers Mafia."

When it was my turn I told the plot of *Kiss of the Spider Woman*.

"That's really meta, James."

"Thanks, Stevie," I said, and reached across Sam to ruffle her hair.

Stevie told *The Big Chill*. "It's pretty boring without the soundtrack," she apologized.

Then I asked her to tell *Clue*, for old time's sake. She did ("Mrs. Peacock was a man?!") and I think we all liked that.

And then we were silent, listening to the lap of the water on the car, the incongruous moo of a distant cow. In the driver's seat, Dan snored the snore of someone who had never had a second thought or regret in his life.

Eventually the skiffs arrived and rescued us. Though none of us saw him do it, Dan had woken up at some point and dropped the gun and his holster into the flood waters. Someone must have found it, eventually, but I never heard anything about it again.

The press was there to meet us, when we made it back to dry ground, which turned out to be an overpass over a road a couple of miles from our highway. A guy with a camera and a woman with a mic huddled under see-through parkas in front of their gray news van.

The woman did a soundbite, "At least one person is dead and two more are missing after a flash flood at Squirrel Creek today."

The four of us looked at each other as the sheriff's deputy wrapped a mylar blanket around Stevie.

The reporter shook her head. "Try again," she said to the cameraman, and she took a breath and started over.

"Terror at Squirrel Creek today, as a flash flood tore through Long Grove. At least one person is dead, with two more missing."

Stevie leaned in to the deputy, "Was the person who died in a black BMW?"

The deputy took his hat off and scratched his stubbly head, "Did you know him?"

"I did," said Stevie, and the deputy looked away, into the distance where a red light from a radio tower blinked and blinked.

"Sorry, ma'am," he said.

I suppose you probably know what happened next.

After the motel, and the showers and the sheriff's rescue clothes that looked suspiciously like prison sweats.

After the landline call to our mom and her tears of relief and then to see her, finally, our mama, our mommy. Mom. She was right there, tiny and fierce, even fiercer for the sling and the bruises. Our tough Viv. I put my nose in her hair and I breathed her in.

"My baby," she said and held me tight and I was small again and the tippy world righted itself for a moment.

After dropping Dan at the Cedar Rapids airport with little fanfare, to file the paperwork with Alamo, and get the last flight out, back to Tallahassee.

After turning down the long blacktop road that led down, down, down to the house where we'd grown up and fought and left each other.

I suppose you know what was waiting there at the bottom of the hill. Why mom said, "Brace yourselves." Why we had to stop halfway down and get out of the car to look.

The river was running *through* the house, through all the houses on our street, boisterous and fast. It looked as if someone had intentionally built a village in the middle of a river, like they do along the Mekong River Delta. Or like someone had taken the concept of a houseboat far too literally. We joined the crowd of neighbors there on the side of the road and we all watched the river devour our homes with grim faces. Our front door stood wide upon and most of the windows were gone. And the sound the water made—like a roaring dragon—as it flowed through our kitchen, through the bedrooms where we'd grown up, through Stevie's room and her boombox, as it soaked vertically up Jim Morrison, so that when we finally got into the house to look around a month later, all that was left of the poster were the words "The Doors," under which there was an enormous hole in the wall where the water had disintegrated the drywall. This made us laugh, actually. What else could you do?

Through the basement, where we'd all been so young and so stupid, and though Dan's hi-fi equipment was long gone, the cedar chest was still there, having been successfully rescued from the first flood, when there had been more time. Time enough to move things upstairs, time enough for our family to be ruined. The chest had floated to the other side of the room and was covered in a layer of grime, but the wedding dress was still inside, slightly mildewed but, miraculously, whole.

In the entire house, it was almost the only thing still in good enough condition to save. Viv said to throw it out, but Stevie said she'd have it cleaned. That grandma had made it, so it was special.

EPILOGUE

I know I told you I don't like happy endings, and this isn't one exactly, but the flood wasn't all terrible news. Elvis's death was too bad, but no one seemed to miss him much. To Stevie's surprise, they offered the management of the pool not to her, but to a nursing student named Sherry, whom Stevie had never met, but who came, it was later said, to her first day on the job with her own full cashbox and a bag full of diving sticks, those empty ones you can fill with water or whatever.

And the state offered buyouts to everyone on our stretch of the river. The 500-year flood plain had shifted, they said, and according to climatologists and environmental scientists and engineers at the University of Iowa, it seemed like maybe now it was going to be more like a twenty-year flood plain. They wanted to make the riverbank into a park and to encourage takers, they offered 2006 prices for the houses and land, even though to call what was left "houses" took some stretch of imagination.

Mom took the buyout, paid off the bank, and actually made a little money, in the end.

With that money, she moved us into a townhouse development on a hill. The duplexes were an ugly taupe color, the color of a flooding river, but they were dry and safe and there were three bedrooms, one for each of us. There weren't many trees, just condos as far as the eye could see, but one night I went out for a smoke on the tiny walk-out patio and heard an owl hoot and I knew I was home.

Eventually, I worked on this book at the new kitchen table. One night, Sam brought by Jen's water-stained journal—he'd smuggled it from her apartment when we ran from Elvis. A lot of the entries were smudged beyond reading, but a few were still legible. I haven't included them here verbatim—like I said, Jen was such a private person—but, with Sam's help, I have recreated a few in what I think of as her voice. The details are different of course. Would you believe her name's not even Jen? Still, I couldn't leave her out. She blamed herself for the harmful choices of the men around her. She thought she'd ruined our lives and that by dying she would be doing us—my family and the whole world—a favor. But, of course, this was not true at all. This book is proof that she was here and that she mattered. We loved her. I love her. And she is forgiven.

Some nights, Stevie did the homework for her social work program beside me, allowing me to interrupt her to check on this or that detail, content to advise rather than author. She had lost the appetite even for her blog by then, and it would go the way of so many early century blogs and disappear into the ether only to be replaced with a "Buy This Domain Name" advertisement. The internet is forever; the internet always forgets.

This was her last blog post:

You Were Wrong When You Said Everything's Gunna Be Alright

Remember back in the day, you liked either Madonna or Cyndi Lauper, Pearl Jam or Nirvana, Bruce Springsteen or John Cougar Mellencamp? Why were these always presented like binary choices? Were there really that few bands back then? One of the rock guys I dated in New York asked me once, "Beatles or Rolling Stones?" as if there is any real difference anyway (Velvet Underground). But if I had to choose, and for some reason someone always used to make you, Springsteen is obviously always superior to Mellencamp *except* in the case of "Jack and Diane" which is frankly more realistic than, say "Glory Days," and is made more true when sung by that nasal depressive, Doug Martsch.

Life *does* go on long after the thrill of living is gone. That is Mellencamp's gift to us.

Jen knew it but she couldn't bear it.

I am learning it, too. Maybe this is just what we call "getting older." I always thought I was funny but all this time I've been writing a tragedy.

The thing I'm realizing, after my move, is that telling the story of my life while I'm living it isn't actually making it better, and in fact may be making it worse. Performing for strangers on the internet is beginning to feel like a poor foundation upon which to build.

I was wrong to move home, I was also not wrong. You can't go back, but you always have to. The more you try to locate that old home, the more it dissipates until it's gone forever. I guess there's a reason they call it the mists of time?

But I'm also realizing that maybe it wasn't that great to begin with. What I'm saying is: I'm going to try something new for a while. It might not be thrilling, but it will be my life, I think. Finally.

In the townhouse, there was a room in the basement for Sam, whenever he wanted. And he did come over sometimes, after he'd finished his thirty days in recovery, paid for by Bonnie. After he'd moved into a bachelor's studio in downtown Taylor over the old farm café where the remaining farmers grumped and worried over their ever-shrinking yields. Always either too much rain or not enough.

He came over some nights and watched TV with us on the couch, Stevie in the middle and Mom on her expensive new zero-gravity recliner, which helped take the pressure off her shoulder, which ached most days, especially when the humidity was high.

And it was enough, to watch *Friends* reruns, arm to arm with Stevie, or down the couch with Sam's feet in my lap wiggling for a rub. I often fell asleep like this, laugh track in my ears, and sometimes when I did, in the moment just before, I would imagine the smell of heroin, that acrid burning vinegar, and that's all I would need to step off the ledge into nothing.

Acknowledgments

This book was a long time in the making and went through many iterations over the years, some of which were supported by a Steffensen Cannon Fellowship at the University of Utah, and residencies at the Virginia Center for the Creative Arts, and Rockvale Writers' Colony. Thank you to early readers, including Melanie Rae Thon, Lance Olsen, Natanya Pulley, Joe Keohane, Alison Powell, Katie Hartsock, and Annie Gilson. Thanks, also, to everyone who supported me in the writing of *2008* by being there during a long, full decade of talking and traveling and working and making art, including Carolyn Sivitz, Jen Sheldon, Bob Stein, Danielle Deulen, Jacob Paul, Tim O'Keefe, Xhenet Aliu, Rachel Hanson, Robert Glick, Rachel Marston, Shena McAuliffe, Dawn Lonsinger, Geoff Babbitt and Kathryn Cowles. Thanks to my colleagues at Salisbury and Oakland for your support and friendship. Thanks to my parents (who are not *these* parents) and to my family. Thanks to my old pals from my first home in Iowa, who inspired this novel, and to Matt Kirkpatrick and Mattie (and Jellybeans) who are my home, now. I love you so much.

FICTION

It's 2008, the age of the blog, the dawn of social media, and the birth of the smartphone. Obama is running for president on a slogan of hope, while in the shadows an opioid crisis emerges and the housing market teeters. Stevie and Sam, two old high school flames who have grown up and grown apart, are brought back together in the aftermath of a tragedy that throws them off the tracks of their lives. On the cusp of a new era of uncertainty, the old friends must find ways to reconcile themselves to the past and find their way home.

•

For a novel of such an exquisitely particular moment, *2008* manages to be profoundly and shockingly prescient. Hilarious and devastating, with hometown heroes and forever-outsiders whose decisions and fates feel both constantly surprising and inevitable, McCarty somehow knits together Middle America, jaded urbanites, bloggers, the publishing industry, adolescence, late early adulthood, climate change, capitalism, and then-and-now into one of the most prismatic contemporary American novels I've encountered in years.

—**Xhenet Aliu, author of *Everybody Says It's Everything***

2008 pulled me in from its very first pages and then never let me go. . . . I can't wait to recommend it, to shove it in people's hands, to talk about it with others who found themselves awed by it.

—**Aaron Burch, author of *Year of the Buffalo***

Susan McCarty is the author of the story collection *Anatomies*, called "deft" and "resonant" by *Publisher's Weekly*. Her essays about consumerism, desire, and motherhood have appeared in *Creative Nonfiction*, *Ecotone*, *Lit Hub*, *Juked*, *Zone 3*, and other journals. She is an associate professor of English and creative writing at Oakland University in the metro Detroit area. She lives with the writer, Matt Kirkpatrick, their child, and a dog named Jellybeans.

CARNEGIE
MELLON
UNIVERSITY
PRESS

Cover design: Connie Amoroso
Cover image: Soraya Silvestri on Unsplash
Author photo: Matt Kirkpatrick